CEYCHELL'S CINDERS

CEYCHELL'S CINDERS

HER SOUL OF FIRE ✦ BOOK TWO

Copyright © 2022 J. V. Fahl

WWW.JVFAHL.COM

Cover and Interior Design by We Got You Covered Book Design

WWW.WEGOTYOUCOVEREDBOOKDESIGN.COM

Ebook ISBN: 979-8-9873884-0-2

Softback ISBN: 979-8-9873884-1-9

Hardcover ISBN: 979-8-9873884-2-6

v1.0.0 - Errata can be found at HTTPS://WWW.JVFAHL.COM/CC-ERRATA

HER SOUL OF FIRE ✦ BOOK TWO

CEYCHELL'S CINDERS

J.V. FAHL

I would love for you to join my spam-free newsletter.
If you want to join now, please visit **jvfahl.com** and sign up.

LET'S GET YOU TO THE STORY

ONE

REUNITED AT LAST

THE SUN BEAMED THROUGH CEYCHELL'S window, warming her store. Though she'd slept soundly since hearing the news, she awoke early each morning excited that today would be the day Kyradel and Miraden returned home. She brushed her auburn hair with a copper comb and pulled it into intricate braids.

It still didn't seem real that Kyradel was coming home. She had been taken by the ashenkin several months ago, and Ceychell had nearly accepted that her sister was gone forever. Until Miraden saved her. Miraden, her loving ranger, who wanted nothing more than to dote on Ceychell. He wanted nothing more than to love her, which she rejected for so long, for something so stupid, she hated herself for it.

But she hoped all of that was about to change. If Miraden got her final letter, it could mean the difference. As she brushed, she stared at his letters stacked neatly on the table beside her favorite leatherbound chair. But a different letter was in her pocket, and she urgently needed to show it to Miraden when he arrived.

She was eager to see him, but she couldn't help but feel she'd lost him all over again. Worse yet, to Simigrin, his *lovely* and brave companion. Simigrin sounded too perfect, she couldn't blame him if her fears were true.

Miraden would be thrilled to find out that Lovo had survived his freezing plunge into Arrowheart Lake. Lovo showed up in Kaehrn looking for him just a few weeks ago and had been helping her brew her potions and chop firewood. He'd also helped out with smelting ore at Bryndyke's forge. Lovo's much friendlier than she thought he'd be. Always happy to pitch in and never complained. It was nice having him around, a wonderful reminder that Miraden was on his way home.

Regardless, time crept along slowly. It had been nearly a month since she last heard from Miraden after he closed the Ashengate and saved Kyradel. It was the single greatest thing she'd heard in her life, but every hour since had felt like a year as she waited and watched for Kyradel and Miraden to walk out of the forest and into Kaehrn's town square. She hoped that all would be forgiven between the three of them.

And then at last, on a warm morning in early spring… she heard yelling from the road. It grew louder.

"They're here!" someone yelled.

The comb fell from her hand. She grabbed her fur coat and dashed out of her cabin shop and into melting snow.

The entire village had gathered around Sulover's ore cart. As she approached, Kyradel darted out of the crowd into the arms of her mother and father.

Ceychell covered her mouth and dropped to her knees. The gods had mercy and her sister was home again, saved from the clutches of the ashenkin. Tears ran down Ceychell's face. She picked herself up and ran, slipping and sliding through the snow, and crashed into her sister. They held each other so tight. Ceychell cried, so happy was she to hold Kyradel after all this time. Two years had passed since she last hugged her sister. That lost time hurt, but the worst was the last six months since Kyradel was taken. She looked up at the sky and thanked the gods that her prayers had been answered.

Kyradel cried, too. Her fiery hair was cut shoulder-length, loose and messy. Ceychell could feel her sister's bones through her clothes. The puffiness in her cheeks was gone, neck was thinner, and collar was exposed. She looked frail like a bird.

Ceychell smiled and brushed tears from her eyes. She couldn't help herself and wiped a smudge of dirt from Kyradel's cheek.

"I thought I'd lost you for good," Ceychell wheezed. "I'm so happy you're home." She embraced her sister again and kissed her cheeks.

Kyra cried in her arms. "Me too. I never thought I'd see you again."

Ceychell's heart nearly stopped when Miraden stepped out from behind the cart. His rusty hair was nearly shoulder-length, and almost wavy. He had a scruffy beard she'd never seen before. He stared at her, his deep brown eyes bloodshot and misty. She lost her breath and thought for a moment that she might faint.

Miraden looked over at her father, Ormus, and reached out to shake his hand, but Ormus grabbed him and pulled him into a monstrous bear hug. Miraden looked like a child in her father's arms. She never thought she'd see the day her father would hug him.

Curasca, her mother, reached out and wrapped her arms around Kyradel and Ceychell. She was crying tears of joy. She put both hands on Kyradel's face and kissed her forehead.

"My baby girl is home. Gods be praised."

Ormus released Miraden and pulled Kyradel carefully into a hug. Ceychell had never seen her father cry with such happiness as he gently squeezed Kyradel.

"Thank you," Ormus whispered over and over to Miraden.

Miraden nodded and turned toward Ceychell. Despite her tears, she calmly stared back at him. She wanted to run into his arms; she wanted to be swept away and told that all was forgiven.

At last, Curasca pulled Kyradel into a hug again to give Ceychell and Miraden some space. Ceychell abandoned her pride and ran to Miraden. She hugged him with every ounce of her strength. They both cried. Ceychell brushed his long rusty hair back, stared into his sandy brown eyes, and rubbed his stubbled cheek. She wanted to tell him how much she loved him, how much she'd always loved him, but instead, she whispered into his ear, "I am so sorry… for everything. I'm so happy you're home."

Miraden looked down, seemed distant, lost in thought. It was something she'd never seen in him. For a moment, she felt like she didn't recognize him. She finally raised his chin to look into his eyes and he came back to her. She saw a glimmer of the affection he'd always shown her since they were children.

"Perhaps Miraden can join us for breakfast. Someone special is waiting for him," Curasca said.

Ceychell was anticipating what Miraden might do when he sees his former companion, who Miraden thought drowned in Arrowheart Lake. The old Miraden would have screamed and ran thinking Lovo had risen from the dead—she was curious what the new Miraden will do.

"I…" Miraden hesitated.

Ceychell took his hand in both of hers. It was rough, dirty, and cold. "Please, Miraden," Ceychell whispered.

His eyes widened. "The robe… you found it?"   "Yes, I love it. It's so perfect down to every detail," she said hugging the garment around herself. They walked together to her parent's house.

The rush of heat from the hearth and the smell of cider and baked bread rekindled so many memories for Miraden. It helped him briefly forget his treacherous journey. He ran his right hand along the top of a couch with a warm brown blanket. The fireplace was burning hot where he could feel it on his face, just how he liked it. He wanted to dive under a blanket and slip into a long nap after the cold ride on the back of Sulover's cart for the last week.

One brown and one golden dog greeted Miraden and Kyradel with barking and whimpering. Miraden petted them eagerly, including the finicky gray tabby cat that tried to ignore him and prance over to Kyradel.

"Miraden!" Lovo shouted and held out his arms.

Miraden jolted so hard he almost knocked over Ceychell. "Lovo!" Miraden broke down immediately. It just couldn't be true. He watched his friend die—it was like a grinning specter had returned to haunt him. He couldn't speak and before he could crumple in disbelief, Lovo grabbed him in a bearhug. Lovo was real and just like Miraden remembered him. Like a blonde ogre.

"I missed you, buddy," Miraden sobbed, struggling to breathe. "You, you"—

"I missed you too," Lovo said, "but it's breakfast time, let's talk about it later."

Curasca brought Miraden a winter greens salad, two freshly cooked eggs, and a chunk of warm bread. It was the finest meal he'd had in months. He sat next to Lovo, whose plate was loaded near to toppling with eggs, greens, winter squash and bread with a layer of preserves. Ceychell leaned over Miraden from behind and placed a hot cup of juno in front of him, a dusting of cinnamon floating at the top. The smell was intoxicating; oh, how he'd missed it. He picked it up and took a whiff of the bitter juno and enjoyed the warm steam on his face. Ceychell ran her hand along his back as she sat down next to him. Curasca grinned and passed her some bread.

Miraden desperately wanted to ask Lovo what happened. He knew something unexplainable, perhaps divine saved him. No one could have survived that plunge. He stared into space for a moment and vividly remembered watching the shifting ice and the stilling water on Lake Arrowheart with Simigrin until it was too dark to see anymore. For the moment, he didn't question it. He was so grateful to see his friend… who just ate an entire egg in one bite.

Miraden ate but said nothing. He'd always wanted to share a warm breakfast with Ceychell and her family, but never did. Curasca had often sent him home with bread or a pie when he finished a few chores for them, but he'd never shared meals with them.

He wanted to savor it, wanted to melt away and just be happy he was home in Kaehrn, but he felt forlorn. He wasn't even sure why. He got up without a word, left the table, and went to sit by the fireplace alone with the warm cup of juno Ceychell made for him. It was extra rich without milk, exactly how he liked it. He'd forgotten how good it tasted. It still didn't feel real to be back in Kaehrn. He stared out through a frosty window at his village. He could even see his little cabin in the woods over a snow drift and down the shoveled path.

"Here, son," Ormus said, stepping up next to him and offering him a metal flask. Ceychell's father was nearly two heads taller than Miraden and broad-shouldered. The sickness he caught took a toll, his shirt was loose and his face was thinner. Miraden had never seen him so thin.

Ormus never called him son, so he was thrown off guard by his comment and the offer. Ormus had mostly shooed him away before his adventure. Miraden took a hearty sip that burned his throat in a good way… or at least a way he had started to tolerate. He nodded and handed the flask back to Ormus, who sat down next to him. He couldn't recall the last time he sat next to Ormus like this.

"I know that look," Ormus said and looked out the window, too. "I know it all too well." He exhaled a heavy sigh.

"I'm not sure what you mean," Miraden said.

"That's a look of having seen far beyond your home, being changed by the risks you've taken and the mistakes you made. It's the look of someone who is no longer a boy. You've seen what torments this world, and by the gods, you found a way to beat them."

Miraden grabbed the poker next to the fireplace and stirred a few coals. He said, "I have closed one gate. I have no idea how many exist, but I know there are more. I… I am not even sure if they all close the same way."

Ormus sighed again and nodded. "Representatives from Storjn and Valijn, Adolehrn and Bilore Des are coming here soon to seek your wisdom. You have had a difficult journey, and I don't want to forestall your needed rest. If you want, I can relay your story to them so you can have some peace before you decide what you are going to do."

"What do you mean?" Miraden asked, a bit surprised.

"I know what's weighing on your mind, Miraden. It is a heavy burden, and I'm sorry, after all you've done, that you must carry it. But always remember this, as long as my family is in Kaehrn, you will have a place to come home to."

Miraden took a sip of his juno and stared into the fire. He had seen the burning devil world and wondered if he would be able to live with himself should he abandon the cause to retire to a peaceful life in Kaehrn with Ceychell. What if their children were stolen by ashenkin? What if his vigilance and the vigilance of others like him were all that was keeping the ashenkin from overrunning the world?

Ormus leaned in a bit to speak softer. "Whatever you may think, know that Ceychell sent many letters to you, though you may not have received them. It's best if she tells you the stories, but the reason

I got sick—the sickness *you* helped cure—was because I was trying to deliver her message as well. It was all I could do to stop her from venturing out to find you herself."

Miraden looked over his shoulder at Ceychell. She was happier than he'd seen her in years. Her cheeks were red from laughing, and her eyes were full of spirit. She caught Miraden's stare and flashed him a shy grin that brought back memories of their younger days.

"I am glad you stopped her," Miraden said. "I do not think she would have fared that journey well."

"Ceychell has a fighting spirit. I am still not sure I did right in stopping her. The other villages have already started stories of Ceychell, the Tyrant of Kaehrn."

Miraden stared at him for a moment. "The Tyrant?"

"You didn't see her commanding the villagers or how she nearly sentenced a cleric to be eaten by wolves. He squealed like a pig just before she let him go free," Ormus said, leaned in and laughed. Miraden grinned and looked back at her as Ormus continued, "Her mother did not want her to leave, so she's kept her busy with her potions. But I think in time, she will lead Kaehrn or go onto greater things."

"She would be a strong leader, thanks to your guidance."

Ormus laughed again. "I'm afraid she doesn't listen to me. But she would listen to you." He handed the flask to Miraden, patted him on the shoulder, and returned to the dining table.

Miraden took a few more swigs of the spirits then walked back to the dining room. "Thank you for breakfast. I need to catch Sulover before he leaves."

"Miraden, you've hardly had time to sit and relax," Curasca said. "Why leave so soon?"

"I need to trade for as much silver as he'll part with to make arrows."

"Silver is expensive now," Ormus said. "All the smiths are making weapons for ashenkin hunters. Perhaps Bryndyke would have some he can part with."

"I will need all of his, too. Please excuse me." Miraden bowed his head, took his fur from the hook on the wall, and opened the door to leave.

Ceychell caught him by the sleeve. "Can I go with you?"

Miraden hesitated for a moment and then said, "Sure."

Lovo rose from his seat, jostling the table. Curasca reached out to stay him. He smiled and sat back down.

"You coming, Lovo?" Miraden said.

"Meet you there, just going to have one more cup."

Miraden lifted his pack, bow, and quivers and he and Ceychell left the house. They walked through the village without a word and found Sulover's cart outside Bryndyke's smithy. Inside, Sulover wrote in a journal at a small table where Hydracks, Bryndyke's dashing jerk of an apprentice, used to work. As he thought of Ceychell's letter, he flushed with anger. He turned to Ceychell—

"Ask me later," she said.

Miraden nodded. Then he turned to Sulover. "Thank you again for the ride. I have a few pelts in my house I can give you for your kindness." He vigorously rubbed his arms. Now that he was back north, he was very cold. The warmth of the smithy tingled on his skin.

"Oh, sure," the old man said, lifting his head from his journal. "No need for the pelts. I'm just happy to see you and Kyradel home."

"Would you sell some of the silver in your wagon?"

"Well, of course. You're lucky I still have some."

"I had silver-tipped arrows, but I used them all beyond the Ashengate."

"Well, I can sell you what I have, but it's not cheap." Sulover left the store and returned with a small sack of silver nuggets. He placed them on the table.

"This entire batch … you can have it for seventy-five hydras."

Miraden almost collapsed. His pockets were nearly empty, and he had nothing worth that much in his home.

"How much can I get for five?" he asked with a sigh.

"I have at least twenty in kams," Ceychell said.

Miraden turned, "What?"

Bryndyke emerged from his storage room and asked, "What is this about? Miraden! C'mere boy!" He waddled over like a keg with logs for legs. Miraden could smell the sweat-soaked smith well before Bryndyke reached him and pulled him into a bear hug. The thick-armed smith's braided red hair was even longer than Miraden remembered.

"These two are buying my silver," Sulover said.

"Eh?" Bryndyke looked at Miraden. "What happened to that saber I gave you?"

"I had no choice but to trade it for safe passage down the mountains. I'm sorry."

Bryndyke slapped his arm. "It's just a sword, boy! It's great to have you and Kyradel home! Now, what do you need all this silver for?"

Sulover looked down at Miraden's empty quiver. He dumped the rest of the nuggets out on the table and rolled up the bag "How about twenty? Can't charge a devil slayer full price."

"Done," Ceychell said.

"You tell me what you want," Bryndyke said, "and I'll make it right away. Alright with you, Chieftain?"

Miraden turned expecting to see Ormus, but saw Ceychell nod. Ormus wasn't kidding, people were answering to her. "Thank"—

"Don'cha dare thank me," Bryndyke said abruptly. He picked up a hammer and two clamps and brought them back to his closet.

"I'll get your kams right away," Ceychell said. She took Miraden's arm and they left.

When they got out to the snow-packed road again, Miraden said, "You really didn't have to do that." He felt guilty. All his old anxieties seemed to be rushing back. He feared she might cut him down like she used to, especially now that she was chieftain.

Instead she smiled at him and said, "You're right, and I wouldn't do it for anyone else." She put her arm around his waist and said, "I can tell you're cold. Why don't you come back to my place?"

The wind whipped down the road. He was already trying to rub some warmth into his arms. "At your parent's house? I can't stay there! Besides, I should get back to my house and chase out the critters. I hope I still have a spare cloak."

"No, Miraden," she said with a laugh. "I live at my store now. I can brew some more juno if you'd like." She smiled, the wind blew her hair into her face but she didn't break eye-contact. She hadn't looked at him like that in so long.

Curasca's shop was at the end of the road, around the wooded gully from her parent's cabin. Smoke rose from the chimney above its snow-covered roof. He was excited to go with her but tried not to show it. For so long he'd wanted nothing more than to be forgiven by her, accepted by her, and now that he was, he felt uneasy. He broke Kyradel's heart. It was nothing he wanted to do, he had fallen in love with Ceychell and not Kyradel. But over the past few months, he'd felt himself falling out of love with her. Something he never thought possible. But when it happened, it left a hole, black and painful inside of him. He thought of Simigrin and how happy she made him. Her determination inspired him to return to the fight and close more Ashengates. Still, when Ceychell took his hand, those thoughts melted away, and he followed her without a sliver of resistance.

Inside her shop, he smelled jasmine and limebloom. Her shelves were stocked on both walls with clay pots, small canisters, and even a few glass jars. Just inside the entryway were two large brown chairs, each with a folded red blanket. Beside it was a short wooden table with papers stacked neatly on top, a pelt on the floor, all next to a fireplace that was sputtering a few sparks. Past the seating area, a counter stood in front of two tall bookshelves.

Ceychell placed two logs on the fire and had it going in no time. They sat by the crackling fireplace, and enjoyed a warm drink. Miraden was quiet. He started to thaw and relax in her comfortable chair. The leather didn't squeak at all, it was old and perfectly worn. The limebloom mixed with the pine smoke and entranced him. It was *exactly* as he'd always imagined the store would smell once Ceychell took over.

Ceychell stared into the fire. The flames seemed to dance in her deep green eyes.

"I thought about you so much out there," he said, breaking the silence.

Ceychell wiped a tear from her cheek and whispered, "I know."

"When I didn't hear back from you, I felt sick. I've never felt that way in my life, and I hated it— " Miraden stopped and caught himself. He thought of how foolish he was leaving Kaehrn, and how terrified he was of being nearly sliced open by the naagling chieftain, or eaten by a ghoul, or killed by the ashenkin, just for her. A vision of Lovo and the snow wolves plunging through the ice into the frozen lake flashed through his mind's eye. He thought of how his mistake cost his friend his life, and he did it for her. "It doesn't matter. All I wanted was to know you still cared. With every day that passed, I felt worse and more alone."

Ceychell's lips were trembling and her eyes were pouring tears. She didn't wipe them away, she just listened.

"When I found Kyradel, I was so happy. But… I dreaded seeing you again. I couldn't bear to have my friendship and loyalty tossed away again. I was over you. I knew I had to grow up and face the fact that what we had, what I wanted back more than anything, was gone. My future was clear when I reached Kander Bondare. Then, I got this letter," he said, drawing it from his reed pouch, "and now nothing is clear." He noticed the letters he sent Ceychell stacked neatly on a table next to her, it made him nauseous with guilt.

"Believe me," Ceychell said calmly, wiping away tears. "I will never understand what you went through, what you're still going through. I truly regret everything I ever did to you, every night. I never wanted to stop talking to you. It was stupid and I only did it for my sister, and it didn't even work. But please know I wrote to you many times, I am so glad you got at least one of them, but if that's the letter I'm thinking, it was probably too little too late." Ceychell's eyes flared, "I don't now how Neandra got one of my letters. Oh, I will kill him if I ever see him!"

Ceychell's rage scared him. He certainly wanted some revenge on Neandra after the bounty hunter betrayed and abandoned him and Simigrin with devils at their back, but not murder. The way Ceychell lit up about killing him, he believed her.

"Gorgundi's bat flew off before I could get my letter many times," she continued. "I would even go as far to say as the gods planned it but… but—" She looked away.

He squeezed the armrests, felt the heat of the fire, and realized he was holding his breath.

She looked back at him with her tear-soaked, green eyes and said, "I must be honest with you, I'm glad I was cruel to you for the past few years."

He could not believe it. Her words stabbed him so deep it took everything he had to not fold his arms over his chest, lean-forward, and crumple onto the floor. Just like he had so many times after she discarded him.

"For no other reason than it motivated you to find my sister."

That stung. "I would have gone after her anyway!" he yelled.

"Would you?" Ceychell leaned in and put her hands on his hand. They were so warm and soft. But she was right. He'd had no intention of leaving the forest, and he wasn't brave. "The truth is, Miraden," Ceychell continued, tears dripped from her cheeks, "ever since we were little kids, I have always loved you. Now more than ever. Even if you leave Kaehrn forever, I will still love you. Even if you go to Simigrin, I will love you. Even if you tell me you will hate me for the rest of your life, I will still love you. I would journey with you until you're ready to rest, and then we would make a home together. It took losing you to realize how much I love you."

Miraden dropped his cup and scrambled to find something to clean the spill. "I'm so sorry I spilled it," he said. "I'm sorry, so very sorry!" Shaking, he took a cloth from his pack. He knelt to clean the juno from the floor. Ceychell crouched beside him, took his arm, and whispered, "It's okay." She leaned forward and pressed her lips against his.

Miraden had dreamt of this moment ever since their last kiss, the one that had turned her cold after Kyradel caught them. The kiss that broke their trio of fellowship. Terror gripped him. He'd relived the nightmare of the fallout so many times that this felt too similar. He felt he might lose them both again.

Ceychell suddenly pulled away. "It's okay—you have every right to be cautious of me. I was such a wretch to you, after all."

"Do you still blame me for your falling out with Kyradel?" he asked.

"It was my fault, not yours. I did blame you. After it happened, we should have talked to her together."

"It wouldn't have mattered. She told me she always knew."

"She probably did. Does any of that matter now? I will never let anything come between us. Never again."

Miraden stared into the fire for a moment. He knew how much she loved Kyradel—they were inseparable—but he couldn't believe Ceychell felt that way about him. He'd wanted that his whole life, but he couldn't ignore how he now felt about Simigrin. He *almost* wished he had dropped Kyradel off and returned south. Juggling his feelings for Ceychell and Simigrin wasn't something he was prepared to handle. "A big part of me wants to stay in Kaehrn, but—"

"Then let me go with you."

"You can't, it too d-d—"

"Dangerous? I know, and I'm not afraid. Ashenkin attacked me in my bedroom not long before you returned."

He couldn't believe it. If he returned Kyradel only to find Ceychell gone, or killed, he would have lost his mind. The fear crept into his thoughts that the ashenkin could come right back and finish what they started.

"I figured out how they mark their territory using a char pen, then saw my window marked. So I was ready for them."

"Did you see who marked your window?"

"Vera."

"Vera? What happened to her?"

"I initially noticed traces of char on Kyradel's windowsill, then checked Klod's sill and found a smudge there as well. I caught Vera outside my shop one night. She said she was looking for her cat, but I came out with a knife and scared her so bad she dropped a char pen."

It didn't seem possible. Why would Vera help the ashenkin? Why would she have them take Kyradel?

"There are more of them, Miraden. That was the last thing Vera told me before she died."

Ormus would have killed Vera when Ceychell told him.

"I knew in that moment that I couldn't sit and wait for things to happen. We ambushed the ashenkin coming through my window, and then I took care of Vera." She smiled.

"I didn't know you had it in you," Miraden said.

Ceychell firmly gripped his hand. It was far warmer than his.

"I guess you don't know everything about me." She winked. "I don't think I could ever swing a sword, but I can enroll in the academy in Kander and learn how to fight them in other ways. I believe they might take me."

Miraden wondered if Ceychell would even be admitted. Even so, it would take years for her to train. "What makes you think so?"

She took a folded note from the pocket of her robe, unfolded it, and showed it to him.

Boonja with the soul of fire. Follow him.

He couldn't believe his eyes. "This is from Gorgundi! Where did you get it?"

"The bat brought it just before you returned. I didn't show it to anyone, not even my father." Her voice started to quaver. "I don't know what it means, but it scares me. I can't explain how different I feel lately—almost like I have thoughts and feelings that are not my own." She rubbed her arms and stared into the fire.

"What kinds of thoughts and feelings?"

"Sometimes it's like insects are crawling under my skin. Or I'll wake up boiling hot, or… this may sound strange, but I can feel my moods. Right now I'm cold and my mouth tastes bitter." She rubbed her neck and said, "My neck really aches. It started the moment you tensed up from our kiss."

"I'm sorry."

"No, don't apologize. I… I shouldn't feel these things but I do. I'm worried what they may tell me at the college."

Miraden put his hand on hers. Moments ago it was hot but now her hand had turned icy cold. "When did these feeling start?"

"Soon after you left, but they've become more intense ever since you sent me this shell." She walked to the counter and returned with a small glass jar. Inside were the charred broken remains of the blue shell. Miraden fetched from his bag the shell pieces he had and dropped them in with hers.

"Now they'll never be apart," he said.

Miraden went home to his cabin shortly after and didn't sleep well. After tossing and turning all night, he woke up early the next morning. His bones ached from the cold as he got dressed. He could see his breath and knew he'd have to cut firewood today. His cold house felt still and smelled old and abandoned. The tokens, paintings, and keepsakes were stiff reminders of who he used to be, and he didn't want to be reminded of that. The smell of old pine and the familiar creaks and closeness of the walls were manifestations of his anxiety. He could hardly stand it and almost ran back to Ceychell's shop. He never wanted to stay in his own house again.

He rubbed warmth into his arms and pushed his front door open. Out front of his house was the large oak where Stormrange used to perch. It was partially covered in snow and dripping on the warm late-winter morning. Below the long branches was a small grave marked with a wooden carving he made of Stormrange long ago. Miraden didn't notice it last night when he came home in the dark. He walked over to kneel by the grave.

"I miss you Stormrange," he whispered and patted the snow. He could sense his bird was close. He shut his eyes and remembered Stormrange as a chick, remembered feeding him and nursing his wing. The bird kept him connected to home when he went after Kyradel. He'd never forget him.

Suddenly, he heard chirping. It came from above him in the tree. Miraden gripped the cold trunk, placed his feet on his old footholds, and climbed up the tree. He found a preddlehawk nest on a high branch. Three small bright-blue hawks chirped and opened their mouths when they saw him. They were newborn and hungry. Miraden recalled the family of preddlehawks that lived there three years ago when he'd rescued Stormrange. These chicks were healthy, and he didn't feel right taking one from their mother. There was a screech from above so he climbed back down the tree and jumped into the snow.

"Still climbing that tree?" Kyradel asked. Her eyes were bright blue and cheeks were pink. Lovo was with her. They both smiled at him.

"Miraden is definitely a much better climber than I am," Lovo said. "Remember the swamp?"

How could he forget? He'd never seen a ghoul before or since and hoped it stayed that way. He nodded to Lovo.

"What were you doing up in that tree?" Lovo asked.

"I thought I heard something."

Kyradel whispered, "Stormrange."

His large friend nodded and lowered his head. His smile faded, but only for a moment. "C'mon buddy, we need to get you ready for the ceremony today," he said and pulled in Miraden for a grand side hug.

"I still don't know why the elders are coming here for this," Miraden said, still shaking in his light coat. He couldn't find any furs that fit him in his house and thought the first thing he would do later is to sew a new cloak.

Lovo released Miraden and said, "I know you're going to hate the attention on you, Mir. Just try to enjoy it."

Kyradel took Miraden's arm. "We need to get you ready to meet them," she said. "I think Ceychell may have something for you."

"Kyradel!" Lovo said. Kyradel reddened and put a hand over her mouth.

They walked Miraden to Kyradel's house. Lovo opened the door for him and out came dogs and cats. Miraden pet them as he walked inside and into the family room and went right next to the fireplace. He smelled cinnamon tea brewing in the tea kettle hanging beside him; it brought back memories of stopping by their house with firewood on cold winter mornings. The wave of heat warmed him. He didn't want to leave the fire after being cold all night.

"Sweet rolls are almost ready," Curasca yelled from her kitchen, "just make yourselves at home."

Lovo sat down on the couch and let out a hearty sigh, then picked up a wooden harp next to him and plucked at the strings. He whispered a tune and tried to play but his fingers were fumbly.

"Are you a musician?" Kyradel asked, plopping down next to him. Miraden rubbed his hands behind his back and hoped she'd play.

"I like to play," Lovo said, "but I wouldn't say it's a gift of mine," he said. He plucked a tune, hitting a couple of wrong notes.

"I know that one, here." Kyradel helped him adjust his fingers. "Your hands are so big— you should try just touching the strings instead of plucking them. Like this…" She helped him strum the strings and sang the song with him.

"She came to the river and felt her love tore
The path from her home was burned and no more
The ashes of the cottage her babe was no more
The wrath of Her name claimed another babe for war"

Miraden was entranced. It felt good to hear Kyradel sing again. It had been years since he last heard her, and her beautiful voice calmed him; her song drew out his sorrow like an ebbing tide. He watched her sing, and as she closed her eyes and helped Lovo strum the tune, she smiled. Miraden felt every word, and the sorrow grew unbearably heavy in his heart. Something about her was different. She was becoming a woman, but it was more than that. He felt a painful weight in his chest. Tears fell from his eyes.

When she finished the song, tears ran down Lovo's cheeks and his hands were shaking. "I don't think I've ever heard anything so beautiful in my life," he said. "Can you teach me a bit more, please?"

Kyradel grinned. "I-it's so good to play again. I didn't think I ever would, but it feels good."

Curasca emerged teary-eyed from the kitchen and hugged Kyradel from behind. "Oh, my love. I have missed your singing," she said and kissed her cheek. Kyradel grinned and stared toward the fire, but seemed somewhat distant. Miraden had never seen her like that. He stared at her, wondering what she might be thinking. Then he smelled something burning. "I should get the—"

"Oh no!" Curasca ran back to the kitchen. A few moments later she came out with a plate of browned sweet rolls and offered them. Kyradel took one; Lovo took the rest. Curasca plucked one from his thick fingers and handed it to Miraden.

Miraden popped it into his mouth. Honey and nutmeg oozed down his throat as he chewed the crispy dough. When Ceychell walked into the room, he stopped mid-chew. She wore leather spaulders and gauntlets, a boiled leather cuirass form-fitted to her body over a green dress. Her hair was tied up in a tail. He was certain she'd tossed it up before she stepped out to see him because she usually put time into her hair. Over her arm was a light-tan leather cloak lined with white fur. Miraden forgot to chew.

The fire crackled and no one made a sound as she stepped up to him and unfurled the beautiful cloak. He stood stiff as a statue as she wrapped it around his shoulders and fastened it around his neck. He noticed a trimming of deep-red trees and a deer sewn into the inner lining. It was his family crest. When he was fully dressed, she announced, "Miraden. I've made you this cloak as a sign of my affection and appreciation of you."

He realized she had just *chosen* him in the tradition of the villages of Baregorin. It jolted him. Normally a cloak is given during Valdenfest, but he didn't mind the breaking of the tradition. He struggled to hold back tears and forced a smile. Her eyes were misting up, and her lips were trembling. He pulled her in and hugged her tightly.

He loved her. He'd loved her longer than he could remember. She was the first and last person he thought of each day. Holding her meant *everything* to him. He could feel her strength, hear her breath, enjoyed her warmth, the taste and smell of her limebloom perfume; he knew her as well as he knew himself.

But something was different now. He remembered the moment that his love for her, the love that he'd felt his entire life, shattered. He'd been sitting on the beach next to Simigrin, and he'd finally admitted to himself that Ceychell would never really love him. When he finally got her love letter, it was too late. And it hurt too much.

"Are you okay?" she whispered.

Miraden said nothing. He wanted to run.

She leaned back and smiled at him but her bottom lip trembled. He wanted to thank her; he wanted things to be like they used to be. But they weren't. When she leaned toward him, he noticed the copper lantern sigil on her chest. Ormus wore it for special occasions. It was the sign of his house and the mark of his office.

"Are you really the chieftain?" he said.

She nodded. "For now."

Kyradel laughed. "Not sure Baregorin can handle the Tyrant of Kaehrn long-term."

"Kyra!" Curasca said.

Lovo put a hand on Ceychell's and Miraden's shoulders, smiling broadly. "I kind of always pictured this when Miraden mentioned you. Praise be to the Mother of Light that I got to see it for myself."

TWO

THE HONOR OF BAREGORIN

KAEHRN WAS CROWDED WITH VISITORS from the neighboring villages
and Bilore Des. People stopped in on distant relatives, drank freshly
tapped mead, roasted swine on spits at the town square near the
Founder's Statue, and most of all, hoped that the ashenkin could
be defeated. Miraden's mouth watered from the wonderful scents
of herbs and oils and meat that plumed from the cookfires. He was
next to the long dining hall near the edge of town. Inside, a feast
was being prepped. Outside of it, the ruling families of the region
were gathered.

Miraden stood next to Lovo near the gathering of the ruling
families. He was anxious and fidgety. The crowd grew throughout
the day, now hundreds of people were in his small village. People
were getting in line to be served food near the cookfires. The
ceremony would start soon.

He was much warmer in his new cloak. The leather was softer
than the fur and it was cozy. It was as if Ceychell had sewed her
love into it and her arms were wrapping around him. He pulled it
tighter. He thought about talking to Ceychell about how he really
felt, but his thoughts drifted to Simigrin. She was often on his

mind. He wondered if she was studying now and preparing for her next mission. He daydreamed briefly and imagined staring into her amber eyes.

"Is all this really necessary," Miraden groaned. "They should have invited Simigrin up if they wanted to honor someone." He saw Ormus and Ceychell talking to Jojhor, Chieftain of Storjn. Ormus was so tall and broad-shouldered that he made Jojhor look like a child. Jojhor's beard was long, red and gray. Deep wrinkles stacked on his forehead. He'd outlived three wives. Miraden remembered he'd asked Ceychell at Valdenfest last year, before Kyradel was taken. When she rejected a village chieftain it was a high insult and Jojhor demanded Ormus convince Ceychell that she should honor his position. Ormus didn't back down, and she was a chieftain's daughter, and now the chieftain herself. Jojhor slouched and cowered as he spoke to her. Miraden started believing there was more to *the tyrant* moniker Ceychell was carrying.

Lovo leaned in and whispered into Miraden's ear, "You can't look at things that way. You've given people a chance at hope. You saved Kyradel and many other children."

"So did Simigrin," Miraden told him. "So did you."

Lovo smiled. "A hero shouldn't wear the title. Don't ever change. Don't think Simigrin isn't being recognized as a hero."

Miraden knew he should be excited, but he did not welcome all the attention. He would rather the other villages send him silver arrows or a horse.

Miraden sighed, he was being foolish. He looked up to his friend, smiling and enjoying himself. "Lovo, I am so glad you're here. But I've got to know what happened."

Lovo nodded. "I wish I knew. I... remember being held. I was certain I died." His voice fell, he was really distraught. "A woman was there, I couldn't really see her, but I heard her humming. She told me I could go back and that I had more to do in my life. I'm not sure how long it was, really, but I woke up on the side of Arrowheart lake and I was wearing these white furs that are just like the wolves that chased us. And then I came here."

Miraden believed a goddess saved Lovo, but didn't know why. He was thankful, and realized not only should he pray more often, but that many of his prayers were answered on his journey.

Kyradel's laughter caught his attention. She was chatting with Elsaria, the new chieftain of Valijn. She was young, only a year older than Miraden. Her hair was nearly white, and she wore black bear pelts with a white streak down the back. Her arms were fit and strong, and two deep scars lined her face. Miraden heard stories of how fierce she was. She hunted bears and fought in their battle against the village of Yoldro a few years back. He'd met her once during Valdenfest when she'd shoved him out of her way on her way to the campfire.

Kyradel was telling a story, and Elsaria listened with a listless gaze. Kyradel tipped her long brim hat and brushed her fiery red hair to the side. She wore the outfit Miraden bought for her in Crestain—a green shirt, dark paints and black high boots— also a shimmering green cape he hadn't seen before. She looked like a gambler or an adventurer.

"Does *everyone* love Kyradel?" Lovo asked. "Seems like they do."

Elsaria leaned against the wall of the dining hall, smiling, and pushed her hair back behind her ear.

Miraden shrugged. "Believe it or not, this isn't like her Ceychell was always the center of attention." People loved Kyradel's singing, but she was usually shy around everyone but Miraden. He was happy to see her climbing out of her shell.

"Really? You could have fooled me," Lovo said.

"What do you mean?

"I've seen a dozen men here chat with Ceychell and she was pretty curt with the lot of em."

"You have?" Miraden said with a twang of jealousy. "I mean, I'm not surprised. So many men in the villages have tried to court her, even some that were married. It's strange not to see Ormus chasing them away."

"Don't think Ormus has to do any chasing. And I've not seen her smile at anyone but you, buddy."

Ceychell interrupted a newcomer to the conversation. The man wore steel armor under a blue tabard, two gold rings at the center of the blue on his chest—a knight of Crestain. He was tan and had dark curly hair and wide dark-brown eyes. He looked rebuked by whatever Ceychell said and glanced over at Ormus. Then back to Ceychell.

"Ceychell scares me a bit more than Ormus," Lovo said, "and that is one handsome knight she just snubbed."

"Ceychell doesn't like the charmers," Miraden said, watching the knight back away. Miraden was glad she'd chased him off.

"You okay Mir?" Lovo asked.

"Yes, just a bit anxious," he said. But he felt the pricking of jealousy each time he caught someone staring at Ceychell or going up to talk to her.

When the knight looked over at Lovo and stared for a moment, Lovo said, "He's not too heartbroken."

Miraden noticed them stare at each other for a moment before the knight walked back into the crowd. Miraden patted Lovo on the shoulder and grinned.

The doors to the feasting hall opened. When a low horn sounded, the ruling families and esteemed guests started to walk inside.

Lovo and Miraden headed inside the hall behind the crowd. Miraden sighed with relief and shook out the cold. Between a roaring fireplace and the flaming torches on the walls, he quickly felt better. Lanterns hung from the apex of the ceiling over a long table that stretched down the center of the longhouse. Their dancing flames illuminated the deep-green and dark-brown walls. People took their seats slowly; no one seemed to be in a rush. Villagers and cooks from Bilore Des started slicing steaming roast pigs, pheasants, and venisons in the open kitchen at the far end of the hall. Miraden smelled the nutmeg on the smashed yams and the sweet scent of the salted pig, and his mouth began to water. He hungrily eyed the warm loaves of bread soaked in sweet cream butter—one of his favorite foods—and there was a loaf down at the end of the table near where he was headed.

Everyone chatted with their neighbors and drank large flagons of mead. At the head of the table sat Ceychell with Kyradel, Ormus and Curasca to her left. Miraden sat to her right with Lovo beside him.

Miraden glanced over at Ceychell. She was sitting up straight and observing her table full of guests. He leaned toward her and she leaned over with a grin.

"I am not so sure about this," Miraden said. Part of him wanted to retreat and escape. He was nervous something bad would happen or that the fun would be spoiled somehow at any moment. Old jokes about him might be brought up by villagers or they might tease him about Ceychell. He wanted none of it. But then he realized he wasn't that boy anymore. They had no reason to tease him, and he deserved to sit at the table. After thinking it over, he felt much better. "But it is kind of nice."

She put her hand on his below the table, looked into his eyes, and whispered. "Be here with me. You deserve a few kind words, Miraden."

"Miraden needs more mead," Ormus told a cook who was filling cups, "His cup isn't full." The cook rushed to the other side of the table to top off Miraden's glass. Lovo drained his to get a refill as well.

Once all the meals were served, Ceychell stood up. The villagers stopped their eating, drinking, and chatting and turned to look at her. Miraden couldn't believe his eyes. Her long brown hair shone under the torchlight, her bangs woven back around her head like a crown. Her bronze pin shimmered on her brown, snug, boiled-leather cuirass. The green dress beneath her armor matched her glittering eyes. She stood tall, chin up and smiling bravely. He'd never seen her so confident. Something about her felt different to him—she seemed fearless or even cruel.

"Thank you, citizens and honored guests of Baregorin," she began. "I, Ceychell, Chieftain of Kaehrn, welcome you to our hall. It has been nearly two years since we've gathered. Ever since the ashenkin began to invade our homes. Our supplies have dwindled and our relations have strained.

"Many of you have lost loved ones—we have too. Our hearts ache with yours, but today we have new hope that these devils can be defeated; that our children will once again be safe to wander our forest, our streams, our mountains; that they will be able to tell our stories.

"We share this joyous moment because of a few heroes. One who, by the grace of our gods, brought my own sister back from beyond the Ashengate. I, along with the leadership of Baregorin Forest, wish to bring us all together to honor them for their triumph and seek their guidance."

Ceychell put her hand out for Miraden. "Miraden, if you would please stand." Miraden swallowed his anxiety and stood up. He brushed breadcrumbs from his arms and chest and stared down at the table before him. He squeezed his fists to stop himself from shaking and wanted to hide. He heard a few whispered comments but he didn't understand them. At last, he raised his head and looked at Ceychell; she grinned and stared back at him.

Ceychell waved to Elsaria of Valijn. The huntress chieftain rose from her seat, lifted two boots from beside her chair and walked up to the head of the table. Her lips were chapped and her eyes crystal blue. She looked tougher than stone despite being a tad shorter than Miraden.

"I, Elsaria of Valijn, honor you, Miraden, and bring you these boots. They are fireproof and leave no footprints. They were blessed by Kho-talic, the mystic of my village. I hope they bring you a quiet step and help you avoid a misstep." She held up the dark brown, scaled boots. Their interior was lined with white fur, and their soles were a strange, mottled black. She bowed and handed them to Miraden then returned to her seat.

Ceychell waved forward Gandolvou of Adolehrn. The snub-nosed man stood from his seat and leered at her. He was gaunt but primped with a fresh haircut that curved far over his ears. Adolehrn was a village of artists and fisherman. They valued a good catch and a painted canvas. Miraden remembered Gandolvou speaking about his sculptures at one of the Valdenfests, telling everyone how he was sought out by great artists in Sentry for his work. He stepped around to face Miraden carrying a scaled cloak over his arm.

"I, Gandolvou, Chieftain of Adolehrn, give you this hood and cloak sewn from the scales of the osiliath, ages ago when osiliath still lived this far north. It will make you invisible and keep you safe. May it protect you from those who would stop a hero in his path." Its scales were hard, greenish-black, thin, weightless, and rolled up nicely. Miraden nodded and set it next to him on the table, noticing its slick surface did not reflect the torchlight. Gandolvou dipped his head and returned to his seat.

Ceychell nodded to the next guest. Jojhor rose from his seat and slowly walked around the table. His people were more mountain folk than forest people—planters, miners, brewers, and dog tamers. Jojhor was a head taller than Miraden, roughly Ceychell's height, and far beyond his sixtieth Passing. He had a blockish face with thin red and white hairs on his chin. He looked at Ceychell, grunted, and then looked at Miraden.

"I Jojhor, Chieftain of Storjn, gift you a seeing lens that has been in our family for generations. It can see through darkness and fog, and shorten distances so that you will always know what is coming to harm you. We appreciate you for what you've done for Baregorin and this world." He handed the silver tube to Miraden. On both sides it had a crystal-seeing glass. It buzzed in Miraden's hands.

When Jojhor returned to his seat, Ceychell nodded to Mayor Updinkle. He was in a black suit that his gut was stretching out at the waist of his pants, but he managed to fasten all his buttons and they had not yet popped. He muttered something under his breath and rose from his seat as if he were pulled up by strings. He grinned gruesomely and walked around the table to face Miraden. Miraden recalled him in his overly-stuffed, decrepit office, and vividly remembers him cowering behind his dagger-pocked desk back in Bilore Des. He had changed his tune when Miraden returned with the naagling chieftain's head in his sack.

"Well, a few of us in Bilore Des still know you as the naagling slayer, but it seems that is no longer a fitting title for you. This boy—"

"Man," Ceychell interjected, even though Miraden still hadn't had his eighteenth Passing. Updinkle's eye twitched.

"Pardon, this *man* came to Bilore Des last year looking for his friend and helped rid us of the vermin plaguing our city. It's good to see heroes never retire from their duty, and to recognize you for what you've done, I extend to you this golden coin with four sapphires and an emerald. May it be known that any bearer of this symbol of heroism shall be given special consideration with guards, prices, taxes, and treatments in the four villages and our own city of Bilore Des." The guests nodded in agreement. He handed the coin to Miraden. "I'm glad you found those ashenkin you were looking for," he whispered. Then he smiled and returned to his seat.

Yoldro's chieftain and people didn't come, which didn't surprise Miraden. All the other villages have had issues with them in the past. He'd hoped there would have been a truce or peace offering while he was away, but that didn't happen. But he hadn't known that relations were so strained that the Yoldro simply weren't even mentioned. The coin Updinkle gave him only had four sapphires, instead of five. He was surprised even Bilore Des no longer recognized them as part of Baregorin.

Ceychell nodded to Ormus who stood and walked around the table holding a sheathed axe. Miraden had always looked up to Ormus but he also feared the man and wasn't sure what he might say.

"I, Ormus, former chieftain of Kaehrn and a very grateful father to Kaehrn's current chieftain give to you a treasure that has been in our family for many years." He revealed from the sheath a silver battle axe with fragments of black stone in the gray oak hilt. "This was my greatfather's axe, my father's axe, and it was my axe when I sailed the Sea of Sarkus for many years. Whenever I was uncertain, I held this close and it always helped me. For a young man who's cut a hundred hundred logs, it should feel natural to you in battle." He placed the axe in its black leather holster and handed it to Miraden. Miraden held it as Ormus hugged him and nearly crushed him.

"Thank you, son," the big man whispered. "Let it always guide you." Teary-eyed, Ormus walked back to his seat.

Miraden stood in front of his chair in silence looking down at the heavy axe in his hands. He wasn't sure what to say, having received all the wonderful gifts. He looked at Lovo, Curasca, and Ormus; they all smiled at him. He turned to find Ceychell also smiling.

The knight from Crestain broke the short silence, tapping his knife on his tankard. "What about the Chieftain of Kaehrn? What does she say?"

Ceychell put her hand on Miraden's shoulder and said, "I've known Miraden my whole life. His father treated me like a princess. His mother wiped my tears and encouraged me to never stop dreaming. And the man you see here has treated me with care, loyalty, and affection—" she paused and swallowed, then said "—beyond that which I deserve. I honor Miraden by allowing him to live any life he chooses, to be the man of his making, and to always honor him as the hero of our village because my love for him is unconditional. That is all I have to give."

Miraden was so stiff he shook. He held his breath and tried to catch his balance. He wasn't sure he could respond. He looked at Ceychell and felt his heart might explode.

Lovo stood quickly and clutched Miraden's arm, steadied him. "I'm Lovo," he blurted, seemingly breaking the awkward silence. "I have no titles. I am not important when it comes to these things. I ventured with Miraden because I believed in him. I felt he believed in doing right and he was devoted to save his friend. He is my best friend, and I would follow him again to the end of the world and beyond the Ashengates. He is—"

The crowd burst into cheers and claps.

"Thank you, Lovo," Miraden said, finding his mettle again. The visitors quieted down again, and Miraden peered around the table. "Lovo sacrificed himself to save me. He is a dear friend. I would not be here were it not for Lovo, and he would never have you hear any of it. Simigrin, a mage of Kander Bondare, followed me without question and fought beside me beyond the Ashengate. And Gorgundi, the shaman of O'kokra and many of his people were also a big part of this mission. They closed the gate. Not me.

"I was just a ranger, a coward, I-I was nothing when I left here." He looked at the people sitting around the long table. They were listening so intently he felt like he might fall apart. Ceychell took his hand in hers, and he took a deep breath. "But I left and found purpose. Even though I'm home now, the ashenkin must be wholly destroyed. I won't stop hunting them. This is why I must … thank you for this. You … really … " He began to worry that they might still think him a coward. He knew it was ridiculous—most of them didn't even know him. Lovo stepped up again to shield him from the crowd.

"Perhaps we should eat, Chieftain," Lovo whispered to Ceychell.

Kyradel stood, everyone turned to look at her. Her short red locks were braidless, combed and curling around her cheeks and neck. She looked healthy again, not gaunt as Miraden found her beyond the Ashengate. He was happy she was home. "I'd like to say something." She smiled and lifted a book off the table. It was leather bound, large, and had a purple tassel holding her place. "I have also known Miraden all my life. He's kind, thoughtful, he's wonderful, and such a good friend. Most of you don't know him like I do. He saved me—he saved many of us. I can never repay him for that, but as he told me about his adventures on the way back, I have started to write them in verse. And when I finish it, I'll make sure everyone gets to read or hear about Miraden's journey because it is a tale that is made for heroes. So…" Kyradel looked at Miraden. Miraden was stunned. "So, we are all here to be thankful for Miraden and we can all enjoy this happy moment together."

Ceychell nodded. "Agreed. It's time to feast."

Everyone at the table began conversing and feasting. The village elders chatted more than they had in years. Even more so than at last year's Valdenfest, throughout which they constantly complained about the ashenkin and tried to drink their worries away.

Miraden ate quietly and drank very little. He glanced at the gifts on the floor next to him and still couldn't believe such treasures were his. He chewed a piece of roasted pig, picked up the coin, and stared at the tiny emerald gleaming in the torch lights. He looked over and saw a similar shine on Ceychell's emerald serpent ring, then up to her matching eyes.

He could hardly believe that she loved him; he'd been so accustomed to her coldness and cruelty these past few years. But even though she'd opened up to him, Miraden still thought of Simigrin and wished she was there with him. When he thought about her, he thought he could feel Ceychell sensing it. As ridiculous as that seemed, he knew that she knew. She looked over at him mid-bite, and he could feel her reading his mind. He pushed the thoughts from his head, and Ormus rescued him, "Do you need any more pork, Miraden? I can have the cooks bring another platter."

"No, sir. I'm quite full." Miraden replied, though he had not eaten much.

Ormus nodded and took a drink from his mug.

Aside from his feelings about Simi, Miraden felt comfortably warm in the cloak Ceychell made him and safe beside Lovo. But he still felt anxious. He wasn't sure why. It seemed everything was in place, but something he couldn't see was drastically out of place. Kyradel winked at him from across the table, she was chatting with Elsaria. The white-haired chieftain played her fork through her food and bathed in Kyradel's honeyed words.

Someone down the table asked when he was going to tell them about his excursion and the gate closure, and the inquiries slowly progressed up the table toward him. He prepared an answer, but as he stood up, the large doors at the end of the hall opened, and the guards of Bilore Des and the villages' militia stood in the doorway. The hall quieted, and the loud chatter of the villagers in the square outside drifted into the hall.

Chandar, the village carpenter, stepped between the guards and said, "Chieftain, Miraden. You'd best come. There is a messenger from Kander here."

"We'll be right there," Ceychell told him. She smiled at Miraden. "After you."

When Miraden started to leave, Lovo pushed his own chair back and stood, and the three of them walked out of the hall. The guests were not far behind them, chattering as they followed the trio and Chandar to the village square, where hundreds of villagers were sitting around the cookfires, enjoying the feast, and chatting.

At the edge of the square was a giant bird, taller than two men, with a sharp beak and long silver and white feathers, and saddle belted to its midsection. Next to it stood a man in a green, hooded robe.

Miraden had seen one of the birds once. It was a grouble. He never realized people could ride them. The bird and the man watched Miraden, Ceychell, Lovo, and the line of distinguished guests cross the square as the villagers parted for them.

The man lowered his hood. His skin was dark, his smile was confident, and his short hair was golden and frizzy. He scratched the grouble's neck, and the bird nudged its head against his shoulder.

"I am Otalogrin, of Kander, city in the clouds," the man said when Miraden and Ceychell reached him. "Are you Miraden?"

"I am," Miraden said.

Ceychell stepped forward and said, "Welcome to Kaehrn, Otalogrin. Would you join us for our feast? Your timing is perfect."

Otalogrin held up a hand. "Thank you, but I cannot stay long. I am sorry to have interrupted your celebration, but I have an urgent message for you." He took a scroll from a green bag at his side that had looked empty. The pouch reminded Miraden of Simigrin's bag, only hers was blue. He handed the scroll to Miraden.

"Are you an ice mage, like Simigrin?" Miraden asked.

"No, I am a caller. There are many orders in Kander."

Miraden stared at the letter for a moment. The bone-white

parchment felt smooth in his hand, unlike the course paper he was used to writing on. It was tied with a purple string, the color of Simigrin's hair.

Miraden slid the string off and carefully unrolled the letter:

Miraden,

My master wishes to speak with Ceychell. He says she is critical to stop the ashenkin. I know you just got home. I truly hope you've had a chance to reunite Kyradel with her family. We have received reports that more gates are opening and children are being abducted in greater numbers. We could really use your help. Please come with Ceychell as soon as possible.

Simigrin

Miraden held up the note for a moment, so Ceychell and Lovo could read it with him.

"When do we leave?" Lovo whispered.

Miraden reached into his bag and found the charcoal pencil he had used to write letters to Ceychell. It was worn to the nub, but he managed to crimp hold of it to write a response.

Simigrin,

I will leave at once. Tell your master I will bring Ceychell. Gorgundi said she is a woman with a soul of fire. I hope someone knows what that means.

Until we meet.

Miraden

He rolled the letter back up and slid the string back over it. "Would you please return this to her?" Miraden asked.

Otalogrin nodded and accepted the message. "I shall. It's good to meet you, Miraden. Thank you for what you've done." He placed the scroll in his pouch and pulled his hood up. Then he climbed onto the black saddle on the grouble's back, and the bird leaped into the air and quickly climbed into the overcast sky.

"What's going on?" Mayor Updinkle asked.

"What was in the note?" another man shouted.

Miraden held up his hand to quiet the rush of questions from the crowd. "I will tell you how we closed the Ashengate, I know that is why you're here. Then, Lovo, Ceychell, and I, must get ready to leave for Kander."

THREE

THE DAGGER'S MASTER

MIRADEN WIPED SWEAT FROM HIS face. He sat at a workbench with a pile of shafts, a row of silver arrowheads, and a ball of twine. Behind him, Lovo was sweeping up metal fragments and soot near the bellows and smelter. After he'd received the message from Simigrin, he and Lovo worked with Bryndyke for hours in his smithy. All Miraden could think about was getting down to Kander.

Lovo was dripping sweat. He had taken off his shirt and was half covered in soot. Bryndyke had already made them a lot of arrowheads, but they helped him complete the work on the silver Ceychell purchased from Sulover.

Miraden held up a cooled tip, only five left to make. His tired fingers twitched as he slid the tip into the shaft and tied it in place.

Bryndyke placed five leather-sheathed daggers on the table next to Lovo. "These aren't my finest work, but they're sharp and silver. You've got the strength to be a smith, young Lovo."

"I've been a lot of things," Lovo said, "but I don't think being a smithy is for me." He picked up the daggers, walked over to his gear sack near the door next to his silver mace, and put them in the sack. "You want help with those, Miraden?"

"Miraden's the fastest fletcher in Kaehrn," Bryndyke said.

"After my father, of course," Miraden said reflexively. He missed his father; he hadn't thought about him in some time. They'd spent countless hours down by the river making arrows, listening to the water and the birds, the sounds of their knives working wood and the tight pull of the knots. He missed those times.

Miraden was amazed by Lovo's strength, but his friend was lacking in dexterity. Lovo fumbled the tools and at one point stubbed his foot on the anvil. Miraden would have to check that Lovo had tired the arrowheads properly.

"Thank you. I'll have these done shortly," Miraden said. He wiped the silver tip with a rag until it shined.

Lovo nodded. "I'm going to jump in the river and wash off. Pray I don't freeze in there."

Miraden almost made a joke, but he was surprised Lovo joked about it himself. He looked over at his big friend who was smiling, not a care in the world, before he closed the door behind him.

"I'm sorry yeh have to leave us again, Miraden," Bryndyke said. "Suppose that is the life of a *hero* though." Bryndyke winked at him. Then he scraped the remaining bits of metal from his arrowhead mold and set it on Miraden's workbench.

Miraden finished the last arrow and placed it in his third quiver. Then he said goodnight to Bryndyke and left the smithy. It was getting late. Many of the visitors had left or set up camp in the village. With so many people chatting at the campsite, Kaehrn was louder than he was used to. He walked down the path to Ormus and Curasca's home. Light shone through the front window, and smoke rose from the chimney. On the hill behind their house, the Kaehrnstone shined like a beacon reflecting the moonlight, as bright as the full moon itself.

He walked up to their house and knocked on the door. Curasca opened it. Her eyes were red and teary. She pulled Miraden into a hug and brought him inside without a word. Ormus was sitting near the fire with Ceychell. She was suited up in leather pants and a shirt of leather armor that was too big for her, covered by a coat and a pack on her back. She held a blue pine walking staff. Trees were carved into the wooden shaft and their outlines and shadows were burnt around the carvings. Miraden had made it for her a few years back; he hadn't seen it since.

Ormus stood up from the fireplace as Miraden petted the dogs and walked over to them. Ormus's beard was shot grayer than Miraden remembered. And though he was tall and heavyset, he looked frailer than Miraden remembered. Losing Kyradel had taken a toll on him, and now Ceychell was leaving. Ormus must be devastated.

Ormus reached out and hugged Miraden. Miraden felt sad to take Ceychell away from her father so soon after he'd finally returned Kyradel. It didn't seem right, but he knew it had to be done. Ceychell wanted to join him, she wanted to find a way to aid in stopping the ashenkin and this was her chance.

Kyradel walked into the room, her eyes were red, but she was smiling. She walked up to Ceychell and hugged her; they held each other for a long time.

Ormus put a hand on Miraden's shoulder. "Promise me you'll both return home when this is all done."

Miraden wasn't sure he could make that promise. He looked at Ceychell, sobbing and holding Kyradel, and wasn't sure about many things, wasn't sure she could protect herself, wasn't sure he still loved Ceychell, wasn't sure Simigrin loved him.

"I will do everything I can," Miraden said.

Ormus gave him a final squeeze, and he was pulled right into Curasca's arms. Her hug felt like angel wings curling around him after Ormus's iron-gripped hug. She whispered, "Thank you, Miraden."

Ceychell and Miraden walked out of the house and down the path south leading out of the village. Ormus, Curasca, and Kyradel all watched from the front doorway of their home. He saw their dark silhouettes and felt he was part of their family for the first time. Ceychell reached over and squeezed his hand without a word. They met Lovo at the edge of the village, leaning on a young blue pine. He hummed and plucked the wooden harp Kyradel had given him. He strapped the harp to his giant backpack, grinned, and lifted it by the straps with his thumbs. "Are we ready?"

Miraden looked at Ceychell and she nodded.

"Tell me again why we are leaving at night?" Lovo asked.

"Because I'd probably change my mind by morning," Miraden said.

"You could change your mind tonight instead, and we can sleep in," Lovo said.

"What's the fun in that?" Ceychell said.

"There is a large bed, a big breakfast, and a nap afterwards. That all sounds fun to me," Lovo said.

"Maybe they'll have all that and more in Kander," she said, "I've heard they have the best food and finest beds in the world."

"Hopefully," Lovo hummed to himself.

Miraden could tell Lovo was imagining Kander as a giant inn with endless treats. He patted Lovo's shoulder and said, "Hold on to that dream."

They walked through part of the night and took a short rest before daybreak. Miraden didn't sleep much. He rested against a tree; Ceychell and Lovo rested against him. He felt proud that he chose to leave Kaehrn and make a difference. He smiled and stared through the red morning sunshine breaching the tree canopy.

It was a pleasant couple of days walking through the forest. The early spring brought out the warmth and a symphony of chirping birds. He realized how much he missed hearing them. It felt like a lifetime ago when he heard them last year.

They reached Pallow Lake early in the afternoon. The sun broke through parted clouds, and its reflection on the still lake was almost blinding. Miraden remembered coming down to Pallow each year with his parents. His mother would sit with her feet in the water and sew clothes. He would help his father catch golden smecks with a net in the shallows and roast them at night. Thinking about their buttery taste made his mouth water.

"Are we going to stop in Yoldro tomorrow?" Lovo asked.

"They refused to come up to Miraden's ceremony," Ceychell groaned. "They don't like us very much."

"Why is that?" Lovo asked.

Ceychell sighed. "They accused us of poaching stags from their land last year, though it was likely Storjn or their own people. They're a savage bunch, cruel to animals and each other. I've never liked them."

"I'd rather go around," Miraden said. "I don't want any problems." He saw the end of a pole sticking out the top of Lovo's pack and kept thinking about the aroma of fresh fish crackling on the fire.

"What problems?" Lovo asked.

"Is that a fishing pole?" Miraden said in reply. Lovo nodded. "Let's stop to catch some fish for the evening, and we can chat about it."

Thanks to Lovo's pole and some grubs Miraden found in a rotting log, they fished for an hour and caught a half-dozen smecks. They made a campfire near the lake and smoked the fish. Ceychell came back from a quick forage holding a small leather bag full of berries. She sat next to Miraden, and with her pocketknife, scraped dust from scortwig she found onto the fish for some salty flavor. Lovo played on his harp while Ceychell and Miraden cooked. Lovo sniffed the sizzling fish and said, "That does smell good, you two." The golden fish were small but delicious, and they ate them up.

After dinner they rested near the smoldering fire. It was chilly, but Miraden felt *so* much warmer in his new cloak. Ceychell laid her head on his shoulder, wrapped her arms around him, and held him tight. She hadn't sat next to him like that in a very long time. It was just like when they were younger, and they would stop after a long run through the woods and collapse to rest against a tree. His body sagged as the anxieties melted away. His arms, hands, and legs buzzed as they relaxed like he was turning into a puddle. He remembered how much he dreamed of being held by her while he was away. Sitting with her now felt surreal. His mind was calm. At last he closed his eyes.

He awoke in a muddle. A hand grabbed his shoulder and pulled him to his feet.

"Well, who do we have here?" a man in brown furs said. His beard was black, and two ram antlers jutted from his cracked iron helmet.

Miraden couldn't believe he had fallen asleep and been caught off-guard in his own forest. He reached for his axe but two men in furs held his arms tight. One of the bandits wore a ram horn helmet with a cracked visor and the other with a steel skull cap. Across from him, Ceychell was held by a heavyset bandit in black bear furs with a large skinning knife held to her side. Three men in furs tried to hold Lovo until one punched him in the gut to settle him.

"This is a pretty catch!" The short bandit wore a helmet with ram horns that spiraled so far forward that the helmet leaned against his brow. He pulled a lock of Ceychell's hair and sniffed it.

Ram-horned helmets, most likely trappers from Yoldro.

"Let them go," Miraden said. "I'm the one you want."

They all looked at him, then laughed. The man in the center stepped closer to Miraden. He was shorter than the rest, but his horns were the largest. He held a boarding axe, and had a thorny whip coiled to his side. "What makes you think we don't want all of you?" he said. "You all look like you can be good slaves."

"I am Miraden. I closed the Ashengate. I would be worth a ransom from Kander. Let my friends go."

The trappers laughed.

"You're the mighty Miraden?" the leader said. "So sorry we missed your party." He laughed again and spat on Miraden's chest.

Ceychell yanked her hand free and elbowed the man behind her in the jaw. The trapper fell back, and everyone gaped at her.

The leader started to rush her, but Lovo lunged and kicked him in the face. The short man crumpled, lost his helmet, and stumbled back into a tree. Lovo pulled away from the three men and drew his mace. The Yoldrons pulled daggers from their belts; one unfurled a net and threw it at Lovo. Lovo grabbed the net, spun it over his head with one hand, and bashed a man in the skull with his mace. He tossed the net onto the other two as they tried to back away.

Miraden elbowed one of the men holding him, spun, and kicked him away. The other pressed a dagger to his throat.

"Wait!" Ceychell hollered. "I am the chieftain of Kaehrn." The fighting stopped. "If they find out you've captured me, the villages and Bilore Des will raze Yoldro."

The leader licked the blood from his lips, shook his head, and picked up his helmet. One of the antlers was broken in half. "Chieftain Drojindaak is going to love having you as a trophy in his longhouse, Ceychell."

Ceychell stared at Miraden's hip where his dagger Hellshy was sheathed. She felt a warm buzz, as if it connected with her. She didn't know how, but she felt it. When Ceychell reached her hand out toward Miraden, Hellshy snapped out of its sheath and stabbed Miraden's captor in the chest several times until he collapsed to the ground.

Miraden jumped away, snatched his bow off his back, drew an

arrow, and pointed it at the leader's head. Hellshy dripped blood as it swayed back and forth midair as if looking for the right place to plunge into the leader.

The two men behind Lovo tore at the net and watched the dagger.

"What… what ashenkin sorcery is this?" The leader yelled. He raised his boarding axe to throw it at Ceychell, but Miraden shot him through the hand.

"On your backs!" Lovo yelled at the two men trying to scoot away in the net. They dropped their weapons and put up their hands. Lovo twisted the net, pulled the rope to bind it, and dragged them closer to their leader screaming on the ground pulling the arrow out of his hand. "What do you want to do with them?"

"Kill them," Ceychell said as Miraden said, "Let them go."

Miraden was shocked. He hadn't expected Ceychell to say such a thing. She was dead serious though. She glared at the men, and her hands were balled into fists. Perhaps she was the *Tyrant of Kaehrn.*

"They will return to Yoldro," she said, "and send their militia after us.".

The two bound men shook their heads. "No," the taller of them said, "we will say we were ambushed by a bear!" Or attacked by ashenkin!"

Miraden dropped his bow and drew his axe. It was heavy but felt good in his hand. The leader got back to his feet, hand pouring blood. Hellshy drifted over and hovered with its point at the leader's forehead.

"It's your call," Ceychell said to Miraden.

Miraden knew Ceychell was mostly right about killing them, but he couldn't kill two men who'd surrendered—it wasn't right. The Yoldro tribe was disorderly and cruel and unfriendly, but killing the men would risk their mission if they got caught up in Yoldro. He walked over to the two men in the net, and took a few deep breaths.

His stomach twisted in knots.

"We are taking the road past Yoldro," he told them. "You try anything, and my friend will get her way."

They both nodded.

"Take their weapons," Miraden said. Lovo rifled through their pockets and took their knives.

One of the trappers, a man with close-set blue eyes and a patchy beard said, "We can take you to our stags if you let us go."

"Shut—" the leader's yell was cut off by Hellshy floating down and pressing against his neck. He tripped and fell backwards. Hellshy balanced precariously on his Adam's apple.

"How many stags do you have?" Miraden asked.

"Two," the trapper said.

"Take us to them," Miraden said.

"What do we do with him?" Lovo asked.

Miraden walked over to the leader, who was still pinned to the ground by Hellshy. He looked far stronger than Miraden, but he lay perfectly still. Miraden reached out to retrieve the arrow next to the leader and was ready to strike. As he gripped the shaft, the leader grabbed Miraden's wrist with his injured hand, and Miraden drove the axed into the leader's neck.

Blood sprayed up in Miraden's face, and he jumped back. He wiped his face with his sleeve; then wiped the arrow and axe clean on the man's pants.

Hellshy floated up from the man's neck and returned to Ceychell.

Lovo yanked on the rope tied to the net. "Let's go."

They walked in darkness for a few minutes, Ceychell and Miraden just ahead of Lovo and the other two. Miraden held his bow ready in case of ambush. Ceychell clutched his bloody dagger and walked beside him. He wanted to ask her about what happened, but not in front of the trappers.

Between a grouping of thick blue pines, Miraden spotted two great stags tied to a tree next to a smoldering campfire. Their eyes sparkled in the light of the embers. He waved for Lovo to stop. Miraden crept toward them and realized he couldn't hear his own footsteps in his new boots.

It was so dark, it was difficult to see, but he found no trappers sleeping or waiting for them. They were at a trapper's campground with cages, a sharpening stone, a tanning station with a bucket half-full of urine, two iron lanterns and three smoothed tree stumps for sitting. A big animal was lying down in one of the cages, but Miraden couldn't tell what it was in the darkness. It was just a large dark mass.

He waved them forward.

Miraden walked over to the two great stags: one was white, the other black. Both had a saddle on their backs. Their shoulders were level with his head, and each had at least twenty-point antler racks. Miraden had seen stags this size before, and even shot one with his father long ago. They were far more common in southwest Baregorin Forest, where it meets Solkjin Woods. They were beautiful, the steeds of kings.

"Let me have that scortwig," he whispered to Ceychell. She took it from her pack and handed it to him. He broke the root in half and kept one half in each hand.

Both stags looked at him and nervously scuffed the ground with their hooves. He could tell they were nervous by their quick breaths. He slowly extended his hand for the black one to smell. The stag licked his hand and started to nuzzle for the scortwig. Miraden petted the side of the stag's face and whispered, "Good, it's okay now." Then he offered the treat to the stag. He gave the other half to the white stag and it nipped angrily at his finger.

The close-eyed trapper said, "We've led you here, as promised."

The black stag snorted at his voice. Miraden heard a loud snuffling behind him and then a growl. He turned and saw the creature in the cage bare its teeth.

Miraden stepped slowly toward the cage.

"Careful, Miraden," Lovo whispered.

When Miraden got close enough to see, he found a razorback bear, a big one. The bear showed its fangs and pawed at the cage. Miraden thought he recognized the bear. He wasn't sure in the dark, but it had a long scar on its snout like the one he had encountered long ago near Preyno.

The other trapper in the net said, "That bear killed a trap—"

"Shut up," Ceychell told him. Lovo yanked the rope to pull them away from Miraden.

The bear rolled in its cage and clawed at the bars. One of the bars was already broken, but the others still held.

Miraden took some dried meat from his bag and carefully dropped it into the cage. The bear sniffed it and ate it. "Good, remember me?" Miraden said. He extended another piece in hand, and the bear licked it and took the meat. "Everyone stand back," he said.

He waited until Lovo and Ceychell had backed away with the bound trappers. Then he popped the peg from the door of the cage. He swung the door open and took a few steps back.

The bear walked out of the cage, sniffing the air a few times and then looking at Miraden. Miraden leaned down, put out his hand, and whistled. The bear bobbed its head a bit and looked at Lovo and Ceychell, who were both standing as stiff as statues. Miraden whistled again and tossed another piece of food to the creature. The bear gobbled it up.

Then the bear stood up on its hind legs; it was huge, nearly ten feet tall, much bigger than Miraden remembered it. Its claws were nearly five inches long. He started to question if it was the same bear and realized he'd put the others in danger by freeing it. Then the bear flopped down on all fours again and sauntered away into the dark forest.

Miraden's heart pounded. He tried to look calm and walked over to Ceychell.

"We don't know what they are going to tell Drojindaak," she told him. "They could attack our home."

Miraden stared at the two trappers, who stared intently back at him. They seemed to be awaiting their fate. When Miraden walked over to them, Lovo pulled the net tighter. "How do I know you aren't going to run back to your village and tell them what happened?"

"We swear it," the close-eyed man said.

"Oaths can be broken, and then what? *You* ambushed *us*. If we set you free, we may suffer for it."

Ceychell stepped up to them. They watched her quietly. She grabbed the close-eyed man's hand and sliced a small cut with Hellshy, then she cut the other's hand.

"Now I can watch and listen to you," she said. "If I even hear a mention of us, you will pay for it. All of you!" She thrust the dagger close to their faces and they flinched. "You will grow sick," she said, pressing the dagger to the close-eyed man's belly. "I'll melt your insides until you vomit them from your burning throats. Then I will turn everyone in Yoldro inside out without even entering your village. Or, you could tell them you were ambushed by ashenkin, go about your lives, and everything will be fine."

Miraden smelled fresh urine. Both men were crying and shaking. He loosened the rope and Lovo pulled the net off them. The close-eyed one fell to his knees and the other followed.

"Please don't, please, I swear I'll say nothing!" the close-eyed man said.

"And you?" Ceychell asked. He took her foot in his trembling hands and kissed it with a frothing slobber.

"He, he can't speak," the close-eyed man said.

"Go. I'll be watching you, always," Ceychell said.

They crawled backward until they were a safe distance from Ceychell and then ran away into the dark forest.

"Can you really do that?" Miraden asked her. He wasn't sure if he really wanted to know the answer.

"I don't think so, but they don't know that," she whispered with a wink.

He removed Hellshy's sheath from his belt and fastened it to hers. "I think Hellshy is yours now."

Lovo chuckled and asked, "You're a sorceress and didn't tell me?"

She stared at the dagger for a moment. It floated above her palm. "I don't know. I got scared, and suddenly felt it was calling to me. I … I saw it and knew I could control it. I feel connected to it. I hear it whispering. It sounds … sad."

Miraden wasn't sure what to think. Ceychell stared impassively at the floating dagger. Then she took the tip of the blade in her fingers and stared at the blood as if she admired it.

"What is it saying to you?" Lovo whispered. His brow furled as he carefully watched.

"I-I'm not sure. Its whispers are so soft and fast."

Miraden had carried Hellshy from Pinderfang all the way to the Ashengate and back to Kaehrn, and had never heard it speak. The dagger was evil. He'd only kept it because it was a compass that pointed him to Kyradel. With the Ashengate closed, he wasn't sure it still had a purpose. Ceychell rolled her fingers, and the dagger pointed to the southeast.

"You should keep it," Miraden whispered. "It led me to Kyradel. Perhaps it will serve you." He grasped the floating dagger and put it into her hand.

She grinned and caressed his cheek. "Always with your tokens of affection, Miraden. I shall hold it for you, for now." She put the dagger in its sheath.

Miraden stared into her eyes for a moment. She seemed much more playful and unpredictable than he remembered.

"We should get moving," Lovo said. "Gain some ground on the trappers."

Miraden agreed. He lifted Ceychell onto the saddle of the black stag and then pulled himself up behind her. When Miraden took the reins, Ceychell put her hands on his.

"Is that why they call you the Tyrant of Kaehrn now?" he asked. She turned her head to the side so he could see her wink at him. His heart jumped. It still didn't feel real to be heading to Kander with Ceychell.

"They call me that because I no longer let them look at me like hungry dogs or talk down to me anymore. I'm the chieftain. They should be scared of me." She squeezed his hands and added, "I like it."

They rode through the night south of Yoldro without running into more villagers. The yellow firs of southern Baregorin were just starting to bloom. The forest was damp and muggy from the rain. They stopped in the early morning to take a short nap before leaving the forest.

Miraden woke first. Lovo was snoring against a tree, and Ceychell was sleeping peacefully in his arms while he ran his fingers through her hair. It was as though he'd seen this before, but something about her felt different. He'd known her so well when they were kids but he'd hardly spoken to her at all in the few years before Kyradel was kidnapped. He wasn't sure if this dark side of hers was new, but he'd never seen it either.

"Why did you stop?" She opened her eyes and looked up at him.

"I… think I was lost in a memory," he said.

"Mmm, as long as I'm lost in it with you," she said. She leaned up and kissed him. He pulled back from her kiss and felt a stab in his chest.

It was time.

"What is it?" she asked.

"Ceychell, I have loved you all my life. But…" His courage was starting to crumble under her glossy stare. He swallowed his fears and said, "But I don't think I am in love with you anymore."

She leaned forward and fell against him. He felt awful about how badly he had just hurt her. Tears ran down his face. Those words were the hardest of his life. He wouldn't have said them before his journey to the Ashengate, even if he'd felt it, but he was proud that he'd been honest with her now, no matter how badly it hurt. She sobbed softly and held him.

They held each other while Lovo snoozed beside them. Ceychell hadn't said a word; she just sobbed. Miraden finally broke the long silence with "Are you nervous about going to the university?" He was more concerned about how she would interact with Simi.

"I am nervous—"

There was a rustling, it was getting closer. They remained still, then the razorback bear walked out from a few trees just in front of him. Miraden put his hand over Ceychell's mouth before she could scream. It moved quietly for a big creature, despite its massive shoulders and head, and huge paws. In the morning sunlight, it was mostly a deep black, almost blue, with a bright white streak on its back. He knew the males' streak turned dusky as they matured, so it was a female, and a very big one.

Miraden should have heard it coming near, but his guard was down. He cursed himself for a fool and picked up a few boldfigs that Ceychell had foraged the previous night. They were bigger than apples, with a hard dark brown outer skin, and sweet as candy. Miraden tossed one to the bear. The bear sniffed it then pawed it open.

"Slowly get on the stag," Miraden whispered. "If the bear looks at you, stop moving. I'll wake Lovo." Ceychell got up and Miraden tapped Lovo's arm. "Lovo, wake up slowly. Don't do anything—"

"Wha, what is it?" Lovo said.

The bear growled low and long. Miraden put his hand over Lovo's mouth. They looked at each other, then back at the bear. "Get up slowly and get on your stag." Lovo pushed himself up and crept over to the stag. Miraden took another boldfig and tossed it to the bear.

The bear leaned down on its front legs then rolled over on its back to scratch itself on a rock. Then it sat up on its rump and looked at Miraden.

Miraden wasn't sure what the bear wanted but it looked comfortable and didn't seem threatening. He slowly walked over, picked the fig up and brought it to the bear. As he got close, he recognized the scratch on its nose and its eyes again. He was certain it was the same bear he'd fed near Pallow Lake a few years back to buy Ceychell time to get away. He pulled one of the silver knives Bryndyke had made him, sliced the fig open, and fed it to the bear. Then he scratched its ear. It growled a bit and nuzzled its large head against his shoulder.

"You were someone's pet," Miraden said.

"Are you done, Miraden?" Lovo said. "We should go before it decides it's much hungrier."

"The bear rolled over again, sat back up, and looked at Miraden."

"I think someone owned this bear," Miraden said. "She wants something and is used to getting fed after a trick I suppose." He scratched the creature's ear again. "I don't have anything else for you."

The bear shuffled against a rock again and laid down next to

Miraden. Miraden took a guess and ran his hands through the thick fur on her muscular back. The bear grunted and stretched its legs.

"Miraden, when you get tired that bear is going to eat you. C'mon, let's go," Ceychell said.

FOUR

THE SCORGIS

BAREGORIN WAS FAR BEHIND THEM as they entered the Flatlands, grassy plains and rocks as far as they could see with only a gray hint of the great mountains to the west. Ceychell did her best to hide her feelings, to pretend she was perfectly fine. She even raised her arms in the air and screamed with joy as the stags ran across the open plains. Not far behind, the razorback bear pounded through the grass after them.

They rode south of Kald Junction, a mossy fortress with four towers built around a hill. It cast a huge, ominous shadow on the valley. Ceychell had never been there. She'd heard it was a safe harbor for merchants and travelers, but it was only midday; they had supplies and no need to stop.

Near evening, they approached the great mountain range to the west. The cloudy orange sky partially hid the tops of the tall peaks. The three travelers were far from the road and there was no cover for a camp. Miraden grumbled that they'd be sleeping out in the open. They'd been trotting for quite a while since their last break, and Ceychell could tell he was pretty grumpy, hungry, and knew he hated vast open spaces.

A few raindrops hit her face. "I hope you were looking forward to rain," she said. Miraden squeezed his hands on the reins and said nothing.

"I don't mind a little rain," Lovo said, as a roll of thunder nearly drowned out his voice. He grimaced. "But a storm might get me down."

A thunderhead loomed before the mountains. It was dark, and the sky above it was nearly black. The bear caught up with them and shook a bit of rain from its hide, showering them with spray. It stood up next to Miraden so he could scratch its face. The stag didn't seem to mind, but the gigantic creature made Ceychell nervous. The bear turned her head to the side and looked at her. She had a flashback of the bear stalking her a few years ago near Preyno Lake.

"We should head for that tree," Lovo said. "It might be the only place to set up a dry camp."

The tree was huge, three times as tall as any Ceychell had ever seen before and completely isolated as there wasn't another tree in sight. It was maybe a thirty minute ride. She wasn't sure they'd get to it before the storm hit.

They picked up the pace, but the rain increased to a steady downpour by the time they approached the tree. It must have been a couple hundred feet tall and wider than two grain silos. Its thick branches were dense with flat, red leaves and blue and black flowers. Its bark was violet with deep red lines, and it seemed to be moving. When they finally rode their stags under it, Ceychell saw tiny people scrambling up the trunk, along branches, and along the ground to it. They were less than a foot tall. And wore basic red tunics made from the leaves of the tree. Their hair was gold, black, or silver, and their skin was dark gray. Many of the little folk climbed into holes in the bark and closed tiny shutters behind them.

"Do you see that?" she asked.

"I do," Lovo said. "I hope the little fellas let us sleep here quietly."

As he said this, a small rock bounced off his head. He looked up as if it were the rain, but Ceychell definitely saw the rock.

"Do you know what they are?" Ceychell whispered to Miraden.

"No, I've never seen them before."

"We are grunkins, you miserable witch," yelled a spiky golden-haired, big-nosed grunkin. "And we can hear you whispering!"

Ceychell stared at the grunkin in bewilderment. She had no idea if grunkins were dangerous or a little more of a threat than talking squirrels.

"We didn't mean to scare you, we— " Miraden started.

"Scare us?" one shouted. "You don't scare us!"

"You don't scare us!" a dozen more grunkins shouted.

Ceychell put her hand out. "Please, we just came to this tree for shelter from the storm."

"Sure, next you'll be cutting down the Scorgis for firewood and cooking us!"

"You'll burn our home"

"You shouldn't be here!"

"We're warning you!"

The grunkins continued to shout at them, but Ceychell dismounted from the stag anyway. She pulled a handful of hannelberries from her bag and slowly approached the tree. They spit and shouted and shook their fists at her.

"Ceychell, what are you doing!" Miraden whispered. "Come back."

"C'mon," Lovo said. "Let's just ride on."

A swarm of grunkins climbed down the tree, but before they reached Ceychell she asked, "What is the Scorgis?"

The question halted their charge; they all jabbered and pointed at the tree.

"I've never seen a tree like this," Ceychell told them. "Are there more like this?"

The grunkins were silent for a moment; then they all began to screech with laughter like children. A grunkin holding a violet twig jumped to the ground and walked toward her. His black beard nearly touched the grass, but only speckles of gold hair remained on his spotted head. "I'm warning you, leave now," he said.

She offered him a hannelberry. It was bulbous like a raspberry, transparent, and filled with pink jelly. The grunkin sniffed it, poked it with his stick, and took it from her. It's as big as a pumpkin in his hands. He took a cautious bite, opened his eyes wide, and took another. The other grunkins began to chatter and swarmed around him. Then, he struck the berry with his stick and there were two berries, again and there were four, and again and again until there were hundreds of berries all over the ground. The other grunkin picked them up and began eating. Their cheeks were full and jiggled like chipmunks.

Ceychell laughed. She enjoyed listening to them all munching and slurping the goo. They were louder than the rain.

Lovo and Miraden came over and stood next to Ceychell. The grunkin with the violet twig, his face covered in pink goo, pointed at Lovo and said, "You look like you could eat a whole forest of berries."

Lovo laughed.

Some of the grunkins kept chewing, but many of them stopped as the bear walked up and sniffed Ceychell's hand. She held out her palm with five berries, and the bear licked them all off her hand it. The grunkins gaped at the bear, chewing with their mouth wide open and watching it.

"I'm hungry for more than berries," Lovo said. "But, I'm certain the Mother of Light wouldn't want me to eat glumkins."

"We are grunkins, you imbecile!" the stick-holder said. "Mother of Light?"

Hundreds of goo-covered faces chuckled.

Lovo's smile faded. Ceychell looked over at Miraden, who was staring at his big friend.

"What's so funny?" Lovo asked. The grunkins kept laughing. Lovo stood and balled his fists. "Answer me!"

The grunkins settled down, and the stick-holder shoved the last piece of his berry in his mouth. He chewed and scowled; his beard swayed to and fro. Then pointed his stick up at Lovo.

"You humans and your feelings. Don't like that I mocked your *god*, do you?" He poked Lovo's shin with his violet twig.

Lovo breathed loudly through his nose. Ceychell hoped he'd stay calm and not start stomping grunkins. "Why you—"

Ceychell reached out and put her hand on his hand. Then she asked the grunkin, "Can you tell me why you mocked the Mother of Light? We've never seen or heard of grunkins, and we—"

"Of course you haven't. You all know nothing. Nothing!" He pointed the stick at her. "We are not from your world. We are from Ghaborion, the one that Levoria, your *Mother of Light*, abandoned."

Ceychell was incredulous. She could see the same disbelief on Miraden and Lovo's gawking faces.

"Yes. It is hard to hear the truth. Isn't it? You shouldn't be seeing us. We've existed here for a thousand years in peace and hiding, but something disrupted the Scorgis and now we are vulnerable. Vulnerable to you pests in *your* world."

Miraden said, "We are headed to the university in Kander. Perhaps the wizards can help you understand what happened to the Scorgis,"

"Bah. Wizards! Charlatans! Thieves!" the grunkin yelled with a raised fist in the air. "Those wizards caused these problems. Be gone with you!" He brandished his stick at Miraden.

"I'm sorry, I was just—"

"Begone!"

The grunkins scurried back to the Scorgis with their berries and disappeared into their little holes, closing the shutters behind them.

"Levoria?" Lovo said, stunned.

"I feel like they know a lot more," Ceychell said, nearly shouting over the hiss of the rain on the leaves. "But they don't want to tell us."

"Maybe something happened at the college?" Miraden said.

Lovo shrugged, "Maybe something to do with the Ashengates?"

Hundreds of heads popped out of the little holes in the tree, and the stick-holder climbed back down the tree. He stomped furiously up to Miraden. "Ashengates? What are those?"

"They are dark gates that lead to a burning plane filled with devils. They come through it to our world and take our children.

"Oh no. No this can't be," the grunkin said.

"We closed one a few months ago," Miraden said.

The grunkins head shot up as the entire lot of them gasped all at once.

"That explains the Scorgis. When you numbskulls destroyed what you call an Ashengate, you disrupted the magic in this world. Those gates come from a dark sorcerer that invaded and destroyed our world. We escaped, but it appears he has finally followed, after centuries of imprisonment. Do the things you call ashenkin have horns? Sharp teeth, burning flesh? Snatch your children in the night?"

"Yes, exactly," Ceychell said.

"They are his cursed servants. He twists them in to following his every desire as he devours worlds and every soul in them. He will slowly genocide your race by eliminating your children. You'll all die out, just like the rest."

"Who is this sorcerer?" Ceychell asked.

"I dare not say his name," he leaned forward and whispered just over the rain, "he hears better at night. The shadows, follow his command."

"If what you say is true," Miraden said, looking down at the angry little grunkin, "please come with us. We can get help from the wizards. Perhaps they can solve this,"

"They have caused it! They are the only way he could have found us!" He shook his twig, bounced and jumped, almost onto Miraden's foot. "Leave us be. We've lived for ages, far longer than humans, and now that we are exposed here"—he lowered his voice—"I fear we won't survive much longer."

Ceychell kneeled down to the little stick-holder. "You need not fear us. We are sorry to have angered you, and would like to help you."

"You humans ruined our world, and now you're ruining this world. If you want to help us, go destroy the wizards before the sorcerer comes. Then we can talk." Ceychell and her two companions returned to their stags and rode for another hour through torrential rain, but they found no shelter. She shook and rubbed her soaked sleeves but it was no use. She just wanted to lie down in front of a warm fire. The cold and wet was all that was keeping her awake. Miraden held her close, but it wasn't enough.

"Should we ride through the night?" Lovo asked.

Lightning cracked ahead of them, and the stags bucked. Miraden pulled to the left to avoid running into Lovo's stag. Ceychell held on as Miraden pulled the reins and got the stag back under control.

"We are near the storm," she said. "It's dangerous to stop here."

They continued riding and saw burning patches ahead where lightning had struck. The warmth of the fire was tempting, but the rain would surely put it out before long.

"How far are those mountains?" Lovo yelled.

Ceychell put a hand above her eyes to see through the rain. She saw nothing but darkness and the frequent flash of lightning. She wasn't even sure they were going toward the mountains.

"I don't know! Hours! Maybe a day!" Miraden yelled.

The hair on Ceychell's neck stood up. She felt a tingle in her hands. A surging crackle and boom. Lightning struck the ground less than 30 feet away.

"I've never seen it that close!" Lovo yelled.

"We better ride fast and hope we don't see it closer!" Miraden yelled back. He kicked the stag into a gallop. Ceychell held on. There was a sizzle and a crash behind them. They pressed on as fast as the stags would take them while lightning erupted around them.

A few hours later, the rain had passed. The sky was still pitch-black, but they were beyond the storm. Ceychell lay curled up next to Miraden and the bear. Lovo was beside the two stags. They hadn't spoken since they stopped, and she was glad to rest, despite being cold and wet, exhausted and miserable. But she was alive.

Miraden was almost face to face with her. She could barely see his eyes, but she hoped he was at least happy to be next to her. "From your letters, it seemed difficult like this often."

"Sometimes," he said. "It was never easy."

She put a hand on his face and brushed the cold water from his cheek. "Do you remember the night you spent in the darkness, in Bleak Gale Pines?"

"I do."

"I'll never forget how hurt you were that I wasn't there for you." She folded her bottom lip into her mouth and held back her tears. "I was so scared of losing you then. I wanted you and Kyra back more than anything, more than my own life. And now that you're back, now that I can finally be with you and be there for you, I've lost you." She paused for a moment and then added, "It's so cruel."

She tried to stare into his eyes but couldn't see past her own uncontrollable tears. She would have never questioned his devotion to her before, but she could feel his doubt and hesitation. She finally understood how he must have felt during the two years she had ignored him, and it was tearing her apart.

FIVE

UNIVERSITY IN THE CLOUDS

THE MORNING WAS DREARY, AND the trail leading up the mountain was soggy like a riverbank. Through breaks in the mist, Ceychell saw Bondare's sprawl of caravans, tents, and small shops, a mass of dwellings extending to the sea from so high up she could barely make out one building from another. Above the city, the mountain tops disappeared into a blanket of dense clouds. It was just as she had always imagined it from stories.

Loose shale made for a slow and slippery climb, but the stags were surefooted enough. The bear had a much easier time keeping up now that they were moving slower. It rambled next to them and almost seemed to be enjoying itself.

Higher up, the pass was reinforced with stone railings and bridges, and the trail was wide and as safe as mountain travel could be. She realized the wizards valued their imports enough to ensure the road was easy to travel on.

There were no travelers this morning but she was amazed at how many fat black and white goats were on the trail. The goats stared at them and chewed the grass between the rocks, completely unbothered by their passage. One bleated at the bear. The bear growled in response, and the goats scattered up and down the mountain side.

The ride uphill was slow but steady. Ceychell shivered in the cool breeze. She was still wet, had barely slept, and was not in the greatest of moods. Luckily, the terrible weather and exhaustion were all that were keeping her from thinking constantly about Miraden. She'd sensed he felt differently the moment he arrived home. She'd hoped it was only in her mind, but now she knew it was real. She wanted to cry; she wanted to hide, like he always did when they were younger. But that wasn't her. And if she had any hope of finding love with him again, she would do it with her strength, not seeking his pity or exploiting his guilt.

On top of feeling crushed, all the anticipation of entering the university was shrouded by having to confront Simigrin. She knew Simigrin would be kind; at least Miraden never said anything that implied she would be mean. But Ceychell wasn't sure *she* could be kind. She wasn't sure she could see Miraden close to her. She wanted to scream at the very thought of it.

"Have you a name for your stag yet, Lovo?" Miraden asked.

"I thought I'd call him Snowball," he said. He patted the stag and handed him an apple from his bag.

Ceychell laughed. It was a ridiculous name. Perfect for Lovo, though.

Miraden grinned and shook his head. "Snowball doesn't sound very majestic."

"Well, what is Your Majesty's steed's name? Lord Antlerwrath? Prince Tundracrush of Baregorin?"

"How about Eclipso," Ceychell said.

"Yeah, I think that's probably a good name," Miraden said.

"What about the bear?" Lovo asked. "Does it get a royal name?"

Ceychell looked over at the bear, casually rambling alongside them. She was grateful for the creature's warm fur last night.

"Maybe she can be Princess Tundracrush," Miraden said.

Ceychell giggled. She locked eyes with Miraden for a moment, grinned, and looked back at the road. "Very tough."

At last, the blue-green stone of Kander's great towers and high walls appeared in the mist up ahead. She'd never seen anything like it. It looked like it was carved from a mountain of blue-green gemstone. Its dark glass windows contained painted images she couldn't quite make out, but she could imagine how beautiful they'd be from the inside, with the light shining through them. The wall walks stretched around the entire mountain topped with burning basins at even intervals. She wasn't entirely sure, but the university looked to be the actual peak of the mountain. It was the most beautiful building she'd ever seen.

"Would you look at that," Lovo said. "I hope Simi has a fire and some warm food in there."

"I am sure they will, Lovo," Miraden said. "Do you hear—" Miraden snatched his bow from his shoulder and nocked an arrow.

Ceychell took Eclipso's reins. Her hands trembled. There was a gust of wind, and the mist swished above them. A blue wyvern swooped down and landed on the rocky mountainside in front of them. Sitting atop it on a black saddle was a hooded woman in green robes. The wyvern had a long, spiny neck and tail. Its legs were muscular, and its talons were like great black hooks clinging to the rocks. It had long, scaled wings, no arms, sharp teeth, and a sinister glare to its eyes. Ceychell sunk back into Miraden and shook in fear from the wyvern.

"Whoever you are," the woman said, "you've taken the wrong road, our road. You are not an authorized merchant. Go back to Bondare and send supplies through the approved caravans into the mountain."

"We are not merchants," Miraden said, removing the arrow from the bow. "Simigrin invited us."

"I see," the mage said. "My apologies, you must be Miraden, we are honored to receive you." The wyvern snapped its jaws; the rider pet its neck. "Please continue. The gates will be opened for you. And thank you for coming to help us." The wyvern sprung into the air, roared, and rose into the mist.

Ceychell took a deep breath and tried to relax. "Luckily you're famous here too," she told Miraden. She wiped the tears from her cheeks and tried to push the image of the wyvern from her thoughts."

"I may not be famous, but At least I'll be a good surprise for Simigrin," Lovo said. Ceychell wasn't amused, but she smirked at him anyway.

A short time thereafter, they reached the castle. They rode through two columns of hundred-foot high statues of hooded figures, carved of a green stone with orange specs. Every scale of their boots was perfectly carved, the seams and ripples in their robes looked real. The statues were holding something over their heads, but it was so high up that she could barely make out what it was, books perhaps.

They passed through an open doorway of black metal. It was thick as a tree and hummed as they rode through. The doors closed behind them.

Floating sconces suddenly ignited. Ceychell was so startled she almost fell off Eclipso. They entered a perfectly arched, blue tunnel, leading deeper into the mountain. The heat of the sconces felt good on her goosebumpy skin. She wished she could sit by a sconce and warm up for a while, but they kept riding.

At the end of the tunnel was another black door, and before it on both sides of the tunnel was another tunnel that opened up to a large pen surrounded by bollards, where stable hands tended to horses, drakes, groubles, and rams.

A person in a brown robe stood near the door. They walked up and waved. "Hello. Your stags will be perfectly attended to here." The hooded person took the reins from Ceychell and Lovo. "Is your… bear friendly? If not, you must leave it outside. I'm afraid I can't have it eating one of the other animals… or me."

Lovo sighed and slid off Snowball. He shook hard and stretched his arms and legs.

Miraden and Ceychell also dismounted. Her arms and legs were chilled to the bone.

"I think she's friendly," Ceychell said. She wasn't totally sure about that, but she reached over and scratched the bear's ear anyway. The hooded person reached a hand out, too, and when the bear growled, quickly pulled it back. "Maybe not *that* friendly."

"I'd like to keep the bear with me," Miraden said.

"Indeed," the hooded person nodded. "Keep it away from trouble." They opened the stone door and waved Ceychell and the others inside.

Ceychell followed Miraden into a brick tunnel. To the right was a room of boxes, barrels, and bins neatly stacked. As they continued through the tunnel, more floating sconces appeared. Dancing blue-green lights lit up an entire passage that was chalked up in shiny pastels: starry nights, dragons, people, villages, and mountains. Most looked like children's drawings, but some were very good. A drawing of two little girls holding hands reminded her of a picture Kyradel and she had carved on the Kaehrnstone years ago. She missed Kyra and wished she could have come.

"Lots of little artists in here," Lovo said. He picked up a piece of purple chalk from the floor and quickly drew a self-portrait. It looked a bit more like a monster, but for a quick drawing, it was very good.

"Wow, I didn't know you could draw," Miraden said. "You and

Kyra could have made something while you were in Kaehrn."

Lovo drew horns on himself and added a few buck teeth. "I have no shortage of talent," he said, "just a shortage of useful talent."

They continued into a grand hallway. Lights floated throughout; it was brighter than daylight. Several people in various colored robes were chatting in small groups. Above them, precious gems shimmered in the smooth stone, fifty-foot-high ceilings. Pillars of blue-green stone stood from floor to roof.

"These pillars aren't actually sitting on the floor," Ceychell said, looking close at the bottom of one pillar. "This university isn't on *top* of a mountain. It is part of the mountain."

"Yes, it was carved from the mountain," a mage yellow robes said, walking up to them.

"It is amazing!" Ceychell said. She'd never seen anything like it. The pillars were polished and the few gemstones she saw sparkled. Even the floor reflected the light as if they were walking on a mirror. A spread of fruit and bread sat on a table ten feet from her near the wall. Every peach and plum looked perfect; the perfectly cut tarts didn't even look real to her. Young people, no older than thirteen Passings were hurriedly pushing carts with books and scrolls. One scroll fell from a cart, and the young girl ran back to get it as her cart kept gliding toward a mage. She screamed, "Look out!" and ran to catch it. A mage in orange robes turned and raised her hand. The cart stopped instantly, and the girl crashed into it.

The green-robed guard whom they'd seen on the wyvern walked toward them. Her hood was down. She had dark skin, short black hair, copper hoop earrings and held a golden wand with a silver stone at its head. She smiled at them.

"Welcome to Kander University. Many of us call it Ohmalo or the Center." She looked past them. "Did that bear just follow you in here?" The bear was sniffing a bowl full of fruit on a table.

"Tundracrush is my companion," Miraden said. "I just call her Tundra."

"Hmm. Simi did say you were good with animals. Well, follow me, and make sure your bear comes to." She walked a few steps down the great hall, then turned back. "Oh, I'm Kaliagrin. If you need anything, let me know."

The mention of Simigrin talking about Miraden stung Ceychell. She didn't say anything, she dreaded meeting the woman.

Miraden whistled and patted his leg. The bear looked at him, then back at the fruit. He went to the table and picked up a melon, pulled a knife from his belt and sliced it open. The bear walked toward him and he fed her a chunk.

They followed Kaliagrin through many hallways. Hooded mages, and few with their hoods lowered, walked past them and nodded. One hall had a floor-to-ceiling mirror on the wall that stood nearly thirty feet tall and reflected a side hallway. Its reflection made the corridor look endless, but mostly she noticed how shabby she looked. Her hair was caked with mud, her clothes wet and filthy, and her furs soiled and saturated with muck. She looked more like a tanner's assistant than the Chieftain of Kaehrn. She tried to straighten her hair, but it was no use.

She grabbed Miraden's wrist to stop him. Lovo kept walking. "I can't meet Simigrin like this," she said. "I look awful." She hated sounding self-conscious, or even vain, but she was nervous. Simigrin was intimidating, and the last thing she needed was to feel worse.

"She's not going to care," Miraden said quietly. "How do you think we looked most of the time?" He looked impatient; she could tell he was eager to see the mage again.

"I guess I don't know how you looked," she said. She felt foolish and nervous about what he must think of her.

Miraden put his hands out to his sides and said, "Well, we looked a lot like this. He was just as soggy and disheveled as she was. His rusty hair was muddy, and his face was dirt-smeared as well.

"Everything alright?" Kaliagrin asked.

"Yes," Ceychell said, and they rushed to catch up with their escort.

Several more tunnels led to a white door covered with frost. Kaliagrin put her hand near the door, and it yawned open and blasted them with cold air. The chill took Ceychell's breath away. She nearly slipped and then grabbed on to Miraden. The walls were frozen, the floor was icy, and the air was filled with crystals that burned her cheek. She couldn't see much through the icy fog except a few figures and a small ice creature skating in circles. Long icicles hung overhead like the ceiling was made of spikes. Her lungs burned a little, but as a proud woman of the north, she couldn't let her cold show.

"I forgot to mention, L-lovo" Miraden stammered, "Simigrin is a—"

"Miraden!" Simigrin shouted. Her hood was down, and her purple hair bobbed as she ran across the ice to him. She slid and tried to a stop but veered toward Lovo. "Lovo! Lovo is that really you!" She crashed into him and squeezed. Lovo hugged her back and lifted her off the ground.

"By the Mother of Light," he said, "you're a woman!"

"Surprise!' She said, but her lips trembled. "How could you possibly be here? What … wh…" She stopped and started to cry.

"Surprise!" Lovo said. "Sometimes, it's best just to be grateful."

She put her hand on his arm, and Ceychell could see how happy she was to find out he was alive. Then the mage turned and pulled Miraden into a big hug. Ceychell stood silently by as they held each other. It was a bond forged through real hardships, one she wished she had with Miraden. She hated watching it.

And finally Simigrin looked at Ceychell. Ceychell couldn't place the look in the woman's eyes: it was not jealousy, but it didn't look friendly. "You must be Ceychell," the mage said. "I heard so much about you." Ceychell sized her up and felt Simigrin was doing the same. Other mages in blue robes approached but remained silent while the friends were reunited. Ceychell wanted to hate Simigrin, she really did, but this was the person who helped Miraden rescue her sister, who closed an Ashengate, and selflessly followed Miraden almost to their deaths. Despite her petty resentment, Ceychell reached out to shake Simigrin's hand. Simigrin pulled her into a hug. Ceychell wasn't sure what to think. She was holding a person who was too close to Miraden, and she didn't like it. She began to hate herself for being so childish about it.

"You're all so wet!" Simigrin said. They were also shivering hard from the cold.

"We went through some serious storms coming here," Miraden said. He had a wide grin that burned Ceychell. She would not stand to be rejected.

"Oh, I saw that storm go by," Simigrin said. "Well, let's get you some dry clothes and warm quarters. A feast is being prepared for you. Lord Umorogrin can't wait to meet you." She seemed to drain her voice of enthusiasm before she said, "Especially you," to Ceychell.

"R… right," Ceychell said. She was so jealous she couldn't think properly.

"I can take them to get cleaned up," Kaliagrin said.

Simigrin grabbed Lovo's hand. They were both grinning ear to ear. "It's good to see you, you ogre!" She swatted his shoulder.

He grabbed her into one final hug. "Do you always train in this cold? No wonder Keldenfelds didn't bother you. And why didn't you tell us you're a woman?" Lovo was so loud his voice echoed in the ice chamber.

Simigrin paused for a moment. "It's just best for me when I travel."

Kaliagrin cleared her throat and said, "If you'll follow me…"

The green-robed mage escorted them to a corridor with a dozen doors on each side and a door at the end. She opened the door farthest from the far end and waved for Miraden to enter. Ceychell peeked in. There was a fireplace and a servant filling a bath next to it. He was a short and stocky man, nearly bald and fat around the mid-section. A thick hide was spread on the floor in front of a small bed with black silk sheets. At the side of the room was a table with spirits and a few beauty items.

"I'll see you both at dinner," Miraden said and stepped inside. Kaliagrin closed the door behind him.

The mage led Lovo to the room next door. He opened the door and said to the young man inside, "Let's get that fire roaring."

Ceychell pointed to the room across from Miraden. "May I—"

"You're down at the end of the hall," Kaliagrin said, pointing. Ceychell found the mage's eye makeup fascinating now that she was standing right beside her. Gold glistened beautifully on her upper and lower lids and came together as a point going toward her ears. "Come." Kaliagrin waved her along. The mage strolled with her chin high and opened the door with a smile. "Please enjoy your stay."

Simigrin made Ceychell feel even grubbier than she already was. She was not easily embarrassed, but she suddenly felt unprepared to come to Kander. She forced a grin and nodded at the woman. Then she stepped inside, and her door was shut behind her. The room was similar to the others but was also furnished with a dresser and mirror. The assistant was not robed; she wore a red silk shirt and pants and white slippers. Her hair was pulled back neatly into a bun but was otherwise unremarkable.

"I will get your bath ready, madam," she said and unhooked a caldron from over the fire.

Ceychell pulled some muck out of her hair and doffed her furs and leather. Then she sat down near the fire to shed the cold from her bones. "Is it possible to keep the bath water after I'm done, so I can clean my clothes?" she asked.

"I'll clean them for you, madam" the servant said.

"Are you, are you sure?" Ceychell asked.

"Yes, I'm here to make your stay pleasant. It is my duty." She dumped a cauldron of hot water into the bath.

Ceychell looked her over. The woman was as young as her, plain and pale. "What's your name?"

"My name is Alva, madam"

"Well, Alva. I'll stoke this fire while you get more water. I am looking forward to a hot bath."

When the bath was finally ready, Ceychell nearly melted in it and almost fell asleep until Alva reminded her that a feast was being prepared. She got out, combed out her hair, and put on a silk dress Alva brought her. It was green like her eyes and lighter and chillier than anything she'd ever put on. Wearing such finery felt strange. She didn't care for dining dresses,

She sat in front of the mirror and brushed her long hair out. A simple braid wouldn't do, she braided a double crown braid, then combed the rest of her long locks. She fetched a small phial of limebloom perfume from her pack and dotted it on her neck.

"You are so beautiful, madam," Alva said.

Ceychell thanked the young woman, but didn't smile. It brought her no joy to be beautiful, but when she thought about it, she realized she wanted Miraden to find her beautiful tonight. She wanted to see that spark in his eyes again. She looked at the little brushes, powders, and jars on the dresser. She knew ladies in the cities wore makeup, but it was never practiced in the villages of the north and she knew not what to do with them. "Would you help me?"

"Of course."

Alva used just enough paste and powder to bring out Ceychell's stunning features. Ceychell stared at her image in the mirror and could barely recognize her own face.

There was a knock at the door. Alva shuffled up to it and cracked it open. Ceychell slipped into her new golden sandals and tried to listen but couldn't make out their whispers.

"The feast is ready," Alva said, after closing the door. "I'll take you there."

Ceychell followed Alva down another long, stone corridor lined with doors. They all looked the same to her. Each had a wood block outside the room, on which were written a few symbols she didn't recognize.

"Do you know which room Simigrin is staying in?" Ceychell whispered to Alva.

"She is a mage. She stays in the east wing. You are in the south wing, but I'm not sure exactly which room on the east wing is hers. I can find out if it would please you."

"It would, thank you," Ceychell said. Alva didn't respond. She kept her head tipped forward and continued down the corridor.

A black carpet lined the floor of the hallway and shone in the light of the blue sconces. It was beautiful and so dark. When she arrived at the banquet hall and saw the floating gem chandeliers, her mouth fell open. The lights sent sparkles across the red-lit walls. She walked over to the wall near the doorway for a closer look and found the walls were smooth and reflective gold. She wondered if they were real solid gold, but she dared not ask and risk seeming like a bumpkin.

A table in the center of the room was set for twenty, with black chairs topped with red silk cushions, silver plates, crystal cutlery, and piles of sumptuous-looking delicacies. It was so over the top she wanted to love it, but she suddenly missed simpler things like her longhouse banquet hall and a hearty bowl of mutton stew.

Four men, each holding a goblet, were standing on the other side of the room chatting. All four were dark-skinned, well groomed, and well dressed in silky dress robes, two blue, one green, one silver, and each with a unique pattern sewn into its fabric. The embroidery glinted, even sparkled, in the chandelier light. The sleeves and robes were much tighter than the robes she saw worn around the college. All four turned to look at Ceychell as she entered the hall. One spilled his drink on his robe as he gaped at her. Two servants hurried over to clean up the mage and the floor.

"Enjoy, madam," Alva said and turned to leave.

All four mages came over to her, the one in the green robe wearing an overweening grin. He waved a servant over with wine. He looked muscular and healthy. His eyes were brownish-purple and hair was in black braids that she adored. "Why hello, who might you be?" he asked and offered Ceychell a cup.

Ceychell didn't like being a showpiece, and the man's fawning smile was grotesque. She'd been stared at before in the other villages when she'd gone for meetings or celebrations, and she hated it. But she didn't want to cause a problem. More and more, she thought she didn't belong at the university. She was struggling not to feel like an imposter. Flight and fight were firing in her chest. "I'm Ceychell," she mumbled at last. "Chieftain of Kaehrn."

"Oh my, a chieftain?" the man said. "I must say, you are absolutely stunning, Chieftain."

The comment made her skin itch. "If you must." She took a sip of her drink and found it exceptionally sweet for wine. Too sweet.

"I am Stardagrin," he said, dipping his head slightly. Many here call me Star."

"Well met, Stardagrin," she replied.

A pair of blue-robed mages stepped forward, much to Stardagrin's apparent annoyance. He was shorter than the other three, with thin braids in his black hair. He had deep brown eyes and a kind grin. "I heard you were a brewer, but I didn't know you were *noble* as well."

"More of an alchemist," Ceychell said. "Where did you hear that?"

A man in silk clothes and a blue sash across his chest with two gold rings walked into the hall to Ceychell's left. He was darkly tanned, had long wavy black hair, and his posture was perfect. Ceychell recognized him instantly: he was the knight from Crestain that she'd met at the celebration for Miraden. She recalled her childhood fantasy of moving to Crestain and finding a handsome knight like him, but that dream made way for newer ones.

Star leaned indecorously close to her ear and whispered, "A knight from the northwest—he arrived a little before you did."

The knight walked over and dipped his head to Ceychell. "Chieftain, it is good to see you."

"Do you just frequent banquets?" Ceychell said. Her terse words stopped him in his tracks. The mages leaned back a little, most gaped at her with open mouths.

"No, I don't just mingle at parties, though I enjoy them. I came here because I believe in your cause."

"My cause?" she asked.

"You have a cause?" Star said. "Oh please tell us about it?"

"I-I am here for someone else's cause," she stammered.

Star snickered to his colleagues and said, "Well, you are in the right place. I do believe we have all the answers."

She admitted to herself that she was semi-fascinated by Star's long, braided hair. He was quite handsome when he finally stopped grinning, and she realized he may be more of a jokester than a jerk.

Lovo walked into their circle and interrupted her thoughts. "Well look at that feast!" He slapped his hands together. He was finely dressed, but his silk shirt strained to contain his belly and his black pants were too tight in places she'd rather not think about. He didn't seem to care. His hair was combed for the first time ever, and he was smiling like he was at his own Passing party.

"You look well, Lovo" she said.

"Milady," Lovo bowed slightly and winked at her. "This one's not bothering you, I hope." Lovo exchanged a warm smile with the knight.

"I don't believe we were introduced at Miraden's honoring," the knight said, "I am Chintaja, a knight of the Second Status of Crestain."

The mage in the silver robe, a tall man with short black hair and a scar on his right cheek, gawked at the knight asked, "Miraden?"

Star's eyes also widened as he turned from the silver-robed mage to Ceychell. "Miraden—the Miraden we have heard so much about? He's sort of a celebrity around here as of late. You know him?"

Ceychell nodded and said, "I do, quite well. We grew up together."

"Mmm hmmmm," Star hummed, stealing a sidelong glance at the green-robed mage. "Have you by chance met Simigrin yet?"

"I have," Ceychell said more easily than she felt. "She's wonderful."

From behind her, Ceychell heard, "Awfully nice of you to say."

Ceychell turned to see Simigrin standing in the doorway. She wore a blue robe-like dress. Her purple hair was freshly cut in a reverse bob, her eyeliner drawn out from her eyes, long slender gold earrings dangling just above her shoulders, and a simple silver necklace with an amethyst below her collarbone. Ceychell thought her stunning, but she was not intimidated. She wanted to say something mean, she really did, but she knew Simigrin had done nothing to deserve it.

After a moment of awkward silence, Simigrin told her, "My you cleaned up nicely."

Ceychell struggled to come up with a retort, but was saved by a chef calling everyone to the table.

The room had filled up considerably, and more mages were still entering the hall, along with several servants holding silver wine goblets. A black man with short, graying black hair, wearing black robes walked into the room. He had a single gold ring on his left ring finger, but his outfit was not nearly as ostentatious as the others. In fact, it was quite plain. He smiled and looked around the room. Then he stared at Ceychell.

Lovo was whispering to Chintaja about nearly getting cooked by lightning, when Miraden entered the room. He wore a white shirt and black pants. His hair was freshly cut, and his face was clean shaven. He looked so much like the young man she remembered, not the scruffy and unkempt adventurer who had returned from the Ashengate. He looked at her with that boyish grin she loved. But before she could say or do anything, the man in black, standing at the head of the table, pointed his hand to the chair on his right.

"Ah Miraden, please sit beside me."

"Can you scoot down?" Lovo said to the mage with a scar on his face who was trying to sit down next to Miraden.

"I was—"

"Scoot down two or three," Lovo said. He waved Ceychell over and held his hand out for her to sit down beside Miraden, then he sat down beside her. Chintaja sat down next to Lovo. Simigrin sat across the table from Miraden and exchanged smiles with him. Then she glanced at Ceychell, and her smile faded.

The man in black turned to Lovo and said, "You are quite protective of him."

Lovo's cheeks reddened. He was at a loss for words until he said, "I am just looking out for, for his—"

"You're a good friend," the man said. "I can tell. It's good to have loyal friends." Lovo nodded and sat down, red-faced.

Ceychell found the man in black warm and intriguing. She suspected he was in charge, but she wouldn't know it by his humble smile and plain outfit. He didn't have to speak up—his voice was deep, calming—and everyone listened when he spoke.

When everyone was finally seated, servants brought out wine and bread in abundance. Ceychell smelled fresh herbs and butter melting on soft bread, and her mouth began to water.

When the man in black finally introduced himself—"I am Lord Umorogrin—he was looking right at Ceychell. "I welcome you to Kander and hope you found your accommodations acceptable. I am most pleased that you have come to join us."

Ceychell was still nervous and excited at being invited to such a prestigious place, but she calmed her breathing and said, "Thank you, Lord Umorogrin."

Miraden leaned forward on with his elbows on the table and said, "We are from a humble forest village and are grateful for your hospitality." He nodded to Lord Umorogrin and when he looked back at Ceychell, she smiled at him. She saw little of the boy left in his warm brown eyes, the love she'd always known, but she loved him deeply despite his rejection. If she could, she would regain his love.

"We wanted to have a celebration when you all arrived," the man in black continued. "An Ashengate was closed. A feat we thought impossible. Children were saved, many are now safer because of our guests."

The mages clapped and looked at Miraden, Simigrin, Lovo, and Ceychell, though she was not part of that effort. Nevertheless, she clapped with them and then took a heavy sip of her wine. She was going to need it. Lovo patted her back and whispered, "It's alright, you belong here too."

She nodded slightly to Lovo and she couldn't tell if he was being overly nice for some reason.

Two mages in golden robes walked into the room, one carried a coiled string, the other a kite-shaped silver shield. It was polished to a mirror. There were four small symbols, one in each corner that glowed from the light.

The mage with the shield stood behind Lovo, the one with the string behind Miraden.

"Lovo," Lord Umorogrin started, "Simigrin told me of your sacrifice when she returned home. You could imagine how surprised I was to hear you arrived, but I'm thankful for it. For your bravery, and your sacrifice, we've enchanted a silver shield especially for you. It can resist fire and guard you from any blow. May it continue to protect you so that you can protect others."

Lovo was red and almost in tears. He looked back and took the shield from the mage. He held it without a struggle and admired its shine.

"Thank you," Lovo mumbled. He wiped the tears from his face. Everyone clapped for him. The mage wearing gold leaned down and said, "I'll put it back in your room so you can enjoy your dinner." Lovo handed it back and turned to Ceychell. She put her hand on his shoulder and smiled. He hugged her.

"Miraden," Lord Umorogrin said. Miraden was looking down at his plate. "I've heard about your bravery, we all have. Simigrin told me how you fired every arrow you had beyond the Ashengate. She told me how you stood your ground against a great demon and fired your last arrow to shatter the necklace. I want to make sure you never run out again. This enchanted bowstring will allow you to fire magic arrows, and it will never break." Everyone clapped at the table, Lovo clapping the loudest.

Miraden accepted the string from the mage in golden robes and held it. He looked sad and glanced over at Ceychell. She wanted to reach her hand out to his to comfort him, but she knew it could make him more uncomfortable. She looked over at Simigrin who was looking at her. The mage didn't look away; she smiled confidently at Ceychell. Ceychell realized Simigrin knew every secret between her and Miraden. She'd thought herself thick-skinned, but she was beginning to feel that she should not have come.

"I hope you honored Simigrin, and gave her another spellbook," Miraden said.

Lord Umorogrin leaned back and started to smile. "Miraden, of course."

"She deserves to be recognized," he said.

"Miraden, Simigrin gave me a full report, every detail. Part of the reason she went on this mission is because she's as ambitious as she is prodigious. I'm not surprised at all that she achieved. None of us are. Which is why when she suggested reaching out to all of you for help, we listened. But, if you are concerned, she has a new staff, and a new spellbook with all the spells from her order."

Miraden nodded. "I'm glad to hear it. Thank you."

Lord Umorogrin returned the nod with a calm smile.

Ceychell's skin burned. Miraden's devotion looked so familiar, but it wasn't for her. She wanted to cry; it took everything not to. She just smiled and suffered in silence.

"I would like to raise a toast," Simigrin said. Everyone lifted their glasses, even Ceychell, reluctantly. "To my dear friend, Miraden, for coming, and my friend Lovo, who I didn't realize was coming." A few people laughed. "We really need your help. But tonight, we can enjoy a party." Everyone cheered. Simigrin tipped her glass toward them, and they returned it.

The man in black waved his hands toward the servants in the back. They brought in more plates. One began carving a cooked bird, another a roasted pig.

Ceychell remained quiet for much of the feast. Lovo occasionally whispered to her. Miraden was also quiet. She wished he would talk to her. She didn't know if he was uncomfortable with all the attention or because *she* was there.

She reached for her wineglass; it was nearly empty. A bottle floated toward her and started to pour itself into her glass. Across the table, Star flicked his wrist at the bottle and winked at her.

She couldn't help but wink back. Out of the corner of her eye, she saw Miraden looking at them and felt his jealousy spike in her bones. For a moment, she thought Star was charming, and thought perhaps his charm might influence Miraden. She took a sip of her wine and pointedly ignored Miraden.

"So I hear you are quite the alchemist?" Simigrin said to her unexpectedly.

Ceychell coughed on her wine, cleared her throat, and smiled. "I can brew a potion or an ale, depending on the occasion."

"We have a large alchemy lab here," Simigrin said. "Perhaps you'll find it interesting."

Ceychell couldn't get over the mage's confidence. Simigrin's smile looked unrehearsed but set in iron. She was just as strong as Ceychell had imagined. Ceychell really wanted to like her, but she had to find out what Simigrin's relationship with Miraden was first.

Star interrupted her thoughts by telling Simigrin, "I can tell you she knows how to brew a love potion." He fluttered his eyelashes at Ceychell. "It's like I'm in a dream that I don't want to end."

Simigrin rolled her eyes and swatted Star with the back of her hand.

"What?" Star spoke softly to Simigrin, "I'm just saying, I'd love to brew a potion or two with her— "

Ceychell sat up straighter and said, "In my village men treat women with respect. Even the illiterate, uneducated ones." She was starting to like Star, but she didn't like the way he was looking at her.

Star rolled his eyes and sipped his wine.

Lord Umorogrin had apparently been eavesdropping. "They are our guests," he said. "Show respect, Stardagrin, or I'll have to ask you to leave."

"Can't say they're all like that in Kander, Ceychell," Simigrin said, flashing Star a sidelong glare. "Miraden was a breath of fresh air. Lovo was too, mostly."

Lovo laughed hard and then spouted, "Do you know we had no idea she was a woman for a long time." Lord Umorogrin and the other mages looked over at Simigrin, but she was still glaring at Star.

"There are a few reasons why I hide my gender," she said.

"You must be a master of disguise. You sure you're not an illusionist?" Star said, smirking and looked at his fingernails.

"Enough of that," Miraden said. "What's wrong with you?"

Everyone, including Ceychell, turned to stare at Miraden who hasn't said a word all dinner. He was a gentleman, but she had never seen him rise to defend anyone but her. She tried her best not to burn with jealousy but her face went pale. Stardagrin looked at Miraden and then at Simigrin. Then he smiled and said, "Oh, I thought there might be something—"

"Stop it," Simigrin whispered.

"Enough!" Lord Umorogrin said. "Stardagrin, leave us."

Without another word, Stardagrin stood up, still smiling, straightened his robe, looked at Ceychell, and then walked out of the hall.

"Let's bring in dessert," Umorogrin said into the awkward silence, "and try to make this a pleasant evening, shall we? I apologize—the young mage needs a hard lesson in diplomacy."

Dessert was custard and honey and filled with nutmeg and an orange slice. It was quite delicious, but her head was starting to spin.

After dessert, the guests and mages stood around and chatted while the table was being cleared by servants. Ceychell stayed next to Lovo and Chintaja, who were talking about Crestain.

Miraden finally broke away from his conversation with Umorogrin and approached Ceychell. She was so glad. She grinned coyly and took another sip of her hot spiced wine. When Miraden grinned back her heart fluttered. The old Miraden would have flirted with her at any chance. When he said nothing, she felt his distance. After a brief spell of goosebumps, she considered testing if Miraden was serious about his rejection.

"Would you like to try some?" she asked him. "I think you may like this one."

Miraden took the cup and drank a sip, nodded and handed it back to her. "Wish we'd had some of that on our way here."

She laughed but inside she was badly hurting. "Yeah." She leaned closer, put her hand on his chest and whispered, "I know this is all a lot. But I am here for you."

Miraden turned as red as an apple.

Lord Umorogrin walked up to them and said, "Miraden, Ceychell, I want to thank you again for coming to help us. While you are with us, I want you all to feel at home here and come to us if you need anything at all."

Ceychell and Miraden smiled and nodded politely, and Miraden said, "Thank you. I am glad we can help."

Lord Umorogrin put a hand on his shoulder and smiled. He looked at Ceychell. "Chieftain Ceychell. Can I speak with you privately for a moment?"

She looked at Miraden, and he nodded. She didn't want to get pulled away from Miraden but said, "Of course." Lord Umorogrin put his hand on her shoulder and led her out of the room. She felt safe next to him. He reminded her of her greatfather, a gentle teacher, and a wise caretaker. She wanted to know more about him.

As they walked through a tunnel away from the dining hall, she said, "Can I ask you," she began.

"About your soul of fire?" he said. He was stern, his smile was suddenly gone. "I'm sure you've been experiencing a lot of strange things lately … like odd dreams, flashes of heat, seeing into minds?" he whispered.

She felt her eyes open wide. "Yes. It's like I'm two people—one on the surface and the other just below it."

"Who told you that you have a soul of fire?"

"The shaman Gorgundi. He sent me a note from O'kokra."

Lord Umorogrin nodded. "I am quite aware of Gorgundi. He is a wise shaman, and Simigrin has told me much about her conversations with him." He put both hands on her shoulders and leaned in where only she could hear. His eyes were large and bold and took her all in. "Before Simigrin and Miraden left the island, Gorgundi told her about you and your soul. She was sworn not to tell anyone, not even Miraden, until she talked to me."

Ceychell was confused and intrigued. She didn't understand why Miraden couldn't know.

"I feel like I know Gorgundi, like I know what he looks like. Miraden's letters were so vivid."

"It's difficult to comprehend the power of the shamans. Some have great, unnatural power, but most rarely use it. Who knows, I wouldn't be surprised if you saw him in your dreams. Their magic is very old and guarded. Unlike you and me, they are natives in this world." He stopped and removed his hands from her shoulders. "There are not many like you left in this world; in fact, I thought there were no more."

"No more? And what do you mean native?"

"You have a soul from the old world."

Ceychell almost choked on her own tongue. She looked around to see if anyone was listening. "Do you mean from Ghaborion?"

"How could you possibly know that?" he asked.

"I … heard of it only recently," she said and thought of telling him about the Grunkins.

"Only a few people in this world outside of Kander know Ghaborion even existed. A world where our ancestors lived before coming here to Kanderlus, abandoned and then locked away, but…"

"But what?"

"But a link to Ghaborion was reopened and…" He looked like he might start crying.

"And what?" she asked. She didn't want to seem brash, but she had to know.

"You see, Ceychell, The Liches, our *gods,* founded Kander. They were the forefathers and foremothers of all of us in Kanderlus. They were all-knowing and passed to their direct descendants as much knowledge as they could before they left us."

She realized her mouth was gaping open and closed it. "Where did they go?"

"None of us truly know. Some believe they traveled to a new world, but most believe they transcended, which is why they are worshiped as deities. But they brought the mages, our ancestors, and the rest of the humans to our world before theirs was destroyed. However, they left one god behind, a being referred to in text as Carbrojl. They sealed him and his dark magic in Ghaborion so that it wouldn't pass into this world. Over time, his name faded from the thoughts and stories passed on by the people of this world.

"But, part of his power still exists in this world. You see, each discipline of Kander scouts the world and retrieves children gifted to wield magic by soul, though few are found anymore. We are the decedents of those mages, those gods, who made the leap, and each of us belongs to one of the eleven disciplines. Any mage can learn any of the eleven disciplines but most specialize in their chosen discipline on their twelfth Passing."

Ceychell was enraptured. She had so many questions, but blurted, "Is having a soul of fire a discipline? Why wasn't I found?" She'd never heard of anyone taken as a child by Kander.

"It is… yes. Many years ago, we had a twelfth discipline, Vfindisiss Kar, roughly translated to *the burning guardians*. Those who were in it learned the powers and spells the gods stole from Carbrojl before they trapped him in the old world. The texts tell of Carbrojl's fire spells but also his power to raise the dead and create demons. The gods took only what *they* deemed useful and tried to teach it. But unlike mages who can learn any discipline, only those children born with a soul of fire could become burning guardians. No others could wield Carbrojl's power."

She realized she was shaking when Lord Umorogrin steadied her. His dark eyes stared into hers. "To know Carbrojl's magic, a mage has to be able to channel it from *him*. It is a wild, chaotic discipline," he leaned in, "your discipline. In layman's terms, we called you fire mages."

Ceychell said, "I'm not a mage. I—"

"You have the gift, Ceychell. I will show you very soon. It is good you came here because you will be the key to turning the tide on the ashenkin and helping us close the rift between worlds. Your power is what we've needed all this time!"

Ceychell felt weak; she swam in her thoughts for a moment. It was too much. "Where did the fire mages go? Why are there no more?"

Lord Umorogrin clenched his jaw. "They're gone, along with someone I loved very much." He glanced at a golden ring on his left hand. It had a single purple stone in it.

"I can tell they meant a lot to you," she said.

"*He* did. He meant *everything* to me. Now he's gone forever." He seemed to stare through her for a moment. His hands dropped from her shoulders and his head dipped. He looked on the edge of tears.

"I am so sorry. When did this happen?" She knew all too much about loss.

"Eighteen years ago, but it feels like an age."

Ceychell was near her eighteenth Passing. She wondered if she would have been found and brought to the college had the other fire mages not been lost. "There must be others with souls of fire. I can't be the last."

"Very likely, but with the burning guardians gone, no one here can detect the soul of fire in children. But now that we have found you, I have hope. Finding you changes everything."

"But, Miraden and Simigrin and Gorgundi. They closed the gate. Not me."

Lord Umorogrin put his hand on her shoulder again. "Without you they would have never entered the gate or returned from it. You were a big part of it. Gorgundi knew this and sent you the note to get you here. I am thankful you're here."

SIX

WANTED

MIRADEN PICKED UP HIS SPICED dessert drink and took a sip. It burned in a delightful way. He could smell all the herbs; it reminded him of something Ceychell brewed for Valdenfest two years ago. He could tell she was hurting, could feel it. It tore him up that she was so supportive despite knowing he wasn't in love with her anymore. As he stood next to the long table alone, he wondered what she and Lord Umorogrin went to talk about. He was also full and exhausted, and he didn't feel like socializing. He was ready to leave the party. Next to him, Lovo was telling a joke to Chintaja. He put his hand on Lovo's shoulder and got his attention. "I'm going to turn in," he told his friend. "See you in the morning."

"Of course," Lovo said. He took Miraden's arm, pulled him closer, and whispered, "You want me to go correct Star's manners?"

"No, I think the embarrassment alone taught him a lesson."

Chintaja said. "It may have been difficult for him to be among honorable people." Miraden hadn't spoken to Chintaja, but the knight seemed to be friendly with Lovo, so Miraden trusted him. He nodded to the knight, smiled, and said, "Possibly."

Lovo puffed his chest out. "Well, I *am* pretty honorable."

Miraden smirked, turned toward the door, and was pleased to find Simigrin standing behind him and smiling. She was radiant; her blue robe-like dress shimmered in the yellow light. Golden wristbands and earrings gleamed as well. She had glossed her lips to a brilliant shine. Her very presence made Miraden feel safe. When they arrived at the base of Kander less than a month ago, he thought he may never see her again. He's so thrilled to be back so soon that he wanted to laugh out loud. He'd missed her very much and by the way she stared at him, felt she missed him too.

She reached out and held his hand and said, "It's good to see you, Miraden." Then she pulled her hair back from her face and smiled again.

He wished he could speak to her privately, wished they were on the road and sharing an adventure again "It's great to see you, too. I never thought a place could be so magnificent. Is this how you all normally have dinner?"

She laughed and squeezed his hand. "No. Not often. But we enjoy a good feast when there is something to celebrate."

They looked each other in the eyes and said nothing for a moment. Miraden's chest sank into his stomach, and the rest of the party seemed to melt away. Everything about her was lovely. "I bet you were surprised to see Lovo," he said.

She laughed and put her hand to her mouth. "Yes, quite a surprise. Would you… like to take a walk?" She looked out the archway Ceychell had walked through with Lord Umorogrin. "Or, if you are waiting"—

"I'd like to go for a walk."

They left through the archway opposite the way Ceychell went. Three servants, dressed similarly to his chamber man, were hanging painted boards. Dozens of children in gray robes stood behind them in a line, holding their artwork. All the children turned to greet her.

"Hi Simi."

"Hi Simigrin."

"Simi, hi hi."

"I'm happy you're home, Simi."

She said hello to each of them in turn, high-fived a few, fist bumped another, and hugged a very small girl. She was the youngest, no more than her fourth Passing.

"You look so pretty tonight, Simi," the girl said.

Simigrin blushed and squeezed her hand. "Thank you, Scala!" She waved goodbye to the children and took Miraden's arm, to which a few of the children *ooohhhed* and giggled. Then they all watched her go.

"The kids really like you," Miraden said.

"I tutored many of them. A lot of us do. How is Kyradel doing?"

"She's doing much better and happy to be home. It almost feels weird to say that."

"I bet her parents were ecstatic."

"They were. Ceychell, too."

"I'm sure."

Miraden suddenly remembered what Ceychell had told him. "She discovered who led the ashenkin to steal Kyradel, Kjod, and the others."

Simigrin stopped and stared at him. "What do you mean? Who would do that?"

"An old woman in our village. They mark the windows with a char stick that signals the ashenkin. She told Ceychell there were many like her. I think I found a char stick after I killed a naagling chieftain before we met. They were capturing children as well."

"That is fascinating. We must tell Lord Umorogrin tomorrow. He can spread the word quickly."

"Of course. She told the village elders and mayor of Bilore Des when they were up for the banquet last week. I was really hoping the ashenkin would be stopped when we closed the Ashengate… but it makes me sick that there are people out there helping the devils. And I'm sure they will help them come back. When I left Kaehrn, all I could hope for was that someone like Lord Umorogrin knows how to stop them for good."

"Lord Umorogrin told me he has a plan. And it involves Ceychell." Simigrin paused for a moment and looked away. Then she added, "She is definitely pretty. I can see why you'd like her," she smirked and added, "and she certainly likes you."

"She is my best friend," Miraden said. "And she's far more than pretty." He realized how defensive he sounded and wished he could take it back. He hoped she'd change the subject.

"This probably sounds ridiculous coming from me but, she's awfully cold. I heard Baregorin women were like her, then I met Kyradel, who was a joy to be around."

Miraden fidgeted with his fingers behind his back. The last thing he wanted was for the two women to dislike each other.

"Oh, I'm sorry, Mir," she said. She ran her hand through the crook in his arm and put her head on his shoulder.

He enjoyed being close to her, but he still wanted to change the topic. "I'm glad they gave you another spellbook?"

She laughed. "I am grateful my master overlooked my losing the last one."

"I would hope so'" Miraden said with a laugh. "It's not like you threw it away or lost it gambling."

"Or gave it to the I'la tribe for a cooked grub." They exchanged a look and laughed again.

"I did like that sword, but I got an axe in its place. It was Ormus's, my chieftain's, or he *was* my chieftain. He's Kyradel's father." Miraden reached for it and realized he'd left it in his room.

"I remember, you sent him an antidote. It must be a special axe."

"So, has anyone said anything about your hair?" He touched the ends beside her chin.

"Yes! Many people have. Star said it looks like a silly helmet."

"What's with him? Is he always so rude?"

They continued into a round courtyard. Glowing green bugs fluttered around wide-leaved plants. Flowers as tall as an adult, with large, drooping, blue, white and gold petals grew in a rectangular garden next to the path. Yellow ivy with shimmering purple thistle ran along the ground.

"He really liked me, or maybe he still does," Simigrin continued. "I am not sure anymore. We were sort of close once, but he could never see me as an equal. When I realized that, I lost interest."

Miraden was doubly jealous that Star had eyes for Simigrin *and* had flirted with Ceychell. He felt intimidated by the mage. Star was tall, strong, handsome, and likely more intelligent than he was. Miraden felt himself falling inward, his anxiety getting the best of him, so he stopped and lifted the petals of a white flower. It was bigger than any he'd ever seen. Simigrin leaned over to smell it.

Miraden caught a glowing bug on his finger and stared at it. He'd never seen one like it. It was fat like a pill bug. When it flapped its wings, it spread glowing green dust into the air.

"We call those chorbles," Simi said. "I think they only live here in Kander." She poked the bug off his finger and laughed when it buzzed up into his face. He tried to gently bat it away, but it flew up into his hair. Then he breathed the dust into his nostrils, gasped, and held back a sneeze.

Simi kept laughing, "Miraden, stop! You're going to squish it."

"I got it," he said, turning his head to sneeze, and nearly squished it.

"Wait, hold on." She stepped chest to chest with him and carefully removed the bug from his hair, holding its thorax between her fingers as it fluttered. The glow lit up her face. She slid her other arm over his shoulder and ran her fingernails up the back of his head.

Miraden's heart raced. He was close enough to feel her breath; it was wonderful, like spiced wine. She grinned and unexpectedly pressed her lips to his. It felt wonderful, but he also felt like he was betraying Ceychell. She let go of the bug, and put her hand on his cheek, which calmed his nerves. Suddenly, though, his lips and tongue chilled. He pulled away and breathed out a bit of frost. Simi smiled and said, "I feel—"

There was a rustle in the garden. They both turned to look. The foliage was thick. Miraden brushed past giant fronds and wide flowers to investigate. Simigrin walked around the side of the garden. They heard another, fainter rustle. Miraden ducked below a black-leaved shrub. He was certain that was where the rustling was coming from.

"Did you find anything?" Simigrin whispered.

He saw a freshly broken stem just above a slight footprint on the mossy ground, then went back to Simigrin on the path.

"Someone was spying on us," he whispered.

"Who would be doing that here? Besides, we weren't doing anything. It could have been a kid. They sometimes play hide and seek here."

"The footprint *was* small," he said.

Someone giggled and a shadow passed quickly through the shrubs.

"I know that laugh," Simi said, shaking her head. "Taurus. Taurus!" She sighed. "He is one of Star's pupils. Well, I'll talk to him tomorrow about this," she said and smiled again. "Care to walk me back to my quarters?"

They walked back through tunnels, past a large kitchen, and down two flights of spiraling stone stairs into the eastern housing wing. The stairs continued to spiral down and branch out for a dozen or more floors and disappeared into deep darkness. He wondered where and how far they went.

They stopped just outside the open door of a spacious room. Miraden peaked inside. There were large plush couches, some floating and others nestled into enclaves in the walls. Mages were playing cards at one table, another group were reading next to a row of bookshelves and some just lounged on couches. Three mages were sending a ball flying across the room by waving their hands.

Simigrin's fingers curled around his. "This is my floor. I am not allowed to bring you in, I'm sorry."

Miraden smiled, "It's okay." When he put his arm around her she leaned against him.

Miraden noticed all the people inside were wearing blue. "Are they all ice mages?"

"Each discipline stays together. My order is called Khaldriss Sar, which means a frozen core, but most people call us ice mages."

A man in the room shouted, "Hey Simi, you up for a game?"

Simigrin leaned into Miraden's ear and whispered, "Let's pick up where we left off in the garden." She pecked his ear, then said to the man in the room, "I am." She winked at Miraden and entered the room.

Miraden walked back up the stairs and retraced his steps through the tunnels back to the banquet hall. The table was cleared, and only servants were still in the hall. He walked through it and continued back toward his room. His mind was swimming with thoughts of Simigrin and Ceychell. He briefly considered leaving Kander after helping Lord Umorogrin with what he needed. He didn't want to, but he worried that Ceychell wouldn't get the full benefit of being at the university if he stayed. She had an opportunity for greatness. He didn't want to be a distraction.

His biggest fear, though, was that one or both of the women he cared for would get hurt because of him. It was the last thing he wanted to happen. Ceychell told him she'd support him no matter what, but deep down he knew he had broken her heart. She'd hidden her pain well, but she was always good at hiding her feelings. Simigrin was just too good to him. He didn't want Ceychell to flirt with him, but he couldn't muster the courage to shut it down. He remembered what his father once told him, *Ignoring your heart will only lead to deeper despair.*

Miraden found his way back to his room. Aldus, his chamber servant, was waiting on a small stool outside his door. He stood and straightened his shirt.

"Milord, y-y-y-your bed is r-r-r-readyyy and I've kept y-y-your f-fire w-w-warm. A s-s-stable hand c-came up e-e-earlier and f-fed y-y-y-y-y-your b-b-bear. N-n-n-eed anything else f-from me this e-e-e-evening?"

Miraden had a hard time following the man's stuttering speech and felt bad for the poor fellow. "Please don't call me milord, and you didn't have to wait for me. Thank you, though, for taking good care of my bear."

"It is my d-d-d-duty," Aldus said. He bowed, picked up his stool and walked away down the corridor.

Miraden stepped inside. A lone candle was lit, and the fireplace was crackling with a hearty blaze. Tundra was asleep on a rug near the fire. When he closed the door, the bear popped her head up. He walked over and kneeled down near her, and she bared her teeth playfully. Miraden scratched her ears, and after a moment started on her neck with both hands. The bear growled and rolled over.

"You were definitely taken care of by someone before me," Miraden told the creature. "I'm lucky I found you."

The bear snorted and started to snore.

Miraden couldn't help but think about Ceychell and how lonely she must feel. He felt bad for leaving her after the party. He thought of how aloof he'd been, out of habit and fear, and how, the moment she opened up to him after two years of her rejecting him, he'd rejected her. It was crushing him. He loved her so much, yet was afraid to love her.

His conscience nagged him, and he cracked open his door and looked down the hall. It was quiet. Light from the flickering blue-flamed sconces danced across the stone floor. He hesitated for a moment; then he walked down the hallway to her door and stopped. When he reached up to knock, he froze with fear. He thought he heard something. Holding his breath, he could hear sobbing from inside. He felt terrible. He wasn't sure exactly why she was crying, but he knew it must be because of him. She rarely cried. The last time he'd seen her do so was on the day he kissed her in front of Kyradel. He wanted to rush into her room and comfort her. The guilt was suffocating him so badly that he'd forgotten he was holding his breath. He struggled to hold back tears, dipped his head, and accidentally struck the door with his forehead.

His skull made a loud *thud*. She'd certainly heard it. His heart pounded faster and his palms began to sweat. He started to run back to his room, realized he wouldn't make in time, stopped, and tried to find a shadow to hide in, but there were none. The door squeaked open. He wiped his face and turned toward it. Her room was dark, but in the flickering blue light of the corridor sconces, he saw the cascade of her brown hair and the shine of tears on her cheek.

"Miraden?" she whispered.

Miraden scratched his head. He tried hard to calm down but he was shaking. "Hey Ceycha, I was just seeing if you were okay."

She straightened up and shrugged her shoulders. "Oh, I'm fine. Just thinking of home. I wish I could have spent more time with Kyradel."

Miraden cracked his knuckles behind his back. He felt foolish.

"Maybe she'll come to visit."

She smiled. "I hope so. This place could use some music."

"I could ask Lovo to grab his harp. I bet he'd come out and sing for you."

She giggled, leaned against the wall, and smiled at him. He felt goosebumps pop up on his arms.

"Well, I better get to my room," he said. "I hear tomorrow's a big day."

She stared at him and didn't say anything. He grinned and turned to walk back to his room. The whole way he kept thinking he should turn back and talk to her, tell her he was sorry for being standoffish. He just wasn't sure it was the right thing to do. He opened his door, stepped inside, and as he turned to close it, felt her brush by him into his room.

She was wearing a light brown robe and barefoot. She kissed him, thrust her soft tongue in his mouth, and caressed his face with her long fingers. Then she slid her arms around him, leaned on him harder, and wouldn't let him come up for air. He felt a warmth wash over him like so many dreams coming true. He didn't want her to let go.

Their lips smacked as she pulled away. He opened his eyes and looked deep into hers. They were green like emeralds, so beautiful. He felt for a moment they could see into each other's souls.

She leaned her head against his and whispered, "Thank you for coming to check on me. I just wanted that kiss. I fear I won't get another. I won't get between you and Simi, but know that I'll be thinking about you. Always."

Her words shattered his self-confidence. He felt he was on slippery ground, that his desire might betray his emotions.

"I know how badly I hurt you," he finally admitted. The old Miraden would have cried and ran, but he felt stronger now. He could face her. "I never wanted to. For years I avoided hurting you in any way and it led me to a bad place. I realized how dependent I was on your opinion of me. Every time you disapproved of me, I thought I would die."

Ceychell didn't say a word. She just stared at the floor, deep in thought.

"I do love you, Ceychell," Miraden continued, finding his courage. "You've always known that, and it's true as it was the day—"

"But you also love Simi. I could see it." A tear ran down her cheek. "I saw you look at her like you used to look at me."

"You're right, Ceycha."

She bit her lip and ran her nails lightly along his face. She pulled away and walked out as quietly as she'd come in. He peaked out the door and watched her sway silently toward her room.

He stepped back into his room and wondered how he could possibly sleep tonight.

SEVEN

A CLASSROOM RUSE

A SINGLE RAY OF MOONLIGHT lit the black walls of her dry, bone-chillingly cold tower cell. Her breath frosted against her face. She was so hungry. A portcullis dropped, and Ceychell woke to the sound of a door closing. The dream faded, leaving her filled with dread and despair.

Ceychell propped herself up on her elbows. It was Alva, holding a deep-red robe in her hands. Ceychell blinked away sleep, caught her breath, and looked at her candle. She had slept only a few hours.

"I'm sorry, madam," the servant said. "I didn't mean to wake you." She set down the robe on the dresser along with a folded note. "I can return later if you would like to get more sleep."

"No, that's alright," Ceychell said, climbing out of bed. Her mind was still clearing, but she couldn't shake the horror of that freezing cell. "What is all that?"

"It is your uniform, though I can't remember seeing anyone wearing a red robe here."

Ceychell stood, nearly fell over, and stumbled over to Alva. "Really? Ever?"

"No, madam. It's a forbidden color at the university."

Ceychell looked at her with a stern gaze. "Then why should *I* wear it? Who sent it?"

"Lord Umorogrin did, madam. I can tell by the material that it's never been worn, it's freshly made. He caught me in our dormitory last night and gave me strict orders to deliver it."

Ceychell had thought she was being pranked, but now she was just confused. It didn't make any sense to her, and she worried what would happen to her if she wore it… or if she didn't wear it.

"I also brought you fruit in case you were hungry," Alva said, placing the biggest green apple Ceychell had ever seen on her dresser.

"You don't have to bring me food," Ceychell said. She picked up the letter and opened it.

"It's my duty to serve you and make your stay comfortable." The way she said it sounded rehearsed. The young woman had no fight in her. Her skin was pale, her fingers had calluses, and her nails were worn to the nub.

"Why is that? You're not my servant. Where I come from we don't have house servants."

"My master wishes me to serve you, so I serve you." Alva took a step back and kept her head down.

"This… you aren't employed by the university?" Ceychell asked. She wasn't sure she wanted to hear the answer.

"No, madam. I'm sorry if that upsets you."

"You aren't upsetting me. I'm disappointed that such enlightened people can live in savagery," she said.

"You are as kind as you are beautiful," Alva said.

Ceychell did not like the way the comment was juxtaposed. Few regarded her as kind and many thought her beautiful, a quality she didn't value. She held her tongue and read the note.

Ceychell,

Please report to the Alchemy Lab today after you break your fast. Before the post-sunrise.

She laid the note on the dresser, pulled off her nightrobe and slipped into the red robe. The fit was slender and held her waist snuggly. Gold lace adorned the cuffs and the hem just above her boots. It felt strange, like a costume.

"It fits you perfectly, madam. Shall I brush your hair?"

Ceychell picked up her own brush and pointed it at Alva. "Stop calling me that. Call me Ceychell, or Chieftain if you must be proper." She brushed her own hair, spun it up in a bun, and punched two pins into it to hold it. She picked up the apple off the desk, took a bite, and mumbled, "Where is the alchemy lab?" She fastened her belt over her robe with Hellshy in its sheath.

Alva bowed and led her down many tunnels and to the lab. It was round and vast; red vines like the ones that grew in her garden climbed its bark, interior walls. It looked like the inside of a tree trunk. About twenty tables were spaced throughout the room. Shelves along the back wall, five sets of them, the highest over thirty feet tall, appeared to be natural outgrowths of the tree trunk and were stuffed with books and parchments. The shelves along the left wall were laden with empty phials, flasks, and potion bottles of all sizes, and along the right wall shelves were filled with a few hundred small crystal cabinets stuffed with reagents. Giant spider leg tips stuck out of one cabinet, a putrid green scaldshroom from another. It dripped stinking yellow ooze onto the floor and sizzled.

There were over thirty people inside. Most were younger than her, and a few were older. Mages in various colored robes were chatting with each other at tables laid out to surround a center podium, and most were next to cauldrons. The mages robes were at least nine different colors: blue, yellow, green, orange, purple, tan, white, dark brown, silver; but there was not one red robe. Many of them gasped when they saw her; she guessed it was because of her robe. The only person she recognized was Star, who was casually chatting at a table with three women. He noticed her walk in and grinned. Alva bowed and said, "Mother of Light, Ceychell," and left. Ceychell walked through the room, trying not to let her angst show, and headed to an empty table.

"My my my," Star whispered. "You seem to cause a stir wherever you go."

A few mages giggled.

Ceychell stopped at a table by herself and waited. She didn't want to be there. She wondered if they wanted to test her brewing skills and hoped she wasn't there only to learn how to make potions. She tried to mind her own business, but she saw Star walking over to her.

"Mother of Light, Chieftain Ceychell," the mage said. "Looks like we are in class together today. I'd be happy to show you around the lab." Then he leaned in and whispered, "But you may want to change out of that robe before Master Brewer Dakhimadigrin gets here."

"Why?" she asked with a shrug.

"Well, this isn't appropr—" He touched her sleeve and she slapped his hand away.

"Do not touch me," she said, glaring at him.

He smirked. "Are you villagers always so rude? You need friends here, Ceychell. Not enemies ... or more enemies."

"I am not. Wait, what do you mean 'more'?"

Someone behind her said, "Alright, everyone. Settle down."

Ceychell turned around and saw a woman in her autumn years. She was dark-skinned, and her hair was graying black that frizzled out a half-foot. She had thick glasses and wore a black robe. She looked straight at Ceychell, lowered her glasses and narrowed her eyes.

"Young lady," she said and beckoned her with a curled finger to approach the podium at the center of the lab.

Ceychell realized she had no choice and walked up to who she assumed could only be Master Brewer Dakhimadigrin. The woman's chiding gaze made her regret showing up to class.

She leaned forward only for Ceychell to hear and whispered, "I don't know who you are, but we have rules in Ohmalo and one of them is red is *forbidden*." She emphasized the word by slapping her hand on the podium with each syllable. "Why have you come to my class dressed like this, and why should I not send you to see the Lord?"

"Lord Umorogrin gave this to me," Ceychell said, extending her red-draped arms. "It's the only mage robe I have, Master Brewer."

"Oh, did he? And what kind of mage are you, a wayward mage?"

"I-I am not a mage at all."

Dakhimadigrin leaned back and gave her a sidelong look. "Get back to your desk before I turn you in. And don't you come to class tomorrow like that."

Ceychell bowed and returned to her table. Star was waiting for her. He winked at her, and she coolly looked away.

"Today," the master brewer began, "we are going to be brewing a fireproof potion, so get out your quills and take notes."

Ceychell listened as intently as she could, but she was bored. She already knew how to brew the fireproof potion, and when she went over to get the impstool, flak moss, ginseng, and haltic grass, many of the students tried to question her. She wasn't in a chatting mood and ignored them while she gathered the ingredients. Then she returned to the cauldron near her table. Star was waiting there patiently adjusting his sleeves.

"Are you just going to watch me brew this?" she asked.

"I would watch you brew anything, Ceychell," he said.

She groaned and focused on making the potion. The cauldron was small and sitting on an unnatural pink flame that burned hot on a stone. She'd never seen anything like it.

Master Brewer Dakhimadigrin approached them. "Star, are you supervising our new student."

He stammered, "Why, Master B—"

"I don't need supervision," Ceychell cut in. "I know this recipe."

"Well," Dakhimadigrin said, looking down her nose at Ceychell, "I didn't realize we had an alchemist here. Perhaps you should teach the class. I'll go sit down and relax."

"Perhaps you should," Ceychell said without giving it much thought.

Everyone gasped, even Star.

Master Brewer Dakhimadigrin's eyes grew two sizes. "Well, young lady, I never thought I'd see—"

"With all due respect Master Brewer," Ceychell said, keeping her voice calm, "I am an alchemist. Of all the classes here, this is the one I could teach." There was another wave of gasps.

"Alright then, buttercup," Dakhimadigrin sneered, "brew me a teleportation potion. Let's put on a good show for all these... aspiring alchemists."

Ceychell looked at her small cauldron. "I need a hotter flame. It has to be hot enough to melt gold. And do we have giant's tongue or riddleroot here? And I need to know where I can find apperhorns quickly because once the potion is boiling, it has to be added before the batch spoils."

Master Brewer Dakhimadigrin's eyes slowly widened. She pulled her glasses off, set them on the table, and stared at her. "Who are you, pretty thing?"

"I am Chieftain Ceychell of Kaehrn."

"Chieftain? Are you Curasca's little girl?"

Ceychell was thrown off guard and softly said, "I am."

"She was one of my finest students when I worked in Bilore Des. Well, you just might be an alchemist."

From the doorway, someone said, "Excuse me, Master Brewer."

It was Lord Umorogrin. He was holding a large red sack over his shoulder. All the students bowed, except Ceychell.

"Yes, Lord Umoro, please come in," Dakhimadigrin said. She smiled adoringly at him. "I hope you've come to see some of our experiments today. We have a new student that is shaking things up a bit."

"I am very sorry for the disruption," the lord said, "but I need to take Ceychell out of your class."

"We were just getting started," the master brewer said. "Why does she have to go?"

"She is supposed to work with me today," he said. Then he turned to Ceychell and asked, "Did you not get the note?"

"I am very sorry, Lord Umorogrin," she said. "I got a note about reporting to this class."

He paused to look at her for a moment, then said, "I am certain a letter was delivered."

She looked at Star, who was peering out the window, quite deliberately avoiding her gaze. She walked toward him, clenched her jaw, and tried to bump him out of her way. He was solid though, and she bounced more than bumped. Then she walked down to the podium where the Master Brewer stood, reached out, and grasped the older woman's hands. "Maybe I can come back another time and give you the day off." The Master Brewer grinned and winked at her.

"I am sorry for the disruption, please, Ceychell," Lord Umorogrin said again and waved for her to follow him out.

Ceychell and Lord Umorogrin walked down a long hallway lined with paintings. "I am so sorry for the confusion," he started. "You probably got some unusual stares and comments about your red robes?"

"I did," she said.

"Red is the color of your discipline and I forbid anyone to wear it after the fire mages were lost, but now that you're here, you have breathed life back into your order."

Ceychell followed the master, her mind spinning with questions. "Why forbid it?"

Lord Umorogrin slowed down and pensively stared at her. "It was a painful mistake. I—"

She wasn't sure what to say. He seemed frail, searching for words. "Should I leave?" she asked.

"No no no, child. Please." He closed his eyes, took a deep breath, and opened them. "All the mages in your order were stolen from us."

"Mages are so powerful—how could that happen?"

"They were… consumed by Carbrojl. Twisted, and forced to serve him."

The hair stood on the back of her neck. "When the pathway to his world was opened?" she asked.

"Yes."

She wanted to ask more questions, but was afraid of the answers she might get. They walked down several flights of stairs, and entered a large, dusty room draped in cobwebs. A few tables were covered in rubbish, and the bookshelves were thick with dust and seemingly forgotten. Lord Umorogrin held out his hand, and a floating light appeared.

"Where are we?" Ceychell asked. There was a wide red banner on the wall emblazoned with a black-horned creature of shadow in a field of flames. Its emerald eyes sparkled from Umorogrin's light.

"This was the entertainment room for Vfindisiss Kar." Lord Umorogrin pointed down the hallway lined with at least twenty doorways, extending into darkness. "The sleeping quarters are there. But we need to go to the training room. I want to show you something."

They walked down the hallway and into a grand room with a stairway leading down into darkness. There were no torches lit, and she could only see reflections of paintings on the walls from the light that floated beside Lord Umorogrin. She smelled hints of sulfur and coal.

"This was where your order practiced their arts. The fire mages became very powerful."

Lord Umorogrin snapped his fingers. The wall sconces flickered a few times, then burst into deep red flames, painting the entire tunnel blood red. They continued until the end of a hallway that opened up into a great arena carved from black stone. Many tiers of steps encircled a hard dirt pit, surrounded by eleven more archways like the one they walked through. The ceiling was mountain stone.

"This where all the orders train for combat and often summon creatures. Our people can practice their dangerous craft safely away from society."

"Why are you showing me this?" she asked.

"Because this will be your laboratory for now." From the sack over his shoulder he drew a thick red spell book with black shadowy veins spread over its cover. It looked like a book of nightmares. "This was recovered from the ashenkin realm, before the temple inside the Ashengate was destroyed."

She stared at the book. The writing looked familiar, but she couldn't place where she had seen it before.

"This here," he put his hand on the cover of the book, "belonged to a very good friend of mine. He too was taken from me. He was the master of your order. And the book was infected by Carbrojl. I am certain of it."

She was scared of it and resisted when he took her hand and placed it on the book. He brought the book up to her hand. It was burning hot. Its heat rushed through her. She'd felt the burning before, when she'd been angry, when she killed Hydracks. She felt it when she controlled Hellshy.

"I beg you to stay here at the university and learn everything you can as fast as possible. I realize it is no small request, but we need you. Eventually I will send your companions to recover a powerful artifact that I know will help us control the ashenkin and sever Carbrojl's tie to this world. But you must train first and perfect your skills or the artifact will consume you, and the ashenkin and their master Carbrojl will destroy us."

Ceychell didn't feel ready for such a heavy responsibility. She was out of her depth. She wondered how much time she had, and what the artifact would do to her should she fail. A hundred such questions raced through her mind; she didn't know where to start.

"My pupils will guide you and teach you the arts, but only you will be able to understand the contents and wield the power of this book."

Ceychell hands were shaking.

Ceychell swallowed the knot in her throat and asked, "How can I stop Carbrojl?"

"Learn. Everything you can. Part of why he is so powerful is because everyone who understood his power and how to draw from it is gone. But we will discuss this later. For now, we must get down to business. I have arranged a tutor for you, she will help you learn the basics of being able to bring your power into focus so that you can cast basic fire spells. Then, more of us can help you with other spells, such as summoning creatures to serve you. I will attend your lessons as well. Bringing you up to speed quickly is my top priority and the top priority of the university right now."

Ceychell felt numb. She was elated and terrified. She wanted to thank the lord, but thanking him for propelling her into a dangerous task seemed awkward. She was about to say something optimistic, but Simigrin walked into the arena and saved her from embarrassing herself.

"I believe you met Simigrin last night," Lord Umorogrin said. "She is one of our finest mages." Simigrin smiled and walked over to join them.

Ceychell just couldn't believe it. She tried to smile but her cheeks felt like stone.

"We meet again Ceychell," Simigrin said. She looked at the book, at Ceychell's hand on it. "Why are you touching that book?"

"Simigrin," the lord said quickly, "Ceychell will be able to use this book, but she must understand the basics first. And she must learn quickly, the first four years of training in the next month."

"What!" Simigrin and Ceychell said simultaneously.

Ceychell and Simigrin stared at each other. Lord Umorogrin handed Ceychell the book, and she grasped it with both hands. He tucked the sack below her belt at her side. "I am entrusting the book to you now. Guard it with your life. You two will want to get better acquainted before you start lessons. Servants will clean up parts of Vfindisiss Kar hall, so you can move in later in the week." He extended his hands in front of him, and hard-packed dirt transformed into beige flagstones. A table appeared, then another, a cooking fire with a cauldron, bookshelves, notes, quills, instruments, baubles, and glowing armor all appeared in the arena. Sconces lit on the walls and banners bearing the insignia of each order appeared above the archways."

Ceychell looked around in awe, gaping at the incredible transformation. She'd never seen magic at work. It was fantastic and intimidating all at once. She clutched the book in her arms and turned enough to again face Simigrin, who was smirking at her.

"I shall return shortly," Lord Umorogrin said and walked toward an archway with a two-headed dragon banner over it.

Simigrin and Ceychell said nothing while Lord Umorogrin was still in the arena. Ceychell briefly ruminated on how her situation had turned into a mess so quickly. She stared at Simigrin and her tutor stared right back at her. Ceychell wondered what she was thinking. She couldn't possibly be happy with the arrangement either. Then Ceychell thought about her conversation with Miraden the previous night; now she was staring at the women who'd stolen Miraden's heart. She was hell-bent not to let Simigrin keep it.

Simigrin finally broke the silence. "I hope you take good notes because I won't repeat myself."

"Don't worry, I'll keep up."

"Maybe. So long as I don't ask you to write me a letter."

Ceychell gasped and squeezed the book. More than anything, she wanted to knock Simigrin out.

Simigrin looked at Ceychell's fingers shaking on the book cover. "Go ahead, punch me like a barbarian. Prove me right."

"What do you mean?" Ceychell said. "You know *nothing* about me."

"I know you only care for yourself. You're vain and overly concerned with how others perceive you."

Every word stung Ceychell deeply. The poison spread under her skin and numbed her stiff. She hoped that was only the person she *used* to be.

"You are wrong," Ceychell said.

"I was there—every day. You broke his heart. I watched it; I saw him suffer. He nearly abandoned our search for your sister; he almost gave up on himself because of your lack of compassion."

Tears welled in Ceychell's eyes and tumbled down her cheeks. "I failed to get my letters to him. But I do love him, and I would do anything for him."

Simigrin barked a laugh. "Try climbing the steps of an ashenkin hell beside him. I dragged him unconscious out of a temple consumed in flames after one of those devils nearly choked me to death. He stitched up my guts and helped me walk for three days. He even helped me scale the wall of an abyss in the freezing cold. You have a childhood crush, but *we* stuck together through miseries that you only experienced through his letters."

It was the very conversation Ceychell had been afraid of, and every retort she could think of was petty and base. "I lost Kyradel and Miraden on the same day. I—"

"Oh I heard all about it. But the reality is, you lost Miraden years ago. You *threw* him away over a spat with Kyradel. It was your own fault."

It was too much all at once: the fire mage training, the responsibility for Lord Umorogrin's mission, and now confrontation with Simigrin. She wanted to scream, wanted to cry, wanted to attack.

She shoved Simigrin with the book into a table. Then she set the book down, ready to fight, and Simigrin tackled her to the ground. Ceychell climbed on top of the mage and pinned her arms. Simigrin wriggled one free and slapped Ceychell.

Ceychell grabbed Simigrin's hair and slammed her head on the ground. Simigrin yelped, grabbed a tuft of Ceychell's hair and yanked her down. They rolled over and Ceychell threw her off. Simigrin jumped up, but Ceychell grabbed her in a head lock and flung her onto a table. She could hardly believe her own strength. She seized Simigrin's robe at the collar, pulled her up, and shouted, "Miraden already told me he doesn't love me anymore, but I still came to help. So you can be a little nicer!" Then she punched the mage in the jaw.

Simigrin spat blood on the dirt. "He got your last letter because of me." Her hair was a mess and her lip was bleeding. "Gorgundi gave it to me when we left the island and told me about your soul of fire. He told me to give Miraden the letter before he returned home. I could have thrown it in the sea. Think of how much he'd hate you if I did."

Ceychell was stunned. Her chin and arms shook; she wanted to strangle Simigrin to stop her from talking lest she'd find out how much more she's indebted to her.

Simigrin grabbed Ceychell's wrists. Ice spread from Simigrin's hands up Ceychell's arms until Ceychell yanked them out of her grip, backed away, and slouched from the weight of the thick blocks of ice congealing on her forearms. She screamed and slammed her arms on the floor, but the ice barely cracked. Simigrin kicked her in the chest, knocking the wind out of her, and she crumbled to the ground.

Simigrin knelt next to her and whispered, "Don't ever push me again, barbarian."

"Are you quite done, ladies?" Lord Umorogrin was standing in the two-headed-dragon archway, glowering at them and shaking his head. He walked over to them. "Whatever *that* was about is now *over*." He pointed at Ceychell, and the blocks of ice on her wrists melted away. "*You* will begin training immediately." Then he pointed at Simigrin, "And *you* will do everything in your power to help her. From this point forward you will eat together, sleep in the same room, and train together every day. If I see one of you I'd better see the other close by. Am I understood?"

"Yes, Lord," Simigrin said.

"I didn't hear you?" he screamed. His voice boomed like thunder in the great chamber.

"Yes Lord!" both women said.

"Good." Lord Umorogrin straightened his robe. "Now clean up this mess and get to work."

"Lord," Ceychell said. He turned and glared at her. "I am sorry. This was my fault."

EIGHT

A FIGHT?

MIRADEN WOKE EARLY. HE HADN'T had a leisurely sleep in so long that he had forgotten how nice they were. It made him realize how much he took for granted a good snooze in the afternoon sun back in Baregorin Forest. He lay against Tundra while the big bear snuffled and snored. He hadn't heard Aldus come in. The servant sat on his stool quietly near the door.

"Greetings, m-m-m milord," he said.

Miraden stood up and stretched. His leathers, cloak, boots were all cleaned and set out. "Thank you for cleaning these, Aldus. I really appreciate it." He changed into his gear, holstered his axe, and felt much more comfortable. He pulled a bit of smoked meat from his pack and a few pieces of fruit from a small bowl on a nightstand next to his bed, and set them next to Tundra. Then he left the room.

Across the hall, Chintaja was standing outside Lovo's room, straightening his collar and looking a bit flustered.

"Hi Chintaja," Miraden said.

"Master Miraden, good to see you." Chintaja wiped a bit of sweat from his forehead.

"Have you seen Lovo or Ceychell?"

"Lovo is in his room getting ready. I've not seen the Chieftain since early this morning. Say, that is a fine axe at your side. Are you good with it?"

Miraden looked down at the axe Ormus gave him. "I've chopped a lot of wood, but I've never used one in combat."

"Lovo and I were going to work on drills today, perhaps you should come so I can show you some techniques. I've trained quite a bit with an axe."

Miraden nodded. "That would be great." He walked up to Lovo's door and knocked.

Lovo opened the door and stepped out holding his new shield and the mace attached to a sling on his belt. He was in a brown linen shirt that almost covered his belly and long charcoal pants.

"Master Miraden is coming with us to train today," Chintaja said.

Lovo smiled and put his arm around Miraden. "Let's go break a sweat."

He trained most of the day outside on the mountain trail with Chintaja and Lovo. His arms hung from his sides and felt like they might fall off. His back ached from top to bottom and his fingers haven't stopped buzzing. His legs felt like jelly. Lovo was wheezing and catching his breath. His linen shirt was two shades darker from the sweat soaking it.

"You both did well today, but I think you'll need a late morning before we drill again," Chintaja said.

Miraden thought he may need a week's rest to feel better and wasn't excited to train tomorrow.

"I'm going to go exploring, I'll see you both tomorrow," Chintaja said and turned down a hallway to their right.

Miraden and Lovo talked and laughed about their time drinking at Kagan Jack's Inn in Muckmog as they walked back to their rooms. Argus nodded and left when Miraden entered. The room was clean, there was food on the table, his bed was turned down, and fresh linens were set out for him.

Tundra rolled over when she saw Miraden. She wanted her belly scratched. He leaned over the giant bear and scratched her sides. She purred like a tiger and rolled back and forth happily. When he finished, she licked his hands, pulled him into a hug with her large paws, and lapped his face with her thick warm tongue. He'd have to spend some time with her tomorrow, take her outside and play with her.

There was a loud thud against the wall outside his room. He walked to his door and peaked out. Lovo was doing the same from his room. Four servants were carrying a bed down the hallway. They were taking it to Ceychell's room. Miraden was perplexed. Why would she need another bed? Had she met a friend already? Two more servants walked by carrying bags of items, books, and a folded stack of blue robes. Miraden stepped out of his room and stopped one of them, a short young woman with blond hair and freckles.

"What is all of this?" he asked.

"Master Simigrin asked for her things to be moved up here."

"What?" he asked, but the servant kept walking.

Ceychell and Simigrin entered the corridor from behind Miraden and saw him at the same time he saw them.

"Hey Miraden," they both said slightly out of tempo.

"Hi," he replied as casually as he could. "Why is Simi moving into your room?" Ceychell shrugged her shoulders as if it wasn't very strange. "Simi… is going to help me train and—"

"We felt it best to stay together so we could study at night." Simi said.

Ceychell smiled at Miraden. Her lip was slightly bruised and cut. Miraden touched it gently with his index finger. "What happened?"

"It's nothing," she said, turning her face away. "I'm fine."

"Did someone hurt you?" Miraden was furious. Why would someone hurt her? He'd never been violent, but seeing her hurt made him ready to fight.

"Really, it's okay. I can take care of myself."

Lovo put a hand on her shoulder and leaned into the conversation. "No one scares me quite like you do, but if Miraden and I need to take care of someone, just this one time, give us a name. It won't ever happen again."

Ceychell glanced over at Simigrin; the two men looked at her, too. Simigrin had a bruise on her jaw and a cut on her lip as well.

Miraden looked between them, "What's going on here?" he asked, but he was pretty sure there was a fight.

"It was a hard day training," Ceychell said.

Simigrin nodded, "Yep."

The two women exchanged conspiratorial looks, before Ceychell kissed Miraden on the cheek. Annoyed, Simigrin looked at her and then kissed him on the other cheek. He stood frozen. Stunned.

He watched them walk down the hall and into Ceychell's room.

Lovo and him exchanged a look before Lovo whispered, "I don't envy you, buddy." Then he went back to his room.

NINE

30 DAYS

MIRADEN GASPED AND FELL ON his butt. He set his axe down and leaned it against a rock. His chest heaved as he tried to breathe the thin, high-altitude air. Nevertheless, he felt strong and invigorated, and as much as he disliked Chintaja's drills, they kept his mind off of the world and the ashenkin.

He fell into a routine at the university. Every morning, he sparred with Lovo, using steel clubs and shields. After a small snack of fruit and rice, they ran the mountain trails with Chintaja up to snowy drifts in the thick clouds, never venturing from the path, as a misstep would lead to a several thousand-foot drop.

Chintaja and Lovo built wooden dummies and placed them on the path, and Chintaja would instruct Lovo and Miraden on how to attack them. Miraden felt like he was starting to get the hang of his axe. He thought about his time trying to wield the silver saber Bryndyke had given him, and was glad he hadn't been killed, because he now realized what little skill he had with a weapon. After training each day, he usually took Tundra for a walk, sometimes all the way down to Bondare to buy a snack or around all the wall walks, enjoying the views of the tree countryside beyond the caravans of

Bondare and the blue ocean to the east.

One day, after about a month of the routine, Chintaja told him, "Master Miraden, we are ending early today. I'll save the dummies from your wrath." The three men walked down the trail toward the university. Though he was still sweating and hot from running, a gust of wind on his neck sent a chill through him. He looked up and saw a dragon fly overhead. He'd seen smaller drakes and wyverns but never a serpent so large. It had golden scales, broad wings and spines lining the sides of its back. He couldn't see a rider but *hoped* there was a mage controlling it. Its roar sent his blood cold.

"Would you look at that," Lovo said.

"A magnificent beast," Chintaja said.

The dragon rose into the air and continued north.

Miraden shook the chill from his bones and rubbed his sore hands together. He was invited to see Ceychell's progress and couldn't wait. He'd hardly seen her or Simigrin the entire month.

Tundra was sleeping in the shade of a jutting boulder lower on the trail. When they got near, she clambered up and walked up alongside Miraden. He gave her a hearty scratch behind the ears.

Chintaja laughed. "I still can't figure out why that bear follows you like a dog."

"It's all in the treats," Miraden said, "and knowing how to scratch, my father used to say."

When Miraden got back to his room, he realized how much his arms ached and body hurt. He lifted his shirt and checked a welt on his side that Lovo had dealt him in their sparring session. Miraden didn't enjoy combat, but he knew he needed to improve his hand-to-hand combat skills. Unfortunately, the ashenkin wouldn't always be at arrow's distance.

After cleaning himself up, he changed into his nice white shirt and black pants. Then he brushed Tundra's fur with a crude iron and thistle brush he'd purchased in Bondare the previous week. He'd worked her matted hair into a smooth shine.

"You ready to go see how Ceychell's doing?" he asked the beast.

Tundra sighed and rubbed her head against his leg.

Lovo met him outside his room, looking and smelling much cleaner as well. As they walked through the hallway toward Ceychell's training ground, a few people nodded at him and he smiled and returned a nod. Some of the other mages pressed themselves against the wall to avoid Tundra. He passed the alchemy classroom and smelled sulfur and immediately thought of the ashenkin. Instinctively, he patted his side for Hellshy, but of course he'd given it to Ceychell. Even though Lord Umorogrin had said that though the ashenkin had increased their abductions, they had time before they arrived in force, it just didn't feel consistent with what Gorgundi had told him about the demons. And he wasn't sure how long he could stay in Kander and wait for the ashenkin to fully invade, despite Lord Umorogrin's insistence that he do so.

He walked with Lovo into the training ground arena. He looked back at the archway he walked through, above it was a purple banner. In its center, a crystal heart. Icy veins spread from the heart to the edges of the banner like a spider web.

Lovo grabbed his shoulder before he bumped into two mages walking in front of them. When he corrected himself, Tundra bumped them anyway. One of the mages, a woman in orange robes, tan skin and spikey blue hair jumped back with a gasp. Her friend, another woman who looked like her but had green spikey hair said, "Do you have to bring that bear everywhere?"

Miraden felt bad initially, then said, "Yes, I do."

Both ladies scoffed, then shuffled away.

A handful of mages sat up in the stands of the coliseum-laboratory. Huge scorch marks covered one wall, and a few were on the ceiling and the seats. On the coliseum floor were some tables and chairs and bookshelves, but they were ethereal, like illusions one could pass right through.

Miraden sat between Tundra and Lovo near the bottom seats. Mages continued walking in through the dozen archways and slowly filled the seats. Out the corner of his eye, he saw Stardagrin making his way over with a few of his friends. He wished he'd walk right on by but Star sat right behind him. He was tense and could hardly focus on the arena.

Star whispered to his friends. Miraden wished he could hear but there was so much noise in the coliseum.

"You okay?" Lovo leaned over and whispered to him.

Miraden clenched his teeth and stared forward. Lord Umorogrin escorted Ceychell down onto the laboratory floor.

Then a yellow sphere appeared, encompassing the whole lab. It slowly changed to red then dissolved into heat waves that rippled in front of the lower seats.

"I can't wait to see what she can do," Lovo whispered. He handed Miraden a green apple and gave another to Tundra.

Ceychell looked at Miraden and snuck a wave at him while she listened to Lord Umorogrin's instructions. Miraden was so curious about the lab that he didn't notice Simigrin walking up beside him.

"Hi!" she said.

She looked beautiful but exhausted. Miraden stood and hugged her and waited for a comment from Star. It felt good even though he was nervous. She hugged Lovo as well.

"Oh Tundra," she said, "it's good to see you too." She scratched the bear's neck up, and Tundra rubbed against her side.

"It's great to see you finally," Miraden whispered. "Do you ever get any breaks?"

She rolled her eyes. "Not really. We don't teach like this. We start mages young so we can take our time and really mentor them. Cramming isn't fun, but she has the knack for it. Have to say I'm surprised."

"She was always a quick study," Miraden said.

Ceychell was listening intently to Lord Umorogrin, standing up straight with her hand on the red silk bag at her side, and somehow ignoring the growing crowd.

"What have you been up to?" Simigrin asked.

"Chintaja has been training us. So I get beat up by Lovo in the morning, run til I'm sick and hit a wooden man that doesn't fight back in the afternoon, and then do it all again the next morning."

"The wooden man fears him more every day," Lovo said, laughing.

Simigrin smiled, took Miraden's hand, and leaned against him.

Star giggled. All three turned to look at Star, who grinned along with his friends. "It's great seeing you Simi. Hugs for me and my mates too?"

"I'll give you a hug," Lovo said. He was terse and Star didn't like it.

They turned around without another word. Miraden was on edge and sat with his hand on Tundra's back. Simigrin squeezed between him and Lovo.

"Hello everyone," Lord Umorogrin addressed the audience, which had filled the coliseum. "We normally do not demonstrate like this but you all have asked me so many questions that we felt it was time to share some of what our new student of Vfindisiss Kar has learned."

Ceychell nodded to him and held out her hand, the book jumped from her bag and opened itself, just like Miraden had seen Simigrin's book do. Ceychell whispered a few words Miraden couldn't understand and then she extended her hand, palm out. Nothing happened.

She repeated the phrase, thrust her palm forward, and three plumes of fire flew from her fingertips. Ceychell shook her head. Miraden's stomach started to knot. Some of the mages in the crowd began to murmur and a couple chuckled. Ceychell yelled and threw out her hand again. A gout of fire struck the barrier with such force that the entire sphere shuddered. Flames licked the sides of the barrier, and it rippled with such intense heat he couldn't see through it. Then the flames disappeared with a loud bang. A green barrier rippled around Lord Umorogrin and Ceychell as the force of the blast harmlessly passed over them.

The crowd went silent. The two men who'd laughed at Ceychell moments ago were gawking at her with their mouths open.

She flipped her hand, and pages turned in her book.

Simigrin turned to Miraden and whispered, "Wait until you see this if she pulls it off."

Lord Umorogrin walked outside the forcefield and stood with his arms across his chest. Ceychell whispered and reached her hand out to the book. Red sparks and lightning leaped from the book up her arm; she hurled the energy at the barrier, splitting and cracking it and casting the entire arena in blood red light until the sizzling sparks died out and the barrier reformed around her.

Ceychell focused for a moment. Her book flipped pages and suddenly stopped. Ceychell lifted both hands and then thrust them in front of her. A burning portal opened, and then another on the other side of the lab.

Miraden stared at the portal and felt his skin crawl. It was smaller than an Ashengate but looked like it. He grew nervous about her power.

She ran into the portal and out the other side before both gates burnt out into a thick cloud of black smoke.

Ceychell flipped more pages.

"There's more?" Miraden asked Simigrin. She winked.

Ceychell drew a long tooth, like a slag wolf's fang, from her red silk bag. She held the tooth up and said some kind of spell. The tooth caught fire in her hand, then sparked and fizzled out. She tried it again, but the flame flickered and died.

Miraden didn't realize he was squeezing Simigrin's hand until she squeezed back. Whatever it was that Ceychell was doing, he hoped she'd succeed.

Ceychell tried the spell several more times with the same result. Then drew a pattern in the air with the tooth, though there was no flame, and traced the pattern several times.

"I just don't think she's got it yet," Simigrin whispered. "Summoning is really hard for us non-callers."

"C'mon!" Ceychell screamed and drew the pattern again; the tooth burned a line into the air and then a pattern that looked like letters. The shadow of a drake twice the size of a person burned momentarily and then fizzled into smoke. She lowered her head and closed her book.

Lord Umorogrin began clapping, and so did Miraden. The mages in the audience seemed confused for a few moments, but they eventually joined in and applauded. Lord Umorogrin looked quite pleased with Ceychell. He walked over and said something into her ear. Miraden felt like a thousand pounds just slid off of his shoulders. He couldn't quite understand what she'd done, but it was impressive, nonetheless.

"You okay?" Simigrin said, patting his leg. "It might be the forcefield. You can't stay near them too long or it starts to mess with you."

"Did she learn a lot this month?" Miraden asked. Several spectators walked down to the lab and gathered around Ceychell.

"Yes! Do you have any idea how hard it is to teach someone to use fire so fast and how dangerous her spells are?"

Miraden shook his head. He felt stupid for asking.

"I'm sorry," Simigrin said, "I'm just exhausted. I've worked with her non-stop as have many of the other mages."

Miraden noticed Stardagrin standing next to Ceychell, nodding and smiling with his hands clutched in front of his chest. Ceychell grinned at him. He *knew* that grin, and it didn't sit well with him. "I'd like to congratulate her," he said finally, and they walked down to the lab.

"Wow, that was amazing!" Miraden said and reached out to give Ceychell a hug. She hugged him back, but she seemed slightly reluctant. She hugged Simigrin too.

Then Lovo pulled her into a big hug and said, "You get to start the campfires now, Ceychell."

"How did you create that exploding stream of fire?" Miraden asked. "And the portal, how did you do that?"

Ceychell giggled. "It wasn't easy. The spells are in the book, but I feel the power coming from inside me, like a deep laugh."

"Except there is an explosion at the end," he said.

Ceychell laughed, Star looked down and chuckled too.

"You did well today," Simigrin told Ceychell. "When you first got here, I thought you'd only be able to light a few candles, but the fire-tooth spell was better than I expected even though it still needs work. You should be proud of yourself."

Ceychell beamed and clutched her book to her chest with both hands.

"Indeed," Lord Umorogrin said. "Quite impressive. There is still so much work to do but your progress gives me a lot of hope. Please enjoy the rest of the day however you choose. You've earned it." He nodded to her and walked away with most of the other mages.

"Maybe I'll see you later," Stardagrin said to Ceychell.

She waved and smiled at him as he left.

"Tundra!" Ceychell said. The giant bear lay down on to her back and put her paws up to get a grand scratching. Ceychell rubbed her with both hands, and Tundra closed her eyes and purred.

Miraden wondered about the change in Ceychell. A month ago, she couldn't stand Star, and now they are fast friends. He felt jealous; then he felt annoyed for being jealous. He knew he should be happy for her, and he knew it couldn't be easy for her to see him with Simigrin.

"How… have you been, Ceycha?" he asked, though he knew the answer. He wanted to slap himself for the silly small talk.

"Really busy," she said. "Tired, but I'm learning a lot. How about you?"

Miraden scratched the back of his head. "Oh, Lovo beats me up most mornings. Then Chintaja chases me up a mountain until my legs are ready to fall off. By lunch, I pass out and hope tomorrow will be better."

Lovo lifts the sleeve on his arm and reveals a large welt. "Miraden gets in some good hits too, don't let him fool you," Lovo said. "It's great to see you, Ceycha. I'm going to catch up with Chintaja and get some lunch."

"Would you like to grab some lunch with us?" Miraden asked Ceychell.

"Uhh, that's okay, but thanks," she replied. "I'll probably grab some on my way back to my room and sleep the rest of the day. It was great to see you, Miraden." She shuffled toward the exit where Stardagrin was waiting by the archway.

Miraden watched them go.

"Something on your mind?" Simigrin asked him, arching a brow.

Miraden realized he was staring and looked over at Simigrin. "I can't believe she's—"

"Over you?" Simigrin said.

It cut him deeply, but he wasn't sure why. After all, he *thought* he was over her. He hadn't really thought about her much in the last month. Before he'd met Simi, she was on his mind all the time.

"I guess so," he said with a shrug. "I am glad for her." He took Simigrin's hand and they headed toward the exit.

"I spent most of the last month with her," Simigrin said. "I still don't know her very well because she's pretty aloof. But in case you were wondering, we never talk about you."

Miraden looked at the hard-packed dirt on the ground and said, "I do wonder sometimes. Thanks for telling me. Should we take a walk?"

"I'd love to."

Tundra followed them out and lay down in the sun to wait for them.

Simigrin held Miraden's arm as they walked through the market in Bondare. He paid no attention to the vendors; he just enjoyed the time with her. She looked at trinkets, bought a roasted fish snack, and wandered beside him.

They sat down on a bench for a bit, and Miraden slowly ran his fingers over the flame carvings on her silver vambrace. He remembered the day he got them for her.

"I wear them every day," she said.

"I'm glad you like them. They look perfect on you." He remembered what Kyradel had said to him at the tailor shop in Crestain and put a hand over his mouth to stifle a laugh.

"What?" she asked.

"No… it's nothing."

She squeezed his arm tighter. "Tell me!"

"No, it's ridiculous."

"Your face is getting red. What is it? Tell me!"

He could feel his cheeks flush. "Alright, but you can't get mad."

She leaned back a little. "Well I can't promise that. Tell me anyway."

"Remember when we were at Crestain with Kyradel and went to that tailor?"

"Yeah. What about it?"

"Kyradel told me that, instead of buying you vambraces, I should have bought you a brassier."

"She did not!" Simigrin said and slapped him on the chest. His chest was already sore from training, and he winced. "That sounds like her, though." She paused a beat and added, "What did you say?"

Miraden shrugged. "I don't know, something about not talking about you like that and that they were all out of bras. Might have mentioned something about needing a lot of silver."

She whipped her head around at him. "You did not!"

"I may have."

"You dog, Miraden. Didn't think you had it in you," she said and kissed him.

They sat beside each other for a while. Miraden stared into the bazaar and realized he didn't see a single child. He searched and searched and couldn't find one no matter where he looked.

"What is it?" Simigrin asked.

"There are no children," he said.

"There usually are; perhaps we just aren't seeing them."

"No. I've not seen one down here since I arrived. I think the kidnappings are getting worse," he said and looked over at her. "I really hope your lord knows how to stop them."

Simigrin nodded to him and said, "He does, Miraden."

They hiked back up the mountain that evening. Tundra was still waiting for them where Miraden left her. She stood up on her back feet and then dropped to all fours with a groan. Miraden removed a piece of grilled lizard Simigrin gave him at the bazaar and tossed it to Tundra. The bear caught it and started to follow.

"I am I got to see you," he said. "Suppose you'll be back to teaching, and I won't see you for awhile."

Simigrin hugged him from the side, and he put his arm around her. "Probably not." Then they entered the university.

At their housing corridor, Miraden stopped and opened his door. "Would you like to come in before you head back to your room?"

She looked at him bright-eyed and flashed a coy smile. Then she stepped inside and waited for him to close the door.

TEN

90 DAYS

CEYCHELL POPPED HER HEAD UP, surprised she had fallen asleep in her library. She wiped her face and looked down at her open book. She'd read the spell on summoning a fire drake five times before it put her to sleep. She was still very tired. She felt like she'd been studying for nearly thirty hours straight. It was early in the morning and quiet. It was hard to study in her quarters because there was always so much activity and revelry into the night.

She closed the book and saw a cherry tart beside a note. It was Stardagrin's handwriting.

I didn't think angels could sleep so beautifully.
See you in the morning

She ate the tart, it was her favorite treat from the kitchen. Ceychell smirked and snapped her fingers. The note ignited and burned to ashes in seconds. She liked Star, more than she thought she would, but it seemed like an empty crush, like he was temporarily filling a void in her heart that would never be truly filled. Regardless, he'd been kind to her and had helped her study.

She walked over to a mirror she'd hung on the wall outside of her library. She had dark rings under her eyes and her hair was a mess. She didn't want to be vain, so she simply straightened her hair with her fingers. She wanted a bath, a nice long sleep, and perhaps a holiday. But this was not the time. She walked into the hall and saw Simigrin coming down the steps to her level with some swagger to her stride. She smiled and they hugged.

"Aren't you chipper this morning," Ceychell said. She was suspicious: Simigrin didn't always come back to their room at night.

"The birds are chirping and it looks to be another lovely Spring day. You look tired—fall asleep studying again?" Simi asked.

"I did. Star was helping me and I guess I passed out."

"Let's get something to eat. I'm tutoring you today."

Ceychell and Simigrin walked into a chamber that stood a hundred feet tall. Four stone stairways led up to different towers on top of the mountain. Ceychell had only been up one tower once and it was on a stormy day so she didn't get to practice. She couldn't wait to see the view.

"Ceychell, a word." They both turned at the base of a stairway.

Lord Umorogrin came in from another tunnel. She hadn't seen him for a few weeks. They bowed their heads.

"I come with news but it's not good news," he began. "I've heard back from the mercenaries I sent to Crestain, Sentry, Bilore Des, and Oddion. They all return the same report. They found no leads or evidence of chalk on the windows. What they did report is that abductions have increased. It would appear closing the Ashengate had the opposite effect."

Simigrin groaned. Her eyes filled with tears.

Ceychell wasn't ready to hear that. She shook her head and said, "That can't be right. They rely on surprise, I saw it! They came for me when Vera marked *my* window. She admitted it!"

"I'm sorry. She likely lied to you."

Ceychell couldn't accept it. She shook her head and said nothing.

"Miraden found a similar char pen," Simigrin said. "That can't be a coincidence."

"Are you suggesting that I am presenting lies or that all four of my investigators are in conspiracy to mislead me?" His eyes were dark.

Ceychell felt cold as she stared at Lord Umorogrin. She was scared to question him any further.

"No, Lord, forgive me," Simigrin said. Her head dipped and lip trembled.

"Now, I suggest you double your efforts. Ceychell must be ready."

Ceychell just nodded angrily and then turned toward the stairs.

It was a crystal-clear day. The two women leaned against the stone wall and caught their breath. They'd trained for hours on one of Kander's highest towers. She stared out at clouds over Bondare, forests to the south, mountains to the east, and the sea to the west. It was all so tiny it looked more like a painting than the real world. Her breathing was shallow from the altitude but she liked the rush of cool thin air in her chest.

She'd been training in Kander for three months, but it felt more like three years. Each day ran into the next, and she could hardly remember a time before she'd come to the college.

"You're really coming along, Ceychell," the mage said. She took a drink of water from her wineskin.

"I feel like there is a *but* coming," Ceychell said.

"Not really. You're picking up concepts that it takes kids years to learn. Really makes me wonder if we are training the right way."

Ceychell was surprised that the compliment wasn't barbed.

Simigrin had not exactly been generous with positive reinforcements.

"I worry constantly," Ceychell said. "Worry that it won't be enough for whatever is coming. I feel like the ashenkin could attack us at any time, and I won't be ready."

Simigrin nodded. "I hear you. Honestly, I wish there was something more we could do. I sometimes feel like we—" Simigrin stopped. She looked up at the sky. The stars were barely visible in the sunlight.

"Like we are being lied to?" Ceychell said. "That's how I sometimes feel. Lord Umorogrin disregarded the chalk-bearers and scoffed about the Grunkins. Something is not right. And…"

"And what?"

Ceychell wanted to share her thoughts, but she feared what Simigrin might think. Ever since she'd started training, she'd heard someone whispering to her in her head. It wasn't constant, but in quiet moments, whenever she blocked everything else from her mind, his whispering was there. She hoped she wasn't going crazy, and she surely didn't want Simigrin to think she was. And for all she knew, perhaps mages hear voices all the time. "Nothing," she said at last, "I—I sometimes feel like this power is changing me."

"I have to tell you, Ceychell. I didn't want you here. You probably know that. I thought you were a novelty, a pet project."

Ceychell had thought the same thing for a while, and it hurt. She held back her tears and looked out at the vast sprawl of trees and hills. She didn't want to hear what else Simigrin thought about her.

"I am rarely wrong," Simigrin continued, "but I see what Miraden sees. There is a lot of grit in you. You were born to be a mage. Seeing what you've done in so little time, I'm glad you came to study with us. And I'm glad I got to know the Ceychell that Miraden talked so much about."

Tears finally spilled from Ceychell's eyes. The praise felt good, especially coming from Miraden. She was relieved that she wasn't the imposter she felt she'd been for the past few months. She still felt alone, though. She wanted to belong, to make a difference. She just didn't know how she could.

"I'm glad I got to know you too," Ceychell said. "Miraden told me a lot about you in his letters. I imagined you to be a giant, a legendary known only by her deeds. I wanted to be like you, and seeing you now, and knowing you, gives me hope."

"Gives you hope?" Simigrin asked.

"Yes. That I can be a hero, too, if I am called to it."

ELEVEN

180 DAYS

AFTER SIX MONTHS IN KANDER, Miraden became used to the routine. Thanks to Chintaja's drills, he felt stronger than he'd ever been. His stamina was boundless, his legs never tired, and his appetite was ravenous. He spent his free time teaching Tundra tricks and riding Eclipso around the mountains. He took an early morning ride before training most days unless it was raining, or the fog was too thick. The mages of the college always said hello to him and treated him with great respect. But he didn't consider them to be his friends. Stardagrin, especially, kept his distance, and the annoying mage seemed to be spending more and more time with Ceychell.

Lord Umorogrin had barely spoken to him, and he wondered why Simigrin even sent him the letter to rush to Kander. But Lord Umorogrin had told him to be patient, and he didn't want to leave Ceychell behind. He would do anything for her.

Lovo spent a lot of time with Chintaja. They trained outdoors for hours at a time, laughing and joking, running and sparring, carrying massive stones and sometimes each other up and down the mountain pass. There was more than meets the eye to their friendship; he was glad Lovo found someone like Chintaja.

Lovo and Miraden started playing cards in the evenings to kill the boredom. Miraden had never played cards before, but Lovo had bought a deck in Bondare and taught him the Bone Teller, Soul to Tolls, and his favorite, Kandarli. While they played, they chatted, mostly about what they would do after the ashenkin were gone. Miraden realized he had no idea what he would do, so he came up with some outlandish plans, like becoming a sea captain, to entertain Lovo.

At times Lovo mentioned the Grunkins and how they denounced the Mother of Light, made her sound mortal, weak and corrupt. He seemed confused and upset. He talked about going back and seeking more answers, and even asked around the college about Levoria, but no one knew much about her. They gave him access to the library for information, and he regularly told Miraden about the fascinating stories he found in some of the moldy books there.

After they'd played cards and chatted for a while, Lovo would usually play his harp, and Miraden would shut his eyes, lie against Tundra next to the fire, and try to forget about the world.

Ceychell and Simigrin became inseparable. They seemed to spend every waking minute together, and whenever Miraden saw them, they were always off to do *something*. On a rare day or evening he got to spend with Simigrin, she wouldn't speak of their time together. He felt left out of the story, but he tried to keep a smile on his face.

Mostly, he missed them, both of them. It was like he'd lost both their friendships. What he found oddest was that they sat together in the dining hall and slept in the same room at night. Ceychell had never been tight or chummy with anyone, but suddenly, she and Simigrin were the best of friends. It just didn't seem right.

Mostly, Miraden wondered what he was waiting for. He should be chasing an Ashengate, traveling, anything besides waiting for the ashenkin to attack again. The gifts he'd received at the ceremony lay unused in his travel pack, but he cherished Ormus's axe and wore it on his belt every day.

He felt more connected to Tundra than anyone else. He loved teaching her tricks, and she followed him around and listened to him like a 1400-pound dog. He liked riding Eclipso around the mountains, too. The stag was fast and a bit ornery at times, but it listened to him.

One evening, as he was going to bed after playing cards with Lovo, he kicked off his boots and heard something outside his room. A letter slid beneath his door onto the tile floor of his room. Normally Aldus brought his communications, so Miraden was surprised but also intrigued.

He picked up the letter and opened it next to his bedside candle. He hoped it was from Simigrin. She came to see him occasionally at night.

Meet me at the bathing chambers at midnight.

He recognized Ceychell's handwriting immediately. It was artful and flowing. What could she want?

He left his room just before midnight, shut his door quietly, and snuck down the hall. Then he stopped and laughed at himself—he didn't have to sneak. Nevertheless, he felt like he was about to do something forbidden. He walked down six flights of stairs, passed the discipline halls and away from the living quarters and laboratories. The long tunnel to the underground hot springs grew darker and damper and hotter as he progressed deeper into the mountain. He heard water dripping from the ceiling into puddles and the hissing of steam. The smell of floral bathing oils, to which he was allergic, wafted up his nose, and he nearly sneezed.

He hadn't come down to the bathing pools often, and certainly not this late. There were ten secluded bathing chambers and two larger community chambers in the hall. From what he was told when he first arrived, the smaller chambers were for privileged guests, but he wasn't sure who could use them. Typically, people set their shoes out front of their bath chamber, but there were none anywhere. As he walked past the baths, he was sure he heard his name.

He stepped backward and saw Ceychell in a bathing pool in one of the small chambers. The walls glowed pink in the light of the sconces from the reflection of the natural salts in the stone. The humid air smelled like lemons, and he could barely see Ceychell through the thick mist. When he entered the chamber, he saw her standing up to her neck in the small pool. There were stone seats along the sides of the large rectangular room. Metal jars with oils sat on stone shelves next to the pool. He walked inside and smiled at her, and she smiled back.

He kneeled next to the edge of the pool, and she reached up and pulled him into a hug. It caught him off guard, but he didn't fight it. It was good to see her. He couldn't bear to lose her friendship again.

"I've missed you so much, Miraden," she purred, her moist lips on his ear. She wrapped her arms around him and held him tight.

"W-why haven't I been able to see—"

"Shh," she said, putting a finger to his lips. She rested her cheek on his to whisper, "Lord Umoro demanded that Simi and I spend every waking minute together. It's exhausting. He scares me. He's so pleasant on the surface, but something's weird about him… I don't trust him."

She glanced over his shoulder toward the door, and Miraden turned his head that way, but there was nothing there.

"Just thought I heard something," she whispered.

Miraden shrugged, "I didn't he—"

Then they both heard footsteps.

"Quick, get your clothes off and get behind me," she whispered.

"Wait, what?"

"Quick," she whispered, waving him in. Miraden threw off his clothes and boots and shoved them behind a stone seat. Then he slid into the water. The water was uncomfortably hot, stinging his skin. He crept behind Ceychell and leaned against her back. He was so nervous he began to tremor.

"Well, I really had to search for you." It was Simigrin's voice. "You're lucky I found you and Lord Umorogrin didn't, or you'd be wearing a bell from now on."

Miraden ducked down into the water. If Simi saw him with Ceychell, he'd be dead!

Ceychell stood tall to hide him. "Sorry, I thought I'd get a bit of quiet time. We always work so hard. It may be easy for you, but I feel like I'm wearing myself out."

"It's not *easy* for me," Simigrin said. "I'm helping you because I've been ordered to. And Lord Umorogrin is closely guarding *why* he needs you and I want to know why. I want to be there when he tells you."

Miraden saw Simigrin's robe fly through the air and land on a side bench. Then he heard her plop into the bath to his right. Ceychell tried to turn him so she could face Simigrin, but he was struggling with his footing. He was shaking so hard little ripples were spreading across the water from him. He tried to stay perfectly behind Ceychell so Simigrin couldn't see him.

"Can we talk about something not related to study?" Ceychell asked. "I feel like we rarely talk about anything but books and spells."

"Sure, have you heard from Kyradel?" Simi asked.

"Yes, she's doing great. She's singing and painting again. I hope you can hear her sing one day—she has an amazing voice."

"I've heard quite a few singers. There is a choir here at the college as well."

"Not like Kyradel. Her voice is a gift of the gods. If the queen of Sentry or king of Crestain ever heard her she'd be singing for them."

"I had no idea she had any artistic talent. She didn't sing on the island."

"Oh, Simi. She is so talented. She can paint, and sing, and write poetry. I'd love for you to hear them sometime."

"Speaking of singing," Simigrin mused, "Star seemed full of poetry yesterday in the lab."

Miraden cringed.

"Oh yes, he's always trying to get a reaction from me. If he wrote like Kyradel, perhaps he would," Ceychell said. She wringed out her hair behind her back, showering Miraden's head. "He wants another date, but I'm always in the lab. Maybe on our next night off I'll go down to Bondare with him."

Another date? Miraden hadn't known they'd even had one. He thought he might burst.

"I love seeing him squirm when you stand up to him, though," Simigrin said. "He's so needy. And he's always used to getting what he wants. I don't think I've ever seen him so rebuked. It's kind of fun to watch."

"Well, he's really growing on me," Ceychell said.

"Oh, I know, he grows on you. It's that smile of his."

Ceychell shrugged. "He does have a cute smile, but he's a little too arrogant at times." She wrung her hair out again.

Miraden almost went underwater to avoid hearing more about Star and Ceychell. He was so jealous and annoyed with himself for being jealous. He wanted to stop her from seeing him, but he knew how unreasonable that was. It would make him a terrible friend, and a hypocrite.

"Indeed. Your hair is so long and beautiful, like a real southerner's

—I wish mine was still long."

"I didn't realize yours was long."

"It was longer than yours… until it caught on fire beyond the Ashengate. It was so scorched and shriveled that I had to cut it short, which women don't usually do here until they are married. But not every woman cuts their hair. It's their choice."

"I see."

"Now that you're here with us, maybe you should dye your hair? It's customary for women here. It is a privilege we have; men are not allowed to. Would you hand me the lavender oil behind you?"

"Sure."

Ceychell turned and her breasts brushed against Miraden's face. He closed his eyes and tried not to think, but he was so excited he could hardly contain it.

"Here you go," Ceychell said, tossing the little can of the oil over her shoulder. Simigrin had to reach up for it, which gave Ceychell the moment to turn back around and still keep Miraden behind her.

"Thanks," Simigrin said. Miraden heard splashing and then the bottle being popped open. "So, what do you think?"

"What do I think about what?" Ceychell asked.

"About dying your hair. I can take you down to the salon tomorrow if you want."

"Hmm, maybe I'll dye it… purple," Ceychell said. Miraden poked her for being mean. She jumped a bit and reached back to pinch his face. It hurt, but he didn't make a sound.

"You really want me to seal you in a block of ice don't you," Simigrin said. Miraden wanted to laugh, but he held his breath.

"Maybe red then."

"Like Kyradel's hair?"

"No, not all blended together, maybe several colors so it looks like a flame."

"Well, if anyone can do it, Candraliss can do it."

"Do you really think we have to be attached to the hip the whole time I'm here?" Ceychell asked.

"As long as Lord Umoro wants it, it will be. He may lighten up when he sees your progress, as long as we don't do anything else to piss him off. Like wandering off in the middle of the night to take a bath."

Miraden was curious what had happened. Ceychell hadn't said anything about angering the lord, not that he'd had a chance to talk to her without Simigrin around. And Simigrin never really talked about Lord Umorogrin.

"I hope so," Ceychell said. "I think we could be better friends if we had some space once in a while."

"Perhaps," Simigrin said. "Well, I think I'm clean enough. My fingers are starting to prune." Miraden heard Simigrin get out of the bath. "Try not to wander too far without me. I don't want to get reprimanded because *you* need your space."

"Yes, of course. Sorry about that. Let me just rinse my hair," Ceychell said. She turned to face Miraden again, squeezed him to her chest, dipped her hair in the water, and flung it back. Then she winked at him and slowly pushed him down.

Miraden hated being in the water, hated being *under* the water even more. He saw a blur of Ceychell getting out of the bath and heard their voices, but they were distorted by the water. He slowly scooted toward the far edge of the pool and stayed under as long as he could. When he finally surfaced, the room was empty and could barely hear them talking down the hallway. He got out of the pool quietly and took several deep breaths. He'd never been so aroused and scared all at once.

Miraden thought about Ceychell with Star all night. He shouldn't be jealous, but he was. The next morning Lovo was crying when

Miraden came to his room. Chintaja had been summoned back to Crestain; Lovo wasn't sure for how long. Lovo had really taken a liking to the strict trainer, and he'd gotten into great shape, started combing his hair regularly, and even began watching his manners. Miraden felt bad for him. They walked down the tunnel and sat together on a yellow-cushioned seat at the end of the corridor. Miraden put his arm around the sobbing ogre.

"He'll be back," Miraden said. "Don't worry. Seems like we will probably be here for a while."

Lovo hugged Miraden and then left for breakfast. Miraden sensed he needed alone time and didn't offer to go with him. He looked down the hallway at Ceychell and Simigrin's room, and thought about what had happened the previous night. Then their door opened, and he waited for them to come down the hall. He rarely got to see them in the morning because he was normally out training by now.

"Mother of Light, Miraden," Simigrin said with a smile. They were carrying their spellbooks as usual. Miraden still wasn't used to seeing Ceychell carrying that black and red book they'd pulled from beyond the Ashengate. It creeped him out.

"Mother of Light, ladies," he replied.

"I'm getting my hair dyed today, Miraden," Ceychell said, pushing her long chestnut hair into a mountain on top of her head. "I want to blend in with the southerners. What color do you think I should get?"

"Maybe, red up top and orange and yellow tips. Like a fire." He stole a quick glance at Simigrin's shocked expression. It was a harmless game.

"I love it," Ceychell said, winking at him. "I think I'll do just that." She walked toward Miraden, but Simigrin grabbed her hand and held her back.

"How in the world did you guess that?" Simigrin asked.

Miraden shrugged. "Just seemed like something Ceychell would like." He's shaking a little, and he bit the inside of his lip to try to stop.

Simigrin took a long look at Miraden. He'd never felt threatened by a stare until now. She turned back to Ceychell who said, "Miraden just knows me, I suppose."

"He sure does," Simigrin tersely said. Miraden shrugged and smiled. "Let's go to the salon now and see if they can do it." They both waved and walked away.

Miraden wandered the battlemented wall walk around the college with Tundra in tow. He passed through an open archway, wind in his face, and looked out beyond the mountains and down to Bondare stretching out to the edge of the sea. A sprawl of tents and vendors crowded the roads. Most of the lanes between vendors were packed with livestock, household goods, stacked cages, hanging fish, or piled garbage. He was happy to be standing far above it; he couldn't even hear or smell it. The air was perfectly warm, and the sky was clearer than any he could remember since he had come to Kander. He could see all the ships at the harbor and far out to sea. He imagined he was looking right at O'kokra, watching Gorgundi tell a story at the bonfire. He remembered trekking through the cold of Keldenfelds and Bleak Gale Pines, and the thought chilled him, but he was finally starting to feel that all that hardship was in the past.

The wall walk wrapped around every tower of the university and extended around the mountain for several miles, lining towers and large hexagonal buildings. After they'd strolled for an hour, Tundra started moaning, and Miraden realized it was time to go get the bear a snack. He turned back into the university at the next archway, through one of its many libraries with its chairs, ladders, four story bookshelves, and helpers to retrieve books. He still didn't like the feeling of the high walls and grand rooms. He missed his forest, and though he felt safe, he was always uneasy in the university. He reached down to scratch Tundra's head, and she purred and rubbed her head against him.

Miraden looked up and saw a group of children in gray robes surrounding their instructor in orange robes standing near a bookshelf. The kids stared at the bear in wonder, like they generally did. Miraden waved to them and most of the kids waved back.

"Well, if it isn't Miraden and his enormous bear."

Miraden turned and saw Star walking down an aisle with a few colleagues, all in green robes, and holding green spellbooks. He'd heard they could summon monsters and found it ironic that Stardagrin would mock *him* for having a beast companion. Mostly, he imagined Ceychell laughing at his jokes and it burned him up. But he swallowed his pride and figured he should try to be nice to Star, for Ceychell's sake, no matter how much he didn't want to.

"Is your bear friendly?" one of the mages asked. "Can I pet it?" Miraden didn't know his name, but he remembered the scar on the man's face. He always seemed to be with Star.

"Only when I've fed her enough, and she's pretty hungry," Miraden said. Tundra growled low and deep.

The scar-faced mage withdrew his hand and said, "Perhaps it should be outside in the woods where bears live. The only creatures allowed in in the college are at the stables or in the Caller's Menagerie."

"And this one." Miraden wasn't up to being pushed around today.

Stardagrin stepped up to Miraden. "So does Ceychell like animals then? I was thinking about getting a kitten, perhaps a miralcat."

"Why don't you ask her yourself?" Miraden said.

"I plan to. I just thought, since you two were friends, you might know what could melt that icy heart of hers. You seem to know how to do that." Star smiled at him, more like a wolf would, and not a friend.

Star was taller and far stronger than Miraden. But as Miraden stared at Star, he found his own strength. "Maybe you should try listening to her," Miraden said. He cracked his knuckles, but wasn't sure why. Star's talking about Ceychell was making him even more jealous than he was before.

"I'd listen if she'd talk to me, but, honestly—" Star leaned in to speak softer "—you don't mind talking about her, do you? I suspect you two were close, but you and Simi seem… closer."

"Simi and I are good friends," Miraden said, trying not to clench his jaw.

Star put his heavy hand on Miraden's shoulder and gripped it tightly. "Miraden, who are you trying to convince? I've seen how you look at Simi. And I've never seen Simi jump into someone's arms. Or wait, don't tell me you're leading her on? Because that would be *coooold*. I don't think you would survive that!"

Miraden started to question his own feelings and integrity. Maybe he *was* leading her on.

There was a scream; then many screams.

Miraden ran toward the disturbance and heard Tundra's heavy clopping behind him. He ran out of the library and down a tunnel. Three younger mages were running frantically toward him. He heard a loud crash.

He continued down the tunnel into a connecting chamber from which one tunnel led toward the orders' living spaces and another led to a kitchen. Dozens of servants and mages were fleeing the living quarter tunnel. They scrambled past him, wide eyed. He passed through them and ran down several sets of long spiraling steps. On the landing was a female mage in yellow robes on the floor, holding her own arm. Blood was spilling through her fingers.

"Are you alright? What's happening?" Miraden asked. A loud blast rocked the hallway. Dust and pebbles fell from the ceiling.

"Ashenkin!" she screamed. "They're swarming! Help them!"

Miraden helped her up then ran down another set of winding stairs, which opened into a massive chamber leading deep underground and seemed to stretch forever into the darkness. He reached for Hellshy, which wasn't there, checked his back for his bow, and then drew his axe. There were stairs leading down to tunnels and bridges connecting to other tunnels. Then he noticed a few dead ashenkin and mages slumped near a doorway less than a hundred feet from him, and ran inside the room.

It was a large salon. Simigrin and a few other mages were standing near the back wall. One corner of the room was charred and covered in melting ice. Chairs and tables were strewn about. Ten servants and five mages were crumpled on the floor, many lying in their own blood, some ripped apart. There were a few smoldering ashenkin bodies, many blown to burning bits, but what he found odd were the bits of ashenkin splattered on the walls, tables, outside the door; pretty much everywhere.

"Miraden," Simigrin shouted when she saw him. He rushed over to her.

On the floor beside her, next to a desk, Ceychell was crouched down holding her face in her hands. Her hair looked like a soft blanket of flames. She didn't look hurt, but she was trembling and sobbing. Her spell book lay on the floor next to her.

Miraden knelt and put his arm around her. She was burning up. "What happened?"

"A gate opened right over there," Simigrin said, pointing at the blackened corner of the room. "They started rushing out. As soon as they saw her, they swarmed us."

Miraden thought about that for a moment. "Have gates ever opened here before?"

"Never," Simigrin said, shaking her head. "We've never lost any children."

It seemed strange that ashenkin would never come to the college. There were plenty of children. "Why would they come here? Why now?"

"They came for either her or that book," Simigrin said. "I'm sure of it. There were so many so fast, they overran us. Until she… stopped them."

Ceychell turned and hugged Miraden. She was still shaking.

Simigrin leaned down to Miraden and whispered, "She did *something* and then the gate just exploded. The ashenkin turned and fled. Some of them just flew up into the air and sort of… blew apart. Then the flames went out—" she snapped her fingers "—and they were gone."

"I could hear them," Ceychell muttered, pushing her fingers through her hair, "in my head." Her eyes were full of tears. "They begged me to help them. They sounded like children." She began to sob again and leaned on Miraden's shoulder. "Why!"

"We need to see Lord Umorogrin immediately," Simigrin said. "And you need to pull yourself together, Ceychell. This won't get easier."

TWELVE

THE BIG LIE

CEYCHELL SAT QUIETLY IN A small chamber below her discipline hall with Miraden and Lovo. They were waiting for Simigrin to get Lord Umorogrin. The room had a simple desk and a couple of chairs. A few old books lay on the table and nothing else.

She was scared. The pressure of being at the university was beginning to feel like too much for her: the book, the endless speed lessons, the ashenkin attack, the children screaming. She'd heard whispers in her head for the past few months, but they were becoming a full-throated voice that she couldn't ignore. Her dreams sent her to places she'd never been, where the sky is reddish-orange, the water is green and tepid, the ground is dry, brittle and cracked, and the air smells like the inside of a clay jar, empty and dirty.

She's tried to calm herself down. She could tell from Miraden's expression that he was worried about her.

She assumed all of Kander would be in an uproar after the attack. She, Miraden, and Lovo had walked to this room from the chaos of the salon. The vision of a young girl crying over a mage cut open and lying in a pool of his own blood and gore kept flashing in her mind's eye.

She remembered when the ashenkin saw her, they screamed their cries for her to help them. She thought they perhaps didn't want to attack her but were forced to. She worried that more would come for her and when they might come. If Simigrin was right, *she* had caused them to attack.

Miraden held her. He said nothing, but it helped her calm down a little. Lovo paced around clenching his fists and mumbling to himself.

When Simigrin returned, Miraden stood up to greet her. Ceychell wiped the tears from her face and stood as well. Lord Umorogrin followed Simigrin into the room, raised his hand, and the doors closed behind him.

He was calm, but his smile looked forced and his eyes were a bit glassy. "Are you okay?" he asked Ceychell.

"Yes, Lord."

"Good. We are so very fortunate you were not harmed, and they didn't steal the book. But they know for certain now that you and the book are here. Next time they will send more ashenkin. If we lose you and the book we will lose this war. I am certain of it.

"I thought we'd have much longer to prepare but the fact that they are finally bold enough to come to Kander means that we are out of time. I didn't tell you this before because it would have affected your training, but we have received reports from every city, town, and village begging for our help.

"We have?" Simigrin asked. She looked as shocked as Ceychell felt.

"Yes. Every report is the same: the children are all but gone. The few remaining have been hidden away and remain under heavy guard. Now, I'm going to finally tell you why the ashenkin are abducting, but the information is critically secret. You must tell no one. *No one.*"

Ceychell exchanged a glance with Simigrin. Whatever he was

about to tell them, Ceychell wondered if Simigrin knew it all along. Miraden looked nervous.

"The realm beyond the Ashengate was created by a powerful sorcerer in the old world. As such, it can be created again."

Miraden sagged, and Ceychell patted him on the back gently.

"Who was this sorcerer?" Lovo asked. "And how do we stop them?"

"His name is Carbrojl."

"Carbrojl? The myth?" Simigrin said, incredulously. Perhaps she did not already know.

"He is no myth," the lord said. "He is alone in his world. The Liches came to our world and brought what was left of humanity long ago and left Carbrojl there. It's clear from the texts why, Carbrojl tried to eradicate all life and nearly succeeded. I believe he intends to finish what he started and bring us to extinction."

"By taking our children?" Ceychell asked.

Simigrin nodded and said, "If they take our next generation, we will die out very soon."

"What is the Devil's Bargain then? One of his spells? Everyone was sick in Crestain," Miraden asked.

"Perhaps," Lord Umorogrin said, "We've only heard reports of it in the larger cities. It could very well be a plague people have just attributed to the ashenkin but there may be no relation."

"What about the people helping them find children?" Ceychell asked.

"I told you we looked into it. There were almost no markings in the cities we investigated, and those we found were old and little more than a smear."

Ceychell shook her head, then realized she was doing it and stopped. They weren't trying hard enough, and she knew it. "Where are the others who came through to our world?"

"They are our ancestors, and some of them founded our magic

disciplines. They made Kander the height of society. This was their center. There were wars fought with the natives of this world but our ancestors conquered them, passed on their knowledge, and then they disappeared."

"What happened to them?" Lovo asked.

"We're not sure, Lovo," Lord Umorogrin said. "Most of us believe they transcended or simply left for another world."

"Was Levoria one of them?" Lovo asked.

Lord Umorogrin's eyes widened. He nodded and said, "Her name is known by only a handful of people in this world. How do *you* know it?"

Lovo ignored the question. "Is that the Mother of Light's real name? Was she a mage?"

"From what I understand, yes. She was one of the Liches and they were so revered people started to worship them. Their names faded over time, but belief in them remained. I believe merely in the magic I can control and create, not in deities, but I agree their magic and teachings have touched our world in a way that will last forever."

Lovo sat down and put his face in his hands. Miraden put his hand on Lovo's shoulder. Lovo raised his head; his eyes were twitching and his face was red. He looked to be on the verge of a breakdown. "I saw her," he said. "She saved me."

"What you saw was likely a dream," Lord Umorogrin said.

"No," Lovo said. "It was not a dream."

Miraden said, "I saw Lovo die. He fell into the frozen water of Arrowheart Lake. We waited for him to surface until… he didn't. A few months later he shows up in Kaehrn, and you think this has nothing to do with the gods?"

"I saw it too," Simigrin said. "There is no way he could have survived."

"Miraden," Lord Umorogrin said, "I do not claim to know

everything. And whatever saved Lovo was not from this world. Who knows? Maybe it *was* Levoria."

Lovo clenched his teeth and breathed heavily through his nose. "How do we stop Carbrojl?"

"I do not know if we can," Lord Umorogrin said, "but I do think we can break his link to our world."

"How?" Miraden asked. Ceychell noticed his eyes light up, the first time she'd seen it in a long time.

"Queen Siennah of Sentry used to be a just and kind ruler until the day princess Kalionite died. Clerics from the temple of the Mother of Light determined that Kalionite was bitten by a halok snake in her bed. But Siennah was convinced it was an assassination. She scoured her kingdom for healers and mages to find a way to bring Kalionite back to life. Just as eagerly, she was removing their heads when they'd fail. She was desperate and a deal was made with Carbrojl to bring her daughter back to life through an enchantment he placed on the princess's crown. It didn't, but years later, the ashenkin showed up. I believe if we destroy the crown, it will sever his link to this world and end the invasion."

"It would break the link to Ghaborion?" Ceychell asked.

"I believe it will."

"And I am from Ghaborion?" she asked.

"A part of you, yes. Your power comes from Carbrojl," he answered.

"What?" Simigrin said.

Ceychell felt a pang in her chest. She was extremely concerned something might happen to her if that bond was severed.

"You never really told me what happened to the rest of the fire mages?" she said.

Lord Umorogrin's face twitched. He stared up at the ceiling and seemed to be choosing his words carefully. "It is a long story, but what I can tell you is there was a terrible accident eighteen years ago. Master Khronigrin and all of your order was lost. As I told you, we could no longer find children with souls of fire."

"*How* were they lost?"

Lord Umorogrin didn't answer at first, then said, "Carbrojl took them all."

Ceychell was uneasy. She wondered if the ashenkin that just attacked were coming to take her for him too. "What will happen to me if we destroy the crown?" Ceychell asked.

"I don't know," Lord Umorogrin said. "But you are the only one we know of that still can tap into the power of fire, and I believe I can teach you to control the crown and destroy the enchantment. That is why you are so critical."

She clenched her teeth and stood tall, though her confidence was feigned. The challenge felt too immense. Her fire magic scared her, but the thought that she was somehow linked to Carbrojl and the ashenkin scared her far more.

"Do you think the Grunkins know more about this?" Lovo said to Miraden.

"Grunkins?" Simigrin asked.

Lord Umorogrin chuckled. "There are no Grunkins."

Ceychell couldn't suffer that. "I told you, a Scorgis east of Kander is filled with them. They were quite upset with all of you."

"She's right," Lovo said.

Simigrin looked at Lord Umorogrin. "Lord, why would they make this up?"

"I sent mages to investigate this claim and none returned with any information. The fields you described were as desolate as we expected. No giant tree, and no Grunkins."

Ceychell again felt she was being tossed aside. If only Simigrin were with them and saw them, perhaps Lord Umorogrin would take it seriously.

"Originally," Lord Umorogrin began, "I was going to send you three to get the crown, while Ceychell stayed here to study, but now I believe that Ceychell should go with you. I've sent word to a sea captain I know. He will take you east across Syindella Channel. You will be disguised as merchants bound for Sentry. You will arrive at the palace at Queen's Edge where Siennah will be and steal that crown."

Simigrin shook her head. "If Ceychell's magic is from Carbrojl, then she will only jeopardize our mission!"

"This is not a debate, Simigrin," Lord Umorogrin's tone was fierce. "You will need her help and it is too dangerous for her to remain here."

"Can't you use magic to send us there?" Miraden asked.

"You speak as though that is a small feat. Most mages learn basic blinks. Creating teleportation gates is something only fire mages can do, but from here to Sentry would take a master."

Miraden, Lovo, and Simigrin looked at Ceychell.

"Don't look at me. I've read some spells for it, but I can't do that. We could end up in the middle of nowhere, and I don't even know where Sentry is."

Simigrin looked annoyed and said, "What about the additions to your book?" Got any *dark* secrets that will transport us there?"

Simigrin was right. There were sections added to the book that were written in a different language. She could understand the strange text, but she couldn't speak the words.

"I—" Ceychell stopped herself.

"What is it?" Miraden asked.

Ceychell turned to Simigrin. "You're right, Simigrin. There are many obvious additions to my book. They are dangerous and terrible. The book speaks a lot of ..."

"Of what?" Simigrin asked impatiently.

"Demonology," Lord Umorogrin said.

Simigrin's eyes widened.

"Is this true?" Miraden asked.

Ceychell nodded and shrugged. She was embarrassed, but for no reason she could think of. She hadn't chosen to be a fire mage or to have an altered spellbook.

"It is too late for judgement," Lord Umorogrin said. "Ceychell knows secrets only Carbrojl knows. What is important is recovering that crown and stopping this invasion."

"Well," Lovo began, "Sentry is directly east. Why not just ride there? Much easier than taking a boat."

"Would merchants be riding stags with a bear loping after them? Or suddenly arriving by teleportal? That would alert every guard and Henslemen in the city. They'd capture you without question. Arriving by sea in disguise is the best cover."

Miraden perked up. "Why would they arrest us?"

"Sentry has been hit hardest by the Devil's Bargain and the ashenkin. They fear everything unnatural. It is now heresy to use magic."

Miraden looked at Lovo and then back at Lord Umorogrin. "What kind of merchants will we be?"

"I can arrange a place for you on a ship that brings spice and medicine from Bondare and the islands to Sentry and Queen's Edge." Lord Umorogrin pointed two fingers, one at Lovo and the other at Miraden, "You both can help harvest spices. Simigrin and Ceychell can assist with making medicine. That will give you enough cover, which should get you access to her keep. You must be inconspicuous and cunning. The queen will have no mercy if you're caught. She's lost her sanity in recent years and removes the heads of anyone she even suspects of subterfuge."

Miraden turned to Ceychell. He looked distressed. "What kind of terrible spells?"

Ceychell swallowed. She had hoped no one would ask, there were many spells she feared in her book, but she read them anyway. She hesitated, then said, "Things like… mind control, spreading insanity, transformation, summoning devils and banishing them."

"Is that what you did?" Simigrin asked. "You banished the ashenkin with dark magic?"

Ceychell tucked her lip and nodded. She looked down and held back her tears.

Simigrin said, "Lord there are strict rules here that no dark magic is to be practiced!"

Lord Umorogrin raised his hand to silence her. "What is done is done. You all have a job to do. I suggest you start packing."

Ceychell spent the rest of the afternoon packing up her things. They were leaving at dawn aboard the Sand Caster. She was excited to sail, but knew Miraden wouldn't be. Simigrin was packing, too. The two women hadn't spoken to each other since they'd returned to their shared room. She felt betrayed by Simigrin at the end of their meeting but wasn't going to confront her about it. She didn't need extra stress.

Ceychell stared at her leather and furs from home folded beside her bed. It reminded her of Kaehrn, of Kyradel and her parents. She missed them so much and wished she could see them before her adventure. The leathers would stay behind for this trip.

She pulled off her red robe, rolled it up, and put it in her pack. Then she picked up the gray, merchant's robe from her bed and put it on.

Ceychell felt she ought to be grateful to Simigrin for all the help that the mage had given her over the past few months. They'd not shared many kind words, and Ceychell was fairly certain that Simigrin would have preferred going alone with Miraden and Lovo.

Simigrin set a chest wrap and a pouch of makeup on her bed. Next to her bed was a blue staff that looked like a solid piece of sapphire. There were gold veins that wrapped around it with a single opal embedded into the sapphire rod at the top. Ceychell hadn't seen it before.

"When did you get that?" Ceychell asked.

"My master gave it to me when I returned," Simigrin said. She held her hand out to the staff and transformed it into a small blue sphere that floated in mid-air beside her. The sphere shot into her blue enchanted sack where she kept her spellbook. "Unlike you, the rest of us need reagents, staves, wands, and such to cast our spells."

Ceychell was annoyed. She said, "Was that an insult or—"

Simigrin snapped, "It scares me that your power comes directly from Carbrojl. And that book is *evil*. I don't believe you can control your power when the time comes. I think Lord Umorogrin is making a big mistake sending you with us."

Ceychell sighed and rolled her eyes. "I'll do my best to not disappoint you."

Simigrin scoffed, and then put on her chest wrap.

"Miraden mentioned you had traveled as a man," Ceychell said.

"I did. I don't like to attract attention, or be treated like I'm lesser than a man." She slid the silver vambraces over her forearms and admired them for a moment.

"Me neither," Ceychell said. She'd had plenty of experience with men looking down at her when she'd started out as chieftain.

Simigrin looked at her sharply. "Could have fooled me. I've seen men *and* women ogling you here at the college. I think Star would—"

Ceychell groaned. "Yes, Stardagrin, my hapless admirer, is always ready to flirt with me."

"I thought you two were more than friends," Simigrin said.

"I'm sure he'd want you to think that, and I do like Star—he's so handsome—but I don't completely trust him. And the truth is, I don't want the attention. I'm here to learn, not for attention. But you shouldn't feel the need to conceal yourself because of what other people do. Their behavior and prejudice is on them, not you. We are traveling as potion merchants. We don't have to hide." Ceychell walked over to Simigrin and looked down at the far shorter ice mage. "And I'm not about to let anyone give you a hard time. If you haven't already frozen them solid, I'll burn them to cinders."

The two women stared at each other for a moment. Ceychell hoped this expression of friendship would work. She couldn't afford to have her as an enemy on their journey.

"I disguise myself to help me survive. Perhaps you should do the same."

There was a knock at the door, and Alva entered the room. She bowed her head. "I wish you both a safe journey. I hope you shall return," she said, looking at Ceychell. Ceychell was going to miss Alva, she hoped someday to take Alva back to Kaehrn where she could live free rather than scrubbing the floors for elite mages.

"There are letters for you both." She handed Ceychell and Simigrin each a scroll.

Ceychell slid off the tie and unrolled it. She immediately pulled it to her chest and said, "It's from Kyra! I miss her so much!"

Ceycha!

I hope life as a mage is treating you well. Things are mostly good here. There was a band from Yoldro here recently accusing us of stealing stags, father dealt with it. They worry me though. Those blackguards are always causing trouble. Mom and dad miss you terribly. They are okay though. Mom is feeling much better. I think it's because spring is finally here. Anyway, I hope you're being nice to Simigrin and staying out of trouble. I miss you. I'll come see you soon. I wrote a new song to play for you!

Love,
Kyra

Ceychell glanced over at Simigrin, who looked pensive. She was rolling up her scroll. Ceychell hugged her; she was stiff as a board. "Thank you for saving my sister." She too easily forgot that, despite their tension over Miraden, without Simigrin, she'd have lost Kyradel forever.

THIRTEEN

ANCHORS AWEIGH SAND CASTER

MIRADEN SAT ON A BARREL down at the docks in southern Bondare, staring out at choppy waves. The sea and sky were slate gray. A rainstorm had wrapped the crowded piers in a gloom that swallowed his spirits, despite Lovo's playing his harp beside him. He'd never wanted to be on the water again, but he agreed it was the easiest way to get to the bottom of the ashenkin invasion. He just hoped the sea crossing would be short.

The Sand Caster, a large merchant ship with twin brown sails, two dinghies tied to its sides, a fresh coat of yellow paint, and the prow of a two-headed serpent, bobbed up and down against the dock. It looked much sturdier than the fisherman's boat he'd taken to the islands and the ship he'd sailed on back to Crestain.

Lord Umorogrin had told them to be down at the pier just after dawn, and they were. But they'd been waiting for hours for the crew to wake up and lower the accommodation ladder. He was uncomfortable in his dew-damp gray robe and wished he was back in the university, dry and in his bed.

Simigrin and Ceychell were sitting together on the dock a few feet away, both in gray robes with their hoods up. Lovo also wore a gray robe, but his chainmail showed at the collar. Chintaja had bought it for him from a trader in Bondare after Lovo had beaten him in a race to the mountain top. He knew Lovo missed his trainer. Miraden glanced at Lovo's mirror-faced shield propped next to him and hoped it was a good luck charm.

Tundra was sitting on the dock on Miraden's other side. She seemed unbothered by the rain, though she smelled like wet fur. Miraden could tell she was hungry. She was restless and sighing loudly. He reached out to scratch her chin.

"Ahoy down there," someone shouted from the ship. A man with a black cap, gray beard, and a yellow shirt was leaning over the rail.

"Are you Captain Dulgir?" Miraden asked.

"No, but if you have business, I can take you to him," the man shouted back.

The sailor untied the locking knot and lowered the accommodation ladder. Miraden and his companions hefted their packs, trudged up the ladder, and followed the sailor below deck. It was dryer, but it reeked of fish and feet and perhaps a stew that smelled even worse. The boat rocked lightly, but Miraden kept his anxiety to himself.

"Name's Korgan, but most folks call me Kore. Out of the way Lud." Evidently, the man passed out on the floor was Lud. He begrudgingly rolled out of the way and under a cot, and Kore led them to a gold-painted door with a red stripe. He knocked on it twice.

"Who is it?" someone yelled.

"Visitors, four of them, looking to see you, captain," Kore said.

"Bah … is it mornin' already?" Captain Dulgir grumbled. "Send them in."

Kore pulled open the door. The room was dark except for a candle that seemed to be moving through the air by itself until it lit a lantern, and a man in white pajamas was staring at them sullenly.

His gray whiskers were as uneven as his teeth.

"What do you want?"

"Lord Umorogrin sent us," Miraden said. He hoped the captain was a better sailor than he looked.

"You're the potion merchants?" he asked. He pulled a coat on and stepped out to see them. "The hell is that monster doing on my boat!"

"That's my bear," Miraden said, forcing a smile. "Her name's Tundra."

"A bear?" The captain's bleary eyes went wide. Miraden heard a few murmurs of *bear* from behind them.

"You know how some merchants have dogs or a wolf?" Miraden said.

"Yeah?"

"We have a bear. She deters bandits."

"That ain't no brown bear! It's a razorback!" he yelled. "Where's your money?" He reached out his hand. His middle and ringer finger were missing and his nails were nearly black.

Miraden pulled the sack of fifty hydras Lord Umorogrin gave him from his side. It was a lot of money, too much for a boat passage, he thought. The captain took it, opened it, eye-balled it, then closed the bag.

"Alright, show them a cot, Kore. And you listen," he pointed at Miraden. "That bear hurts or eats anyone and it goes into the deep. You got it?"

"She won't."

"Good."

Tundra laid down on the deck and started to snooze. Lovo, Ceychell and Simigrin followed Kore to their sleeping quarters. Miraden woke the bear and caught up with them, he found Ceychell arguing with Kore.

"Hey, you're in charge, right?" Kore said to Miraden.

"What's going on?" Miraden asked.

"I was giving them a cot, when—suddenly—I realized that we had a woman on board, which is an even worse idea than having your monster here."

Miraden was uneasy. He glanced at Simigrin who pursed her lips and slowly nodded to him. He signed.

"Listen," Miraden started, trying to remain calm, "Lord Umorogrin of Kander paid good money so we could bring our potions to the queen. Where you can you put us where we won't be bothered by your crew?"

"She can stay in the galley?" a sailor said, popping his head up from under his ratty blanket. "She can keep busy there."

Ceychell stepped toward the sailor, but Lovo put out his hand and stopped her.

"Helloooo, pretty lady," another sailor said. Another whistled.

"She can start cooking right—"

Lovo swung for the sailor, but the sailor ducked his head just in time. The sailor stood up grinning, and Ceychell punched him in the jaw, knocking him back onto his cot. The other sailors jumped out of their cots and rushed Lovo. He knocked one back into the wall before Miraden jumped in and pushed them apart.

"Whoa! WHOA!" Kore yelled. Lovo stared down the sailors, and the sailors stared back at him and Ceychell. Ceychell was scowling at them, and Miraden didn't blame her.

"We need a place where the four of us can stay," Miraden told Kore. "It can be small, but we have paid for safe passage."

Kore nodded. "Alright, come with me."

They followed Kore below into the hold. It was even damper and smellier than the living quarters below decks, but at least no one else was down there. Kore lit a couple of lanterns so they could see. Ten barrels of water and fifty barrels of rum were lined up along one side. Boxes of onions, potatoes, flour, salt, and other goods were stacked nearly everywhere. But there were a few aisles where a bedroll could be laid out or a cot could be strung. A rat scurried between Miraden's feet, and Kore stomped on it. "It ain't great, but if you want privacy, this is the place. Where is that lazy cat… anyway?"

"We'll take it," Lovo said.

A few hours later the ship left port. Miraden sat with Tundra, Ceychell, and Simigrin at the bow of the weatherdeck. He watched the dock grow farther and farther away. The slow sway of the ship, the splash of waves, the gusts of wind, all of it turned his stomach.

Lovo came up from the galley, carrying a bowl of soup and a few pieces of bread. Tundra rolled over and put her paws in the air. Lovo handed the bowl and one piece of bread to Miraden. He tore a piece and gave one to Ceychell and Simigrin.

"Who's a good girl," Lovo said, scratching the giant bear's belly. Tundra licked his hands and let loose a long guttural purr. At least *she* was happy.

The soup smelled of fish and *something* else that Miraden didn't recognized. No ship food was ever any good. Simigrin and Ceychell dipped bread in the bowl, and they all ate quietly.

A sailor with an iron boot clanked toward them. The bottom half of his leg was missing. His face was pocked and his beard was black and patchy. "The bear friendly?" he asked.

Lovo stood up straight. He was probably the biggest man on the ship. "She ate the last fool who tried to pet her. I'd rather not watch that again."

Miraden stifled a laugh. "Perhaps if you bring her a bowl of vegetables and a bit of meat, she might let you pet her."

"I think I can manage that, be right back," he said. Then he *clop-thunked* his way aft toward the ladder well.

"Never thought we'd be on a ship again so soon, did you?" Simigrin said.

"I sure didn't," Miraden said. "Though I'm glad we're not on that fisherman's boat."

"The barnacles were definitely holding it together!"

She and Miraden exchanged laughs. It relaxed him a bit, and even though he was still anxious about being on the water, he was getting more comfortable with it.

Soon the rain stopped and the late morning sun broke through the clouds behind them, painting the sky deep red. When the rain stopped, more sailors came above deck and started working. A few looked pale, sweaty and sick, most likely hung over. Three sailors started repairing frayed mooring lines near Miraden and his companions. The iron-boot sailor returned before noon with a large bowl for Tundra. Miraden let him pet her while she ate, and she seemed unbothered by it. Miraden looked back at the harbor and asked Simigrin, "Isn't the channel east?"

Simigrin stood up and looked for herself.

"Why are we headed west?" Ceychell asked the iron-legged sailor.

"You all sure you're on the right ship?" he asked.

"Isn't this the Sand Caster?" Ceychell said.

"It's the Sand Caster all right. We pick up a load from the islands before we cross the channel. Queen loves her nutmeg and hot peppers."

Miraden's heart sank. The delay would make for a longer boat trip than he expected. "I see. Are we going to O'kokra?" Miraden didn't recall any spice ships visiting while he, Simigrin, and Kyradel were marooned.

"Nope, we trade with Ja'bon'ja and Akudu tribes. Pick some of our own too."

"How many days until we get to the first island?" Miraden asked.

"Five, maybe six. Depends on the wind. Captain will be by later to give you your jobs. And if you get seasick," he pointed over the rail, "aim that way." A few nearby sailors chuckled and kept repairing the mooring lines.

"Jobs?" Ceychell whispered.

Simigrin leaned toward Miraden and whispered, "Didn't you give the captain a lot of hydras?"

Miraden nodded. "I didn't expect to have to work, but I guess I shouldn't have been so optimistic."

"Don't worry," Lovo said, patting Miraden's back. "I'm sure it won't be bad."

Not too long after, Kore came back to them with a tentative grin. "Well looks like we need to get you all to work."

Miraden was about to answer, but Ceychell beat him to it. "We're not working." Everyone looked at her.

"Come again?" Kore asked, furrowing his brow.

"We're brewing potions for the queen, and we paid a hefty sum for this transport. We aren't deckhands. However, if you want me to make a couple of tonics to get your"—Ceychell pointed at a sailor vomiting over the side—"crew back in shape from their night drinking, I can do that."

Kore stared at Ceychell for a moment. "You got a deal." He waved her closer. "Try to keep your insubordination to a low roar next time."

Ceychell got up and asked Miraden to give her hand. Miraden was delighted.

"I'll go with you," Simigrin said, clambering up from the deck. "We don't need Miraden for this."

Miraden watched the two women walk away. All he could think about was Kyradel's letter that he received yesterday. The one thing she wrote him that stuck in his head:

Don't break <u>both</u> of their hearts.

Though he felt he'd already broken Ceychell's heart, he hadn't wanted to, and he was glad she was with him. It felt right to have her there.

Kore walked over to Lovo and Miraden. "Try to look busy, eh? I don't want my men asking questions."

Miraden was very good at tying lines. He'd helped his father make rope back home, so he joined the three sailors and helped them repair frays in the lines coiled below the aft mast. Lovo helped the sailors move some heavy crates from the top deck to the hold. He had a lot of pep in his step. His training with Chintaja seemed to have turned him from a lackadaisical loafer to a bundle of energy. The big man had told Miraden earlier in the day that he'd sent a letter to Chintaja to tell him they were heading to Sentry. Miraden hoped Chintaja might meet them there. They could use his help.

The creaking of the ship grated on Miraden's nerves. He kept glancing over the side, expecting a giant serpent to emerge from the bubbling froth, but there was nothing more than a few tiny flying fish. He began to wish he'd stayed in Kaehrn.

Soon Ceychell and Simigrin came back with a few jugs of a brew and some cups, and offered it to the sailors. The men seemed appreciative and gulped it down. Miraden could smell juno and something else he couldn't place, but he wanted some. Lovo, holding a barrel under one arm, took the cup from Simigrin and sipped the hot drink down.

"That's what I needed," he said with a grin and trotted off.

Miraden stared at Simigrin for a moment, thinking about how little he'd seen her since he'd arrived at Kander. She'd spent all of her time with Ceychell, and he missed her. As much as he would have rather have spent the time with Simigrin himself, he hoped their time together had prepared Ceychell for whatever it was that Lord Umorogrin had planned for them. He glanced over at the mage woman. The morning sun shone into her hood and lit up her amber eyes. She winked at him. He grinned and went back to repairing the line.

That evening all four friends and the bear went up to the top deck. Lovo played the harp Kyradel had given him and sang a mellow tune. Most of the sailors listened; one played a fiddle and another a flute. Miraden leaned against Tundra and scratched behind her ear. He hated being on the water but found peace in the evening calm and the delightful harmonies of the music. He just smiled and rested against his bear.

"Miraden. Miraden?"

He was so groggy he could barely open his eyes. Simigrin was standing over him. He realized he'd fallen asleep against Tundra. It was dark, and the boat was listing hard to the side. He reached out and grabbed onto her silver vambrace. "What's wrong?"

Simigrin's eyes were wide. "There is a storm coming!"

He stood up on the deck and looked out to starboard. Lightning flashed, there was a gray funnel whirling down from the clouds not far from the horizon.

"It's heading toward us!" she said.

"Where are Ceychell and Lovo?"

"I don't know. I just woke up from the rocking. I saw it just before I woke you."

FOURTEEN

THE WATER THAT SWALLOWS THE WIND

CEYCHELL FELT A STINGING SUNBURN on her face. Her whole body was hot. She opened her eyes and saw cracked earth loosely covered in orange sand below her cheek. She looked up at the smoke-filled sky blotting out the sun. The oppressive heat weighed on her as she struggled to get to her feet.

She walked in a random direction, head turned and arm up in front of her face to shield her from gusts of sand-filled wind. She didn't know where she was or where she was going, save that she was walking toward the faint outline of an obelisk in the distance. In every direction were endless dunes and blistering wind. Her throat was parched and her tongue was dry and thick. She wondered where Miraden was and how she'd left the ship and arrived here.

She walked for hours through the heat. Her throat cracked when she coughed. It felt full of sand. She wanted to collapse. At the peak of a high dune she saw someone standing near the obelisk in the distance, seemingly waiting for her. She shambled ahead.

The obelisk was plain stone and hundreds of feet tall. At its base, a gray-skinned man was staring at her. He was bald and wore a white robe. His eyes were dark sockets, his skin was cracked, yet he smiled at her kindly. He put his hand out for her, but she tripped and fell to her knees.

"Water…" she rasped.

"I have some, but you may not like it," he said. He took a clay jar from his pocket, removed a stone cork, and handed it to her.

She took it and splashed some on her face and down her throat. It was salt water. She gagged, shuddered, vomited, and dropped the jar.

"I am sorry." He put his hand on her head. His long, boney fingers were freezing cold, like they were made of ice. "However, I am glad you are here."

"Where am I?"

He leaned down to her. She tried to see him but the wind blasted her eyes with sand. "Why, you are home, my dear."

She rubbed the sand away and looked at him. "Home?"

"Indeed. I've been waiting for you for many years. I thought you'd never come."

She could barely hold her head up to ask, "Are you the one who controls the ashenkin?"

"They will not bother *you* again. I'll make sure of it."

She craned her neck to stare at him. She recognized his voice. "I've heard you whispering to me, sometimes in my dreams, sometimes when I am awake. Are you—"

"I am sorry, my dear, but they are taking you from me. Another storm—it's as if they have it out for you. I look forward to seeing you again."

Ceychell vomited another gush of saltwater and felt the world blacken around her.

"Ceychell! Ceychell!"

She woke up to Miraden shaking her. She flailed in his arms as a massive wave washed over them. Rain pelted her face. She coughed out more salt water and leaned up to see Simigrin and Lovo, drenched, staring at her with concern.

"I couldn't wake you for a few minutes! I thought you were dead!" Miraden shouted.

"I… I was…" She pushed herself up to her feet. Torrential rain swished in every direction. The winds blew the Sand Caster toward its side. Lightning flashed, and she jumped. It crashed through the air, illuminating the roiling sea. A wall of water rose in the distance, stretching up toward the back sky.

"Do you see that?" Ceychell muttered.

"See what?" Lovo said.

"That giant wave!" she said.

A torrent of lightning flashed; the wave was slightly closer.

"Oh my—" Simigrin said.

"Lovo, go get our bags from the hold. Hurry," Miraden said. Lovo slipped, he started so fast then got up and shot across the deck toward the hold.

"Miraden," Ceychell said, clutching his elbow, "we need to get to the lifeboats and get off of this ship. That wave is going to take us out."

Miraden nodded.

The sailors scrambled on deck to furl the sails. A line snapped. Miraden grabbed Ceychell and Simigrin and pulled them down to the deck. The line shot over their heads and sliced through a sailor's midsection, cutting him in half. The other sailors screamed and barked orders, but Ceychell couldn't make them out through the howling of the storm.

"Miraden," she yelled. "As soon as they realize this ship is going down, we won't get onto those boats. Hurry!"

"She's right," Simigrin said.

Lightning struck the central mast with a loud *crack*; it split and the wind snapped it. Sails, ropes, and beams fell onto the screaming crew, tangling them and yanking some of them over the side of the ship.

Ceychell and the others ran to the lifeboat on the starboard side. The portside boat was already floating nearly fifty feet from the ship.

Lovo ran up with their four packs, Miraden's bow, Tundra, and his own mace and shield slung over his shoulder.

"Lovo get in there and help Miraden and Tundra in," Ceychell hollered.

"You and Simi should go first!" Lovo yelled.

"Go!" Ceychell yelled.

Lovo looked over at Miraden, who shouted, "GO!"

Lovo hopped into the lifeboat with the gear; it rocked and bounced off the hull. Miraden jumped on next and reached up for Simigrin and Ceychell, standing at the ship's rail.

Lightning lit up the sky again—the giant wave was getting closer. It was taller than the walls of Kander and curling toward the ship.

"Tundra is over 1000 pounds," Simigrin yelled. "She'll sink us!" The wind had blown her hood back. Her makeup was smeared across her face; her purple hair whipped in the wind.

"Rogue wave!" someone yelled.

"Abandon ship!"

"Brace for impact!"

"Get to your stations!"

The sailors were shouting conflicting orders at one another. She knew they were done for. A group of them rushed toward the lifeboat. Ceychell drew Hellshy from her belt and sliced the ropes in one quick motion. The boat splashed into the sea. Waves and wind pushed it away from the ship quickly.

"Ceycha, Simi, jump!" Miraden yelled.

Tundra climbed over the rail and jumped. After a massive splash, the bear surfaced and paddled for the lifeboat.

"Why did you cut them!" Simigrin screamed. "I can barely swim!" Simigrin punched Ceychell in the face. Ceychell stumbled back and grabbed a chock to keep herself from falling.

Ceychell roared and rushed at Simigrin, "You dare—"

Miraden and Lovo screamed, "Jump!"

Another wave crashed against the ship, and the squall pulled the lifeboat out on the churning waves. Ceychell didn't think she could swim that far, she knew Simigrin couldn't. Sailors rushed past them and leapt into the sea.

"I did it for Miraden!" Ceychell yelled. "Those sailors were going to take the boat! You—" A giant wave crashed over the deck. She grabbed a stray line in one hand and wrapped her other arm around Simigrin. The wave washed them over the railing along with half a dozen sailors and cargo. Ceychell held onto the rope with all her might. "Grab the rope!" she yelled. Simigrin grabbed it but still held onto Ceychell.

"We're going to drown!" Simigrin yelled.

Ceychell held the rope as they dangled over the side of the ship. She didn't know how long she could hold.

There was flotsam everywhere. She looked out to sea; the lifeboat was at least a hundred feet away. Miraden was screaming at her, jumping up and down in the rocking dinghy. She was happy she had saved him, but sailors were swimming frantically toward the lifeboat. They would capsize it if they tried to take it over.

"Simi! Can you protect them?" Ceychell yelled. "The wave will crush their boat!"

Simigrin held Ceychell, let go of the rope and raised her hand in the air. Her blue book flew from her enchanted bag and opened in front her. Rain deflected from its pages as they flipped and finally stopped. She reached out her hand; the dark blue sphere shot out of her sack, it turned back into a staff as she grabbed it. She yelled her spell as the water froze around the ship. It rose from the sea until it created a shell surrounding the lifeboat. The book closed, the staff turned back into a sphere and both plummeted back into her sack.

"We're going to die, Ceychell," Simigrin said. "I wish I could have done a few things differently!"

"We aren't going to die," Ceychell yelled as the rogue wave finally towered directly over the ship. It was a black, cresting wall that blocked out the rain. "We're in this together!" She thought of her teleportation spells and knew how unpredictable they were, but she had no choice. She lifted Simigrin with all her strength until the shorter woman was level with her. "Hold on to me!" Simigrin wrapped her arms and legs around Ceychell like a child. Ceychell raised her free hand, and the black-veined red book flew up and opened in front of her. Heat radiated from the book as it whipped through its pages and then stopped. Ceychell closed her eyes and focused on the spell, clutched Simigrin to her, and kicked off the ship. A burning gate opened before them, and they tumbled into it as the colossal wave crashed over the ship and buried it under the sea.

Ceychell and Simigrin passed through the gate. The boat came apart all around them, but the roaring of the sea and the howling of the wind faded to a dull buzz. It was so quiet Ceychell heard her ears pop. Deck planks exploded, cabins collapsed, water gushed through corridors, sea creatures swam through the wreckage, and a great abyss of darkness was below her, but the two women passed through it unharmed. Then fear started to overwhelm her, breaking her concentration. She heard the rain hissing on the surface of the sea, and she and Simigrin popped up above the waves. She coughed out a mouthful of water, paddled frantically with one arm, and held Simi above the surface with the other.

She spotted several long planks held together by a crossbeam and paddled them toward it.

"I've got this!" Simigrin shouted. Simigrin cast a spell that whipped the boards around and cemented them together in ice. She pulled herself on it and then hoisted up Ceychell. Simigrin pulled out of the water a torn shred of sail still connected to a line. Ceychell helped her tie the line and sail around the flotsam to hold it together for when the ice melted.

The rain pelted her face. She lay on her chest, clutching the edge of the raft with one hand and Simigrin's vambrace with the other. "Hold on to me! We will make it!"

FIFTEEN

THE FJISHERS

AFTER A LONG NIGHT DRIFTING at sea, Ceychell woke up with the sun beating down on her. Her throat was parched. Simigrin lay next to her, still holding her hand. They were both on a few broken planks barely held together by the line and clumps of melting ice. She rolled to her knees and looked up. In the distance, past a heavy haze, was an island covered in thick jungle. It was hard to see, but it looked like part of a jungle archipelago. She was only mildly relieved. She needed to find Miraden and Lovo and make it to Queen's Edge.

Simigrin was sleeping peacefully, half on a makeshift raft and half in the water. The woman who Ceychell initially saw as a rival was more of a mentor, and not really a friend. Nevertheless, she was glad Simigrin was alive and with her.

The current slowly pushed them to the verdant island shore. Ceychell couldn't wait to step onto dry land. On the shore was a large sandy mound that looked out of place on the beach. It was a short way down the beach from where they were headed. She shook Simigrin awake.

"Wha, what is it?" Simigrin asked, raising her head.

"What does that look like to you?" Ceychell asked.

"I'm not sure," Simigrin said. She reached up, the sphere shot out of her sack and transformed back into her staff.

When they were close enough to the beach, Ceychell slid off the raft into the surf and pulled the raft and Simigrin toward the beach. She helped Simigrin to her feet, and they sloshed through the water to the land. Ceychell lay down and looked up at the heavens. "Thank you, Son of Seas."

"Thank *you*," Simigrin said, half smiling. "There are no gods listening." She knelt and hugged Ceychell. "How in the blazes are you so strong? I don't think Lovo could have lifted me with one arm. And I'll tell you, I thought for sure we would go down with the ship."

Ceychell straightened the ring Miraden had given her. It had saved her again. "You're not the only one with secrets."

"Well, I'm grateful, honestly. I guess Lord Umorogrin was right. We needed you," Simigrin said, then she pointed down the beach. "We should head east, this way."

Ceychell loved the kind words from Simigrin. She grinned and looked over to the dense wall of palm trees. She wanted to go in the jungle and search for food and water. "Why? How do you know?"

"No matter where we landed, Queen's Edge is east of us. We have to find our way in case—"

"Okay!" Ceychell said, raising a hand to stop Simigrin from mentioning Miraden and Lovo. She just hoped they were safe. They continued along the beach toward the sandy mound. As they got closer, she saw it move.

"It moved," Ceychell said.

Simigrin gripped her staff tighter. They slowed their approach. "It's bleeding," Simigrin said.

Ceychell could see it too. There were runs of blood along its side. Past it were drag marks in the sand mixed with smears of blood, as if it were moving toward them. It groaned in pain.

"Tundra?" Ceychell said. She wiped her eyes and knelt beside the bear, Simigrin next to her. Tundra's fur was caked with sand. The bear's eyes opened but she did nothing.

Ceychell lifted Tundra's head. "Tundra, what happened?" she whispered.

Simigrin carefully pulled fur back from a wound, and then another. The wounds were round and deep. "Stab wounds?"

Ceychell hugged Tundra's large head. "We will find Miraden and Lovo. They can help you."

Simigrin stood up and scanned the beach. "It looks like a few bodies east of here. We should check them out."

"There are footprints everywhere and most of them are leading into the jungle," Ceychell said. "If Miraden and Lovo are anywhere, they have to be in there." She said and pointed to all the footprints. "Tundra came this way, she would have followed Miraden."

Simigrin nodded.

Ceychell heard a loud grunt and scanned the line of palm trees beyond the beach. Then she heard it again. "Did you hear that?"

"I did," Simigrin said.

A man shuffled out from thick green leaves just beyond the palm trees and fell to his hands and knees on the sand. He had frizzy blond hair, and his pale skin was splotched with tan and red sunspots. He wore only grass-woven pants and was covered in filth. He grunted again, gestured at the two women, hooted, and struck his loins. Then he turned in a full circle on all fours on the sand.

While Ceychell was wondering if the man needed help, he suddenly charged them, drooling and barking as he ran. Simigrin's whipped her staff across his face. A flash of light burst from his skull, then he skidded into the sand, twitching.

"He didn't seem very friendly," Ceychell said.

"Uh… no," Simigrin said.

Ceychell looked down at the crumpled figure of a man. His skin was spotted with insect bites and just plain filthy. His eyes were too close together, and one was smaller than the other. His gums were black and his jagged teeth were unnaturally sharp. Ceychell's nose burned from the smell of excrement.

"What in the burning hells is he?" Ceychell asked.

"We are in the Fjishers," Simigrin said. "We need to get to the desert, now."

"Fjishers, what? Why?" Ceychell asked.

"Inbreeders. Cannibals live here. I read about them in the library. They're barely human."

Ceychell's heart sank. "Okay, that sounds awful. But Miraden wouldn't leave Tundra. We have to look for them."

Simigrin peered into the jungle and then back at Ceychell. "Tundra is dying. How do we know they didn't run east?"

Ceychell looked down. "These footprints. I am not as good a tracker as Miraden, but these are the only boot prints I see, and they go straight toward the jungle."

Simigrin looked down at the tracks. "You're right."

"I…" Simigrin said. Something moved in a tree and some palm leaves rustled. "We are exposed out here," she whispered.

They trotted into the jungle, pushing through brambles and dense brush. Ceychell smelled a stench that took her breath away and nearly gagged.

"Human flesh cooking," Simigrin whispered.

"Don't tell me why you know that," Ceychell said.

Simigrin nodded. "We need to hurry."

They trekked deeper into the jungle. Strings of bones dangled from some of the palm branches. Then they heard some more grunting. It sounded close.

They crouched in some brush and stayed perfectly still. Several men emerged from the trees, sniffing and looking around, on what appeared to be a path. Ceychell assumed she and Simigrin smelled like seawater; she hoped jungle dwellers wouldn't sniff them out.

One of the Fjishers crept right up to the brush in front of Ceychell. He was so close that Ceychell could see the bugs in his hair. His large nostrils flared, and he licked his lips. His bottom lip was pierced with a palm splinter. His sharp teeth poked through his lips when his mouth was closed. His eyes were crooked and blinked a lot. His face was lopsided and cheekbones stood out like stones in his face. He wore a necklace of severed fingers. They were dirty below the fingernails and the stub end ends were crusted with fresh blood. She hoped they weren't Miraden's fingers.

Ceychell crouched as still as the dead and held her breath. She squeezed Hellshy in her left hand. Sweat ran down her neck, and her fingers tingled each time the man sniffed. She slowly raised the blade to eye level, but a sudden cacophony of grunting started somewhere east and toward the beach, and the savage scampered away toward it.

Ceychell slowly removed her spellbook from the red enchanted sack at her side, clutched her book under her arm and slowly pushed through the thick jungle with Simigrin close behind her. She stepped out into a shallow clearing and stopped. Simigrin bumped into her, almost sending her into a deep pit in the sand full of bones. Smoke sifted through the brush around them.

They stood there for a moment, breathing heavily and staring into the pit. Then they knelt down next to it. Fresher bones with a little flesh on them were at the top of the pile. Older dried bones were below them. Flies buzzed all around. Ceychell couldn't tell how deep the pit was.

Simigrin picked up a skull with two black horns from the top of the pile. Its fangs were broken out of its jaw.

"Ashenkin," Simigrin whispered.

Ceychell noticed several more ashenkin skulls in the pit. She didn't want to know how the savages had killed and skinned them.

They walked around the pit. She waved away a bunch of smoke wafting around the reeds and leaves. Ceychell's eyes watered; she held her nose, coughed into her sleeve as quietly as she could, and kept moving, following the stench.

She heard more grunting, closer now. Between the constant chirping of birds she heard stamping feet and the rattle of bones. The smell grew fouler and thick smoke stuck to her like a stain.

They continued through the brush. Up ahead, they saw cages made of bones and reeds hanging from the trees. Each cage was stuffed with people. Ceychell crouched behind a clump of ferns and Simigrin settled down behind her. What looked like an entire tribe of Fjishers, at least five hundred men and women, were dancing around a bonfire. They were dirty and mostly nude other than some grass tied around their waists to cover their genitals. Many of them had deformities, from half-formed arms, missing legs, missing eyes, oblong heads—all the deformities of inbreeding.

There were no huts or buildings. Ceychell wasn't sure if this was a village or just a place to cook people. She desperately peered up at the cages, but didn't see Miraden or Lovo. Then she dry-heaved into her sleeve.

"Do you see them?" Simigrin whispered in her ear.

Ceychell shook her head.

The Fjishers danced around, beating sticks against trees and blowing into reed flutes. Even if she found Miraden and Lovo, there were far too many of the Fjishers to hope to save them and escape.

She spotted a spit with hunks of meat on it over a fire pit, just beyond the main crowd of revelers. A man in an ornate headdress of palm leaves and colored stones walked up to the fire pit, turned around to face the mob, and held out his hands. His left hand fingers were all short stubs; in his right hand he held a long painted stick with palm fronds tied to the tip. He grunted loudly and the massive crowd cheered.

Simigrin grabbed Ceychell's elbow and then pointed over Ceychell's shoulder past her ear. In a cage near the central fire were four men. One was large with his leg hanging out. Another had rusty hair. She could swear it was Miraden.

The man in the headdress danced around, twirling his painted stack. He bounced from cage to cage and then pointed at the cage she thought Miraden was in. Multiple Fjishers scampered over to it.

Ceychell gasped—Simigrin put her hand over her mouth.

"We aren't sure that's him," the mage whispered, "and if it is, how are we going to get to him?"

"I'm not going to wait to find out. Can you freeze their cage, just for a moment?"

"Probably, why?"

"I have an idea."

Simigrin held her staff in front of her, and her book popped out next to it. Then she whispered a spell. Ceychell drew her book and flipped to a page.

"What are you doing?" Simigrin said. "You can barely control your spells." A block of ice formed around the cage, and the savages began grunting and growling. Many spun on all fours in a panic.

"You're going to want to duck," She held her hand out toward the bonfire. She could feel the energy burning in her. The bonfire flared up and then settled, and then again, and then it exploded. Ceychell grabbed Simigrin and pulled her to the ground. They lay face-down in the brambles as the massive blast thundered through the forest.

Ceychell raised her head and peeked through the scorched bush. The palm trees and brush all around was smoking and flaming. Hundreds of Fjishers lay on their backs, faces charred, blood everywhere. Many of the savages, including the man in the headdress, seemed to have disappeared completely. Most of the cages were blown to pieces. The ice prison was mostly gone but she saw the men moving in the wet cage. The reeds holding it snapped, and it fell and shattered on the ground.

A charred body fell from a tree and struck the ground ten feet in front of Ceychell. She extended her hand toward a burning tree. The flames coursed toward her hand and she gathered it.

They both stepped out of the bush, Ceychell holding the fireball in her hand. The man who fell was charred and still smoking. Another body dropped, and another. A moan came from above. Ceychell turned and threw the fireball toward the sound. another eruption of fire shook the trees. Twenty more bodies rained from the burning spires. They ran toward Miraden's cage to escape being struck by a falling Fjisher.

"Are you trying to kill us?" Simi yelled.

"Yes, Simi! That was my plan!" Ceychell yelled back. She didn't expect the explosion to be so massive. Their books floated next to them.

The smoke from the burning trees and underbrush was getting so thick, Ceychell could barely see. Trees burned and toppled, knocking down other trees, and smashing to the ground. Through a gap in the smoke, Ceychell spotted Miraden and Lovo still in the melting cage, trees flaming all around them. "Miraden!"

The cage fell and broke apart.

They ran through smoke to the cage. Lovo and Miraden were fighting through the tangle of reed ropes and broken wood bars. Ceychell coughed and drew Hellshy from the sheath on her belt. She sliced through the ropes holding the side of the cage over Miraden. Simigrin coughed violently as she pulled the wood bars off and helped Miraden out of the cage. Ceychell offered a hand and pulled Lovo to his feet. Lovo coughed so hard he doubled over.

Ceychell screamed when a large tree crashed behind them.

"We better run!" Simigrin said.

Lovo led the charge out of the smoke-filled jungle. As they were getting closer to the beach, the smoke thinned. Ceychell took a deep breath of clean air and coughed hard. Everyone was catching their breath.

Ceychell reached out for Miraden when Lovo lifted her and squeezed her in a hug. She smiled but couldn't breathe.

"I can't believe you made it through that devil wave!" Lovo said.

Ceychell glanced over and saw Simigrin hugging Miraden. She hugged Lovo back. "I'm a little tougher than that," she said.

He set her down. "You sure are," he said and gave her a friendly slap on the arm. She grinned and slapped him right back.

Miraden turned to Ceychell and pulled her in for a hug. It felt so good to hold him. She missed him so much and was almost too late to save him. Tears fell from her eyes.

"Thank you for coming for us," he whispered.

That wasn't what she wanted to hear. Her smile soured and she said, "I always will." She was still holding him, looked over and realized Simigrin was staring right at her. It made her uncomfortable enough to let go.

"Is that…" Lovo said.

"Tundra!" Miraden yelled.

They all ran to the mountain of sand by the beach. Miraden frantically started wiping the sand off of her. Everyone jumped in and helped. There were at least ten stab wounds. Drool and blood stained the sand below her mouth. Her eyes were closed.

"Tundra, no. No, you can't leave me," Miraden cried. He went for his bag and patted around his waist for a moment then screamed.

"No! No!"

Ceychell realized Miraden didn't have his trappings. Normally he carried needles, threads, and some ointment.

Miraden dropped to his knees and wept as he held the bear. "I'm so sorry," he sobbed. He held her head and cried into her sandy fur.

Ceychell wiped the tears away, Simigrin did the same.

"It can't end like this," Lovo said. He cracked his knuckles and knelt behind Tundra's back. His large hands rested on the bear's shoulder, his head dipped, and eyes closed.

A soft glow slowly appeared around the bear's body over every wound. Bloody and sandy, the wounds started to close. The light fell dimmer and dimmer but the bear wasn't moving.

Lovo started sweating badly. He grimaced and dipped his head. The lights flashed brightly, then went out.

"It's not working," Simigrin whispered.

"Can we help him?" Ceychell asked.

"We can try," Simigrin said and put her arms on Lovo's shoulder's. A blue aura surrounded her hands, it slowly spread around Lovo's back and soaked into him. His healing lights flashed hotter and brighter.

Ceychell took a deep breath and put her hands on Lovo as well. At first, she just felt a buzz on her hands, nothing else.

"Focus," Simigrin whispered. "Think of when you first start your spell, how you draw your energy from within. Instead of transforming it, try just letting it go."

Ceychell closed her eyes and thought of casting one of the most powerful spell in her book. A spell to summon a fire-breathing monster. She never cast anything close to it successfully but focused like Simigrin said. Her hands burned hot and skin goosebumped. Red energy pulsed around her hands and they started to hurt. She gritted her teeth as the energy faded to black before it shot into

Lovo's body.

Simigrin screamed.

Lovo snapped back so violently he knocked both women over. Tundra jolted just as hard.

Ceychell's head spun as she got back up and helped Simigrin to her feet. The bear groaned and leaned up. She held Miraden with one paw and put the other paw on top of his head. Miraden started to laugh as her big tongue licked the side of his face. Lovo pulled back a bloody mat in her fur only to find a red scar.

Miraden got up as did Tundra. The razorback bear shook hard as sand flew in all directions. Ceychell didn't mind getting sprayed with sand and by everyone's smile, neither did anyone else.

Miraden hugged Lovo, Simigrin and Ceychell joined in. For a moment, all was calm.

They walked east along the shore. Tundra was now less sandy but soaked in sea water. Everyone walked beside her just past where the tide was washing up on the beach.

"Did the boat make it?" Simigrin asked. "It had all our supplies."

"It did," Miraden said. He threw up his hand, "but those savages dragged it into the jungle. Who knows if it's still in one piece."

"They didn't get our supplies," Lovo said.

Simigrin turned to him, "What do you mean?"

"Our boat was leaking badly. Mir and I scooped out water fast and needed to find shore. We saw this island through the mist," Lovo started, "the current helped us get here but there was a horde of people gathering on the beach. They didn't look friendly."

"We didn't want to lose or things if they captured us," Miraden said. "Lovo found a seabag under the seat."

Lovo nodded, "I did, and we stuffed our things in it and dropped it with the anchor."

"That's great," Ceychell said.

Miraden said, "We are still going to need a boat."

"And some food," Simigrin added. Tundra groaned at that.

Lovo pointed to the wide boat-like drag mark going from shore to jungle. "We landed there,"

"How are we going to get the gear?" Simigrin asked.

"Be right back," Lovo said. He stripped down his robes and jumped into the water.

"We may have to go back in the jungle to find food," Miraden said, "but we will have to be quiet."

Simigrin nodded. "Yes, hopefully we can find some food without any explosions."

Ceychell narrowed her eyes but said nothing. She would have blown up the entire jungle to save Miraden. She listened to the birds chirping in the trees while they waited patiently.

"It's been over a minute," Miraden said.

Ceychell grew nervous and scanned the surface of the water. He was gone for too long. Miraden was fidgeting as he got closer and closer to the surf zone.

A minute later, Lovo surfaced and took in a huge breath. He paddled to shore; everyone helped him up. He was dragging a white seabag.

"The anchor," Lovo panted, "It wouldn't budge. Had to untie the line."

Miraden pulled his bow, axe, and pack out of the bag. Simigrin and Ceychell retrieved their own packs.

"Your quivers?" Ceychell asked.

Miraden searched the bag again, but his quivers and silver arrows were gone.

"I couldn't get them in the bag. They were still in the boat," Lovo said. He tied his merchant robe closed, slung his shield over his back and latched his mace to belt. He patted Miraden on the shoulder and said, "Should we go find them?"

Miraden stood in thought for a moment and then said, "I hope these enchanted arrows will work on ashenkin."

"You don't want to go find the boat and arrows?" Ceychell asked.

"No," Miraden said. He removed a soggy melon from his bag. He cut it open with his axe and offered everyone a piece, giving the rest to Tundra. "It's too risky. I don't know how many you killed to save us but we saw a thousand of them."

A few grunts came from the jungle. The sound of sticks beating trees went from a few to hundreds within seconds. Birds scattered from the thick canopy as a horde of Fjishers ran out from the jungle.

"Good gods," Lovo said.

"Simigrin," Miraden whispered, "Can you—"

"Freeze them all?" she said. Her book jumped from her pack. She cast quickly as five twisters of frosty wind mixed with sand. They grew and grew and created a wind wall in front of them. The Fjishers were coming fast and halted their advance. Most were confused by the winds, only a few charged with spears.

The twisters struck them with bolts of frost. Ice grew around the blasts and covered parts of their bodies. They screamed as the twisters continued blasting them. The tempests expanded into an arched wind wall fifty feet long around them, but their backs were to the ocean. They were trapped.

The Fjishers backed away from the wind wall and bounced, hooted, and waited.

Simigrin yelled, "I can't hold this much longer. We may have to run for it!"

Miraden drew his bow and fished the enchanted string out of his pack. Lovo tried to help him restring the bow but the wind was tossing sand into their eyes. Tundra was crouched beside Miraden with her back facing the wind.

Ceychell considered a fireball, then summoning a creature, then throwing streams of fire. They weren't enough. She remembered a spell she saw, written in the other language of her book. Her book popped out of her pack, turned pages and stopped. A black fire burned from her book as she thought of the words of the spell.

"Everyone, cover your ears, quick!" she said as she lifted her hands in the air.

"What?" Simigrin yelled.

"Do it!" Ceychell yelled back.

Lovo and Simigrin covered their ears. The twisters ceased. Miraden covered his, then moved his hands to Tundra's ears.

Seeing the frost tornados dissipate, the Fjishers charged.

Ceychell clenched her fists and released a banshee's scream. The Fjishers' eyes went black. They dropped their weapons, screamed, and scattered in random directions.

Miraden also screamed. His eyes were as wide and black as river stones. Lovo and Simigrin grabbed him and held him.

Ceychell coughed hard enough to double over. There were blood spots on the sand; the taste of iron was overpowering. She gagged.

"What madness did you release from that awful book?" Simigrin screamed. She tried to restrain Miraden but his flailing was too much for her.

Lovo picked up Miraden, threw him over his shoulder, and held him tight. "We've got to get out of here before we are caught up in this mess." A woman with a second half-grown head jutting up from her shoulder grabbed Lovo's legs, her eyes black. He stared down at her inbred deformity for a moment, and then kicked her in the head. She crumpled and lay flat on the ground. Suddenly, the half-grown head looked up at him and winked. He screamed and started running down the beach, Tundra right behind him.

Ceychell and Simigrin ran after him, but struggled to keep up even though Lovo was carrying Miraden. He trampled over sand berms like a raging beast, knocking over Fjishers and leaping over driftwood.

Lovo continued to gain distance and was starting to vanish in the haze. She heard Miraden scream. Her power had hurt him, and she felt terrible. She didn't even know if the spell was permanent. Her lungs were on fire. She slowed and glanced over her shoulder; the Fjishers were only blurry images in the distance.

"Good job back there!" Simigrin yelled, breathing heavily. "It's almost like you're a witch right out of the Ashengate."

"What?" Ceychell screamed. She coughed and wiped blood from her lips.

Lovo was still running ahead. Ceychell couldn't keep up; she had to catch her breath. She coughed and gasped for air. Her mouth tasted like iron and ash. She spit out more blood and felt her lungs burning. Moments later, Simigrin stopped beside her and doubled over coughing. Their books hovered beside them.

"What did you call me? A witch?" Ceychell yelled at her again.

Simigrin took a few deep breaths and turned to face her. "You're worse than an ashenkin. You're like a devil—"

Ceychell punched her in the face, and Simigrin tumbled to the sand. "That's for punching me on the ship *and* for calling me a devil! How dare you!" Her lips were trembling. "I could have let you drown!"

"You would have drowned too!" Simigrin yelled.

Both women breathed heavily for a moment. Ceychell heard Miraden screaming further down the beach.

Simigrin wiped blood from her lip. She looked Miraden's direction and started to tear up. "Look what you did to Miraden! That book should be destroyed. You're a danger to everyone!"

Ceychell finally caught her breath and she wiped her tears onto her sweaty robe sleeve. She'd been strong for so long, but everything was crashing in on her. And Miraden… what had she done to him? She held out a hand for Simigrin. Simigrin just stared at her.

"Let's put this behind us," Ceychell said. "We need to keep moving."

Simigrin grabbed her hand and Ceychell helped her up.

They jogged down the beach. A long berm over ten feet high ran for miles about twenty feet from the tide. When they caught up to Lovo, he was waiting for them between berm and shore, holding Miraden in his arms and praying. Miraden had quieted and his eyes were closed. He was shaking a bit, but his breathing had calmed. A fresh gash poured blood from his forehead, Ceychell thought it was perhaps from his own flailing. Lovo put his hand on Miraden's head above the gash and prayed. A bruise over Miraden's eye shrank to nothing and the gash closed.

Ceychell and Simigrin watched in silence. Ceychell was relieved to see Miraden getting better. She prayed with Lovo to the Mother of Light that her spell would not have lasting effects.

She heard a laugh in her head. No one saw her jump. A flash of heat made her sweat. She shook for a moment then she kneeled beside Lovo and held Miraden's hand. Simigrin did the same.

Miraden shivered. His eyes were closed, and he seemed to be settling down.

Lovo looked around and whispered, "You think there are more of the savages on this island?"

Simigrin looked grumpy. She whispered, "Far as I know there are many islands, and the Fjishers are on all of them."

Ceychell groaned. She was exhausted, sweating, cold, hot, sore, and nauseous. She was terribly hungry, but wouldn't dare go back into the jungle to look for food.

"You still got fishing line?" Ceychell whispered.

"I might, but I lost my pole in the storm. I'll keep an eye out, maybe there is some driftwood I can use," he whispered.

Tundra caught up to them and nuzzled her head against Miraden's cheek. Miraden moaned and turned.

"Miraden, are you okay?" Simigrin whispered. She put her hand on his face.

Lovo held on to him and propped him up to a seated position. "C'mon buddy, you got this. Snap out of it."

Ceychell said, "Miraden, I'm so sorry. Please wake up." She prayed to the Daughter of Forests that she bring Miraden back.

She isn't listening. None of them do. Only I listen to you.

Ceychell jolted, *almost* screamed. She *definitely* heard the voice in her head as though he was standing beside her.

"You okay?" Lovo whispered to her.

She said nothing and nodded.

"The tide is going to go up this berm," Simigrin whispered. "Maybe we should rest here for the evening if we can."

Simigrin found a long piece of driftwood near the water. Lovo pulled some line and a hook from his pack and tied it around it. He dug his hands in the sand and plucked out a small red shell, cracked it beneath his mace and a rock, and plucked out the clam for bait. "Hey Ceycha, if I catch something, you think you can cook it?"

"Sure, but it won't taste good," she replied with a wink. She pulled locks of hair from her face and held the blanket of hair up from her neck. She began to wish she had short hair like Simigrin.

"You smell like the tide, but a little worse," Simigrin said. She turned up her nose and looked out to sea.

"Thanks, I needed that. You want your fish extra crispy, right?"

She grinned, but the mage wasn't looking at her.

"I can't believe you punched me," Simigrin said and rubbed her lip, "you filthy savage."

"I'm sorry. I shouldn't have hit you."

"Uhhg," Simigrin groaned. "I suppose I should be more grateful that my pupil can swim."

Ceychell laughed a little. "I guess at the university you had chamber servants swim for you."

Simigrin's jaw dropped. "I don't have to take this from an ungrateful potion maker."

"At least I can brew my own potions."

"Too bad you can't write your own letters."

Ceychell scowled and clenched her teeth but when she saw Simigrin smiling kindly, her animosity melted away.

"Hey, look at this!" Lovo said. A 10-pound yellow-and-black stripped fish was dangling on his line.

SIXTEEN

AN ENEMY NO MORE

CEYCHELL OPENED HER EYES. ABOVE her, a red sky shone through a broken roof. She got up and walked out of the ruined building, stepped onto the red dirt and headed up a road. She was in a sprawling, seemingly abandoned village. The homes had caved-in roofs, broken planks and doors torn off; other buildings had crumbled completely into their foundations. There was no one in sight.

She walked up to a fountain that was square, two levels, with a fish carving at the top that was probably supposed to spit water, but the fountain was bone dry.

"Where are you?" Ceychell yelled.

She looked around for the gray man. She knew he was there. A gust of wind blew red sand in her face and made her eyes burn. She wandered through the town toward a half-crumbled leaning tower. It reminded her of a giant's curled finger. There was an open archway at the bottom. She stepped inside and looked up. The red sky seeped in through missing stones and cracks. A broken staircase spiraled up to the top. Some of the steps had crumbled away.

"They all left me, fled from me, you know," echoed down the tower.

Ceychell yelled up, "Who left you? The Grunkins?"

"You know them?" He appeared in front of her so suddenly she screamed and fell back. His face was smooth like stone, his eyes black. He wore a regal white gown, laced with silver and gold. The cuffs glittered with gems.

"I've met them," she said.

"Oh. I do miss the Grunkins. They were mine, you know. Loyal. Faithful. They only left because they thought I was going too."

"Are you… Carbrojl?"

He arched his brows and then sat on the red dirt with his legs crossed. "You're full of surprises. Much like your book."

Ceychell felt her heart racing, and she scooted back to the wall behind her. She wanted out of the tower, but she had no idea where to run to. Her throat was so dry she could barely swallow.

"I am glad you are here," he said. "I need your help. And only *you* can help me."

"What sort of help can only *I* do?" she balked.

He put his hand to his chest. "I know that look. Do you not trust me?" He rubbed his face, and it sounded like he was rubbing two stones together.

"You send ashenkin into our world, steal our children. You've infected us with the Devil's Bargain—"

"None of that was me."

Ceychell paused at that. She'd felt Lord Umorogrin had been lying to her, but now she wondered how much. "I was told you sent the ashenkin after Queen Siennah had made a deal with you."

"Is that what you were told?" He laughed. "That's quite a tale."

"Why were you sacrificing children?"

"It wasn't me. It was Khronigrin."

"No," Ceychell said. She wasn't ready to believe another liar, but was he lying?

"And they weren't sacrificed." He extended a long stony finger below her chin and raised her face to look into his eyes. "The ashenkin *are* the children."

Her heart sank; she shut her eyes and screamed.

"Ceychell!" Lovo grabbed her and held her tight. She stopped flailing and realized she was on the beach again. The early morning sun was just rising over the ocean where they were headed. She could see the end of the island only a few miles away.

Simigrin blinked away sleep and whispered, "We better start running before the Fjishers come looking for the crazy woman."

"I am sorry," Ceychell said. "I was having a bad… dream." As if the dreams weren't bad enough, controlling herself during sleep was becoming a real problem.

"You're still having one." Lovo said. "We are still on an island full of cannibals."

"How—" Ceychell started to get up and kicked Miraden on accident. "Oh, I'm sorry!" she said. He began to stir.

All three of them gathered around him. Ceychell ran her fingers through his hair. "Are you alright, Miraden."

"We are so worried," Simigrin said. She held his hand.

"Mmmm, I love you," he said.

"I love you too," Simigrin and Ceychell said in unison. She looked over at Simigrin who glanced at her, then she looked down and saw Miraden's eyes pop open. He looked at them both in turn.

Lovo bent down to pull him into a big hug, "I love you too, buddy."

Miraden hugged him and patted his back. "I had horrible dreams and… were those cannibals part of my dream?" He rubbed his head.

"No, the cannibals are real," Simigrin said. "Unfortunately, your dreams were caused by *Ceychell's* dark magic."

"Let's be glad they're over," Ceychell said, "and we are safe… for the moment." She glared at Simigrin; Simigrin glared back at her.

"They will hunt us again," Simigrin said. "But, I've heard they won't step onto the desert sands east of here. We need to get there before they get to us."

"How far is it?" Miraden asked.

"I don't know," Simigrin said, "Could be five miles or a hundred." Lovo and Ceychell sulked.

"I guess we better start then," Miraden said. "Do any of you have any water? I'm so thirsty."

"I do," Simigrin said. She tapped her staff to his wineskin and lifted it to his mouth. Miraden gulped it down.

"Here's your gear, Mir," Lovo said, handing him the sack.

They headed east along the beach and caught Miraden up on what had happened while he slept. The morning air felt good on Ceychell's face.

Lovo bragged to Miraden about the fish he caught. "It was huge. A real monster. It got away though, it was so hard to pull it in with my bare hands. Then I hooked—"

Lovo was too loud for her comfort, but she didn't believe he could whisper anyway.

"Simi," Ceychell whispered. Simigrin looked over but didn't say anything. "I need to talk to you about what Lord Umorogrin told us right before we left."

"What about it?" she snarled.

"I think he… I think he may have deceived us."

"What!"

Lovo stopped mid-story; all three of them looked at Simigrin.

"Sorry," Simigrin whispered. "Too loud."

"We should pick up the pace a bit," Lovo said.

They jogged down the beach. Ceychell glanced around along the way, but didn't see any Fjishers following them. The berm ended and beach gradually narrowed, and when they stopped for a breath, the jungle was barely thirty feet away.

"Look there," Lovo whispered and pointed. A tusked pig was foraging less than fifty feet away, at the edge of the jungle. It was round and fat, probably one hundred pounds, and had orange-thistle fur. "Think you can shoot that? I'd love some sweet bacon."

"Boar are awfully tough to bring down in one shot," Miraden whispered, "but I'm hungry enough to try." He took the bow from his shoulder and drew the string. A glowing golden arrow appeared between his fingers. He fired, and the arrow burned a hole right through it and through a palm tree behind it. The pig squealed and scrambled away. Lovo took off after it.

Ceychell worried about the boar's noise. But it was nothing compared to Lovo's crashing into the jungle after the fleeing pig.

"Lovo. Stop!" Simigrin whispered but he didn't.

"Let's go!" Miraden said.

Ceychell, Simigrin, and Tundra followed Miraden into the jungle, past where the boar had been shot, and deep into a maze of gnarled trees and leafy vines.

When they caught up to Lovo, the pig was on its side at Lovo's feet.

"Lovo, are you nuts?" Miraden hissed. "You'll get us all killed."

"That's alright, it was worth it," Lovo picked up the pig and tossed it on his shoulder. "Let's find a safe place to cook this."

Ceychell heard a whistle and then a hoot. She peered into the jungle but saw nothing. "Let's get out of here," Simigrin said.

"They're coming," Ceychell said.

Suddenly, they heard grunting all around them, as if it were coming from the jungle itself.

"Let's go!" Lovo yelled, drawing his mace in his free hand and hefting the pig more securely on his shoulder.

Lovo bolted toward the beach and the others followed. Even carrying a fat pig, he was faster than the other three. Ceychell was starting to get winded. A Fjisher leaped down from a tree in front of Lovo. Lovo smashed its face with his mace, sending it tumbling into the undergrowth.

Another Fjisher, it's face full of sharp yellow palm piercings, sprang from the brush next to Ceychell. She screamed and kicked him in the stomach. He grabbed her as she tried to run. His eyes went wide as Tundra pawed huge gashes in his chest. Ceychell barely saw him drop as she started running.

When they reached the beach again, Ceychell fell to her knees on the hot sand to catch her breath. She heard grunting behind her and stole a glance over her shoulder. There was movement in the tangled greenery, but no Fjishers had made it to the beach.

There was no more east-bound island left. They were at the edge of a long stretch of lagoon that looked out to an island at least a thousand feet away. It was small, just a copse of palm trees and some underbrush. A bigger island was less than three miles past it in the haze.

"Uh… that's a long swim," Ceychell said between heavy breaths.

"Simi can you freeze a path?" Miraden asked. He was barely winded.

"Maybe?" she said, still gasping for air.

"That would be—" Ceychell started, but a dart stuck her in the arm. She screamed and pulled it out. It was a burnt palm needle with green gunk on the tip. "Poison!"

"Look out!" Simigrin said and waved her hand. A thin sheet of ice appeared, walling them off from the jungle. About thirty darts pelted the ice before it shattered.

Miraden turned and shot one arrow after another at the Fjishers at the edge of the jungle. Several of the savages howled in pain, and a few fell to the ground. Simigrin held her staff out toward the seas and started casting. Ice froze along the surface of the water, but the movement and the salt cracked it as she cast.

Ceychell's vision blurred for a moment. A painful knot numbed her arm. It burned and moved fast toward her shoulder. She was terrified she could die at any moment, but pushed through her fears. "I'll buy you time!" Ceychell said. She pulled out her book and focused on its whirring pages. Heat rose in her chest and flowed down her arm; she launched a fireball at the jungle. It puttered into the sand about ten feet from her. Another blurring moment nearly dropped her to the sand, she had to catch herself. She tried her spell again and sparks popped from her hands. Then she screamed and put all her energy into the spell. A stream of fire exploded against the trees and spread along the tree line and into the jungle. The shrieking Fjishers disappeared in the fire or back into the jungle, she didn't really care which. Her vision became too blurry to see what she had done, and she felt violently nauseated. She fell down on the sand again and closed her eyes.

"Ceychell!" Miraden yelled.

"I got ya, Ceycha," Lovo said.

Ceychell looked at Lovo. His blond hair blurred with the sun overhead. She could see his eyes, they shined. She thought he might be whispering prayers, but she couldn't make out his words.

A minute later, Ceychell opened her eyes and saw Lovo and Miraden. They were holding her. Miraden looked frightened, she knew the look so well.

"Ceychell! Ceychell, my gods, you're back!" Miraden said and smothered her with a hug.

"Thank you," she said to Lovo.

"Nasty poison," Lovo said. "You'll be okay but the jungle won't."

She leaned up and looked behind her at the ruin. Her fire was out of control, burning through the trees as if they were dry reeds. Dozens of dead Fjishers lay in molten sludge in the sand.

Simigrin was at the shore finishing the spell. The ice bridge had spread to the small island, but it was starting to melt already at the shore in front of them. "We have to move quickly," Simigrin yelled, "but be careful—it is going to be slick. I'll keep freezing it for you." She was sweating and slouching and breathing very heavily.

Miraden raised his hand. "I'll stay—"

"No," Ceychell said, gathering her strength. "I'll stay with her. We'll make it."

Miraden looked at Simigrin. "Last time we separated I thought I lost you forever." Ceychell thought he looked on the edge of tears and panic.

"Well, you didn't," Simigrin said. "Now go. Take the pig and Tundra."

Lovo hoisted the pig over his shoulder again and started walking across the ice bridge. Miraden followed, holding the back of the big man's pants for balance. Tundra moved without much trouble thanks to her large claws but cracks spread quickly once the bear was on it. The duo and Tundra shuffled and slid carefully out over the channel, pausing as waves swept across their feet.

Simigrin continued to focus on her spell. The bridge was holding, but sweat was pouring down her face and her staff was trembling almost uncontrollably. Ceychell took her hand, shut her eyes, and focused on transferring energy to Simigrin. The pages of Ceychell's book flipped in front of her. But she was terribly nauseous and her whole body ached with sickness.

Nevertheless, the bridge doubled and thickened and crackled as it hardened. Frost rose from the bridge and the ice hissed when a wave passed over it. Ceychell watched Miraden and Lovo scamper across and jump onto the shore at the little island.

"Thank you," Simigrin said. She wiped her face and took a deep breath.

It was the first time Simigrin ever thanked her and Ceychell felt a beat of pride in her chest. "You're welcome."

The jungle behind them was a massive wall of smoke above a roaring inferno. "Let's go," Simigrin said.

The two women stepped carefully onto the ice and shuffled toward the small island.

Ceychell held Simigrin's shoulders as they shuffled their feet in unison. Simigrin turned her head and said, "I really was wrong, we do need you," Simigrin said.

Ceychell couldn't believe her ears. It was hard for her to say, "I sometimes feel like your enemy, but you're not mine."

"Hold on!" Simigrin said. She struck her staff against the bridge, it froze in place. Ice spread over hers and Ceychell's feet. Ceychell squeezed her from behind as a large wave blasted them over their heads and took a few seconds to pass and subside. She shook her clogged ear.

"My gods that was close," Ceychell yelled. Simigrin started laughing and Ceychell joined in. She wasn't sure why, perhaps the adrenaline, perhaps the danger. She felt so free and alive in that moment.

The ice broke from their feet when Simigrin lifted her staff. They shuffled again, but it was really slippery now. They were nearly to the shore when the bridge started to break apart behind them. They skated, slid, hopped, and ran as big slabs of ice cracked and floated away, and were barely into the shallows when the span of ice beneath their feet broke apart, dumping them into the channel. Ceychell grabbed Simigrin's arm and pulled her to shore, and they lay on the sand, gasping for air.

Miraden and Lovo knelt and smiled down at them.

"Ceycha?" Simigrin said.

"Yeah?" Simigrin had never called her that.

"If you don't start cooking that pig, I'm going to eat it raw."

SEVENTEEN

TO THE BURNING SANDS

WHEN MIRADEN LEFT O'KOKRA, HE hoped he'd never be stuck on an island in the middle of the sea again, but after escaping the Fjishers, the little island was like paradise. He laid his gear down and tried not to worry for a few minutes. Even if the Fjishers had boats and figured out where they were, they had time.

Miraden stripped down to his pants, grabbed his axe, and climbed a palm tree. The warm breeze felt good on his skin. When he got to the top, he chopped away some black coconuts, and Lovo caught them below. He had a good vantage point to see the entire island. It wasn't large, he figured he could walk all the way around it in twenty minutes. There was a rocky shoal on the north side of the island where he saw a marooned boat.

"Lovo!" Miraden yelled.

Lovo bashed open a coconut and yelled up, "Yeah?"

"There is a boat right over there," Miraden pointed. He climbed down while Lovo opened the other coconuts and passed them around.

Lovo followed Miraden to the north shore. They carefully hopped rock to rock and found the boat listing to one side.

"Well, the goddess provides. That looks like the other lifeboat from the Sand Caster," Lovo said.

When they got closer, Miraden realized it was caught by a rock that had broken through the hull. They managed to lift it free of the rock but it wouldn't float without taking on water.

"Let's drag it back and figure out what to do," Lovo said.

They brought the boat back and pulled it up onto the sand to let it drain.

Ceychell and Simigrin came over. "Is it going to float?" Ceychell asked.

"All five of us will barely fit," Miraden said, "and I'm not sure we can scoop out the water fast enough."

"No way to plug the hole?" Ceychell asked.

Simigrin looked at the boat. She shook it, the boat creaked. "A lot of loose boards. I'd be worried it could fall apart out there. I could freeze it. May be enough to get us to the next island, but it won't last."

"Let's get our rest today," Miraden said. "We'll try that tomorrow."

Simigrin and Ceychell went to scout the rest of the island while Lovo and Miraden dressed the pig and laid it out to cook.

Simigrin and Ceychell returned holding fist-sized stones. They dumped them by the pig.

Miraden looked up at Simigrin and she said, "Remember how they cooked the pigs on O'kokra?" He did remember how they cooked them, and it wasn't over a spit, but in the ground.

"Lovo, can you start digging?" Miraden asked. "Ceychell, let's get these rocks nice and hot."

Within an hour Lovo, with Tundra's help, dug a pit, Ceychell had roasted a pile of washed stones that Simigrin carefully placed in the pig and Miraden covered it in palm leaves. It was smoking and needed to be cooked.

He took his clothes down to the water and tried to scrub the stink out of them. They smelled like low tide, sweat, fear, blood, and smoke.

Ceychell ran past him completely naked and screaming, "Woohooo!" and dove in the water.

"Waaahhhhhh!" Simigrin ran past him too, also naked, and jumped in.

Miraden washed his clothes and tried not to stare at the two naked women frolicking and laughing in the shallows. He was glad they were at peace. He went back and picked up their merchant robes from the sand, brought them to the water, and did his best to work the funk out of them. The tears and scorch holes were too much to pass as respectable potion merchants. His and Lovo's robes were in similar shape. He draped them over some palm fronds he'd propped up in the sand for his and Lovo's robes. He felt better being back in his leathers anyway.

Miraden went through Ceychell and Simigrin's bags and removed their mage robes and set them on the sand for them. Finally, he sat down on the sand across from Lovo and let the wind, the hissing of the waves lapping the shore, and the smell of roasted pig soothe his exhausted mind.

"Don't think I've ever seen you relax like this," Lovo said.

Miraden lay with his eyes closed for a moment, took in the fresh sea air, the birds singing, the women's laughter, the smoke, the peace. He couldn't remember the last time he'd felt such harmony. He knew it wouldn't last more than a day, but he let himself enjoy the moment.

"Would have been funny to hide the boat and tell Simigrin she needed to make an even greater bridge to the next island," Lovo whispered.

Miraden chuckled to himself and said, "Or ask Ceycha to boil the ocean so we can walk across."

"Yeah, don't tempt her. Those darn Fjishers'll be lucky if Ceychell's left a sapling alive on their island."

Now that he had a moment to reflect, Ceychell's power scared him. She was no longer the sweet young woman he'd grown up with. She was a powerful mage with a bad temper. "I still can't believe she had it in her." He shaded his face with his hand and looked out at Ceychell and Simigrin splashing around in the water. She didn't look like the fire mage who'd just burned an island to ash; she looked like the love of his childhood, happy and eager to enjoy life. He also hadn't seen Simigrin so playful and happy before. She'd always been so serious, quiet, and private. But the two of them looked like sisters playing at the beach.

Lovo took a sip from a coconut. "I don't know, Mir. Seems right to me. Lots of fire in her. Be glad she saved us."

Miraden *was* glad, just nervous. "You know, it's nice to not have to worry about Fjishers for a moment and just breathe. Do you know anything about the Burning Sands?"

"What do you say we enjoy the sun, chow down on this pig, and leave that for tomorrow?"

"Perfect."

It took all day to cook, but when the pig was done, they devoured it. Miraden was painfully full, Tundra was napping after her meal and Lovo could hardly keep his eyes open. Simigrin and Ceychell sat on the sand in their warm, dry robes, drinking the last of their coconut milk. Their hair was matted from the seawater, but neither seemed to care.

"Lovo, thanks for getting this pig," Simigrin said. "I thought you were going to get us all killed, but this was worth it."

"Mmm? Yep," Lovo said, half asleep.

"Mm hmmm," Ceychell chewed and nodded.

"I'm going to get another coconut—anyone want one?" Simigrin said.

Ceychell waved her hand, and Lovo shook his head.

Miraden knew Simigrin could barely climb. He grabbed his axe and stared sidelong at her as she walked over to a tree and looked back at him. She started to climb, but she barely got her feet off the sand.

Lovo extended a handful of pork rinds to Ceychell, "Try this, Ceycha. Culinary perfection!"

Miraden walked over close enough to whisper to Simigrin, "Would you like some help?"

"I think I got it. It's not a scary tree like in the Bleak Gale Pines—the bark is rough."

He hopped on the tree and shimmied up. Then he leaned down and took her hand. He instructed her to step on his foot to get a foothold, and he pulled her up with him. At the top, they wrapped their arms and legs around the tree just below the spikey palm fronds where a few coconuts hung.

"I doubt you came up here for a coconut," Miraden said, smiling. "Especially since you hate heights and climbing."

"It was worth it, though," she whispered, taking his hand. She grinned and looked down at her vambraces. The dragons, the fire plume, gleamed spectacularly in the moonlight as they had the day he got them for her. "I think of you whenever I look at them."

Miraden sighed. "I feel like we haven't had a private moment in so long." He chopped a coconut from the tree and dropped it to the ground.

"I hope we can change that one day." She leaned over on the side of the tree away from the campfire, and when he leaned over, she planted a big kiss on his lips and held them there for a long moment. Then they both backed away and smiled at each other.

He hacked down another coconut and then helped her down with his free hand. When they reached the bottom, she pulled him in for another long kiss. He slid his hands into her robe and she bit his lip lightly.

"Okay, I think we should head back," she said.

Miraden didn't say anything for a moment, then realized he was daydreaming. "Right."

When they returned to shore, Simigrin got Lovo to crack open the two coconuts, and she handed one to Ceychell.

Soon nighttime settled in. A full moon lit up the sky and stars twinkled at the edges of Miraden's vision. The Fjishers' island was mostly charred trees and embers and reminded Miraden a little of the land beyond the Ashengate. There was no sign of boats or any attempt to follow them. And they all lay down to sleep.

Miraden woke mid-morning. The sky was beautiful and clear except for the lingering black smudge of smoke. The island east of them was only a few miles away.

"You think the desert is beyond that island?" he asked Simigrin. "Oh wait," he said and went through his bag until he found his telescope. The scope was light and the optic lens brightly shone multiple colors from the morning sun. When he put it to his eye, he had to adjust it by turning the end but the zoom was incredible. It was like he was standing next to an orange sand dune. He slowly scaled back and saw the desert just beyond the next island. "It is."

"Let me see," Simigrin said. He handed it to her, "It's not a good option, but we have to keep moving. The ashenkin aren't going to wait for us to get to Sentry and back."

"We may have a little more time than we thought," Ceychell said.

Simigrin gawked at her. "The ashenkin could come at any minute."

"I've had more dreams," Ceychell said, squinting and trying to see the desert. "Carbrojl is in them. I-I've spoken to him."

Miraden was wary. "What did he say?"

"He told me the ashenkin would no longer bother me—he

assured me."

"They are probably just dreams," Miraden said.

"No," Simigrin said. "She's got that book and a soul of fire. He's contacting her, and that scares me more than the ashenkin."

Lovo nodded. "Which means we need to get moving."

Simigrin looked pensive. She handed the telescope back to Miraden. "You all should know that the desert will get the Fjishers off our backs, but what we may find is worse."

"How so? Lovo asked.

"You've never heard of the Suffering Sands?" Simigrin said. "It's desolate, cursed, no one goes there."

"Maybe we should take the boat back north?" Ceychell asked.

Miraden shook his head. "I don't think so, the boat isn't going to make it far."

Ceychell held out her hands and said, "Then to the desert?" Everyone nodded. Miraden hoped they'd find trees or a better boat on the next island. He wasn't ready to venture through a desert.

They got their gear and walked over where the dinghy was pulled up on the bank. Lovo and Miraden pushed the boat over so the bottom faced up. There were a few holes apart from the one hole a leg could fit through. Simigrin's book and sphere popped out of her bag. She started casting as a thick sheet of ice covered the bottom of the boat.

"I don't know how long this is going to last," she said.

"Hopefully enough to get us a few miles?" Miraden said. He pushed the boat with Lovo into the water and it floated without trouble but when Tundra got in, it sagged.

"Let's paddle quickly," Lovo said.

Lovo was on one side using his shield to paddle. The others leaned over and paddled by hand. Tundra sat in the middle of all of them on her hind quarters and seemed to enjoy the ride.

"No chance you can get Tundra to paddle?" Lovo said.

Miraden saw water at his feet and knew the ice was starting to fail. He paddled as hard as he could.

They barely reached the island. Miraden stepped out of the boat and helped Ceychell out. When Tundra jumped out the boat fell apart.

"Glad we didn't take it north out to sea," Lovo said.

There was thick jungle ahead of them that stretched for miles north and south but the desert wasn't far east, maybe two miles away.

Miraden waved his hands and they huddled up to whisper. "We don't know if Fjishers are here, so we should stay quiet. Let's see if we can get some coconuts to take with us because it's going to be a long trek." Everyone nodded.

They headed into the jungle, Lovo in front and Miraden closely following. Ceychell was just behind him, then Simigrin and Tundra in the back. There weren't many coconuts, and many of the palm trees were over forty feet tall.

Vines hung from the palm trees and bramble bushes were everywhere. Miraden noticed there were well grooved paths, which they followed. That made him nervous; there were people on the island.

Ceychell put a hand on his shoulder and whispered, "Miraden." She pointed to their left to a tree that had ten coconuts on it. It was off the path through some dense brambles.

Miraden removed his axe and took the lead, chopping away the bramble when it got too thick. It was hard to be quiet as he hacked away the twists and turns of the thorn bushes.

"Kinda wish you could just burn this all away," he whispered to Ceychell. She returned a wink.

Lovo took the axe and cleared the rest of the way.

"I'm going to climb up and chop them, you catch them," he said to Lovo. Miraden climbed the tree quickly. It wasn't difficult and he started enjoying the breeze. There were blue and green birds nesting above him, smaller than hawks. He got up to the coconuts and held on tight, he was a ways up and there were no branches to catch him should he fall.

Miraden cut the first and dropped it toward Lovo. Cut the next and when he got to the ninth he heard rustling. As he peered through the other tall palm trees, he saw well over a hundred Fjishers wading through the jungle. He didn't think they had seen him yet but they were headed in their direction.

He took a deep breath and shimmied down the tree.

"We got to go!" Miraden whispered.

"Why?" Simigrin whispered.

"They are coming," he said between pants. "A lot of them."

Tundra sniffed and roared.

"Shhhh shh shshh," Miraden said, but it was too late.

The grunting started and they all ran back to the path.

Lovo was in front. He weaved between palms, and slipped under vines. Miraden drew his bow. The golden arrow appeared and he loosed it at the first Fjisher he saw. The arrow ripped a hole right through a spear-wielding Fjisher and stuck in a palm tree. He fired another and another, cutting down two more Fjishers. Some of the savages howled and turned to where the arrows were coming from. Lovo advanced with his shield and mace ready. There were ten Fjishers in view. One bounded at Lovo with a jagged knife. Lovo barreled him over with his shield and pounded his head into the underbrush with his mace. Another leapt over the fallen Fjisher—Miraden shot him through the chest and he fell. Tundra charged the tribesman from behind, swatted one's head of with her massive claws and bit another's arm off at the shoulder. Miraden shot another in the eye—the man screamed, whirled around, and fell against a tree.

The five remaining savages fled into the jungle.

"Miraden, Lovo" Ceychell said, "They are on us!"

Between the trees to his right, Fjishers were galloping after them on all fours.

A dart flew past his face. One twanged off of Lovo's shield.

Simigrin's book sprung from her pack. She tried to yell a spell but stumbled and almost fell. She pointed her staff toward the tribesmen and coated the trees in frost and scattered blades of ice.

To Miraden's left, a woman dropped from a tree with her dagger held out. Tundra slammed her in the chest with a massive paw, sending her tumbling into the brush.

A horde of grunting Fjishers clambered after them and more were leaping down from the trees. Way too many to fight. Up ahead he saw Lovo burst into the sunlight. Ceychell and Simigrin were right behind him, but they were heaving and running for their lives.

Fifty feet from the opening in the trees the Fjishers caught up with him. His only choice was to turn and fight or be cut down from behind, but when he turned around, Tundra was swatting and clawing the tribesmen to pieces. Blood and gore and limbs were flying in all directions, and the savages were retreating.

"Tundra! Let's go!" Miraden shouted. He dashed for the opening in the trees and heard the big bear trampling the undergrowth behind them. At last, they burst through the opening onto the beach and tumbled to the sand. It was so hot, Miraden thought he might be frying.

"I see why they call this the burning sands," Lovo said. "My feet are on fire."

Miraden didn't feel the heat. He glanced down at the boots he'd been given and was thankful. Glancing back, he saw an angry mob of Fjishers standing at the border. Many were making threatening gestures with their hands.

"Hot, hot, awful sand!" Simigrin said and ran past him.

"Well," Ceychell said and took many breaths, "Should we go back into the shade of the jungle?"

"Ugh." Simigrin rolled her eyes. "Yeah, can you go get me some water from the ocean to cool my feet?"

They continued north. The sun beat down on them and the red-orange sand radiated the heat up at them. There were no trees for shade, no shrubs, no birds, not even insects. Tundra sagged and plodded along, covered in sand, her mouth hanging open.

"Can you spare some water for her?" Miraden asked Simigrin.

"Maybe a little for all of us?" Lovo added.

The mage held out her staff and filled up their near-empty wineskins. She flipped through her book and waved her staff at them. A cool breeze and even a few flakes of snow blew over them, and Miraden recognized the spell she'd used beyond the Ashengate. Tundra licked at snow flakes flying around her head.

"Ohhhhh," Ceychell moaned. "Why were you saving that one?"

"Thank you," Miraden said and hugged Simigrin. It felt good to hold her again. "I noticed you're not pulling out as many ingredients. Do you not need them anymore?"

"My staff is created with most of the ingredients I need. It's not limitless, but it's a big help."

"Simi," Lovo said, "I take back everything I ever said about you."

She gave him a hard look. "What do you mean? What *did* you say?"

Miraden and Lovo laughed for a moment.

"Nothing," Lovo said, covering his laugh with his shield, "At least you don't have to worry about me hounding you to conjure a campfire in this heat."

"Why would you want a campfire?" Ceychell asked. "And does anyone know where we are going?"

Miraden smirked but didn't answer her.

"We can't just wander through the desert. Is there anything here? Uh… besides those things?" she pointed up ahead

There were three giant, six-legged, copper lizards in the near distance. They looked like they were digging holes.

Simigrin held a hand up to shade her eyes. "Those look like basilisks. They aren't aggressive but we need to avoid them. They can turn you to stone with a look and their bite is deadly."

"Happy to avoid them," Miraden said. "Which way should we go?"

"We could go north and run into Syindella Channel," Simigrin said. "Maybe get lucky and catch a ship passing through, but the cliff going down to the water is shear for hundreds of feet. It's a treacherous climb, at least for me."

Miraden knew climbing was not a great idea. "Any other options?"

"There are harbor towns on both sides of the channel," Simigrin said, "but I'm not sure how far each is. If we travel northwest to the harbor town, we will have to pass through the Ruins of Arbaan which we should avoid at all costs. They say a sadness befalls anyone who goes to close, and they are drawn to the ruins where the dead keep them forever."

"So… that's out," Miraden said.

"Let's just go to the channel, this heat is going to kill us," Ceychell said.

"This desert is uncharted," Simigrin said, "it's supposed to be huge. I don't think we could cross it even if we had water. It could take weeks."

Lovo let out a huge sigh; it was exactly how Miraden felt. They slouched from the rising heatwaves and oppressive sun beating down on them relentlessly.

"There are no towns?" Lovo asked.

"None that I know of, unless you believe in the myth of Fe Jet,"

Simigrin said. She wiped sweat from her brow. "There is a legend that the natives of this world were banished here long ago and can't return to the north, but those are just stories. You can see," she said and outstretched her arms, "nothing could live here."

Miraden noticed how much the rest of them kept their feet moving up and out of the sand. It looked miserable.

Miraden said, "Let's go north and try to stick to the coast to cool off once we get around those basilisks. Hopefully we can signal a ship that might bring us back to Bondare or ferry us across the channel where we can find passage up to Queen's Edge."

"Wait, Fe Jet?" Lovo asked. "From the children's stories?"

Miraden suddenly remembered his mother telling him about Fe Jet when he was little. It was a land of mystical creatures, magic and flying, a city where dreams were made. It sounded silly, he hadn't thought of Fe Jet for more than ten years.

"Well," Miraden said, "since there are no good choices, let's head north to the harbor and hope we find some food along the way."

"Let's start by avoiding those basilisks," Lovo said.

EIGHTEEN

THE TRUTH?

CEYCHELL STOOD IN THE CENTER of an amphitheater. Black vines had cracked through the tiers of stone benches. The dirt ground was sun-scorched and fractured. It looked like rain hadn't fallen here in years. The amphitheater reminded her of the coliseum lab at Kander.

She remembered falling asleep in the desert under the stars. She didn't know how she'd arrived in this desolate place.

A purple storm spiraled in the red sky, blew sand and hot air across Ceychell's face. She walked out of the amphitheater through a broken archway and into a barren town. The buildings were run down, some were merely piles of rubble. One rock heap was so enormous it looked like a mountain. She could see smooth walls in the rubble and ornate travertine arches, possibly from a shrine, but the engravings were worn smooth by the wind-blown sand. There wasn't a soul in sight.

Her throat was parched, and the hot, dry air scorched her lungs. She wandered through town, came to a half-standing building with a large open window, and peeked inside. There were boxes and crates. Mostly crushed by fallen stone, along the far wall, and vases, mostly broken, on shelves behind a counter. She crept in the window and saw a bowl below the counter. She touched it, and it crumbled into dust. On the wall was a painting. It was faint, but it looked like a woman standing by a lake, a brown-haired woman in a yellow summer dress.

"She was beautiful."

Ceychell screamed and whipped her head around. Carbrojl was standing right behind her, smiling, his arms folded across his chest.

Ceychell wheezed out a long breath. "Can't you say hello from a little farther away?"

"The painting is of a woman named Maladaria. She was a shopkeeper and herbalist, long ago. The people of Lithia loved her."

"Why am I here again?" she asked. She was worried that Miraden and the others would be gone when she woke up.

"You came here on your own. I came to see you and offer any help I can. Come, walk with me."

She walked through the city with him and they talked.

"Why does Khronigrin steal children and turn them into ashenkin?" she asked.

"Because that was what he bargained for—it was his debt to pay. So tragic."

"Is he gone now?"

"Yes. Defeated actually." Carbrojl walked with impeccable posture, as though he had perfected each step.

She was confused. "Was he the giant demon Miraden killed?"

"Indeed he was. But inside, he was only a man consumed by power he couldn't control."

"What was the deal?"

Carbrojl shook his head. "Tragic really. He needed help with magic that he couldn't obtain in your world. You see, there are some arts, some secrets that they left here with me."

"Who is *they?*" she asked.

"I believe you call them the *Lady of Light*, the *Daughter of Forests*." He laughed quietly for a moment, his face contorted and ugly. "I knew them as Levoria, Kastalynn, and the rest. They were the knowledge bearers, the leaders of this world who brought their followers into your world, ages ago."

"Why couldn't you go with them?"

He smiled at her; it felt like sand was blowing on her face and in her eyes even though there was no wind.

"I look forward to our next chat."

Ceychell was shaken awake by Simigrin. It was still mostly dark. Miraden and Lovo were sleeping soundly.

"You were groaning." Simigrin whispered. "I thought you were in pain."

"I keep going to the old world. I was just speaking to Carbrojl."

Simigrin stared at her for a long moment, but didn't say anything.

Ceychell realized how crazy she must sound. She couldn't explain it. "I've... recently started waking up there... or going there in my dreams."

"Is that where the Grunkins are from?" Lovo asked. He wasn't asleep after all.

"Yes. At least I think so. It's a hot, desolate place."

"Worse than here?" Lovo asked.

"Yes," she said. "I'm just so happy to see you all again. I never know if I will make it back."

Miraden turned over as well. "Were you *trying* to go there?"

"No, it just happens. The past few months I've started having vague visions of desolate places, like this desert, and hearing voices during the day. But lately, the dreams have become very vivid, like I am actually in Ghaborion. The first time was right as the storm hit our boat."

"Maybe that's why you sometimes scream while you're dreaming,"

Miraden said.

"Yes… it's really strange, but I feel like I'm supposed to learn something while I'm there talking to Carbrojl—"

"Wait?" Simigrin said, propping herself up on her elbows. "You talk to Carbrojl every time?"

"Yes. He told me Khronigrin was the one summoning ashenkin. I didn't want to believe him, but he seems to know everything that has happened in our world."

"I see," Simigrin said. She looked deep in thought.

"He told me"—she wasn't sure she should tell them, but they were all looking at her expectantly— "that the children weren't sacrificed—they are the ashenkin."

"What?" Miraden said.

"He is lying to you," Simigrin said. "Lord Umorogrin said he was a deceiver, and he is obviously manipulating you."

"But why would he lie to me? I'm nothing to him."

Simigrin took Ceychell's arm. "Don't trust him, no matter what. They left him in that world for good reason."

"What reason?" Lovo asked.

Simigrin didn't seem to have an answer.

"Whatever the reasons," Miraden said, sitting up, "we are heading north. Let's hope we can keep your mind here so you won't have to talk to him again."

An insect flew at Ceychell's face and she batted it away. She was hot, and the sun hadn't even crested the horizon yet.

They walked for two days. Simigrin kept their wineskins full and cast a cool breeze over them during the worst parts of the day. At night, the desert became cold, and they huddled with Tundra.

Tundra groaned a lot. Ceychell figured she was hungry, but there was nothing to harvest or hunt. They were low on food, and Miraden shared as much as he could with Tundra.

They woke before sunrise to gain ground before the heat struck them like a roaring hearth fire. Ceychell's stomach felt like it was turning inside out. Water tasted good on her tongue, but it just made her hungrier.

Lovo's stomach grumbled so loud it sounded like distant thunder.

"I'm so hungry!" he yelled. "Can one of you ladies summon a pot roast? Or even an apple, anything!" Lovo said.

"Why didn't I think of that!" Ceychell said, rolling her eyes.

Simigrin laughed. "I don't have the right reagent to create a magic pot roast, or a fruit tree and I doubt it would grow here anyway."

"Maybe we could eat the bear?" Lovo joked.

"She might eat you first," Miraden said.

"She wouldn't do that." Lovo scratched her ear, and she groaned. "Hmm, maybe she would."

At midday, the sun felt like it was just overhead, beating down on their burnt faces. Ceychell dragged her hot feet through the sand. She was exhausted, hungry, and miserable. Each step felt like she was squishing her toes through sweat and sand. She could only imagine how foul she smelled because her companions smelled like a trash heap covered in fish roasting in the sun.

At night, the moon was giant over the desert, painting the red sand pink, and the stars twinkled brightly, which would have been peaceful had Ceychell not been beyond hunger. But she did not complain because she knew her companions were equally as wretched. Lovo looked like a plodding golem. Miraden slouched forward with his mouth open and his tongue out. He'd given the last of his food to Tundra, who slowly pawed through the sand behind him. Simigrin seemed in the best spirits of them all and walked almost upright. She was tougher than she looked.

"When do you think we should stop for the night?" Lovo asked Ceychell.

Ceychell wanted to stop even more than she wanted to eat, but she worried about her dreams. "We can stop when you find something to eat."

Suddenly, they heard screaming up ahead, beyond the next dune.

"C'mon, we have to help," Miraden said.

They ran over the dune and spotted a small camp. Two basilisks were attacking a group of travelers in orange linen robes. The creatures were big and muscular with long snouts and jagged teeth that shone pink in the moonlight; they had six short legs and scales that looked like slate. A third basilisk was dead on the sand with spears sticking out of its head. One of the travelers screamed and charged a lizard, then turned to stone and tumbled onto the sand.

"Basilisks," Simigrin said. Might be the same ones. Whatever you do, don't look them in the eyes or get bitten." As Simigrin said it, one of the traveler's arms was bitten off, and he stumbled away, spraying blood, and then dropped to the sand.

Ceychell and Simigrin's books both shot out of their sacks.

Miraden ran down the dune, pulling his bow from his shoulder. He loosed an arrow at the massive creature. It plunged into the basilisk's neck, and the beast turned his head toward Miraden.

"That one is looking at you Miraden," Lovo shouted. "Don't look up!" He ran down the dune toward them. Miraden slowed and drew another arrow, but he struggled to aim without looking at the monster.

A bolt of water flew and struck the other basilisk in the face and froze in a block around its head. The basilisk flailed its head around and clawed at the ice.

The basilisk Miraden shot ran toward him. Lovo held out his

shield and crashed into its side. Then he slammed it with his mace, looking away from its eyes. The beast swung its tail around and knocked him to the sand.

Several of the travelers shot arrows at the creature, sticking it like a pin cushion without much effect. Lovo jumped up and bashed its tail with his mace, and the lizard swung around and bit onto his shield, gnawing and tugging at it. Lovo slid below the basilisk, hiding beneath his shield, trying to pull the shield free from its jaw. Miraden shot the creature through the eye, and it collapsed on Lovo.

The other basilisk had nearly clawed the ice from its head. Ceychell cast a flaming spear that pierced it, and it detonated, sending blood and guts spraying all over the travelers and Ceychell.

Miraden and the travelers ran up to pull the basilisk off of Lovo. He pushed from below, and the travelers pulled the creature's legs from the other side. Lovo was able to crawl out, jump up and bash the bleeding beast's head into the sand.

When everyone was sure the basilisks were dead, they bent over panting and coughing.

Simigrin pulled a chunk of meat from her robe, flung it on the sand, and smirked. "Thanks, Ceychell, that's just what I needed."

Ceychell and Simigrin walked down the dune to check on Lovo. She turned over his wrist and looked for punctures. His arm was covered in hot sticky slobber, but he had managed to avoid being bitten. The shield was covered in it too and there wasn't a scratch on its surface. Miraden brushed the hot sand off of Lovo's back.

"Are you all okay?" Ceychell asked the travelers. Five of the seven survived. All of them wore hooded orange-linen robes, roughly the same color as the sand, and their scaled hands were blue-green.

One of the travelers pulled her hood back. "We are, yes, and we give thanks to you." Light-blue scales covered the sides of her smooth face. She had a short jutting nose and her white hair looked like a spider web. She had long, thin arms covered with green scales, and sharp white claws. A tail stretched out behind her. Ceychell had never seen anything like her. The rest pulled back their hoods. They were all serpent-people.

Ceychell's stomach growled. As her adrenaline wore off, she remembered how hungry she was. "Anyone know if basilisk is poisonous to eat?"

"It is not." The snake-woman said. "We eat it often. As you can see, there is not much else out here."

They joined the travelers' camp. Ceychell relit their fire while Lovo and one of the travelers cut some meat from a basilisk's rump after they'd managed to hack through its scales. Lovo cooked while Miraden helped one of the travelers skin the three basilisk corpses.

Ceychell and Simigrin sat next to the campfire with the other four travelers, and Lovo handed them pieces of meat skewered on copper sticks the travelers carried for the purpose. While they ate, they talked with the snake-people.

"I've read about you," Simigrin said, "You are lortaraas."

"We are," said the snake-woman, who seemed to be their leader. "I, Kopreis, greet you. I am surprised you know of us and more surprised you are here. Few northerners come here to our land. Those who do rarely leave and never have I seen a human in the Burning Sands." She smiled at the two ladies; her fangs glistened in the moonlight. "We thank you for your kindness here. We do not trust humans. Many of you are irrational and deceitful, and your thoughts are muddled by spirits."

"Many of us… but not all of us," Ceychell said. "We're glad to have found you. We were heading east when our ship was sunk and we landed near the Fjishers."

"Pssss," Kopreis's tongue darted out. "Vile creatures. The worst. Seers saw their islands burn. We go to investigate. We care not for

Fjishers. We like their gems to trade."

Simigrin and Ceychell exchanged glances. Then Simigrin said, "We can save you the trip. It's burned to ash."

"I started the fire," Ceychell said tentatively. "They were…" Ceychell got lost in her thoughts for a moment, realizing that she and her companions had landed on *their* islands and destroyed *their* homes. She hadn't thought about what she was doing. She had only wanted to rescue Miraden. "They were…" she swallowed a lump in her throat, "trying to kill us."

"Indeed," Kopreis said. "Why do you tread on our land?"

"We ran to the desert to escape the Fjishers. Now we just want to get up to the channel," Simigrin said, "We don't mean to trespass."

Ceychell and Lovo glanced at Simigrin. Ceychell hoped their trespassing wouldn't be taken the wrong way.

"We didn't mean to trespass?" Lovo said, smelling the chunk of meat on his stick.

"We will escort you to Fe Jet," the snake-woman said. "There you must face Fe Jet law."

Ceychell looked at Simigrin, then at Kopreis. She couldn't believe Fe Jet was real.

Miraden joined them, holding a bundle of hides. "What laws? We are in the middle of the desert."

"The Lorden's desert. Humans, she favors the least. By her mercy."

NINETEEN

THE CENTER OF THE WORLD

LITTLE WAS SAID WHILE THE companions and the snake-people traveled east the next day. The snake-people stayed a fair distance behind Miraden and his companions to avoid being cooled by Simigrin's spell. When she first cast it, they hissed at each other and looked frightened and annoyed.

The sand sea seemed to have no end. Miraden periodically checked on everyone. Lovo told him quietly that he thought they were being led into a trap. Simigrin agreed, but also asserted that getting the snake-people's help was their best chance to get to the channel. She apologized for not telling the other three that lortaraas don't like outsiders. Ceychell recommended heading north and braving the cliff.

Miraden just wanted to get a clear idea of how far it was to the channel and how they could get more food and supplies. He intended to make it back to Kander alive, one way or another.

Ceychell was reading her book much of the day. It floated in front of her as she walked behind it. She seemed determined and whenever he asked her what she was reading she just whispered, "Portals."

They camped with the lortaraas and stayed quiet that night.

Miraden didn't like the feeling of being escorted as a prisoner but that's how it seemed. They didn't need to be bound because there was no escape in the desert. The next day was even hotter. The sweat crawled like spiders down Miraden's scorched skin. He felt like he was melting. "Simi," he whispered. "Is the spell failing?"

"My staff is losing its charge for that spell. I'm afraid it will run out soon."

He wasn't sure they could survive without the cool breeze. He cut off a chunk of charred basilisk and handed it to Tundra. They had plenty, but it would spoil in a day. Then he poured some water on the back of her neck. The bear moaned and chewed and plodded along beside them.

Miraden lingered and allowed the others to walk ahead while he waited for the lortaraas to catch up. "Kopreis, how much longer?"

"Tomorrow," she said. "You have made it this far, which is good. You are lucky to have the sorceresses."

"What's going to happen when we get there?"

"Not your business," one of the other lortaraas said. He was the tallest and had brown scales on the side of his arms.

"It's happening to us, so I'd say it is my business." Miraden clutched his bow and wondered how pushy he should get.

"Go ahead," Kopreis said. "On this side, is Fe Jet and the Suffering Sands. You all will die. I speak truths."

"Will the Lorden set us free?" he asked. "We were just trying to get to the channel and we did save you."

"Before, I say yes. Now, I say no," she said.

Miraden's heart sank. He considered using force but he had no idea where they were or how long it would take to get to the channel. He looked up ahead. His three companions and his bear were waiting for him. He turned back to Kopreis and said, "And why is that?"

"The Lorden *hates* wizards of Kander, we all do. There is a long history that will not be forgotten by us for ages. The wizards shall be at the desert's mercy. If you cooperate, perhaps you will live."

Miraden went numb. He didn't want to pry further. It was unjust and he couldn't understand it. He couldn't understand the blind prejudice. He wanted to fight them since at least they stood a chance of surviving in the desert but did they really.

"Return to your friends. Rest soon," she said.

Miraden turned and walked back to his group. He didn't say anything to them. Lovo asked him what they'd talked about, but Miraden couldn't answer. He continued walking eastward.

They all camped together that night, and the next morning the heat was even worse. Miraden felt like they were walking in an oven. When they'd separated from the lortaraas by a few yards, he whispered to his friends that if they continue to Fe Jet that they may be imprisoned or killed. Simigrin said they had no choice because they had to get to the channel and they had no idea where they were. Everyone agreed.

Around midday, they saw a sandstone city that sprawled for miles in the distance. Ten great towers stood hundreds of feet tall over a wide central building. Squat sandstone edifices seemed to surround an oasis of palm trees.

As they got closer, Miraden felt a cool breeze blowing over the city. The air smelled fresh, unlike the cities up north.

A company of tall, muscular guards in blue chain-metal tunics and holding double-ended spears stood at the city gate. Their upper bodies looked human, but instead of legs, they had split serpent tails. Miraden peered beyond the gate and realized that none of the people bustling on the dirt streets were human.

"Kopreis?" the guard said, his tongue whipping on the *s*. The guard spoke to her in a language Miraden didn't understand.

"Humans here?" Simigrin translated in a whisper.

Kopreis hissed something to the guard.

"Prisoners," Simigrin said. "They caused the fire. I'm taking them to the Lorden."

Miraden was surprised she knew their language. He had so many questions.

The guard waved his spear for them to enter. Miraden walked in slowly, the others right beside him.

Kopreis slithered up to him and said. "You walk without chains. Be stupid humans and I will bind you and drag you through the streets."

Miraden nodded as did the others.

"How do you know their language?" Ceychell whispered to Simigrin through her teeth.

"I know ten languages. They call this the First Tongue. Never knew why until now."

"Humans. Come," Kopreis said. The guards pushed them along with the butts of their spears.

When they entered the city, many of its denizens stared at them and some yelled what Miraden assumed must be curses and some even spat at them. Some of the people appeared to be half-human and half-wolf, others were mostly lizard, some had a dark upper body with arms and their lower half had four legs and a long base like a striped-horse.

Miraden had never felt so out of place. Simigrin and Ceychell stayed close to him and Lovo walked just behind him. Tundra growled at a lizardman who got too close; most of the others gave her a wide berth.

The streets were lined with pillars carved with idols of birds and snakes and topped by lanterns of green flames. The homes and shops were large, simple square structures built from solid sandstone.

The windows were just holes, and the doors were little more than shutters of palm reeds. Water flowed from the oasis along gray marble channels on the edges of the streets. Some channels led through buildings or around parks filled with trees. The streets were immaculately clean, but there was a strange smell, like an animal den, earthy but not offensive. Kopreis led them toward the tallest building. It looked like a palace or temple.

Miraden kept looking for any humans, but he didn't see any. He whispered to Simigrin, "Do you—"

"Quiet," Kopreis said, staring at him.

The palace or temple, or whatever it was, stood next to the oasis. Large palm trees were filled with hundreds of colorful birds, some swam on top the crystal clear lake. Miraden was dying to get a drink and just splash into it, but he didn't dare.

The building stood five stories tall and was bigger than any shrine or palace he'd ever seen. Windows more than ten feet high lined the front of each story. Music echoed from inside. It was beautiful but unusual. He didn't recognize the wind instruments, but overall it had a twangy sound and a low pitch.

Six tall guardians met them at the front doors, which were open and looked to be solid stone three feet thick. The guardians had six, pointed legs and a hard exoskeleton like a scorpion but their upper torsos were more lizard-like. Each guard had four arms and carried a long spear in both sets of hands. Miraden stared at them nervously. They were big enough to skewer him from ten feet away.

Kopreis stopped and waited for Miraden to catch up to her. "We'll soon be at the Lorden. She will not give quarter to your lies or honied words. Answer her questions and perhaps you will escape the desert's mercy." She whipped her tongue in and out and then she grinned. Kopreis said something in her language.

Simigrin yelled, "No!"

The scorpion guards grabbed Tundra and bound her in shackles. It happened so fast she didn't have a chance to struggle.

Miraden grabbed his bow but Lovo grabbed his hand and held him. When Miraden reached for his axe, Lovo whispered, "Don't, not now."

"No, you can't take her!" Miraden yelled at the guards who weren't listening.

"One more word, and you'll join her," Kopreis said.

Kopreis escorted them inside. As they entered a main hall, the draft and shade felt delightful. Miraden was so exhausted, he wanted to drop down and take a nap on the floor on the diamond-shaped silver tiles. The walls were painted with gold, greens and blues, stretching all the way up to the full five stories to the impossibly high ceiling. Sunlight shone through the windows and reflected off mirrors, illuminating the entire chamber.

In the center of the hall were two statues of a half woman–half serpent that appeared to be made of solid diamond. As they refracted so much light, Miraden found it difficult to look directly at them. He stared at them for a moment, just imagining what they might be worth.

Then he realized that the floor was likely pure ryzalian silver, incredibly costly and so polished the tiles shined like glass. The sandstone walls were painted with abstract and bright colors. Kyradel would have been amazed by it all.

Miraden tried not to get distracted by the opulence. A guard prodded him with the butt end of his spear, and Miraden moved along.

They walked past the massive scorpion guards and into a tunnel. At the end of the tunnel, a lortaraas was sitting on a giant throne of amethyst and gold with three diamonds on the high chair-back over the lortaraas's head.

The lortaraas was petite. She wore a blue shimmering dress that covered her chest and part of her long dual tail. Her scales were light-green, almost yellow, and hair was jet black and long. She sat upright with both hands on the armrests of the throne when Miraden and his companions entered, then leaned back and peered at Miraden with sharp, clear eyes.

The hooded travelers bowed. When Miraden and his friends did not bow, the scorpion guards forced them down so hard he could hardly breathe. He wondered what would happen if they *wanted* to hurt him.

"Kopreis," the Lorden said in a surprisingly deep voice, "I was told you went to investigate the Fjishers, yet you've returned with four humans. That is, unless the Fjishers are standing on their hind legs now." The Lorden laughed at her own joke.

Kopreis started to reply in their language, but the Lorden raised a finger to stop her.

"Let us speak in their tongue," she said, "Least we can do."

"They caused the fire," Kopreis said. "We found them in the Burning Sands, slowly dying."

"Of course. And it appears two of them are wizards, correct?

"Correct, Lorden Flisstriq." Kopreis said.

"My my," the Lorden said and slid off the throne. Still pressed to the floor, Miraden struggled to turn his head and watch the Lorden slither toward him. She slithered confidently toward him, almost radiating in the sunlight as if her scales were polished to a glow. "Before I decide on how to kill you, tell me what happened at the Fjishers. Tell me why you are in my domain."

"Murf..." Miraden couldn't turn his head enough to talk, but Ceychell could.

"I'll tell you, Lorden," she said.

"Alright, you then. Tell me."

"We were sailing toward the channel when a storm sunk our ship, and we washed ashore at the Fjishers. They had captured two of us and were going to eat them. I set a fire to free them, and… it got out of hand. We escaped and crossed two islands, and while we were trying to cross the Burning Sands, we saw your… people being attacked by basilisks and helped them. Then they told us we were your prisoners. We just—"

The Lorden pointed a finger at the guard, and he pushed her face to the floor to stop her from talking. "You trespassed and burned down the Fjishers' island. You see, this is why we don't allow humans here. They bring destruction and death." The Lorden slithered upon her tail over to Ceychell and leaned down between her and Simigrin.

"And you forsaken mages and your damned tricks are the very *worst* of humankind. We are stuck here in the desert because of you. I should call a celebration for your executions. Perhaps I'll have you duel to the death to amuse my people."

"How are you here because of us?" Simigrin asked. The guard pressed her face to the floor, and she screamed. Miraden struggled against his captor to no avail. His neck felt like it might snap under the guard's grip.

"You don't know?" the Lorden asked. "Let up on her so she can hear this. She should know why I am killing her.

"Long ago, civilized humans arrived from another world, but before their arrival, many humans, some intelligent, others not, lived on the islands. The Fjishers, the inbred people-eaters whose island you destroyed, though, were something of a mistake of nature. The new humans entered this world like insects through an open door, chittering and chattering and buzzing all about," the Lorden waved her hands to and fro. "They came well-armed, and with the help of *mages,* they claimed so much land it seemed they would take it all." The Lorden paused for a moment to glare at Simigrin.

"Many, *many* mages came and summoned monsters to aid them and to hunt us. The mages commanded the winds and seas or called fire to fall out of the sky to wipe out our cities. They were the leaders of your people, your guardians, your saviors. But they were our exterminators.

"At first, the races you see here in Fe Jet co-inhabited the lands to the north with you humans. We shared knowledge, technology, and language, but as you bred, much more rapidly than we do, you and your mages claimed all our land.

"Finally, our people had had enough, and there was a war. Our ancestors lost, thanks mostly to the mages, and we were forced to migrate to the southern, less inhabitable, less desirable part of this world where we've lived ever since.

"So—" the Lorden leaned down face to face with Simigrin "—we despise you."

Miraden was floored by this new information. How is it this wasn't common knowledge? He felt there should be justice for the people of Fe Jet, he just didn't want to lose his head for it.

Simigrin turned her head enough to speak from the side of her mouth. "My master said ancient mages came here to research and study. Fe Jet was a land of wonder where the privileged could reach divinity."

The Lorden laughed. "Your master lied. Take them away."

The guards yanked Miraden and his companions from the floor and pulled their arms behind their backs.

"Please wait!" Simigrin said. The Lorden turned to face her and narrowed her eyes. "My master knows how to stop the ashenkin. We were trying to get to Queen's Edge to stop them!"

"You were traveling to Queen's Edge?" the Lorden asked.

"Yes," Miraden said. The guard grabbed his face tightly and jerked his head over to face the Lorden. "To steal her crown and stop the ashenkin."

"What are the ashenkin?" Lorden Flisstriq asked.

Miraden was surprised the Lorden had not heard of them. "They are devils that invade our world and steal our children. They leave a sickness behind that's killing people in our cities. The Devil's Bargain. Don't you have them here? They stand upright like humans, but they are red-skinned, muscular, and have horns and sharp teeth."

The Lorden stared at Miraden and seemed to think for a moment. She grinned and her fangs sparkled in the brilliant light reflected by the diamond statues. "Why that sounds incredibly familiar. Let me understand, they invade your lands, steal your children, destroy your lineage, and cause chaos and suffering for your people?" She waited, seemingly for a response, but no one said anything. "No. You probably don't like that at all and want to stop them. Don't you?" she yelled. "Don't you!"

"Yes," Ceychell cried out. Her guard yanked her off her feet and held her by her arms.

"Ah. Of course, you do. You'd do anything to stop them. But... I am afraid a different band of heroes will have to steal the queen's crown."

"Is there anything we can do to convince you to let us go?" Miraden asked. He would try to fight if it came to that, but it seemed hopeless surrounded by the terrifying scorpion guards.

The Lorden laughed. "Whatever these... ashenkin are, I want them to terrorize you and your people. I enjoy your suffering. Why would I let you go?" She stopped for a moment and stared up at the high ceiling. Her throat was scaly and white like a snake's underbelly. "Remove them."

Lorden Flisstriq waved them away, and the guards yanked them along. As Lovo and Miraden were dragged out of the hall, Miraden saw Simigrin and Ceychell taken away through an archway on the opposite side of the hall. He yelled out for Ceychell, but a claw clamped over his face and gouged his cheek.

TWENTY

THE HOT ROOM

CEYCHELL COUGHED VIOLENTLY. HER THROAT felt like it was burning. She brushed dirt off her face and stood up. Below her was a ledge, and far below it was a cracked, dry basin that stretched all the way to the hazy red horizon. She thought it might have been a giant lake or a sea at one time.

She walked away from the ledge into what seemed like an endless desert, orange, dusty and bleak. The sand pelted her face, and she tried to protect her eyes with her hand.

Forward she walked for hours. The clawing in her throat was driving her mad. She was so thirsty she'd thought she might shrivel up like a snakeskin. She wanted to lie down on the baked earth and sleep, but she knew she would die if she did.

At last, she collapsed hard on the dirt. Her ribs hurt, and her lips were cracked. She spat blood on the sizzling sand.

"You've come back to see me," Carbrojl said, standing over her.

She craned her neck to look up at him. He was smiling cruelly. "Not by choice."

"You're here because your subconscious is bringing you here. You are starting to learn the truth about what happened when your *gods* went to your world and corrupted it, and enslaved it, and did all those unspeakable things to the natives of your world. But you still don't know the reasons why they didn't allow me to join them. You've been told I was sealed away to contain all the dark magic and vileness. But that is all lies. I wanted to fix our world. We had the knowledge, the power, and the people to heal our dying land. But they left to consume another world."

Ceychell groaned. She pushed herself off the ground, wiped the blood from her lips, and stood up in front of Carbrojl. "I'm sorry they left you here, but they must have done it for a reason."

"Perhaps. But your wise and revered Lord Umorogrin came to me for help. He came to *me* for help when all the gods and teachers and knowledge my people left behind couldn't help him."

Ceychell was intrigued, but she felt like he was baiting her. "Why did he come to you?"

"He needed to save the Queen's daughter. She was forcing his hand with the real threat of releasing Fe Jet's hordes should the mages not come to her aid. He realized there was no magic in your world to save her daughter—only I have the knowledge to raise the dead. And then… boom—" he spread his hands out like an explosion "—ashenkin everywhere."

Ceychell gasped for breath and opened her eyes. She was on the floor of a roofless cell surrounded by metal bars with only her robe. They had taken her pack. Three other cells were connected to hers by barred gates, and a wall surrounded all four cages. One contained Simigrin. Two held corpses shriveling in the blazing sun. Ceychell sat up and leaned against the bars.

"You're awake," Simigrin grumbled. She also had only her robe.

"Where are Miraden and Lovo?" Ceychell asked. She was thirsty and sweaty, and the heat was almost as bad as that in her dream.

"I don't know, they were taken another way."

Ceychell crawled over to the bars that separated her cell from Simigrin's and whispered. "I never got to talk to you about Lord Umorogrin."

Simigrin rolled her eyes. "I don't care what you think of him. You barely know him."

"He's more involved with the ashenkin than you realize. I think he wants the crown for another reason."

"And how would you know all this?" Simigrin asked, glaring at Ceychell.

"Because," Ceychell whispered. "In my dreams—"

"You see Carbrojl. I get it. And he's telling you these lies about Lord Umorogrin?"

"He seems to know Lord Umorogrin well. I hear Carbrojl in my head when I am awake, too. I can feel him encouraging my thoughts and helping me. Every time I wake up in his world, he is there, telling me details about what happened with the ashenkin."

Simigrin stared at her in disbelief.

"I know it sounds crazy," Ceychell continued, "but it's true. The ashenkin are the stolen children transformed through a pact Khronigrin and Umorogrin made with Carbrojl."

"No!" Simigrin said and stood up. "Impossible."

Simigrin's cell door swung open and a jailor, giant and hairy with a pig's face and four arms, stepped inside. The jailor snorted and patted an iron cudgel in its hand. "Want to make racket? I help you stay calm," it said and lumbered toward Simigrin. Simigrin backed away with her hands up.

"It was me, pig!" Ceychell yelled. "I made the noise!" The huge pig guard left Simigrin's cell, slammed the door, and came into

Ceychell's. She glanced over and saw Simigrin gaping at her.

"Okay, I help you," the pig grunted.

The pig slammed the cudgel into her mid-section, and she crumpled to the ground. Her breath whooshed out so fast she couldn't even scream. She nearly passed out. Black spots swirled in her vision. When she breathed again, a stabbing pain flared in her ribs. She screamed into her sleeve to muffle the sound.

"Woman better," the pig creature said and slammed the door.

Ceychell lay on the floor crying in pain.

"Ceycha, why did you do that?" Simigrin whispered.

She didn't answer; she just wept.

Hours passed. Ceychell and Simigrin leaned against the bars of their cells in silence. The heat bore down on her but the sun had passed over the cells and the air was starting to cool. Her ribs still throbbed in pain.

"Do you think we could make it over that wall?" Ceychell whispered even though she could barely move.

"I peeked before you woke up. We are on top of a tower. It's at least a hundred foot drop."

Ceychell sighed, and the exhale made her wince in pain. She breathed shallowly and leaned to her other side. Thoughts of Miraden and Lovo brought her grief, and she wondered if she would ever see them again. She missed Miraden and wished neither Gorgundi nor Simigrin ever sent a note to entice them away from Kaehrn.

The door to her cell slammed open, and the pigman stepped inside with two scorpion guards behind him. She clutched her side and stood up to meet them.

"You come quiet?" the jailor asked. "Or I drag you?"

"Quiet," Ceychell said. The pig snorted and waved for her to follow him. The two guards stood at her sides and brought her out. The jailor retrieved Simigrin and they both walked, without restraints, down the tower steps. She shuddered with each step from the stabbing pain through her side.

Instead of walking out on the ground floor they descended another ten flights. The air was much cooler. They walked into a long, torch-lit tunnel that smelled of soot, then turned two lefts and one right and entered a great underground chamber. On the far side, Miraden and Lovo stood twenty feet from the Lorden who sat on a throne on top of a dais. Ten scorpion guards surrounded her. Behind the Lorden was a long oil basin burning hot; the guards cast monstrous shadows across the great amphitheater where stone steps rose a hundred feet high and stretched along the other three walls. The ceiling was so high she could barely see it supported by tall stone pillars.

"It's so good of you to join us," the Lorden said. "I hear one of you needed a lesson in silence."

Ceychell said nothing. She couldn't tell if the Lorden was amused or annoyed.

"I could have you fight to the death. My citizens would love that. Or I could send you out into the Suffering Sands. My scavengers would love that. Or I could impale you on the hooks I use for my most unruly citizens to send a warning to others who may come here. I would love that, but your kind don't often venture here, and you'd be pecked to the bone long before the next human stepped foot in my city. Perhaps I could ransom you, but my land is rich, as you can see, and I don't need your coin. So—"

"Why have you never tried to take back your land?" Ceychell asked.

The jailor drew the cudgel from his belt, but the Lorden put her hand up. "Let her speak."

"Where I'm from, your city and your people are just children's tales. No one outside of maybe Kander even believes you exist. If you were forced from your land, why have you not reclaimed it?"

The Lorden climbed down from her throne and slithered upon her tails over to her. She was much shorter than Ceychell, but beautiful and confident. Her golden eyes shimmered, and her skin looked smoother than silk. Ceychell noticed her face and upper body was more humanlike than the other lortaraas Ceychell had seen, and she was more delicate than muscular.

"What is your name?" she asked, studying Ceychell with her bright gold eyes.

Ceychell didn't think of a reason not to be honest, so she told her.

"And why do you care about our land and our people, Ceychell?"

"I come from a small village of simple people, but I would defend my home against those who would threaten it. When I see your might, I don't think many of the northern cities could stop it. So I don't understand why you harbor anger toward us, yet don't try to reclaim your land. Killing us doesn't solve any of that." She wheezed and wanted to hold her side but instead stayed still. Every rib ached and when she heard the jostling of the cudgel behind her, it made her shake.

The Lorden slithered back and forth for a moment. Then she asked, "And if you were ruler of the north, what would you do if my legions crossed the channel?"

"Knowing what I know now," Ceychell said, "I'd welcome you back and try to help you settle in peace."

The Lorden's eyes lit up.

"But if you tried to banish my people," Ceychell continued, "I'd fight you to the very end."

"No. Your kind would fight first and settle or beg for peace only when faced with defeat," the Lorden said.

Simigrin spoke up unexpectedly. "She isn't our kind. She has ties to the old world."

"Do you?" the Lorden mused.

"I do," Ceychell replied, slightly miffed by Simigrin's admission. "But I admit it was wrong for the people who came here from the old world to force you from your lands."

The Lorden pursed her smooth lips for a moment, and then said, "I like you, Ceychell. Since you were all bound for Queen's Edge anyway, I have a task for you. Complete it, and your sentence will be commuted."

"What must we do?" Miraden asked.

"The queen possesses a certain horn. It is a large tusk with black bands of metal, a dusty trinket that has been at Queen's Edge for ages, passed down from lord to lord, but it is quite special to me and my people. I would like it returned to us. What do you say?" The Lorden grinned, knowing what Ceychell's only answer could be.

"We will get it," Ceychell said. Miraden and Lovo also said, "We will," but Simigrin remained silent.

The Lorden shook her head slowly. Two small fangs showed when she grinned. "Now, I want to trust you, I do," the Lorden said, sliding over to Simigrin. "But I don't. I will return your equipment, provide you with food and water, and take you through the tunnel to the channel so you can escape the heat. But one of you must stay here so I can ensure you'll bring me the horn."

"We need everyone, including my bear," Miraden said, "if you really want us to bring back the horn."

The Lorden snarled and cocked her head to glance at him. A silver tongue whipped out and back, then she said, "Stealing a crown and a horn from a heavily fortified city will be a challenge, but what's to keep you from leaving here and never returning? I need some assurance." Deep in thought, the Lorden slid around Miraden, then Lovo, and then back over to Ceychell before looking up with a grin. "Ceychell, dear, if you would die for any person in your party, who would it be?"

"Miraden," she said without hesitation and pointed to him.

The Lorden looked over at Lovo. "And you, ogre?"

"Miraden," he said.

"And you, mage woman?"

"Miraden," Simigrin said.

The Lorden clapped her claws. She slithered over and then leaned in close to Miraden with narrow eyes and a smirk. "Well, this has made deciding very easy. It seems you are well loved, bear-keeper. I am curious though—what is *your* answer, Miraden."

Miraden stared at the Lorden for a long moment and said nothing. He avoided looking at anyone, then glanced Ceychell's way. Her heart fluttered; it made her so happy.

The Lorden's tongue shot out the front of her pursed lips and flicked his eyes. Miraden flinched but when the closest guard took a step forward, Miraden froze and put his hands down. "It must be hard for you to choose one when they all chose you. But I need an answer."

Miraden clenched his jaw and looked away from Ceychell, Lovo, and Simigrin. Ceychell knew that look—he wanted to get away. She knew he was in love with Simigrin, but surely he still loved her. They'd spent most of their lives together. What if he didn't pick her?

"You are trying my patience, young archer, and I have little of it already. Choose, or I'll choose for you and kill them."

Miraden folded his arms across his chest. He was panicking; Ceychell hadn't seen him this afraid in a long time. He fidgeted and finally looked at his companions. A scorpion guard grabbed Miraden's shoulder with a claw and held him still.

The Lorden sniffed and licked the air around his head. "I can taste the acridity of your anxiety. I do not envy you. You're practically oozing it. It is sweating through you. Which one do you love more?"

"Why do this? You're looking to punish someone? Just punish me and be done with it," Miraden begged.

"I'm intrigued. But mostly, I need to make sure you'll return with the horn. Choose one," the Lorden said with a cruel stare. "I won't ask again and you will be without one, permanently."

Ceychell and Simigrin stared at each other. Suddenly Ceychell regretted trying to become friends with Simigrin.

Miraden looked on the brink of tears. He pressed his eyes closed.

TWENTY·ONE

THE LONG PASSAGE

MIRADEN FELT NAUSEAS. BILE ROSE from his gut and he swallowed it down. He didn't want to answer, but he knew he must. He loved both women—it was cruel and horrible, but it was true. He stared at the Lorden and felt the serpent queen devouring his anguish.

At last, Miraden unclenched his jaw and blurted, "Simigrin." He loved her. She'd always been there for him. As much as he loved Ceychell, he felt he would betray himself if he chose her. He was surprised by how relieved he was to finally say it. He genuinely loved both of them, but his feelings for Simigrin were more than attachment and devotion; they were true love.

Ceychell turned away from him. Even though she'd told him she'd be supportive, he knew how jealous she was and that she'd never get over this. He would have to live with that for the rest of his life. It seemed ridiculous that he'd fought so hard to regain her affection and then tossed it aside. He felt terrible about hurting her again, and he despised the Lorden for forcing him to answer.

Simigrin smiled at him through her tears. He wanted to kiss her, and was thinking about doing it when the Lorden lunged at him, grabbed him, and sunk her fangs into his neck. He nearly screamed before he realized it didn't hurt.

Lovo stepped toward Miraden, but two scorpion guards poked him in the chest with their spears, stopping him.

Miraden wiped his neck. A bit of saliva mixed with blood smeared on his hand. His neck and throat burned, but not terribly.

"Lortaraas carry a slow-acting venom. It's deadly to humans, but you should have plenty of time to get to Queen's Edge and back for the antidote. I would not dally."

"What kind of venom," Ceychell asked. "What does it do?"

"He will sicken as the venom spreads until it eventually shuts down his organs," the Lorden said.

Miraden rubbed the hot spot on his neck. "Why did you make me answer when you were going to bite me anyway?"

She crept up, nose to nose with Miraden. "Watching you wallow in your self-loathing was worth it." The Lorden leaned to his ear and whispered, "And you picked the wrong one."

Miraden thought about that for a moment. How would the Lorden know anything about them?

"Now, my guards will get your things." the Lorden said and turned to her guards. "And you'll be on your way." The pig jailor lumbered off without another word.

"Where is my bear?" Miraden said.

"Your bear stays here. We will study it, and if you make it back, and it is still alive, perhaps you can have it back."

Miraden seethed in silence.

The guards returned their equipment and escorted them through an underground chamber, a wide tunnel, then down a long narrow tunnel. Though Miraden was happy to have his bow and things back, having to crush Ceychell was still top of mind. But he said nothing. He could feel the pressure mounting from Ceychell while she geared up without a word.

The Lorden and a host of scorpion guards walked with them. When they reached the end of the tunnel, the Lorden smiled and said, "I am heartened that you have chosen to accept this mission. My guards have food and water that should be enough for your journey." The Lorden slithered up to Ceychell, cupped her face, and winked. "I know you desire to unleash your power. Save it. Don't abandon this mission. Perhaps I'll have a use for you afterward."

Miraden wasn't facing the Lorden when he asked, "Lorden, can I please take my bear?" He squeezed his bow and clenched his jaw.

"We had to feed it goldroot. It was aggressive and specimens from the north are quite valuable down here. Must you take it? I'd be willing to compensate you for the creature when you return."

"I need my bear." Miraden said. "We are going to get your horn—that was the deal."

The Lorden shook her head and wagged her tongue as she thought. "Very well, a bear will be an encumbrance. I hope you don't regret bringing it. Farewell adventurers." The Lorden waved to a scorpion guard to fetch Tundra.

Twenty minutes later a guard brought Tundra down the tunnel. She looked groggy and tired. Miraden ran up and hugged her. The bear rubbed her neck on him and pushed him over. He scratched her ears, and she licked his face. He gave her a piece of the food the guards had given him, and she eagerly followed him.

They started northbound down the straight tunnel that faded into darkness.

The monotony of walking through a tunnel and seeing nothing but the occasional torch was stupefying. No one spoke about their time in Fe Jet. Miraden felt awful. Ceychell had not even looked at him for hours. She walked with her head lowered. He wondered if she'd ever forgive him. Then Simigrin grabbed his hand and gave it a squeeze. She was trying to cheer him up, but he was too dejected.

Simigrin whispered something to Lovo but Miraden couldn't make it out. Then Lovo walked over to Ceychell and whispered to her. Lovo and Ceychell stopped, and Lovo pressed his hand to Ceychell's injured ribs and said a prayer. Ceychell closed her eyes and shook. Then she put her hand on his face and thanked him.

Simigrin walked up to Miraden and said, "We can find an antidote in Sentry. We should not come back to Fe Jet."

"Don't you remember the tale of the lortaraas and the lord?" Ceychell asked her as they began walking again.

"It is a fairy tale," Simigrin said.

"Are you sure? I'm not anymore," Ceychell said.

"I don't remember it," Lovo said.

Ceychell put her arm around Lovo's and started, "There was a lortaraas who was so beautiful she was adored by the villagers. She was considered the most beautiful creature in the kingdom. The local lord paid to have her captured, and a band of trappers caught her in a net in the forest. They brought her to the lord, and he kept her prisoner at his keep.

"She had a lovely voice, and she sang him to sleep every night, and he quickly fell in love with her. But every time he tried to kiss her, she pushed him away and told him that she was poisonous, and, if he kissed her, he would die.

"The lord hired alchemists, witches, and mages from the far reaches of the land, but none of them knew how to counteract the poison. They all agreed that it was a weak poison, but knew of nothing that could counteract it.

"The lord grew desperate and began to lose his mind. The lortaraas begged him to set her free, for she would rather they love each other from afar and live to be old, than for him to die. The lord called her a monster and refused to free her. The lord cursed the gods that he could not love the one person he desired most in the world.

"So one day, while she was sleeping, he crept into her chamber and kissed her. At first his heart nearly burst with love and passion. But the next day, he grew ill, and his health declined steadily from then on. All the poison brewers and alchemists and healers from the Mother of Light couldn't help him. The lortaraas stayed by his side and wept. When it was finally clear he was dying, he reached up from his bed, pulled her close, and said, "To—"

"To live is to die," Simigrin cut in, "but to love is to live."

The big man shrugged. "If she's right, Mir, there is no known cure for the venom."

Simigrin scoffed, "That story is a thousand years old. There has to be a cure."

"Why not get the horn?" Miraden asked. "The Lorden must know the cure."

Simigrin grabbed his arm to stop him. "Because it is the Horn of Syindella," she said. "The war the Lorden mentioned was an ancient war between monsters and humans. The part the Lorden left out was that the war was very short, and the humans realized that they were losing badly, so the mages created the horn. They marshaled the human armies to meet the monsters for a final battle, which drew the entire monster kingdom to the fight. But instead of fighting them, the mages broke the continent in two, with the monsters on the southern divide. They blew the horn and from that point, the land was cursed. The one human city that was south is now a ruin and forests and farms dried up into this hell of a desert.

"However, humans are able to come south but the monsters cannot go north until the horn is blown again. The monsters to the north are just the fragments of the native beings in this world.

I always assumed that all the monsters trapped here in the south died out."

"I guess not," Ceychell said.

Simigrin started walking again with Miraden. She said, "Everyone in Kander learns this story as a child. I was told the desert was abandoned, and that's why no one traveled to it. Now I see that it was a lie. I always thought these were just stories, but now I think the horn is real, and it is all that prevents Lorden Flisstriq from sending her army north to conquer Kanderlus."

Miraden wasn't so sure. It seemed possible, and very likely. But if he doesn't bring her the horn, he believed he would die. He had little hope there was a known cure, but asked, "What do you suggest I do then, if we don't bring the horn back?"

"We are getting the horn," Ceychell insisted, "and the crown."

Lovo put a hand on Miraden's shoulder. "You okay, Mir?"

Miraden appreciated the compassion, but he wasn't okay, and he knew Lovo sensed it. "No, buddy, I'm not okay."

They walked down the tunnel for a mind-numbing few days. He wasn't sure exactly how long, but they stopped for a long sleep three times. When they stopped again, Ceychell sat down below a torch, and away from Miraden and their other two friends. She still hadn't looked at Miraden since the lortaraas had forced him to choose between the two women. She took a letter from her pack and read it silently to herself. The letter looked like the one Kyradel had sent him. He wouldn't have been surprised if Kyradel had written to Ceychell, and he wished he knew what the letter said.

Miraden got up, stretched his legs, walked over, and sat beside Ceychell. She wiped her eyes and put the letter away.

"Hey Ceycha," Miraden whispered. "I'm sorry."

"Not as sorry as I am," she said, shrugging her shoulders. "The pain I'm feeling is what I put you through. I deserve it."

Miraden's throat tightened. She didn't *deserve* it. He put his arm around her and pulled her close. When she leaned her head against his, he felt like a child again, joyous and free. He hoped they would still be friends when this was all over. "You don't deserve it, Ceycha. You deserve to be happy. And I will always be there for you."

She smiled through her tears, placed her fingers on his lips and whispered, "I want more than that."

Miraden was aroused, but even more anxious. He returned to Lovo and Simigrin, lay down against Tundra's back and tried to fall asleep.

They traveled for what seemed like another two days until they found an exit off the main tunnel. They walked up a flight of stone steps into an empty chamber and out onto a rocky hill near a coastal village. The sun was setting on the dessert to the west. A village was at the edge of a great fjord cut between the two continents. Behind them was an endless sea of golden sand, spotted by the occasional dead tree. He noticed Ceychell staring at him watery-eyed. When he looked at her, she wiped her eyes and looked away.

Simigrin pointed to the channel, "Syindella Channel is right in front of us. That is where we would have come out before heading north to Sentry."

"Let's keep moving," Lovo said.

They walked down to the small port. Next to the docks were fewer than ten buildings and a few score houses that made up the village. The people, mostly fishermen it seemed, had furry goat heads and hooves on otherwise human bodies. When the four proceeded to join them on a dock with a few fishing boats bobbing at its sides, the goat people gawked at them, open-mouthed.

Miraden walked up to one of the people on the dock, a female, he guessed, since she was smaller and had much shorter horns than the others. Her face was covered in brown and white fur. She wore a yellow linen coverall and a great brimmed hat. She had a reed basket filled with silver fish over her shoulder. On her other shoulder was a pole and a seaweed line. Her hooves were barely covered by her outfit. She looked at him with one blue and one green eye then stared at Tundra nervously.

"Hello," he said.

She was startled and then returned, "Hello."

"I… was hoping to get passage to Queen's Edge?" Miraden said.

"What are you doing here?" she said.

Miraden looked at the others. Simigrin shrugged.

The goat woman adjusted her hat. "Humans don't come here," she said. She clicked her tongue and hefted the basket on her shoulder.

"We shipwrecked west of here and just want to get home," Miraden said.

The goat woman looked past them to the west. She coughed and then said, "Ships come through the channel. They always go north. No ships come here."

"Perhaps we could purchase a boat, or a ride … on a boat?" Ceychell asked.

The goat woman's mouth dropped open. She looked at Miraden's companions and then back at Miraden. "Okay. Come," she said.

They followed her from the pier to a shack at the edge of the village. The sun had nearly set, and a guard who looked like the lortaraas's scorpion guards was lighting street lanterns.

The goat woman opened the wooden-plank door of the shack, spoke to someone inside, and then waved Miraden and his friends inside.

The shack had nets, buckets, and harpoons on the wall. Glass containers full of salt-water and fish took up most of the store. A goat man, as big as Lovo, stood up behind a shelf of fish. He was brown and broad-chested, with massive horns that curved down and back then pointed straight out. He wore a white apron covered in fish guts. He and the goat woman bleated back and forth for almost a minute.

"Do you know what they're saying?" Miraden asked Simigrin. She shrugged.

At last, the goat man stepped out from behind his counter. His hoofsteps shook the floor. He grabbed a harpoon off of the wall and pointed it at Miraden. "We trust no humans."

Tundra roared and scared the goat man. The harpoon fell from his hand as he backed away.

"It's okay, girl," Miraden said and scratched her head. He slowly picked up the harpoon and placed it back on the wall hooks.

"We don't want to cause any trouble. We just want to head north. Can you help us get to Queen's Edge?"

The goat people exchanged a glance. "I'll take you to the edge. No further." he said and nodded. "Tomorrow."

The goat man ushered them outside and closed the door behind them. The evening had started to cool down.

"How do you think that went?" Lovo asked.

"They might help us. They might be waiting for us with more of those terrible guards," Simigrin said. "Either way, we should get some rest."

Miraden didn't want to sleep at an inn, so they went to the other edge of town near the rocky top of the fjord and found a cave to camp in.

They lit a small fire and ate some of the rations the Lorden had given them. Miraden chewed on a dried, bitter wafer. He felt ill and his vision was blurry at the edges. He didn't want the others to become overly concerned, so he kept it to himself.

"If they can't go north," Lovo asked, "where will he be taking us?"

"Maybe some of them can go north," Miraden said.

"I don't think so," Simigrin said. "Whatever enchantment is stopping them has been in place for a thousand years."

"Maybe they can at least take us across the channel," Lovo said. "We can start walking north from there."

Miraden looked over at Ceychell. She was sitting at the mouth of the cave staring at the moon over the channel. He wanted to talk to her, but she obviously didn't want to talk to him.

Eventually, they gathered together at the fire, and Ceychell, Simigrin, and Lovo went to sleep.

Miraden couldn't sleep so he sat outside the cave on a boulder overlooking the ocean with Tundra snoring next to him. He had no desire to be on the water again and hoped their crossing would be much shorter and far less perilous than the last one.

His stomach was upset, and his joints ached. He considered what Simigrin had said, and wondered if she was right—they shouldn't go back to the Lorden. His death would be nothing compared to saving the north from an invasion. After all, if they stopped the ashenkin just to be overrun by Fe Jet's army, what good would it do?

Simigrin sat down next to him. Lost in his thoughts, he hadn't heard her coming. She hugged him and held him tight. She leaned back just enough to be face to face with him. Her eyes were puffy and red but she smiled anyway.

"What were you going to tell me in the garden?" he whispered.

She pulled her hair behind her ears and whispered, "I feel you in my heart." Her lips were trembling. "I'll find a way to help you, without the horn. You have to trust me. I can't lose you."

"I do trust you, Simi." He kissed her and felt a rush of warmth in his chest. The coastal wind blew her soft hair against his cheeks. He wished they could sit there forever.

"I know you love Ceychell, and I know how hard it was for you to make that choice. I feel terrible about it too. I've gotten to know her, and she's great, just like Kyradel said. I understand her quality that you spoke of so often in our last journey." She took out a letter that looked like the one he got from Kyradel and handed it to him.

He opened it and recognized her handwriting immediately.

Hi Simi!

I miss you! I hope they made you head wizard by now. You deserve it! I can never thank you enough for saving me. My family is eternally grateful. I hope one day you'll join us at Valdenfest. It's a good time up here in the villages of Baregorin.

I know Miraden has fallen for you. He is so great—you're so lucky, but so is he! It will break my sister's heart. I love my sister more than anyone in the world and if it was anyone but you, I'd come after you with claws and teeth out! Take care of Miraden. And be kind to my sister, she's really wonderful. You'll see when you get to know her.

Give Miraden a big hug from me. I'll come see you all soon.

Kyradel

TWENTY·TWO

THE PACT

CEYCHELL WIPED HER EYES. SHE knew where she was by the cracked earth and the heat. A blue portal was swirling just off the ground a short distance away. She walked to it.

As she approached the portal, Lord Umorogrin stepped out of it. His hair was fully black and an inch shorter. His face looked younger, and he wore a neat black beard. Ceychell ran up to ask him for help but he didn't seem to notice her. Another mage in a red robe emerged from the portal behind him. He was handsome, slightly younger looking than Umorogrin and taller than her. He had long dreadlocks and a long, black beard. Then, around thirty more mages in red robes and a host of children and young mages from the university came out of the portal. The children complained and started coughing.

"Lord, I'm so glad you're here!" Ceychell said, waving at him. "Lord Umorogrin! Hey, can't you hear me?" Still, he seemed not to notice her.

"Okay, let's find him," Lord Umorogrin said and walked right through Ceychell. None of them seemed to see her. She tried to touch the handsome mage's red robe, but her hand slipped right through it. Then she noticed the book he held—it looked exactly like hers, but it wasn't covered in black veins. Fastened to his belt was a red enchanted sack that was darker than hers.

"I don't like this one bit," the handsome mage said. "Why are we succumbing to the queen's threats? I think we need to tell her she just has to mourn her loss." She thought he might be Khronigrin.

"It's not that simple. She has a personal grudge against me and if she is going mad, she may be mad enough to blow that horn," Lord Umorogrin said. "We've come too far to turn back now. Besides, think of how we can change the world if we are able to reach into the afterlife."

"I don't agree with this hubris and I don't think we should reach for anything that's passed on. This sorcerer is not going to help us," the handsome mage whispered.

"Look," Umorogrin said and stopped to face the man. "We just need to learn how to resurrect the princess and then we can close this portal. We just don't have that knowledge in Kander."

The fire mage shook his head. "*If* we can close the portal."

Ceychell followed them over a cracked landscape where she saw Carbrojl standing in the middle of the vast wasteland ahead. Beside him, a glowing, transparent young girl was floating just off the ground. Her golden dress flickered in the pale light, and her long, black hair frayed into wisps of smoke at its ends.

Carbrojl seemed to be waiting patiently, his robe blowing in the harsh wind. The mages and children gathered around him. Ceychell stepped up right beside Lord Umorogrin, knowing he could not see her.

"I am pleased you've come," Carbrojl said. "Young Kalionite here"—he gestured to the floating ghost girl—"misses her mother more than you know." Kalionite wept and hid her face in Carbrojl's robes. "Shhh, it will be over soon," he whispered.

"We are here to start the ritual," Lord Umorogrin said. "Queen Siennah is eager to be reunited with her daughter. I've brought Khronigrin, headmaster of Vfindisiss Kar. These are his disciples with souls of fire. They have come, just as you've asked. Perhaps after this ritual, you would share what happened when the Liches came to our world. Their mentions of you in the texts are quite dark, and we wish to know more."

Carbrojl nodded and said, "I would be delighted."

Khronigrin leaned through Ceychell and whispered to Umorogrin, "We need to walk away. Something isn't right."

"Now," Carbrojl continued, evidently not hearing him. "You've brought her crown?" He held out his gray hand.

Khronigrin glowered and drew a golden diadem from the red enchanted bag at his side. He stared at the crown for a moment. It seemed plain for a princess's crown—a single emerald at the front of a gold band. The emerald reflected the brooding red and orange of the sky, but the golden band gleamed.

Lord Khronigrin walked up to Carbrojl, hesitated, and then handed him the crown.

"Excellent," Carbrojl said. He placed the crown on Kalionite's head. She closed her eyes and seemed to disappear into the golden band. Carbrojl tossed the crown to Umorogrin. "Take the crown of Kalionite back to Queen Siennah. Tell her if she keeps it close and guards it with everything at her disposal, soon her daughter's soul will return to her body."

"It will be done," Lord Umorogrin said. "Thank you."

"My pleasure, truly," Carbrojl said. Khronigrin stood tentatively before Carbrojl, clutching his book to his chest. The children nervously clung to the legs of the fire mages or hid behind them.

"I'm curious what your name was going to be," Khronigrin asked Carbrojl.

"Name?" Carbrojl looked perplexed.

"The Liches came to our world, and before they moved on, they took on new names. They became gods. Surely you had one picked out before you were left stranded here." Khronigrin scowled while he waited for an answer.

"Ahh, yes. I believe it was going to be Greatfather of Dreams. Or some such nonsense. Now, give me that book of yours," Carbrojl said and extended a hand toward Khronigrin.

"Why should I?" Khronigrin said.

"All the power of that book originated with me. Everything. You can't light a candle unless you pull from my power, and so I'm curious what secrets you've discovered."

Khronigrin stared at him. Then he looked at Umorogrin, and the older mage nodded. Khronigrin handed Carbrojl the book.

Carbrojl took the book with both hands. "Quite impressive that my old companions figured out so many of my spells without my ever teaching them." Black lines bled from his palms across the book's red cover, thickening and darkening as they spread around the book. "However, they weren't able to understand most of my power. They thought it was all fire and portals. But it's not, is it?" Carbrojl and Khronigrin stared at each other. Ceychell could feel the tension between them. "You call on my power frequently. You are particularly fond of diving into minds."

Khronigrin flushed and swallowed so deeply his Adam's apple bobbed.

Ceychell recalled a spell to jump into someone's dreams or invade their thoughts. She was curious, having never tried them. She was tempted to dive into Miraden's mind, but she could never forgive herself if she did.

"Now, my children," Carbrojl said, extending the book to Khronigrin, "all of you will stay here with me. I have so much to teach you, so much time to make up. You must be ready when my devoted fleshsacks call you back to your world."

Khronigrin took hold of the book, and his eyes shot open. He stepped back and tried to jerk the book from Carbrojl's grip, but failed, though Carbrojl didn't seem to struggle at all. "We cannot stay here with you."

"It's time for us to be getting back," Lord Umorogrin said. "The queen—"

Carbrojl pointed his hand toward Lord Umorogrin and the lord flew back through the portal. It closed behind him, leaving all the fire mages and children with their new master.

Khronigrin burst into a tower of flames. He screamed as the mages panicked and the children ran.

Ceychell's skin went cold. Her chest was heavy and throat constricted so tight she couldn't breathe. Her vision dotted black and she collapsed.

TWENTY·THREE

THE CHANNEL

SIMIGRIN COILED AROUND MIRADEN AND held him tight. They lay in front of Tundra, sharing a blanket. He still had trouble sleeping, but he lay very still to make sure she did. Ceychell was sprawled near the campfire, jerking and twitching in her sleep. Miraden thought she was hiding something from him, something important. They used to tell each other everything. Perhaps she didn't trust him as much as she used to.

Lovo brought large palm fronds he must have gathered outside. He brought them to the fire near the cave entrance and dropped a few on the smoldering coals. He's been sullen since Chintaja left, Miraden's noticed it getting worse over the past few days. Especially on the long tunnel walk. Chintaja inspired him, made him feel better about himself. He remembered Lovo telling him one evening at the university, *My whole life I've always had two left feet, an unlucky star, and less than a day's wages in my pocket. Everything changed for me the day you showed up in Bilore Des. And it changed again when I met Chintaja.*

"Do you think he got my letter?" Lovo whispered. "I hope I am a bit luckier than Ceychell was in sending letters to you." Lovo sat down and slumped. "I wonder if I will ever see him again."

"I think you will," Miraden told him, though he really didn't know. He was suddenly feeling flush with heat but not from the fire. His stomach twisted and roiled as sickness washed over him. He laid his head back on the rocks and closed his eyes hoping it would pass.

Ceychell screamed.

Tundra growled, stood on her hind legs then fell on all fours and ran out of the cave.

Miraden jumped up, knocking Simigrin off him, and clamped his mouth shut to hold back his vomit. The cave was dark except for the embers of their fire. Lovo rushed over to Ceychell, grabbed her and tried to wake her up. She flailed and struggled against him. Simigrin and Miraden watched in alarm. The big man could barely hold her. Miraden tried to help hold her arms but to no avail. He couldn't believe her strength when she tossed him against the cave wall.

At last, Miraden screamed, "Ceychell!" and she opened her eyes. Sweat dripped from her face and she was breathing hard. She looked at Lovo for a second like she didn't recognize him and then over at Miraden.

"Ceycha, are you okay?" Miraden asked.

She grimaced and pulled herself from Lovo's grip. Then she sat up and wiped the sweat away on her sleeves and hid her face.

"That was quite a dream," Lovo said. "You're burning up. He pressed the back of his hand to her cheek.

"No," she said softly. "It was no dream." She looked over at Simigrin "Your *Lord* started this whole ashenkin problem. I saw the whole thing."

Simigrin balked. "How could you see that? You've been talking crazy about him since we left Kander, and I'm tired of it."

Ceychell and Simigrin stood up and stared each other down. Miraden and Lovo stepped between them.

"He's rotten," Ceychell said. "I don't believe any of that benevolent mentor crap. "He's sending us to get the crown to cover up his mistake."

Simigrin scowled at her. "What mistake? How could you speak ill of him? Look at how far you've come in such a short time! He broke the rules letting you in and took a great risk on you. He spared no resources to teach and prepare you and this is how you repay him? By slandering him?"

"Umorogrin needs me!" Ceychell yelled. "Or something from me. He didn't bring me to the university out of kindness!" She balled her fists in front of her.

"And what if he did? He believes you are key to ending the ashenkin. That's why we are on this mission."

Ceychell shook her head and pursed her lips. "We are on his terrible mission because of his mistakes. I *saw* it. All of it," Ceychell spat. "He brought Khronigrin and the fire mages, even the children, through a portal to meet with Carbrojl. They sought his help to resurrect Princess Kalionite." She pulled the book from her bag and held it toward Simigrin. "This was Lord Khronigrin's book. It turned black when Carbrojl touched it. Khronigrin didn't want to make a deal with Carbrojl, Umorogrin did. And it cost Umorogrin the entire order of fire mages."

"You are sure about this?" Miraden asked.

"Yes," Ceychell said, "I'm positive. Carbrojl shows me what happened while I sleep."

Simigrin shook her head. "I've known Lord Umorogrin my entire life. He's the only father I've ever known. He made me who I am. He is not the monster you say he is. You're letting your dreams and

Carbrojl deceive you. They are only dreams!"

"Uhhg." Simigrin rolled her eyes theatrically. "Can you talk some sense into her?" Lovo glanced at Ceychell and then backed away. Miraden wanted to say something, but he didn't know what.

"You are not falling for visions," Simigrin said. "Even if he is real, he's in some other world!"

Lovo cleared his throat and said, "He feels pretty real, Simi."

"Lord Umorogrin *is* real, and I trust him," Simigrin shouted, throwing her hands in the air, "she's just having bad dreams! What should we do, Ceychell? Go home? Go and tell Lord Umorogrin he's a monster?"

Miraden had never seen Simigrin so upset. He wanted to say something to calm her down, but he was afraid of angering her even more. "Can we all calm down?" he said at last, and wiped sweat from his brow. He thought he might throw up at any moment. "What if Ceychell is right?"

"I *am* right, Miraden," Ceychell said and got in Simigrin's face. "Why would I lie about this?"

"How can she be right?" Simigrin yelled and leaned up on her toes to push nose to nose with Ceychell. "They're just dreams."

Miraden wanted to walk away from the yelling, but then both women would be angry at him.

"Whoa now," Lovo said, like a schoolmaster. "You both need to sleep this off. We'll chat about it on our trip north.." Lovo slid his arms between them and parted them.

Ceychell and Simigrin stared hard at each other for a tense few moments, then Ceychell turned and walked away into the cave. She stopped about fifty feet from their camp and laid down her blanket. Simigrin turned and went back up to the boulder where she'd been sleeping.

Lovo grabbed Miraden's shoulder and whispered, "Best to let

them both have some peace to think through this." Then he pulled out his harp and strummed and hummed the tune Kyradel had shown him. Miraden lay down and fell asleep, and was not awoken until morning.

The sun lit up the cave mouth, and a cool breeze blew over the camp. Lovo and Tundra had already caught some fish, and Lovo was cooking it up. Miraden felt terrible and ate nothing. No one said a word about the previous night's argument.

They met the goat man at the dock, standing in front of a twenty-foot fishing boat. The boat was made of thatched reeds coated in a black sticky goo and seemed to be rotting from the bottom up by the look of the brown reeds below the water line. The vessel bucked and swayed when Lovo stepped into it. The goat man yelled something Miraden didn't understand. Then Tundra climbed into the boat and the goat man screamed angrily.

"Sorry about that," Lovo said. He sat down slowly and took an oar as the others climbed aboard. "I can row—"

The goat man snatched the oar from his hands. He took both oars and rowed them along the coast of the fjord. The current was strong, but the goat man rowed hard. The sway of the boat was too much. Miraden leaned over and vomited. He doesn't feel right at all. He saw spots from the pressure and heard the goat man's grumbling. He didn't dare look back.

The goat man brought them to a small outcrop of dry beach below the sheer cliff on the southern side of the channel. He barked at them and waved at them to get out.

Miraden was confused, as were the others, but it seemed like they were at their stop. He got out of the boat and helped the others as well. As soon as they were on dry land, the goat man rowed away.

There was a sinking sensation in Miraden's stomach but it wasn't vomit. Tundra circled around the group and backed up against the cliff wall. She moaned.

"Is this right?" Simigrin asked.

A cliff wall behind them, three times taller than the largest trees in Baregorin, was covered in cracks. Birds flew far overhead, hardly visible in the morning sunlight. In front of them was a wide channel, possibly two hundred feet across, and then another sheer wall.

Miraden closed his eyes, took in a deep breath and opened them, perhaps hoping he would see something different, but the scene was the same—hopeless. He scratched Tundra behind the ear and realized how beautiful the fjord was in the early morning. The sun was orange and glaring on the ocean horizon. Birds circled over the water and dove into the sea for fish. It smelled far brinier than the Skolace, likely from the stagnant pools on the small land patch where they were stranded. Lovo walked a few steps and lifted his foot up.

"It's soggy," he said.

Simigrin tested the ground for herself. "That means it's probably under water when the tide comes in."

Miraden looked for a path up the cliff, but didn't find one. He didn't think even he could climb it without equipment; he was sure Simigrin couldn't.

"I hope someone else sails through here soon," Ceychell said.

"Can you freeze a bridge to the other side?" Lovo asked Simigrin.

Simigrin shook her head. "Even if I could, then what? We'd have a melting bridge under us and cliff we can't climb."

Miraden dug through his bag and found the silver seeing glass that Jojhor, Chieftain of Storjn, had given him. He stretched it out and looked west down the channel. Everything looked close up but it was also bouncing around and hard to focus. Miraden realized his arm was shaking.

"Let me take a look, Mir," Lovo said.

Miraden handed Lovo the glass; Lovo set the bigger end on

Miraden's head, and peered through it. Miraden almost laughed but he remained still and watched beautiful colors reflecting on the sand from the scope's crystal.

"Hmm, wooden boards," Lovo said. He slowly turned the end of the lens. "Oh, I do see a ship. Let me just turn this slowly." He briefly played with the end. "They are quite a ways out, but they are heading this direction."

"How far out are they?" Ceychell asked.

"Let's hope it's less than a few hours," Simigrin said. "Or else we are going to be underwater.

A few hours passed, but the ship didn't seem any closer, and Lovo was complaining about being hungry. Waves were lapping onto the beach outcrop. There was nowhere to start a fire even if Lovo caught some fish.

"We may have to try the bridge," Miraden said.

"Why don't I just freeze this spot so we can at least get away from the water?" Simigrin said. "It might buy us enough time."

Miraden nodded, and Simi's book popped up in front of her.

Tundra seemed hungry, too. She rolled in the sand, then shook the sand and water from her fur. Miraden and the others shielded their faces.

Simigrin smirked and brushed the wet sand off her chest. "Thanks for that, girl." Then went back to her book.

Lovo put down the scope and walked to the edge of the outcrop; Miraden followed him. A pair of large, green eyes were peering at Lovo from just below the surface. Lovo pulled his mace and smacked it. A gargantuan serpent with a broad jaw full of teeth bucked out of the water. Lovo cracked it on the head again, and it vanished below the waves. Then he turned around and looked at Miraden.

"You okay?" Lovo asked.

"I really hate sea creatures," Miraden said, trembling from head to toe.

At last, Simigrin pointed her staff and drew an arc around their strip of land. A barrier of ice three feet high formed around them and crackled as it thickened.

"That will hold for a while, let's hope the boat gets here soon."

Less than an hour later, Simigrin had to rebuild the wall. The heat and saltwater were melting it away.

"I see a ship," Ceychell said, pointing out where Lovo had been looking.

Miraden shielded his eyes from the sun directly overhead and saw the ship too. He hoped they were friendly even though he didn't really want to get on another boat, especially since he already felt like throwing up.

After another hour, the sea was seeping over the ice wall and they would have been waist deep were it not for Simigrin's. He squeezed her hand and thanked her.

"Hey!" Ceychell yelled.

"Over here!" Lovo yelled, waving his hands in the air.

A large blue galley, five canon portals on its side, and at least twenty men on deck were less than a mile away. The warship's golden sails were full of wind.

"A Crestain war ship?" Simigrin said.

"At least they aren't at war with us," Miraden said.

"Lovo!" someone yelled from the boat.

Everyone looked at Lovo in surprise. Lovo smiled and waved his hands and yelled back, "It's me! Come get us!"

The men on deck scrambled. One of the men yelled something at the others, but Miraden couldn't quite hear what.

Simigrin gaped at Lovo. "Who the—"

"It's Chintaja. We are in luck!" Lovo said. Miraden wasn't sure how he knew.

Before long the ship dropped anchor in the fjord. A group of sailors rowed a dinghy toward them. When it reached the ice wall, Chintaja jumped out on to the beach and embraced Lovo so tightly Miraden thought they might crush each other.

"Thank the Mother of Light you're here. We've had a rough couple of weeks."

Chintaja kissed him and rubbed his head. "Lovo, my friend, I hope you are still chasing the crown. Come." Chintaja waved for them to get in the dinghy. "Let's get you back to the ship." As Chintaja helped them over the ice wall, he asked, "How did you get here? The tide was going to wash you away!" It took both Chintaja and Lovo to get Tundra into the boat.

"It's a long story," Lovo said. "I'll tell you when we get to your ship."

"Chieftain Ceychell," Chintaja said with a slight dip of his head. "I hope the ship will be to your liking."

Ceychell grinned. "As long as it has food and can outrun a storm, it will be to my liking."

TWENTY·FOUR

THE SCURVY DOGS

THERE WERE ABOUT FORTY SAILORS on the ship. None of them were armored, like Chintaja, nor did they wear common colors. Ceychell guessed they were most likely mercenaries or conscripts. She wasn't sure if they were on a Crestain warship, or Chintaja and his men had captured one, but once again, she was on a ship with only men, save Simigrin and herself. She pulled up her hood, crossed her arms, and leaned on the port-side railing next to Miraden.

Chintaja spoke with Lovo, but Ceychell couldn't make out what they were discussing. She glared at Simigrin, who was standing on the other side of Miraden, and Simigrin returned the gesture. She was surprised Simigrin didn't believe her about Umorogrin. She'd thought they shared a close bond, thought she could trust her, but now realized she needed to be more guarded. She'd needed to be guarded against the sailors, too, many of whom were staring at her unabashedly. She turned away from them and looked out to sea.

"You okay?" Miraden asked Simigrin.

"Not really. I'm glad this ship came along, but I don't feel comfortable being onboard with these sailors."

"Don't worry," Miraden said, smiling. "After you freeze one or two of them, they'll all go back to their business." She laughed and kissed his scrubby cheek.

Ceychell fumed but tried not to react. She refused to show any weakness around them.

Lovo came stomping back from his talk with Chintaja. "Hey, good news."

Ceychell swallowed her fury and listened.

"Chintaja bought passage with the Crestain Navy to sail to Sentry after he got my letter. So he talked to the captain, and the captain said he'll take us there and back to the port town with the goat people if we are quick about it."

Miraden nodded. "That is good news."

"Yep. We're in luck," Lovo said.

Chintaja came walking over a moment later. "Let's crack open a rum barrel tonight. You good folks could use a cup." Ceychell noticed that a few sailors had followed him over. "My dear friend Lovo is good on his harp," Chintaja said and the sailors cheered.

Ceychell wasn't in the mood to cheer. She pulled out her book and decided to study up on her portal spells. Next time they're stranded, she might need it.

Later that evening, red clouds blanketed the horizon. A pleasant breeze blew off the water, and there was no land in sight. Ceychell sat on the deck with a bowl of goop that smelled like fish with cornmeal and a moldy piece of bread. There were silvery bits floating on the top. Not exactly what she'd hoped for, but she was grateful for it.

Miraden sat on the deck next to Tundra. He looked a bit green, and the food bowl in front of him was still full. Tundra groaned and nuzzled her head against him. He scratched her chest for a moment, but his shoulders slumped and his eyes were only half open. Tundra leaned over and sniffed his soup and took a large slurp.

Simigrin sat alone on the deck, staring out to sea. Ceychell thought about thanking her for saving them earlier. Had she not created the barrier, they would have had to either climb the cliff or swim the channel.

Miraden nearly toppled over, but he put his hand out just in time. Ceychell slid over next to him, put her arm around him, and offered him some water. Miraden took a sip and barely looked at her.

She took a bite of the pungent soup, grimaced, and forced it down. It was fishy, greasy and, unsalted.

Lovo, sitting on the deck with his harp lying beside him, was lapping at the bottom of his bowl. When he finished, he picked up his harp and started to play. Chintaja sat down next to him and closed his eyes. Lovo's harp playing was improving, and his melodious humming helped Ceychell relax.

A sailor with a fiddle joined Lovo. They began dancing and hopping on the deck, and another sailor with a flute entered the song. Soon all the sailors were singing and clapping, and Ceychell couldn't help but clap along. It was a pleasant finish to a day that had started out precariously.

She glanced over at Simigrin. She was staring out to sea again, the only one not enjoying the song. Ceychell had to find a way to convince Simigrin that Lord Umorogrin was deceiving them. But not tonight.

Later in the evening, when many of the sailors were passed out on the deck, a few of the less inebriated ones tried to come talk to her or Simigrin, but Lovo shooed them away immediately. Then Lovo and Chintaja retired below deck.

Miraden and Simigrin were asleep against Tundra. Ceychell was worried about the toxin. She thought she might be able to slow its progress if they could find an alchemist in Sentry. He was sleeping peacefully, but he was very pale and almost green, and his eyes ringed with black circles. She crawled around Tundra's rear end, took hold of Miraden's hand, and lay down next to him, but she couldn't fall asleep.

When it was pitch dark, she walked to the aft of the ship, navigating between the snoring and drooling bodies of the sailors, and dangled her legs off the side. A year ago she would have loved to be sailing again, but after being shipwrecked and marooned, she had mixed feelings about being out to sea. Nevertheless the creaking of the ship and the lapping of the water off the hull soothed her tense nerves. Occasionally, the sailor on watch passed by her, but he paid her no mind.

The following day, when the scorching sun was at its peak, Ceychell saw land on the western horizon. Her heart filled with hope, and she stared out over the rail until the land faded away. Simigrin stood next to her, staring beside her and holding onto the rail. Her hood was up and she had been quiet all day since they got onboard. Without a word, Simigrin wandered off. Nevertheless, Ceychell needed to talk to her, not about Miraden, but about Umorogrin.

Lovo walked up beside her. His shirt was off and his shoulders were pink. He was coiling a line from a pile around his arms that were broader than her thighs.

He smiled at her and she smiled back. "Don't take the Lorden's game to heart. Miraden had to pick one of you," Lovo leaned down and whispered.

Ceychell was determined not to cry. She looked to her side and bit her lip.

"He did choose. And I do take it to heart," Ceychell said. "I don't blame him at all, but I don't have to like it."

Lovo nodded and started undoing a knot in the line. "Ceychell, I don't know what is in store for us but I'm glad you're here. You are every bit as tough and brave as Miraden said you were."

Ceychell held her tears back and smiled. She looked over and saw Simigrin sitting next to Miraden. His hair was disheveled but he didn't look as green today. He was sitting on a barrel, tossing fish bits to Tundra to the delight of a few crewmembers who had taken a liking to the massive creature. Miraden gently scratched Tundra's face, and the bear licked his cheek. Simigrin put a hand on his shoulder and whispered something into his ear.

Ceychell turned away from them. "Kyra told me that, when they were on the island, Miraden became very depressed when he finally accepted that I no longer loved him. It wasn't true, but it's what he believed. Now I feel that way. Except, for me, it's not a misunderstanding. He just doesn't love me anymore."

Lovo's eyes were tearing. He stopped wrapping the rope around his arm for a moment, but said nothing. She hoped she would get some time alone with Miraden, but he and Tundra were often surrounded by sailors… and Simigrin. Perhaps, she'd have a chance in Sentry.

"Take a look," Lovo said, interrupting Ceychell's rumination. He pointed ahead of the boat. A strip of land, dense green in the sunlight, lay ahead on the horizon. She stared at it as it came into view. The shoreline was lined with massive green trees as tall as the towers at Kander.

"That's the Queensgrove," a sailor said, stepping up beside them. He was the sailor on night watch last night. Now that she saw him in the daylight she noticed he had one wooden eye and a brown uneven beard. "Beautiful ain't it? They say the trees were planted when giants roamed the land more than a thousand years ago. They go all the way up to Queen's Edge."

"They are beautiful," Ceychell said. "How long before we reach Queen's Edge?"

"We'll pass by there at the end of the day, and dock in Sentry tomorrow."

Hours passed. Ceychell decided to go down and help the cooks with dinner because she was tired of the same disgusting meals. There wasn't much to work with, but she managed to spread some garlic on the musty bread and add a few spices to the fish gruel so it wasn't quite so revolting. She hadn't had a good meal since they left Kander, but at least they were getting closer to Queen's Edge. She wanted to get the crown, but even more so, she wanted to get the horn to save Miraden. She didn't care about the ashenkin or Lord Umorogrin anymore. She wanted to go home to Kaehrn and see her sister. She'd try to become a proper chieftain.

She checked on Miraden several times that day. Apart from when he was feeding Tundra, he snoozed, which was unusual for him. Perhaps being on the water was making his illness worse. He woke up when he sat next to her. She offered him some water. Chintaja, Simigrin and Lovo came over and sat around them.

"We are going to be at port in a few hours," Chintaja said. "Do you have a plan?"

"Not yet," Simigrin said. "Perhaps we should look around tonight to find a tailor for the morning."

"Maybe we should leave Miraden onboard to rest," Lovo said. "And this is no merchant ship, so no one is going to believe we are merchants in our ruined clothes. We will have to find another way into Queen's Edge."

"We need to keep Miraden with us in case he gets worse," Ceychell said. "But Tundra would only scare people and attract attention."

Tundra roared in protest.

Chintaja shook his head and said, "The queen has a heavy guard and a host of Henslemen mercenaries. Whatever strategy we take won't be easy. She is paranoid and would remove a man's head if he even *looked* a little suspicious." He made a popping sound and winked at Ceychell. "So we must keep a low profile."

Simigrin's brows arched. "I'd heard she's a strict ruler, but that sounds a little exaggerated."

"Oh no, good lady. She used to be a wonderful queen, but ever since princess Kalionite died nearly twenty years ago, she's become reclusive and lost every bit of her compassion. I've heard she has culling parties where she rounds up alleged dissenters in her city and throws them into lockaways until they starve."

"Sounds like she started going crazy about the time the ashenkin started to invade," Ceychell said. "Almost like Kander has its own version of history." She and Simigrin exchanged a harsh look.

"Let's scout the city tonight and keep our ears open and our mouths shut. The queen still needs her potions. We can get in. Let's find our opportunity," Miraden said.

Everyone napped beside Miraden until that evening. Around dusk, the breeze started cooling off a bit. Ceychell leaned on the railing beside Simigrin, Miraden and Tundra who were sitting on the deck behind them. Off the port side of the ship and less than a mile away was an immense, walled castle on a rocky hill at the end of a tree-covered peninsula. A central tower was surrounded by three adjoining towers. Fewer than ten guards were visible behind the battlements between the towers. As she peered at it, a watchman emerged from a gatehouse on the central tower and lit a beacon. It burst into flame and beamed out over the water, painting the rocky shoreline in reds and yellows.

Up ahead, she could see the lights in the harbor at Sentry and a few ships bobbing at its docks. Beyond the harbor, a sprawling city climbed up the rocky slope of what appeared to be the base of a volcano. The sailors had called it the "Snoozing Giant." A black smudge of smoke rose from its peak into the darkening sky.

Ceychell had never been to Sentry, but her father used to tell her stories of drunken bar brawls there and war in the harbor that had sunk half the ships in the queen's fleet. He told her it was a powerful city once, and became the richest known city after plundering some other cities across the sea in its frequent wars. But over the past few years, the Devil's Bargain had run rampant through it. She wondered if it would ever be the same.

"Ceycha?" Miraden said. He seemed in a daze. He was lying against Tundra.

"Yes, Miraden?" She crouched closer to him.

"Oh Ceycha. I feel so sick. Are we there yet?" She pressed a hand to his forehead. He was sweating badly and burning up. "Have you seen Tundra? I … I haven't seen her."

"He's burning up," Ceychell said to Simigrin.

Simigrin moved his head onto her lap, muttered a few words, and frost formed on her fingers. She rubbed them on his forehead. Her tears dripped onto his chest.

Tundra moaned and laid her head on Miraden.

"We have to find a way to slow the poison," Ceychell said. "He won't make it back to the Lorden even if we can steal the horn."

Simigrin nodded, continuing to rub his head with her frosty fingers. "We'll need to find an alchemist in town. I'm sure they'll have something to help him."

The deckhand rang the ship's bell. They were getting close. The sailors began prepping to dock, drawing in the sails, readying the line to moor, and chattering about their favorite spots to visit, which seemed to be a tavern called Shephard's Yarn, but after hearing about the brawls and whoring that went on there, Ceychell hoped to miss it. "I'll go to the galley and see if there's anything we can feed him. Who knows how long it will take us to find something once we dock."

Ceychell came back a few minutes later with a hot bowl of oily broth.

When Simigrin got a whiff of it, she turned her head. "Oh, that smells like the fishgut barrel. What is in there?"

"Fish oil, marrow broth, crushed garlic and some rum," Ceychell told her. Tip him up." Simigrin held Miraden's head while Ceychell poured some of the broth into Miraden's mouth until he started choking and spit the stinking brew on his shirt.

"Drink all of it, Miraden," Simigrin said. "We need you strong and on your feet."

Miraden shuddered and leaned up. "Ugh, no more. I'm okay, I'm up." Between the frost treatment and broth, Miraden almost looked normal.

Lovo and Chintaja emerged with their packs from the door to below decks.

Miraden leaned up and shook his head. "What are we even talking about?"

"Are you okay, sir?" Chintaja asked. "You look unwell."

"He'll be alright," Lovo said. "Mir, you need me to help you walk or..."

Miraden stood up and leaned against him. "No, I'm okay. The port really looks dead." The city was indeed quiet. Very few lights were on, streetlamps were lit, and few guards patrolled the streets.

A sailor in a red cotton shirt and cutoff linen shorts stepped up to Lovo. His shoeless feet were grimy black. Ceychell overheard him whisper, "Heard you want to get to Queen's Edge?"

Lovo nodded to the sailor and leaned to hear what the sailor said, muffling the sailor's voice from Ceychell's hearing. Lovo whispered back to him and the sailor waved and then headed toward the dock.

Chintaja waved them all together. He pulled a coin out of his pocket and showed it to everyone. It was silver with a bald man stamped into the face on one side and had a yellow stripe on the back. "This is a *C* coin. It's not easy to come by, but they can get you into places, keep you from rotting in jail, that sort of thing. It can buy off the Henslemen, and the Henslemen are the law here. We must be very careful in the city."

"How can we get more?" Simigrin asked. "We might need them."

"They are given," Chintaja said. "You can't 'get' them. And people don't talk about them. Don't be asking around for them—unless you want to be part of the next culling party."

"Can it get us to Queen's Edge?" Ceychell asked.

"Just spoke to a sailor that offered to row us there and wanted that as payment," Lovo said.

Chintaja seemed to hear him, but didn't continue as if he hadn't. "The issue is, if we get caught in Queen's Edge uninvited, one may not be enough."

"You're risking a lot coming with us," Simigrin said. "Aren't you an order knight of Crestain?"

Chintaja nodded. "I am. And this is worth my honor."

Lovo grinned and patted Chintaja's spaulder. He exchanged a warm grin with the knight.

Miraden scratched Tundra and said, "Alright girl, you stay onboard. The city is no place for a bear. I'll be back soon." She moaned and lay down for a final scratch, then she rolled away from Miraden.

Ceychell looked north across the bay at the castle. It seemed like a *very* long walk around the harbor and then up through the grove, but it might be their only way.

TWENTY·FIVE

THE BROKEN CITY

SENTRY WAS QUIET AND CHILLY. The lampposts were beautiful iron and stained glass, but many didn't work. The cobblestone streets had missing stones and were covered in dung. The homes had gorgeous stone foundations and wooden sides, but many were defiled with graffiti. The city was gritty and ugly and retained very little, if any, of its former beauty.

Ceychell held her nose and stepped around piles of horse manure. She did not want to have to walk through horse shit all the way to Queen's Edge. "Lovo, maybe we should take the shoeless sailor up on his offer to row us over?"

He smirked and shook his head. "The stinky fella said he had a contact at the harbor who smuggled people to Queen's Edge—potion dealers, contraband smugglers, and other unsavory sorts—but he wanted a C coin and some kams for the introduction. Too steep, I think."

Chintaja chimed in, "Because getting caught smuggling is punishable by death. It is a huge risk."

Miraden seemed to be feeling much better after the broth. He kept pace and was alert. "I heard onboard that we need to get off the streets soon because after the bell strikes in the tower of the Father of Darkness, it's illegal to be outdoors."

Ceychell looked over at Simigrin who had her hood up and her head down.

"Let's find an inn and lay low," Lovo said.

They left the main road onto a dirt road and walked past dozens of wooden shacks in disrepair. Candlelight seeped through cracks between the planks. Some of the shacks were just ruins, piles of burned wood or eaten by wood-boring pests. They turned down a wide street heavily grooved by cart tracks and pounded by horse hooves. The smell of horse dung made her gag. There were two-story storefronts and a few houses. The street was almost totally dark save for a single flickering lamppost. Everything was closed. The stores and houses were built so close together that Ceychell felt like she was walking through a tunnel again. Some of the stores were just one long building with different fronts, all joined by common walls.

"It's so creepy the way they're built so close together," Ceychell said.

"The planners of Sentry were efficient," Chintaja said. "They knew they could save time by building close together near the harbor where much of the wood was shipped in."

After a long block, the road turned sharply to the right. Three men in hooded cloaks watched them walk past the corner, but said nothing.

"The Sleeping Giant," Chintaja whispered and pointed to the volcano when it came into view between a few broken homes, "is full of pumice and gems. The poorest communities live closest to the mines. We are in the market district."

Ceychell stopped suddenly, walked over to a small wooden house with a purple smudge below the front windowsill and wiped her fingers on it. It wasn't fresh, and only a little came off on her fingertips. She walked to the next house, and found that it, too, was marked. Across the street she found another.

"Ceychell!" Simigrin hissed. "What are you doing?"

"Ashenkin have been to these houses. Nearly all of these windows are marked."

"What do you mean?" Chintaja asked.

Ceychell walked over and showed the purple smudges on her fingers. "People use this purple char to mark windows so the ashenkin know that children live there."

"I have really wondered why they haven't they come back for you since we left the college?" Simigrin asked.

She didn't want to share that Carbrojl had told her they wouldn't come for her again. "Perhaps your lord has them doing other things."

Simigrin stepped up in Ceychell's face, but Ceychell didn't back down.

"Whoa whoa," Lovo said, stepping between them.

Simigrin balled her fists and leaned into Ceychell. "How dare you accuse my master of these horrible things?"

"Shh. Shhh! Keep your voices down," Miraden said. He was sweating and pale.

Ceychell stood over Simigrin by a head and was not afraid. "I've seen how much of a hand he had in releasing the devils into this world. Don't think he's not sending us to get the crown to cover his own mistake."

Someone opened a window and shone a light onto the street. Then another light went on across the way.

"Let's get out of here," Miraden said. And they continued down the street.

They followed the road left and then right. At the next crossroads, to the left the home tunnel went for a long distance before a turn. To the right, it looked similar, except for the top of a tall temple tower behind homes less than a mile away. At the tower's center a heptagram stone star glowed in the moonlight, below it was a bell. She recognized the sigil as the temple of the Father of Darkness. Anticipating the tower bell signaling an end to the night made her heart race.

She sped up and the others followed. Ahead there were two lit lanterns glowing on the building at the end of the street before a right turn. There were a couple people standing out front. Seeing the inn brought her relief.

They stopped at the inn. It was late and this would have to do. Chatter filtered out through shut double-doors. Two Henslemen, dressed in boiled leather armor with yellow sashes on their arms stood at on each side of the doors. They were both smoking a pipe and staring at Ceychell.

One of them whistled.

The other called out, "Hello milady, warm beds in here."

Ceychell ignored them and opened the doors.

"I know you're not going to walk in there without scraping your boots," the Henslemen who whistled said. He was older with thinning blond hair and a pinkish face. A scar had healed poorly over his left eye, which slouched to the side.

Ceychell scraped her boots on the boot scraper by the door and walked inside. The others did as well. The inn was smoky and warm. The front room was spacious and most of the tables and chairs were taken. A small staircase at the back of the room led both up and down. A woman in her autumn years stood at the counter in front of the kitchen entrance. Her gray hair was sloppily thrown into a tail, and she wore a sullen expression.

"Father of Darkness," Lovo said in greeting. "How much is five meals and a couple rooms?"

"Meals are five lumin each," she said. "We only have one room, and it will cost you a kam since there are so many of you."

Chintaja placed four kams on the counter. "We'd like a good helping and a drink."

They crowded around a single table near the back of the tavern. Ceychell guessed many of the patrons were business owners by their silks and decent boots. Three Henslemen were chatting very loudly and eating at a table near them. After a few moments, the two from outside joined them. All the noisy chatter Ceychell had heard outside seemed to be coming from their table.

Miraden was struggling to sit still. He scratched his neck and pulled his hood up.

"You okay?" Lovo asked him. Miraden shook his head.

"Maybe we should find someplace else," Simigrin said.

"Won't they all be like this?" Ceychell said loudly over the noise. The Henslemen's chatter stopped instantly, and the tavern went silent. The Henslemen stared at her for a long moment, then resumed their raucous conversation.

"We can't be on the streets after the temple bell rings," Lovo said.

"He's right," Chintaja said. "It's too risky."

The innkeeper walked over and set down some food on their table. One of the Henslemen got up and took two bowls of stew off her tray. She turned and stared at the man, but said nothing. He had curly black hair and a close-shaved beard, but his chin was still nearly black. He had two swords on his hips. "You all don't mind if we have these, do you?" he asked, with a black-toothed grin. "We're awfully hungry."

Lovo started to get up, but Miraden grabbed his arm to stay him.

"Is something wrong?" the Henslemen asked, grinning at Lovo.

Lovo glared at him, but sat back down.

Ceychell seethed. "There is something," she said. Miraden and Simigrin winced. "You have my dinner and my friend's dinner, and

I want them back."

The Henslemen laughed out loud, and some other patrons joined in. "Well, I'm so sorry, *milady*," he said with a slight bow. "What are you going to do about it?"

"How about a game?" she said.

"A game?"

Chintaja hissed through his teeth, "Ceychell, we can buy more."

"It's okay, I—" Miraden started to say.

"No no," the Hensleman said. "I feel like playing a game tonight. Love games."

Outside, a bell rang three times, low and steady. It's too late to leave now.

"How about a test of strength?" Ceychell said. "If I win, we get our soups back and all the coins in your pockets. And if you win, you get the soups and all the coins in my pockets."

"I want more than what's in your pocket," he said.

The other Henslemen cheered and hollered. Two of them banged their hands on the table and whistled.

"We are going to need a few more drinks here!" one of the Henslemen at the table said. He was as big as Lovo and had a huge plume of hair. His face was painted in a purple moon, and three pins were stuck through his nose.

"Fine," Ceychell said with a casual wave, "you can have whatever you want." She caught a glance of Simigrin simmering but ignored her.

The Henslemen clapped and nodded. "You have yourself a deal." He set the bowls back on the innkeeper's tray, pushed her away, and rubbed his hands together.

"Ceycha what are you doing?" Miraden whispered.

"Is this what you call keeping a low profile?" Simigrin whispered.

Lovo just shook his head.

Ceychell stood up, pushed up her sleeves, pulled a fork off the table, wrapped her hair into a bun, and stabbed the fork in to hold it up. "Before we start, I want to see the coins."

"Of course, milady." He pulled out a handful of lumins, a few kams, three hydras and placed them on the table in front of Chintaja, then slid the pile to the center.

"All of them," Ceychell said. "Don't try to cheat me." He stared at her for a moment then patted his bag. Ceychell took a step closer to him and narrowed her eyes. "All the coins. Are you worried you can't beat me?"

He scowled and reached beneath this cloak, and dropped a small pouch in front of Chintaja.

Ceychell untied a small pouch from her side—it had a few coins in it—and threw it on the table next to his.

"Don't think I'm an honorable man?" he said.

"Never crossed my mind," she said.

The other Henslemen started pushing their tables and chairs toward the wall. One of them closed the door and stood in front of it. The innkeeper quickly cleared glasses and plates from the tables. Before their dinners were taken away, Ceychell grabbed two bowls off of the innkeeper's tray and set them on her table.

"What is the feat of strength?" he asked. He pulled a dagger from his belt and picked his teeth with it.

Ceychell picked up the two bowls of soup he originally stole. They were still piping hot. She handed him one bowl, and he stared at it for a moment.

"The hell's this for?" he asked.

Ceychell ignored the question. She stepped back a few paces, cupped the hot soup bowl in her hand, and extended it out to him. He did the same; his eye twitched and his fingers tapped the sides of the bowl.

"First to drop it loses," she said.

"That's not fair, women are used to holding hot food," he said.

"So you're saying we are just stronger *and* tougher?" she said. A few patrons and the innkeeper laughed. "If only you had helped your mother a bit more in the kitchen."

He clenched his jaw and held the bowl.

Ceychell held hers as well. She wanted to kiss the ring Miraden had given her, it never failed to bolster her strength. She smiled. "Actually smells pretty good, doesn't it?"

The Henslemen grimaced. His fingers were shaking.

"It really must *burn* you up that a girl without a sword, authority, or a little dagger in her pants is simply stronger than you. Take a look at that bowl in your hand. That was my soup, think of how much happier you'd be if you'd just let me have it."

"SHUT UP!" the man roared. Some of the steaming soup lapped over the side of his bowl onto his trembling fingers.

Ceychell stepped closer to him, keeping her arm stretched out. "You can drop my soup now. I'll have enough coin to buy another bowl."

He groaned, and shut his eyes. The bowl wobbled in his hand, soup spilling over his fingers. Then he screamed and dropped the bowl.

Ceychell caught it in her free hand. She set the bowls down on the table and caught his wrist as he tried to backhand her.

Simigrin whispered, and her staff appeared in her hands. Lovo gripped the mace at his belt. Chintaja slid his hand toward the pommel of his sword.

"Who are you?" the Henslemen asked.

"Just a woman from the north who will not be disrespected."

The other Henslemen drew their swords.

The Hensleman dried his hand on his pants and smiled. "Do you realize it's against the law to gamble with a Henslemen."

"Push him!" Simigrin said.

Ceychell shoved the man back into the other Henslemen. Simigrin cast a wall of crackling clear ice around the men. Ceychell put her hand on it. She leaned forward as did the man who lost the bet. He pounded the ice with fist; she winked at him.

"We better think fast," Miraden said. There was a small window on the wall behind them, but it would be too small for Lovo to fit through.

The book flew from Ceychell's bag and its pages whirred in front of her shoulder and came to a stop. Ceychell held one hand toward the back wall with the window, she estimated how far the door was and pointed her hand at it. A black void ringed in fire grew into a portal on the wall, and she felt another appear beyond the door.

"Lovo, go, hold the door!" Ceychell said. He hesitated and then ran through the gate. The Henslemen were slamming their weapons against the ice, a few started to rush the door. "Chintaja, help him hold the door." He ran through next. Simigrin opened the window and crawled through it.

Ceychell's ears popped and skin was on fire. It hurt so bad she screamed, "Miraden go!"

"I can't leave you here," he said and grabbed her arm.

"Get the coins," she said and grimaced. Her arms began to shake. Miraden scooped up the coin bags and she grabbed him and ran through the gate. He shouted something but it was all warbles while they passed through the cold darkness. They stepped out of the portal outside the door just before it dissolved into smoke.

Ceychell flung her arms to the side and cried out in pain.

Lovo leaned against the door with everything he had. It buckled and threatened to break off its hinges. A beam on the door frame split, and the door cracked. A blade slid between the boards and nearly lopped off Lovo's ear. He pulled his mace and smashed the thick frame of awning over the door down; then he and Chintaja grabbed a beam, pressed it against the door, and wedged it against the boot scrapers.

"We better find somewhere to hide until morning," Lovo said.

"Try not to burn the city down," Simigrin said to Ceychell.

Ceychell snarled. "Shut it—"

"Enough, come on!" Miraden said and ran down the narrow street. The others followed.

People cracked open their doors and watched them run by. They went left and right and right again. The homes and shops looked so similar that Ceychell thought they might be running in a circle. She heard distant shouting from behind them.

They ran up to a large building on their right, a mill of some sort. Miraden tried the door, but it didn't budge.

"Should we break it open?" Lovo asked.

"Too loud," Chintaja said. "And too obvious."

Miraden asked Ceychell, "Can you just warp us through?"

"I don't think so. My skin still burns. I should have read the spell more carefully."

"This is open," Simigrin said, nudging a window with the end of her staff. It was high up, possibly ten feet. She prodded the edge of the window with her staff until it swung out.

Lovo ran up to the wall and put his back to it. "Up you go, Simi," he said, making a basket of his hands in front of him. He boosted her up; she struggled but at last tumbled through.

"Ceychell," he said. She climbed up, pulled herself in, and dropped down on a barrel on the other side.

Miraden came up behind her, and she helped him down onto the barrel. She heard some muffled grunting and Chintaja squeezed into the window. Ceychell pulled from the inside. He was a big man and his armor made him even heavier. At last, he tumbled ungracefully inside, missed the barrel, and thudded to the floor.

Ceychell heard people coming down the street. She leaned out but couldn't see them yet. Then she looked down at Lovo. He had his mace out and was looking up and down the street, as if he were thinking of making a run for it.

"Lovo, we'll pull you up," Ceychell whispered. She, Chintaja, and Miraden reached their hands out of the window. He hooked the mace on his belt, reached up and grabbed their hands; then he tried to step up the wall as they pulled. Ceychell thought her shoulders might pop out of their sockets. Simigrin pulled at their backs. Lovo kicked frantically as they pulled him up and through the window. He tumbled inside, and they all fell into a pile.

"My wrist is burning hot," Lovo said.

"Sorry," Ceychell said, looking at her hands.

"The window!" Simigrin whispered. Miraden climbed up the barrel and reached out to pull the window shut. Moments later a gang of Henslemen ran down the street. Then a few horses, then more men.

"I hope you're pleased with yourself," Simigrin whispered to Ceychell.

Ceychell pulled the Hensleman's purse from her bag and dumped it into her hands. Four C coins and a dull copper key.

"You almost got us killed, again," Simigrin said.

"Hey, let's not argue," Miraden said. He looked pale pink in the moonlight and his eyelids were sagging. "We are safe for now and may need these coins,"

"Lady Simigrin is right," Chintaja said. "We got lucky. We cannot get to Queen's Edge by brute force and bravado. I'd prefer not to end up on the gallows at Castle Cliff. Tomorrow, we get disguises and meet the smuggler. It's too risky to stay in town now."

TWENTY·SIX

THE SICK AND THE MISSING

MIRADEN WOKE UP SQUEEZED BETWEEN Simigrin and Ceychell. He felt sick and drowsy, and almost vomited. It was dark and cold and he could hardly see anything. At his feet, Lovo lay with his back to him, holding Chintaja and snoring. Simigrin was curled in a ball with a small blanket to his left; Ceychell was half lying on top of him and holding on to him tightly. She was shaking and sweating in her sleep. Her eyes were tearing and her teeth were clenched.

It was still dark, and he didn't want to wake the others. He tried to shake Ceychell gently. She snuffled and held him so tightly he could hardly breathe. He shook her harder and whispered her name. She woke gasping for air and wiped tears from her eyes.

"I'm sorry," she whispered and turned over.

She lay there and wept in silence. He figured she must be dreaming of Carbrojl again. He poured a bit of cool water from his wineskin onto his hand and rubbed it into her scalp. She was steaming hot, though the mill was comfortably cool. She sniffed and looked over her shoulder at him, grabbed his hand and squeezed it, then turned back and fell asleep.

They woke early. Miraden felt dizzy, nauseous, and very drowsy.

They left the mill before dawn in case any workers arrived. As they walked up the street, he leaned on Lovo for help.

Lovo patted his chest and said, "I got you, Mir."

They walked in the direction away from the tavern they'd fled. The morning was bright and cloudless. Miraden was nervous because Simigrin and Ceychell were conspicuous in their mage robes. They certainly did not look like merchants, but there was hardly anyone on the streets.

Now that he saw the ramshackle houses and run-down businesses in daylight, he guessed most of them were abandoned. Many had dates and names written in chalk across the front doors. Claw marks scarred on some of the window sills. Other homes had burned doors with broken handles, and shattered windows. A lot of the wood on the roofs and walls were orange-red like rust. The air was dry and noxious, and scratched at his throat.

"Is that orange stuff mold or rust?" Simigrin asked.

"I'm not sure," Lovo said, "but the whole place looks damned, far worse than its reputation."

Miraden felt the same way.

"We should find an alchemist," Ceychell said.

Lovo looked at her. "Aren't you an alchemist?"

"I mean a shop where we can buy some reagents, silly." She swatted his arm. "Maybe I can brew something to help Miraden."

"Of course!" Lovo said, shaking his head. "I'm not thinking straight." He was carrying a lot of Miraden's weight.

Simigrin put her hand on his forehead; her cold fingers felt good. Cool condensation ran down his face.

"Shouldn't we find a tailor first?" he asked.

Ceychell nodded. "We can get started on a remedy while Lovo and Chintaja get us clothes."

After several blocks, they found a tailors shop, a tall, slender building with bolts of red and blue cloth behind its cracked window. A weather-worn sign over the door read, *The Perfect Loom.*

"We'll come back to this," Chintaja said. "Let's figure out where the alchemist is."

They continued down the narrow street and came to a tavern. The smell of bread hit Miraden, and he practically drooled. Lovo jerked to a stop, and his stomach rumbled like an avalanche.

"We'll come back," Miraden said, stumbling on a rut in the road. Lovo steadied him.

"Let's get him to that alchemist," the big man said.

Two blocks later, Ceychell and Simigrin spotted a sign at the same time.

"Realta's Reagents," Simigrin said.

"This will have to do," Ceychell said. "We'll take Miraden, go back and wait for the tailor to open."

Ceychell and Simigrin each took an arm. Miraden moved with them. The alchemist's shop didn't look much better than any of the other buildings.

"Simigrin," Ceychell said. She wanted to make sure the mage woman didn't argue with her once they got inside. "Hogmarsh snake venom has similar symptoms, a sleeping sickness, as do fennelshrooms. Both can be slowed with cooked desalt, juno and barrowroot. The fresher the better. It's the best I can think of, any thoughts?"

Simigrin nodded. "Seems like our best option."

Ceychell knocked on the door, waited a beat, knocked again, and then again. She gritted her teeth, shook her head, and knocked again politely, three times, then four times.

The door cracked open. "It's too early, what do you want?" a woman said. She sounded old, scratchy-voiced and coughing, but Miraden didn't look up to see her. "Is your friend drunk?"

"No, he's been bitten," Ceychell told her through the crack in the door. "Can we please buy some ingredients and use your cauldron?"

"This is my shop," the old woman rasped. "You want to use a cauldron, use your own." She started to push the door closed.

Simigrin stopped the door with her foot. "Please, our friend is very sick. We can pay extra."

"Oh … arr alright, come on—*cough*—in," she said. "You're the first patient in a month that didn't have the Devil's Bargain. I don't want to—*cough*—catch it."

The two women helped Miraden inside. His legs were so weak he thought he might just collapse on the floor. The smell of the shop turned his stomach and he swallowed deeply to forestall any vomit that might come up. It was as if all the stinkiest things in the world were gathered into the little shack, half of them fermenting and the other half just rotting. Behind the main counter were shelves of various-colored vials and small jars stacked seemingly arbitrarily. Three cauldrons sat in the middle of the room, surrounded by chairs, below a hole in the roof.

Simigrin helped Miraden sit on a chair.

"What bit him?" the old woman asked. "Snake? I have an antidote for that. Got one for bat, too."

Miraden finally took a look at her. She wasn't nearly as crone-ish as he'd thought. Her short blond hair was streaked gray and pocked skin was bone pale. She wore a brown nightrobe that hung on her like a sheet on a scarecrow and she constantly coughed into her sleeve.

Ceychell walked to the wall near the counter and started perusing the vials and jars.

"Don't touch that," the old woman screeched. "Leave that be. That's delicate!" She shuffled over to Ceychell. "Stop this instant or I'll call the guards and have you all locked up for looting."

She stopped and stared at the old woman. Miraden watched nervously, he wasn't up for more running should she call the guards.

"Just tell me," the woman said. "What bit him?"

"A lortaraas bit him," Simigrin said. "Right here." She pointed at the two red marks on his neck. They were swollen and dark.

"Looks like a snake bite, a very big snake," she said and crossed her arms, "A lortaraas?" She clicked her tongue. "Bah, now you're wasting my time. You sure it wasn't a snake?"

"No," Ceychell said and lowered her voice. "We were on the southern continent and there are lortaraas there. One bit him."

"What in the devils—no one goes there!" The old woman looked down at Miraden. "Well kid, ain't no cure for that. I got an antidote for snake bites we can try. Red castling and ringed mascar, perhaps a few others."

"Thank you, but I don't think that will help," Ceychell said, as politely as Miraden thought she could muster. "By any chance, do you have desalt, juno, and barrowroot?"

"Sounds like you know something about something," the woman said, rubbing her chin. "Trying to slow the poison?"

"If I can," Ceychell said.

Simigrin said, "We think the poison is similar to hogmarsh snake venom."

"We need to buy him time," Ceychell continued. "My mother told me of a way you can inject an antidote under the skin with a tube to treat blood. Have you done that?"

The old woman nodded and narrowed her eyes. "I have. That will cost extra."

The old woman huddled around a cauldron with Simigrin and

Ceychell. The smell of the steam made Miraden's stomach climb into his throat. The potion was reddish and thick like syrup. It was nice to see Simigrin and Ceychell working together again. Ceychell took charge, and the other two didn't seem to mind. She had a knack for it.

"For young women, you really know alchemy," the old woman said. "Are you mages? Your robes look like mages' robes."

"No, I… bought this robe," Ceychell said.

"We're potion merchants," Simigrin added. "We arrived yesterday."

"Oh, well that makes sense," she said.

Miraden woke from a brief doze. Beside him, the old woman held a sharp point with a funnel and vial attached to it. He jerked at the sight of it, and Ceychell grabbed his shoulders and stayed him. Simigrin carefully poured the potion into the vial. Ceychell leaned to Miraden's ear and whispered, "This is going to be very uncomfortable, but you need to stay as still as possible, and whatever you do, don't fidget or scream."

Miraden didn't like the looks of that sharp point near his arm, but he couldn't burden his friends by falling unconscious… or worse. He nodded and shut his eyes.

A sharp pain shot into his shoulder, and heat seeped under his skin. He stiffened and squeezed the arms of his chair. His legs twitched and his feet shook.

Ceychell tightened her grip on his shoulder. "Be still, Miraden."

Miraden woke up feeling much better, though his body was very hot. When his vision cleared, he thought his dream had seeped into his real world. The women had primped themselves as if they were prepping for a ball. Ceychell was in a beautiful long green dress. Her hair was combed. Her face and hands were clean. He had almost forgotten how stunning she was. She pulled up her dress and secured Hellshy's holster to her thigh with her belt. He caught himself staring and looked over at Simigrin.

Simigrin wore a short-sleeved yellow dress with a black shawl around her shoulders. She was also clean, and her hair was beautifully combed to the side.

Lovo wore a black trench over boiled leather and a yellow sash on his arm. A red wide-brimmed hat sat on his head. Chintaja wore a similar coat over a brown hooded tunic. His black curly hair was pulled back into a tail. They looked strikingly like Henslemen.

"Are you feeling better, Miraden?" Lovo asked. His voice sounded strange, like it was in slow motion. He wore Miraden's bow on his shoulder.

"What's going on?" Miraden said and sat up. His mouth was dry and his tongue tasted bitter.

"Are you feeling better?" Simigrin said.

"Yes, much better," he said. "Am I dreaming this?"

"No, you're back with us," Lovo said, handing Miraden a pair of black pants and a blue silk shirt. "And you need to change into this. I'll put the rest of your clothes in my bag. I'm going to run our things back to the ship. We won't need them tonight."

Miraden doffed his cloak, leather coat and dirty shirt, and put on the blue shirt. He was feeling that he'd slept for days. Ceychell sat down next to him, washed his face, and cleaned his hands. Simigrin winked at him and worked the tangles out of his red locks. He hadn't realized his hair was such a long and knotted mess.

Miraden took the axe Ormus gave him off his belt, and put it in his bag as it was too big to take. He felt unworthy to wield it anymore. He wondered how fast Ormus will crush him—should he survive—when he finds out he didn't choose Ceychell. For years, he'd dodged Ormus's ire to win over Ceychell's heart; now he thought about how kindly Ormus had treated him upon his return. Having lost his parents, he had no family, and her family had taken him in. Though, he still loved her. He'd always love her. Nothing could change that.

"Are we going somewhere?" he asked.

Lovo handed the alchemist a C coin, and she left the shop without another word.

"It's going to be a long night" Simigrin said, putting a hand on his shoulder. "I hope you are up to it."

Ceychell walked over to a shelf covered in vials of different colored powders. She removed the vial, examined it and put it at her side where it disappeared. Miraden blinked. He wasn't sure if he just imagined her stealing the vial or not.

"Miraden. *Miraden?*" Simigrin said.

He looked her way, she was annoyed. "Sorry, I feel as strong as steel."

They left the shop after sunset. A fog hung over the dark street.

Ceychell handed him some bread and cured meat. "You must be hungry. You slept all day."

He was. He ate every last bite, and the food didn't turn his stomach. But he was still groggy and almost felt tipsy.

"Did the food help?" Ceychell asked, putting her arm around him. She smiled at him but it looked forced. "Simigrin found some kampsporin hidden in a box on a top shelf. It's probably what helping you most. The hag didn't want to part with it."

Simigrin shrugged and winked at him.

"Miraden," Chintaja said, "I was able to gather some information about Queen's Edge from a merchant visiting the tailor. There is an underground market below the castle. Contraband is smuggled in there, including men and women for the Henslemen's entertainment. We can try to blend in with them to get into the castle."

"What about the south entrance, through the Queensgrove?" Miraden asked.

"It's well guarded," Chintaja said. "The Splinterhides are paid to protect it. Only the queen's soldiers and the Henslemen are allowed to use it. All merchants send their wares into port, and it's carted up by her mercenaries."

"Splinterhides?" Lovo asked.

Chintaja nodded. "Yes. Cutthroat mercenaries and marksmen. Nothing slips past them."

"What about taking the smuggler's boat?" Miraden asked.

"He wants a C coin each now," Lovo said. "A man who suddenly raises his price cannot be trusted."

"Then how do we get there?" Miraden asked.

"We're going through the service door," Ceychell said, "as *goods*."

Miraden realized what she was saying, but he was surprised she or Simigrin would go along with that even as a ruse. When he realized Lovo and Chintaja were dressed as Henslemen, it donned on him that he was part of the *goods*.

Lovo patted his shoulder. "Sorry buddy, we could only afford two Henslemen outfits. We're going to have to be on our guard and sneak away when we can." He patted the small sack at his side and added, "I have your boots and hooded cloak for tonight, just in case."

"In case of what? The priority is the horn," Ceychell whispered.

"No, the priority is the crown," Simigrin said.

"That crown is evil," Ceychell whispered. "We should destroy it, if anything."

Simigrin balled her fists. "Lord Umorogrin wants it to stop the ashenkin, end the Devil's Bargain, stop the children from disappearing!"

"Lord Umorogrin started this problem with that crown!"

"I heard you the first time you told me that lie. You dreamed it. It is not real."

"The Lorden is right about you mages," Ceychell said. "You're all self-interested."

Simigrin stopped and grabbed Ceychell's arm. "And why do you want the horn? For selfless reasons, I assume?"

"To save Miraden," Ceychell said. "You want him to die?"

"You think The Lorden is going to stay true to her word? She was going to execute us just for being humans. She wants that horn to break the enchantment and we—" she waved her hand around "—all of us will be destroyed by her legion. Think beyond yourself, Ceychell!"

"So you'd just let Miraden die to get the crown for your lord," Ceychell said.

Miraden wondered if Simigrin really would sacrifice him to get the crown for Lord Umorogrin. He wasn't keen to die for the lord, but he didn't value himself over the millions of people who may die in war. He doesn't want to make that choice.

Simigrin glanced at Miraden. Her lip trembled and eyes welled with tears. He never thought she'd give him up so easily, but he was suddenly pessimistic. "We can find a cure for him in Kander," she said. "And the Lorden isn't going to help him. She just told us that because she gambled on us being stupid enough to bring back that accursed horn!"

"Ladies," Chintaja said at last.

"Shut up!" they both yelled at him.

"Pipe down, you two!" Lovo shouted.

Three Henslemen were walking toward them. Ceychell and Simigrin stopped shouting at each other.

"Hello there, brothers," one of the Henslemen said. He was Miraden's size but a bit fluffier around the sides and had long black sideburns. Beside him was a muscular man, bald, and missing half of one arm. He had a broad axe slung to his belt. The third man had a long neck and pointed nose. He fiddled with a knife as he eyed Miraden.

Chintaja said, "Good evening."

"I don't recognize you two," the knife fiddler commented. His left eye twitched. "Where you in from?"

"Crestain, came down from Oddion," Chintaja said. "We picked up these three along the way, thought they may be good to bring to the castle."

"Mmm hmm, not bad," the fiddler said. He walked around Miraden, smelled him, looked around his backside. Then he checked out Simigrin. "A fine southerner. We never get enough of you flowers at our hall. But if he picked you up past Oddion, you may have come from Kander, and most of the southern ladies of your color are scholars… or mages." He raised his knife to Simigrin's eyes. "So which one are you? Hmm?" He slid the knife down the front of her dress.

"A dancer," Simigrin said.

"I bet you are," he said with a laugh. "You may be dancing in my dreams tonight," His eye ticked so much he lowered his knife and looked away. His companion with black sideburns laughed at his joke.

The half-armed man howled. "This is a good lot. You should get them over. The ferry only runs once more before midnight."

"Right," Lovo said. "No need to keep our brothers waiting. Thank you."

Ceychell was staring intently at the knife fiddler. She has such a temper, Miraden hoped she wouldn't cause another scene.

"Hang on brother," the fiddler said and walked toward Ceychell. "Got something on your mind, pretty girl?"

She narrowed her eyes. "That's an interesting pen hanging out of your pocket." He quickly pushed the char pen back beneath his cloak.

"Bad stuff happens to people who start looking for things," he hissed. He raised his knife again and leaned it to her throat. "Sometimes they go missing."

"I wouldn't want that," she said. "I was told I was on my way to make some money."

The three Henslemen chuckled. Lovo and Chintaja joined in. The fiddler tapped the knife against her cheek and said, "Well, I wouldn't want to prevent you from enriching yourself." He laughed and waved the Henslemen away. They continued up the street.

Once they were out of earshot, Simigrin shuffled over to Ceychell and whispered, "What was that all about?"

"Those are the char pens I told you about," Ceychell whispered.

"The ones used to mark the houses?" Simigrin whispered.

Ceychell nodded. "The same."

"I found one on a goblin chieftain," Miraden said. "It leaves purple on your hands."

"I think I'm starting to believe you, Chieftain," Chintaja said. He pointed to a ruined house on the roadside. A purple smear was barely visible below a broken window.

"A woman in my town had a char pen like that," Ceychell whispered. "She marked Kyradel's window, and then tried to mark mine, but we were ready for her."

"Do you think Vera was—" Miraden started.

"Absolutely. But I still don't know *why* they're working with the mages to steal children."

Simigrin's eyes widened. "What? How dare you accuse—"

"Remember at the college," Ceychell cut her off, "when the ashenkin attacked, you were so surprised—and you blamed me! You said there were *never* child abductions at Kander. I wonder why that is."

Simigrin looked from Ceychell to Miraden. Her chin trembled and she clenched her jaw. "How could you accuse me and my order of this?" she said. "Why would I go through all that hell to save *your* sister!"

"Because you're not in on it. I saw your Lord bring the children and the crown to Carbrojl. He knows far more than he's leading on and he *is* responsible for the ashenkin."

"Dreams aren't real! I think that book is messing with your mind. It should have never been given to you. You can't handle it."

"It's mine, and I can handle it," Ceychell said and leaned in face to face with Simigrin.

Miraden had a shadow of belief that Ceychell was right. Perhaps they'd been played all along. "Listen," he said. "I think Ceychell is right about the Henslemen. Everything I've seen so far makes me think they are tied to the missing children."

"Speaking of," Lovo said, "I haven't seen one kid since we got here. Not even an urchin begging for food."

"Crestain and Oddion are like this now too," Chintaja added. In the last few years they've all but disappeared or are under lock and key."

"Hold on," Simigrin said. She took Miraden's arm, "Do you think the mages are part of this?" she asked. "How could you think that?" Her eyes teared up. She started to cover her face but stopped. "After all we've been through. After Lord Umorogrin honored you, a non-mage, in our city. You really think he's the monster she says he is?"

Miraden didn't know what to believe. "All I know is that I was sent to find a crown that I'm told with stop the ashenkin attacks and a horn that might save my life."

"People, please," Chintaja said. "We cannot have dissention. Not now. Not tonight. When we get on that ferry, we have to be absolutely on the same team."

"He's right," Lovo said. "If we don't come together now, they will sniff us out, and we will have no chance of getting the crown or the horn. We can't look back now and *we* are all on the same team no matter what."

"We should forget about the horn, and I think Miraden can make it back to the college. When we get there, we can figure out a cure. I know it." Simigrin said.

Ceychell scowled at Simigrin so intently Miraden thought she might attack her. He wanted to get the horn, too, but, Simigrin may be right about the Lorden and that the offer was merely a ruse. Regardless, he wasn't so sure he'd make it back to the college.

"We need you both. We are all tired and upset and worried about Miraden, but we have a job to do." Lovo said. "I'm not going in there to get locked in a dungeon. I'm in this because we set out to get this crown and stop the ashenkin. I don't even care if Lord Umorogrin is responsible. And I'm getting that horn because I am not doing this without Miraden."

Miraden couldn't help but grin. He wouldn't want to try this without Lovo either.

"I am willing," Simigrin said. "Are you?"

Ceychell nodded, "Let's go."

TWENTY·SEVEN

BLACK MARKET REUNION

CEYCHELL SAT ON THE FERRY beside Lovo and Miraden. Simigrin and Chintaja sat across from them. A ferryman in shorts, no shoes, and a white shirt rowed them toward the castle. She and Simigrin hadn't said a word since their argument in the street. She was content for now, but she had no intention of leaving the horn at Queen's Edge. She was going to save Miraden.

The night was dark and cool. Bright stars reflected on the harbor. Waves crashed on the jagged rocks that jutted from the water like serpent's teeth at the base of the cliff below Queen's Edge. They were so close to the cliff she could no longer see the castle above it, only tall stone walls and the tops of battlements. She couldn't see any guards, but she guessed they were up there, walking the wall.

She was nervous about the plan. She didn't like being used as bait while Lovo and Miraden snuck into the castle to look for the crown. They were only going to look for clues tonight and then meet in the kitchen two floors above the guild hall. Chintaja explained the layout as best he could having spent time at Queen's Edge several years ago, but she had a bad feeling about the entire thing.

The ferryman rowed them into a cave with a small dock. Two

torches on the walls barely lit up the walls themselves. The ceiling dripped water from narrow stalactites.

Lovo handed the ferryman two kams. "Alright, let's get to the party."

The ferryman looked the coins over and then tied the boat to the dock.

Ceychell walked behind Miraden and in front of Simigrin, down a cold stone tunnel and up a stone stairway. Her enchanted bag was invisible at her side with her book and a few extra things inside. The concealment spell was one of the first Simigrin had shown her when she arrived at the castle. Now she couldn't help but wonder if Simigrin might stab her in the back.

Ceychell reached into the bag and ran her thumb over the cork on a large vial of powered shofritters root she'd stolen from Realta's shop. She figured they'd paid the alchemist well enough with the C coin and thought it might come in handy.

They walked through an unguarded door into a giant room. The center of the room was set up as a square bar with four counters. The walls were red and diamond-patterned from floor to ceiling, and the floor was polished stone.

Bartenders were pouring drinks in big red cups to patrons who looked at Ceychell like they'd already had enough. Around the bar, men and women were gambling and drinking at tables covered with gold tablecloths. Seven men pounded one table in unison as another of them leaned back and balanced a glass on a knife on his nose. At another table an argument was being broken up by the dealer, who was as hefty as Lovo.

A Hensleman just inside the door stopped them. His saber pommel gleamed in its black scabbard and his short-brimmed hat was dirt free. His mustache and goatee were also well groomed. He smiled and said, "Guild tokens?"

Lovo smiled and nodded to him. "Ah, here it is," he said, pulling a copper coin from his purse. The face on the coin was Carbrojl's. There were letters but Ceychell couldn't read them from where she was standing.

"Carbrojl?" she whispered.

The Hensleman stared at her. "What do you know of Carbrojl?"

"My… mother told me a story," Ceychell stammered, "when I was young of a man that looked just like the one on that coin. She said he was the creator of the world. A man of dreams and power."

The bouncer glanced at the coin and then smirked at Ceychell. "Your mother sounds like a lovely woman. Enjoy your time here." Chintaja handed the man another coin.

"Well, I best get him up to work," Lovo said, putting his hand on Miraden's shoulder. Miraden snapped to and straightened up. He shook himself out of a daze. Ceychell grabbed his hand and squeezed it briefly before Lovo led him through the guild hall.

Ceychell watched them go and wondered if it would be the last time she ever saw Miraden.

"Let's start looking for someone important," Chintaja whispered.

Ceychell and Simigrin made their way into the crowded hall. A few men called out to them and another whistled, but the two women just grinned coyly and kept moving. Chintaja followed them in and bought an ale at the bar to keep up appearances. Ceychell noticed three women staring at them from across the room.

"What do you suppose their problem is?" she whispered to Simigrin.

"We are competition," Simigrin said. "They are probably the most dangerous people in here."

"Hello!" A blond woman, beautiful, at least ten years older than Ceychell, stepped up from behind them. She wore a pink silk dress and a thin gold necklace with a ruby dangling on her chest. Her earrings were also gold with rubies.

"Hello," Ceychell said, trying not to show how nervous she felt.

"You two are new here," the woman said. "I've never seen you before, and I am here *quite* often." She waved to two men gambling at a table nearby. They waved to her and grinned.

"Yes," Ceychell replied. "My friend and I are from the west. It is our first time here, very lovely."

"Indeed," the woman said, "but take it from me, a couple of these harpies don't like pretty new girls coming here. Especially a Kandarian like you, my darling," she said to Simigrin. "It's rare to see a beauty like you outside of a university."

"I suppose," Simigrin said, "If I went to a university I wouldn't need to be here."

The blond woman snickered and then bumped Ceychell gently with her elbow. "I suppose you're pretty enough, too."

"So they tell me… " Ceychell glanced at Chintaja and then back at the woman. "I'm traveling and was hoping to share company, but not with just anybody."

Simigrin leaned in. "I hear these Henslemen are quite the charmers, but I'm interested in someone more refined, maybe older, more experienced, more… uh… powerful, I guess."

The lady winked and took a sip from her glass. "Yes, darling, it's good to know what you want. I'm sure *you* will have the pick of the lot." She put her hand on Ceychell's shoulder. "And I'm sure you'll do okay too."

Ceychell scoffed, then realized she did. She cleared her throat and said, "Thank you."

The lady put her arm around Simigrin and turned to Chintaja. "What is your deal here? If you're just going to follow them around, get lost." She waved him away.

Ceychell and Chintaja exchanged a quick glance, and Chintaja wandered back toward the bar.

"Good riddance," the woman said. "Back to, oh yes, you see that one, gray beard, long green cloak, charming blue eyes." She pointed to an older man at a table drinking with a few other old men. He looked their way, and the lady waved to him. That man did not wave back. "That's Elcortis. He's a captain of the guild and has been through several naval battles. He sunk a pirate vessel a few months back too. He's quite prude on the surface but a gentleman once you get to know him.

"Then there is, no don't waste your time on him—he only likes men." She pointed at a man not much older than Simigrin. He was tall with black hair, slender and wearing black leather armor. "That is Minitolson, and he likes *all* kinds from exotic to androgynous." She turned to Ceychell "But he probably wouldn't like you."

Ceychell wanted to punch the harlot.

"He may look young," the woman continued, "but he talks directly to the boss here. You'd definitely get his attention."

"He's cute," Simigrin said, "Does he know the castle well? I'd love to see it."

"Pff, who wants to see this dreary old keep? Very few people are allowed up there. The mad queen keeps everything pretty tight. There is a saying in Queen's Edge that over-steppers are always caught by the noose." She clutched her neck and stuck her tongue out.

Ceychell glanced over at Chintaja. He was sitting down at a card table, facing them. Behind his table, a portly man with a short, pointed black beard was also watching her intently. He wore a black wool suit and a yellow fez.

"What about him?" Ceychell asked. "He's been staring at me."

"Ugh, that is Borin. He is council to the queen. Don't waste your time on him. He'll *stiff* you… and then stiff you, if you get my drift."

Ceychell narrowed her eyes and stared at the man.

Yes, talk to him. She felt Carbrojl's voice, skipped a breath, and shook it off.

"What do you think?" Simigrin asked her.

"Go keep him company for a moment. I'll buy him a drink?"

"You talk to him. He's looking at *you*," Simigrin whispered.

The lady shrugged and sipped her drink. "I guess you'll learn. Father of Night to you both." She wandered away between the card tables.

Borin stared hungrily at her. Ceychell winked and kept eye contact with him; put her hand to her mouth when she leaned to whisper into Simigrin's ear, "I have shofritters powder to spike his wine. He's council to the queen, so let's loosen his tongue."

Simigrin grinned slightly and said, "Don't take too long."

Ceychell went straight to the bar and stood behind a man who was as tall as she was. He had sharply combed dark hair and smelled like lavender as if he'd just come from the bath. He had a saber on each hip. He turned to a finely dressed older man beside him and said, "I was next, mate." The older man pursed his lips, but waved him to go ahead.

Ceychell pulled a few coins from her bag and waited impatiently. She looked around randomly to avoid eye contact. The man in front of her got his drink, turned to walk away, but did a double take and the drink spilled over the rim of the glass.

"My my," he said, "I didn't realize an angel was standing behind me." He smiled handsomely. On his collar were pinned two silver bars.

She forced a smile, but said nothing. When the older man stepped up next to the bar, the handsome man stopped him and said, "You simply can't keep her from getting a drink. Why, where are your manners?"

The old man looked at her and shrugged. "Piss off, Neandra."

Then he turned around and ordered his drink.

"Neandra?" Ceychell said.

He raised his cup, bowed his head, and took a sip of his drink. "You may have heard of me."

"I have, actually." She badly wanted to pull Hellshy from her thigh-strap and stab it right into his black heart. He had abandoned Miraden and Simigrin when they were trying to find Kyradel. Had he not thrown her scroll away, Miraden would have known she loved him. She considered seducing him and taking him somewhere where she could cut his throat. She was so tempted, but she couldn't blow their cover just to get revenge.

"Well, well, well," he said. "What is your name, dear lady? Perhaps I've heard of you."

The older man slid past her and whispered, "Watch it."

Stepping up to the counter, she glanced over her shoulder. Simigrin was sitting on Borin's lap. He had his hand on her thigh and was chatting her up. They were supposed to stick together. She couldn't abandon her now, even if she wasn't sure she could trust her anymore.

"Are you so vain that you won't even tell me your name?" Neandra said. He seemed to be losing his patience.

Ceychell put a finger to her lips to quiet him and leaned toward the bartender. "Give me one of whatever Borin is drinking."

The bartender, a dark-skinned short man with a receding hairline, looked up at her and nodded. He pulled a bottle of wine down from a shelf and poured a glass.

"That will be a hydra," the bartender said.

Ceychell wondered if she even had a hydra in her purse. She wanted to reach into her sack but that would look especially suspicious when her hand disappeared into thin air. She dug into her purse and came out with nine kams. She was one short.

A hand reached over hers and dropped a kam in it. The bartender handed her the glass and swiped the coins from her with his other hand.

"C'mon, beautiful, what's your name?" Neandra said when she turned around. "I bet it's something like Freydellia or Angelin or—"

Ceychell glanced over and saw Borin grab Simigrin's leg. Neandra grinned and stepped closer to her but she didn't back away. He reached up for her hand as she put it on his chest. His heart fluttered under her fingers; she wanted to squeeze it till it popped. "I believe you know my name," she whispered. She could smell the lemonseed oil in his hair. "Find me later; maybe you can kiss me goodbye?" They locked eyes for a moment; he was close enough to kiss her now. When he leaned forward, she leaned back and winked.

Ceychell sashayed away from Neandra toward Simigrin's table. She held the wine to her side and reached into her enchanted sack, popped the cork from a vial, and took out a pinch of shofritters root. Luckily, Borin had his eyes on Simigrin and wasn't watching her. She went to drop it in her wine, but someone grabbed her wrist.

"Please, I'd love to get to know you," Neandra said, stepping in front of her again. "There is a beautiful balcony upstairs."

Ceychell looked down at the surface of her wine but couldn't tell if any root had made it in. Borin was staring at her.

She leaned closer to Neandra. His breath on her neck made her skin crawl. She whispered in her sexiest voice, "I would love to, I need to help my friend, alone. Perhaps you'll wait for me."

He let go of her wrist and nodded. "I will wait my entire life," he said, drunk with desire. Then he turned and walked back toward the bar.

Ceychell would have to find another chance to drug Borin's drink. She walked over to him and Simigrin.

"So glad you decided to come over," Borin said and snickered.

"Your friend," he raised his finger with a fat opal ring and brushed it through Simigrin's purple locks "is quite lovely, as are you."

Simigrin rolled her eyes at Ceychell, but she otherwise maintained her composure. Ceychell placed her glass down beside his nearly empty cup and said, "I saw you were running low, so I got you a drink."

He smirked. "Why, that's very kind of you. But I generally don't accept drinks from strange women. Why don't you take the first sip?"

"You'd want me to waste some of your wine?" Ceychell asked.

Simigrin ran her fingernails through his beard. He purred a bit. "Are you really worried about the wine?"

"I do love southern women," he cooed. "But I'd really like it if your friend had a sip of the wine. Now." His face soured to a hard stare.

Ceychell started to sweat. If she drank the wine, her plan could go to shit. She raised the glass to her nose, smelled it, and smiled. It was the finest wine she'd ever smelled, hints of cloves and lush pink grapes from the Manocs. She took a sip, then sat it down next to him and slid her hand on his.

"Now can we talk?" she asked.

He took the cup and smiled. "Now we can talk."

They chatted for nearly an hour. Simigrin leaned against Borin with an arm around his neck and lightly rubbing his shoulder. He leaned his head side to side with his mouth open in ecstasy. Ceychell sat in front of him. They talked about his recent work using taxes to buy the queen experimental potions and his time as head adjudicator for the city, sentencing this person to death or that one to the dungeon. He laughed himself silly when he described having a man flogged in the streets for resisting arrest and then hung by his feet over the side of the castle wall for five days. He was getting tipsy, relishing and bragging about his power. A pair of Henslemen stopped at the table and tried to get him to go for a walk to "clear his head," but Borin told them to piss off with their walk.

Ceychell felt a strange kind of selective clarity, like every word he said rang in her consciousness, but the rest of the sounds in the hall were muted and fuzzy.

She put a hand on his shoulder and leaned to whisper in his ear, and he reached up and grabbed her breast. She jerked back. His pungent oniony body odor mixed with cigar smoke made her nearly gag. "I should kill you for that," she said.

Simigrin's eyes widened and she glanced around to see who might have heard that.

Borin just chuckled like a drunk. He reached beneath his black coat and drew a dagger, black and jagged with a few red runes on the blade. It looked so similar to Hellshy that Ceychell thought he might have pulled it from her thigh. She looked down at her leg, pulled up her dress just enough to slide her hand under it and make sure Hellshy was still there.

"That's what I wanted to see," Borin said. "Some nice leg." When she slid her dress back, he grabbed her leg.

"That's a lovely knife" she said. "Where did you get it?"

"It's really quite interesting, but you see..." He curled his finger for her to lean forward and she did. "They are used for finding Ashengates. Only a select few of us have them." He giggled.

"So fascinating!" Simigrin whispered and ran a finger down his chest. "Then who do you really work for if not the queen?"

"My lord, Carbrojl, of course," Borin said.

"No!" Ceychell said and grinned. "I've spoken to him." She didn't realize she blurted it until it was out.

"Why do you serve him?" Simigrin asked.

"Hey, there," Ceychell said. "He was talking to me, I think." She was annoyed that she was rudely cut off. Then she realized she barked at Simigrin. The memory of drugging his drink bounced in her head. The skin on her face burned to a numbing tingle; she ran her fingers through her hair and realized her head was sweating.

Simigrin turned his face toward her and whispered again, "Why do you serve him?"

"We all do," he slurred.

Ceychell smiled and realized the drug was affecting him. She hoped she could hold it together. "He is the Greatfather of Dreams. The Bringer of Doom. The Henslemen are his clerics and I am their coordinator." He leaned forward, ambition in his eyes. "When he walks this world he will be *the* god and we will be at his side while the others wallow at his feet." He chuckled and pet Simigrin's face.

Simigrin stared at him with her mouth open.

Ceychell started, "That's not—" but Simigrin put a hand over her mouth.

Chintaja walked up and asked, "Is everything okay here?"

"Of course, man," Borin said with a wink. "What do you think?" He rubbed Simigrin's backside, and she pulled his hand away.

"He was just telling us about the horn," Simigrin said. "He's such an important man and we love hearing his stories."

"Wait, was I?" he asked.

Ceychell mumbled into Simigrin's hand. She wanted to tell her she was wrong, that they were talking about Carbrojl.

"They both have had a bit too much to drink," Simigrin said.

Chintaja nodded. "Was he? Do continue."

Ceychell stopped wrestling with Simigrin and listened.

Borin blinked a few times and said, "What were we talking about?"

"You were going to tell us about the horn," Chintaja said. "You know, tusk, bound in black metal."

Borin waved them in for a whisper. "The queen says it is the Horn of Syindella, but I don't believe her. Just a silly legend." He reached up to grope Simigrin, and she released Ceychell's mouth and grabbed both his hands.

"Where does she keep it?" Simigrin asked. She smiled with gritted teeth.

"Keep what?" Borin asked. His eyelids were drooping.

"What does she keep?" Ceychell asked. She then remembered Borin was talking about the horn. She pushed through the effects as best she could. She badly wanted the horn.

Simigrin intervened. "She keeps the horn and the crown very safe."

"Oh yes," Borin said. "Sleeps with it even. She has night terrors, but we all know who's behind that." He winked and mouthed *Carbrojl* without audibly saying it.

"She sleeps… next to night terrors?" Ceychell asked. She was struggling to follow and was so thirsty. She reached for the cup of wine but Chintaja moved it before she could grab it. He removed a wineskin from his belt, uncorked it and handed it to her. It only took a few seconds until she chugged it dry.

"No," Borin said, shaking his head as if his neck had come loose. "They come, when she sleeps."

Simigrin rolled her eyes at Chintaja. Borin grabbed her butt and she screamed, then covered her mouth.

Everyone in the hall turned and looked at her. She turned toward Borin and hid her face.

Ceychell looked around at the gaping faces for a moment, then everyone went back to what they were doing.

"My friend *really* needs that horn," Simigrin said to Borin. "Tell me where it is and I'll do *anything* for you."

"No, *I* will do anything for you," Ceychell said.

"Really?" Borin asked.

"Really." Simigrin and Ceychell said.

"She keeps it in a lockbox below her throne," he whispered, almost mumbled. "The key—" he leaned at both women, then whispered "—is in the heart." He giggled and tried to touch Simigrin's hair but she moved his hand away.

"What does she keep in her box?" Ceychell said and started laughing.

Chintaja put his arm around her and said, "Excuse me, I think she could use some fresh air. We'll be right back."

"Why … she's going? Come back!" Borin said.

Chintaja led Ceychell away from Borin. Her legs were riddled with pin-pricks, and he had to hold her up. "Easy, milady. Careful steps now."

"I don't need any air," Ceychell said. "I… I'm so thirsty." She put an arm around him. "Where's Miraden? He'll get me some water."

"I think you might need that antidote," he said.

"What? What are you talking about?" Then she caught her thoughts. She worried about Simigrin and looked back.

"Didn't you make the antidote?"

"Why would I do that?" she said. "I didn't—" but it donned on her that she did take it. Chintaja was a little blurry but she could tell he was gritting his teeth, and she grabbed his cheek. "Oh you're adorable when you're nervous. I see what Lovo's talking about."

"How long does this last?" he asked.

She rubbed her eyes. She wasn't sure how long, or how much she drank. "I don't know. My head is swimming, but I think I am feeling a little better."

"Okay." Simigrin said, startling Ceychell.

They both turned and she walked up to them in a hurry. "Let's get to the kitchen. I have all the information. We need to decide what to do."

TWENTY·EIGHT

THE QUIET COUGH

MIRADEN SAT QUIETLY IN THE corner closet of the kitchen and tightened his silent-step boots. The black mottled leather felt like pumice and scraped his hands. He remembered trying to sneak quietly through Bleak Gale Pines last year and wished he'd had the boots then.

He picked up the fine osiliath scale cloak that the Chieftain of Adolehrn had given him. It was too big for him but it would still work. He wrapped it around his shoulders and tied it. When he pulled his hood up and drew the front closed over his chest, he could see through his body to the floor. He was perfectly invisible.

The door cracked open and Lovo whispered, "Miraden?" When Miraden looked up at him, Lovo jerked back and then laughed. "Ah, your face is floating." Miraden pulled the cloak back over his shoulders to become visible. He opened the door and Simigrin stepped inside and sat down in front of him. She looked beautiful in her dress. He wished he was back on the island with her, carefree. Had he known he'd end up stuffed in a castle closet and dying of poison, he would have never left O'kokra.

"Don't take too long," Lovo said. "It's probably midnight already." Lovo pulled the door closed without a sound.

Simigrin was on the verge of tears and sniffled a few times. "I shouldn't tell you this," she said, "but the horn is in her lockbox below her throne. The key is in the heart. I don't know what that means but that's what her counselor said. He was drugged and drunk, so it may be made up, you'll have to figure it out."

"The key is in the heart," he whispered. "Why shouldn't you tell me that?" He felt like Ceychell would have gladly told him anything, no matter the result.

"Because, Miraden, I am choosing to save your life, though many people could die as a result." She caressed his cheek. "I love you, but I don't know how I will live with myself if the Lorden brings her army north and destroys Kander and kills everyone I hold dear. Because I will know that I caused it."

Miraden leaned his head against hers. "I love you too and I won't let that happen," Miraden whispered.

She started crying and draped her arms around his neck. He'd never really seen her cry. Feeling her tears drip on to his hand made him begin to doubt if they were doing the right thing.

He would have preferred a romantic moment with her, but this moment was precious to him.

"It's okay, Simi," he whispered. "Where's the crown? That's why we're here." He hoped the crown could stop the ashenkin, but he was beginning to doubt that too.

She wiped her eyes and cleared her throat. "She sleeps with it, but she is a light sleeper and has nightmares often. You must be *very* careful when you find her."

"Even if I find the crown *and* the horn. How are we going to get out of here? When she wakes up, they will probably close off the harbor and the whole city."

"Chintaja and Lovo are working on that."

"Where is Ceychell? Is she alright?"

Simigrin sighed. "She is … fine. Chintaja is with her right now. It's kind of a long story."

Miraden didn't like the sound of that; he leaned her back so he could talk to her face to face. "What happened to her?

"It's just, I think she accidentally had some of the shofritters root that she gave to the queen's advisor. So she's just a little confused. She'll be fine."

Miraden nodded. "Okay… well, I'm going to get that crown. That's what we set out to do. I hope Ceycha is wrong about Lord Umorogrin. We have to stop the ashenkin."

Simigrin shook her head, clutched both of his hands, and pulled them to her chest. Her lips trembled and tears flowed down her cheeks. "I'm so sorry. I wish I had never sent you that letter. I wish we never left O'kokra. I wish everything was different."

It was as if she'd read his thoughts. He wanted to shrink and hide, but that wasn't him anymore. "I am done wishing for things."

The door opened, and Lovo peeked in. "Sorry to interrupt, but we should get moving."

Miraden wanted to tell him to come back later, but he couldn't. There was too much at stake. He stepped out of the closet, and Simigrin followed close behind him.

"Okay," Lovo whispered, "Chintaja told me exactly how to get to the throne room and the queen's chambers. We have to walk through the castle, so I'm going to distract any guards I see. If I get locked up, keep going. Meet us back here when you have that horn and crown. If you can't get it done within two hours, come back to the kitchen."

"Don't get locked up. I am not leaving you here," Miraden said.

Lovo put his hands on Miraden's shoulders. "Wouldn't be the first time I was in jail. I wish we had more time to plan this out, but our ship leaves tomorrow. We have to get you back to the Lorden.

That's our first priority."

Simigrin smiled and hugged Lovo. Then she hugged Miraden again and said, "Good luck. I'll see you back here." She walked out of the kitchen toward the party hall.

Miraden felt minor gut twinges, but he was much better than when they'd arrived in Sentry. He walked beside Lovo with his hood up and his cloak closed. When he passed by a mirror on the wall, he glanced over and saw only Lovo.

They walked up a flight of stairs past two guards. As they entered the hallway on the second floor, Miraden swerved behind Lovo to avoid bumping into three servants carrying trays of empty flagons. The corridor was completely unadorned, no tapestries, paintings, ornaments or trophies, just stone walls, a few narrow-slit windows, and a cold breeze blowing through it.

They continued up another stairway and through a gallery. The paintings were drab, dusty, and poorly lit. Crystal chandeliers hung from the ceiling, but they were unlit, thick with dust, and one hung sideways on a broken chain. The floor was covered with dusty, cracked black and white tiles and footprints. A grand orange-wood three-story staircase with smooth marble stood in a far corner with a guard in thick chainmail and carrying a poleaxe at each floor.

Miraden was surprised that the queen of Sentry, one of the most powerful people in the world, lived in a sad, austere palace. He never would have believed it had he not seen it with his own eyes.

A couple of guards saw Lovo but said nothing. When Lovo nodded to them, they half nodded back. Miraden inhaled some dust kicked up by Lovo, and tried to stifle a cough, but failed.

The guards looked at Lovo, but he coughed and thudded his chest with his fist. As they approached two guards in full plate armor at the massive steel double doors at the far end of the gallery, Miraden clenched his teeth, but could not hold back another cough.

Lovo coughed again and whistled. "Dust," he said to the guards. "Always gets me."

"Where are you headed?" the guard on the left asked. He was large. It took twice the steel to wrap around his body.

"Just doing my rounds," Lovo said. "Need to make sure all is quiet in the throne room."

"All is quiet," the other guard said. He was tall and muscular. His suit required extra steel as well, but the way he clinched his fists, cracking his knuckles made Miraden sweat.

"No one has entered since the queen retired for the evening," the muscular guard said.

"This is going to sound a little crazy," Lovo whispered, "but there's a rumor that ashenkin could have snuck into the castle." Lovo continued toward the guards. Miraden stayed close to him, thinking he wouldn't need the horn if he was killed right here.

"Why would ashenkin be *here?*" the heavy guard asked.

"There are no children in the castle," the second added.

"I know, I know. It's just what I overheard from a ferryman bringing some guests here. Just want to confirm that the room is empty."

The guards stared at him for a moment.

Lovo held his arms out and said, "We are all here to protect the queen, aren't we?"

Miraden stood as still as a statue.

The heavy guard on the left looked over to the second guard and shrugged. He opened the door just a crack. Miraden shuffled toward it, but it wasn't open enough.

Lovo stuck his big head in the opening. "Just a bit—" He tripped fell against the side of the door, pushing it open just another few inches, and Miraden crept through.

"So sorry about that," Lovo said from behind Miraden. "It's

been a long day. Everything looks to be in order. Say, can I get you anything from the kitchen? I'm headed that way."

The door closed behind Miraden. He heard muffled talk but couldn't make it out. The throne room was a giant hexagon with two burning torches on each wall. At the center of the room were statues of four kings and four queens, at least that's what Miraden assumed they were. Miraden thought the paintings on the wall were of prior rulers, but he wasn't sure. One was of a young girl holding a rabbit. She was beautiful, with black curly hair, dark skin, and kind blue eyes. She was dressed in high boots for horse riding. He wondered if she was Princess Kalionite.

At the back of the room were two thrones, one large and one small. A banner on each wall showed four blue shields and two crossed flails against a green field. Moonlight shone through a set of windows on the north wall; the others were black. There were no other exits. Miraden walked over to the statues. Each stood on a pedestal, and there was a smaller, empty pedestal he hadn't noticed at first. He read the plaque on it:

Princess Kalionite
Taken before she could be queen – now reigning in heaven

Miraden walked toward the large throne. It was beautiful. It was made from blue pine. He could tell by the teal hue that it gets when it is polished with oil. It had a large black cushion and dragon's feet at the bottom of its legs. A silver backing was pinned in with solid gold studs. At the top of the throne were tiny steel shields with large emeralds and sapphires embedded into their centers. The smaller throne next to it was identical in every way except its size.

He began searching the throne, but didn't find anything obvious. The back of the throne was blue pine worked into a smooth finish and reinforced with steel vines that reached up the back of the throne like long fingers holding it in place. He ran his hands up and down the smooth wood, but still found nothing.

He pulled on the cushions and lightly tapped the wood to search for compartments, still nothing. He sat on the floor and reached under the bottom, nothing.

Then he rested his head against the back of the throne and looked over at the smaller throne. It was dusted, cleaned, and its gems glittered. On its black cushion was an imprint of what looked like a circle. He got up and took a closer look; the circle could have been made from a crown.

He searched the throne thoroughly and found only an empty vial set into a steel clamp on its back. A small wooden plaque above it read:

Below is the horn
The danger is sealed
To the south they rot
We would see them stay there
Forever
To bring the end
The key is in the heart

Miraden read the verse again and again. Did he really want to bring it back to the Lorden? He imagined the scorpion soldiers rampaging through their towns and thought they might even be worse than the ashenkin. He felt guilty about choosing his own life above all others. It filled him with regret.

He knelt there for a moment, wondering how long he had before he fell asleep and left the world and what he would do differently if he was given the chance to live. He put his hand on the throne and leaned his head against it. His stomach churned. Either his sickness was getting worse or his anxiety was getting the best of him.

He slid his hand over part of the steel clamp and felt a depression in the metal. He looked at it closely and pushed it. A pin shot out of the throne above the vial, nicking his cheek. Warm blood trickled down his face.

Miraden stared closely at the tiny hole with the pin in it in the back of the chair. He looked down at the vial, realized there was a thin glass tube running from the vial into the throne. He leaned in and let the blood from his cheek drip into the vial. He thought he heard something faint, distant. He thought about running and then realized, what does he have to fear?

The vial filled, then drained through the tube into the throne, and now he definitely heard *something*. It sounded like wood sliding. It was probably loud enough for the guards outside to hear it. He ran his hands around the throne again, looking for anything. Then he pushed on it. It budged.

Miraden put his shoulder against the throne and pushed and slid it forward about a foot. Below the throne was a square hole with a black wooden case the size of a breadbox inside it. He picked up the box and pulled the throne back. Then the steel door opened from the gallery.

Miraden remained perfectly still. He looked at the floor and realized he hadn't moved the throne all the way back into place, but he couldn't do anything for the moment. He slipped the box beneath his cloak and waited patiently.

"What was that?" a guard said.

Two guards stepped into the room. Miraden kept his head down so the hood hid his face. He heard them walk closer.

"I definitely heard something," the other guard said. "Maybe that Henslemen was right."

"Hey," It was Lovo's voice, just in time. "I brought you some cake with extra figs. Have you tried this?" Miraden heard him walk into the throne room and heard a loud metallic clang that nearly made him piss himself. He dropped the box and grabbed it again in a panic. He hoped the guards didn't see his hands.

"Sorry about that," Lovo said. "I didn't see it."

Miraden took a quick peek. Lovo was picking up the pieces of an armored suit near the door.

"You idiot," a guard said. "You'll wake the queen! Captain Dredtrek will have us hung!"

Lovo put up his hands. "You're right, I'm so sorry."

Miraden started shuffling toward the open door. As he went by Lovo, he tapped him on the leg.

"I was going to share the cake, but I'll leave all for you, gonna get more for myself. I'm sorry I made a ruckus."

"Next time you come up, bring us some of the jellied cakes," the muscular guard said.

"You got it," Lovo answered. Miraden hurried toward the stairs in the corner of the gallery. He figured the queen's room would be at the top. He heard footsteps, turned around, and saw Lovo, searching for him.

Miraden walked over and grabbed his wrist. Lovo flinched, but then kept moving like nothing happened. Miraden slid the box into the bag beneath his invisible cloak and followed Lovo up the stairs.

At the bottom landing, a Henslemen walked over and put his hand up. His face was wrinkled and his hair was white and thin like straw. He had a crossbow hitched to the side of his black suit.

"Where in His name do you think you're going?" the man whispered.

Lovo said, "I was going to apologize to the queen if I woke her."

"If you woke her," the man said, "she would be screaming and you'd have a crossbow bolt sticking out of your eye. You must be new here. Nobody disturbs the queen's sleep."

"Yes, I am just in from Oddion. I could bring her lilies. I heard they are her favorite,"

Miraden knew Lovo was stalling, so he crept around both men and continued up the stairs.

The Hensleman started, "You must be an—"

The stair under Miraden creaked. The Hensleman turned his head toward him.

Lovo said, "Well, lilies tomorrow then, when she's awake."

"Yes, get out of here."

Miraden heard Lovo tromping back down the stairs. He climbed to the second floor. Two guards and a Henslemen were looking down at Lovo.

From the second-floor landing there was a hallway that went in both directions. Each hallway had at least ten doors, all of them were shut and a few had a guard standing outside of them. Miraden continued up the next flight to the top floor. The Hensleman on guard was staring over the rail at Lovo.

The rug and walls were black and hung with portraits that Miraden assumed to be of the queen. In each she wore black, except for one, a painting in which she was holding the princess at a rocky beach with waves lapping the shore and birds flying in the bright blue sky. The queen and princess both wore bright dresses and were smiling. The princess's face and dress were so detailed that she almost looked alive. Her crown, a golden ring with an inset emerald, was too big and hung low around her ears. Her black hair looked like spun silk and her eyes were ocean blue.

Miraden crept past the Hensleman.

The floor had one long hallway to the left that ended at a large silver door. Two guards stood in front of the door. They looked sleepy or bored or both, but he still needed a plan to get the door open. Causing a disturbance would only bring more guards. So he leaned against the wall and waited.

Across from him was another painting. This one was of the queen, sad and holding a baby. Princess Kalionite was very little, standing beside the queen with a solemn expression. Next to the queen was a man in blue robes, also reaching out and holding the baby.

Miraden waited for over an hour, stared at the painting. He felt dizzy and achy; his patience was failing and he needed to pee. He tried to occupy his mind. He thought of running through the woods with Ceychell when they were young, of fishing in the creek by his house, of when he first met Tundra near Yoldro, and of the last time he saw Stormrange.

At last, a guard came up the stairs and walked down the hallway. Miraden held his breath.

"The slop is cold tonight, losers. See you at half-past," the guard said. His armor was sloppily fastened. The other two walked past Miraden and down the stairs. Miraden watched the replacement guard lean against the wall and tip his helmet just enough to cover his eyes.

Miraden crept toward the door slowly and stood less than two feet from the guard. The door had a keyhole; he hoped it wasn't locked. After several minutes the guard snuffled, wiped his nose, and began to snore.

Miraden reached down to the door handle and pulled it slowly, and it was opening. The guard's poleaxe was leaning against him. Miraden kicked the bottom of the pole toward the guard's feet, and it fell thudding to the rug.

The guard woke and looked around, breathed a sigh, and bent to pick up his weapon.

Miraden slipped through the door and closed it behind him. Then he pressed himself against the wall and waited to see if the sound had awakened the queen.

After a few moments, nothing happened so he exhaled and looked around. The queen's bedroom was dark and smelled like sweat. A massive bed, three times the size of a normal bed, lay at the far wall. The sleeping queen was tangled in the silk sheets. A dark wooden dresser and a silver mirror stood against the left wall; several seven-foot-tall armoires against the right. The room was stuffed with chairs and lounging furniture that Miraden couldn't really make out, and a mess of shoes and garments were strewn on the floor and bedposts.

Miraden crept around the room looking for the crown. Nothing was on the dresser, except a few stacks of hydras. He was tempted to pocket the coins but was afraid of making any noise. He walked slowly to the bed. On the pillow beside the queen's head was a crown. It was gold with a green gem, exactly like the painting he'd seen outside, the crown that was on Kalionite's head. The queen's face was sunken and sickly. Her long black hair was spread out on the pillows. Several empty or near empty wine bottles littered her nightstand. She muttered and twitched, and Miraden ducked to hide; then he remembered he was invisible. She seemed to be having an unpleasant dream.

Miraden's heart raced. He reached over the queen's head and carefully lifted the crown off the pillow. He felt like a petty burglar, but it had to be done. The crown was strangely warm in his hands. He slid it beneath his cloak.

"Go ahead, take it," the queen grumbled. "Take that cursed thing, you bastard. I knew you'd come for it, monster." She propped herself up in the bed and looked in his general direction. "Your wizards stole my baby, then they promised they'd bring Kali back to me, I knew you'd come here eventually, you liar. And now your dogs surround me. I can't be rid of you, so take it, take the crown and leave me. Leave me for good." She began to weep.

Miraden pitied her but he was so curious. He remained still with his head hung low so his hood would hide his face. He had so many questions. He felt she had secrets the world needed to know.

Miraden had to become the mage she thought he was if he were to get answers, "Be grateful I don't take more," Miraden whispered.

"You monster! I should blow that damn horn and kill all of you!" Spit flew from her mouth. "You think I don't know your Henslegoons are the ones marking homes, and planting Mandera Spores to make everyone sick? You sent them to guard me from the ashenkin, but they are just keeping me prisoner in my own keep!" She grabbed a bottle from the nightstand and threw it toward Miraden. It sailed by him and shattered on the wall.

"Umorogrin sends his regards," Miraden whispered.

"That LIAR! He stole my baby, he stole my Simi! He promised he would bring Kali back. He is the reason the ashenkin are here!" She threw another bottle. Miraden barely dodged it, falling to his knees. He jumped up and pulled the cloak around him.

"I see you, you monster! I'll kill you!" She threw another bottle. It exploded against an armoire, shattering the armoire's glass front as well. Her momentum tumbled her off the side of the bed.

The throne room door burst open, and three guards filled the doorway. "My queen, what is the matter?" the guard in front asked.

Miraden shuffled slowly toward the door.

"Don't come near me!" the queen howled, clambering back onto the bed. "Arrest him!" She pointed directly at Miraden. "Hang him!" They all looked in Miraden's direction.

"Your majesty, arrest who?" the sloppy guard said. He adjusted the spaulder strap before it fell backward.

"He's right there! He's stolen my Kali's crown! Get him! Kill him, you idiots!" She screamed and sobbed and wailed into her hands.

"The blood of the world's children is on the mages hands! Go tell him. Tell him, you thief! Tell him I am coming for his head!"

At last, the guards stepped into the room, and Miraden slipped behind them, out the door, and into the hallway. More guards were rushing up from downstairs. He pressed his back against the wall, and they ran past him. At the top of the stairs, he felt a dizzy spell and took a few breaths to clear his vision. Then he started down. Escape was top of mind but the very next thought was her mention of Simi. He knew Simigrin was taken when she was a baby, but was she the next princess in line?

When he reached the gallery, four Henslemen were huddled together.

"You three, follow me," the tallest of them said. It was the old Hensleman Lovo had talked to. "One of our brothers was just thrown from a balcony. Lock everything down." They scattered.

Miraden sped into the kitchen. It was uncomfortably quiet. He spotted the top of Lovo's head on the far side of the kitchen behind some shelves full of food.

Miraden rushed over to him and said, "We have to get out of here." Lovo stood with Ceychell and Simigrin. Ceychell's arms were covered in blood. "What happened?"

TWENTY·NINE

HELL HATH NO FURY

CEYCHELL DRANK A FULL CUP of water that Lovo got from the kitchen. She felt better. Her tongue felt swollen, her stomach hurt, and her vision swayed a bit, but her thoughts were clear. She was lucky she didn't drink much of the shofritters root.

She sat just outside the kitchen, worried sick about Miraden. She couldn't imagine returning home without him.

"Hey," Simigrin said, emerging from the kitchen. Ceychell jumped. Simigrin closed the door behind her.

"Is he alright?" Ceychell asked.

Simigrin nodded. "Seems to be. He's off with Lovo. All we can do is wait now."

"Well, we can't wait here. It will look suspicious. Let's head back to the hall."

"It's getting late," Simigrin said. "I hope there are still some people there."

When they arrived at the guild hall it was just as packed as before, possibly more so.

Ceychell glanced over at Borin. Except for him, his table was empty. He seemed to be dozing off, slumped in his chair, his chin on his chest, lightly snoring, and covered in sweat. Chintaja walked over to them casually with a full drink in his hand. "Hello ladies. I take it all is okay?"

Simigrin nodded.

He leaned in between them and whispered. "I have a boatman that will take us back, but it will cost us the rest of our C coins. We will have to move quickly if things go bad."

Ceychell and Simigrin nodded to him.

"Well," he said with a shrug of his big shoulders, "I'm going to mingle. Have a lovely time."

Ceychell wiped her forehead. It was a bit warm in the hall, and the shofritters root seemed to make it far worse. She didn't like being on display and was tired of so many drunks watching her. "Where should we sit and wait?"

Simigrin's eyes opened so large you'd think she'd just seen a dragon fly into the room.

"There you are, darling." Neandra had crept up behind Ceychell. "And who is your lovely friend?" He was swaying slightly and slopping his drink around. He steadied himself against a pillar, narrowed his eyes, and studied Simigrin. Then he smiled, like the idiot Ceychell always imagined he would be, and grasped Ceychell's hand. She let him kiss it, imagining tearing his tongue as he did.

"This is my friend…," Ceychell said.

"Wonderful to meet you," Simigrin said.

Neandra took Simigrin's hand and slobbered on the back of it. "Something about you seems… familiar. I'm Neandra. You've probably heard of me." He rubbed her arm and said, "Your skin is like silk and…" His eyes got stuck on her chest.

"Ahem," Ceychell said, interrupting his ogling. "Maybe you could take my friend and me outside like you promised. I'd love to see the ocean from the cliffs."

"I know just the place," he said.

Neandra took them to a long balcony halfway up the castle. It stretched out over the cliff, and the entire night sky spread out like a great canvas before them. Far below, the ocean battered the jagged rocks with white caps in the brisk wind. The moon was so bright that the balcony was fully illuminated.

Neandra strolled toward the balcony edge, finished his drink, and threw the glass over the side. Ceychell and Simigrin walked up and stood beside him.

"I'll tell you both, it's not very common I'm so smitten, but you both are as lovely as princesses. As a hero of the people, I get a lot of attention. But I hate it."

"What kind of 'hero' are you?" Ceychell asked. She put her hand on his shoulder and rubbed his triceps. Simigrin and she exchanged a glance, Simigrin covered her mouth and hid a giggle.

Neandra puffed out his chest and said, "I've saved *many* children from the ashenkin. So many I lost track." He looked at Ceychell, and she nodded and tried to look impressed. "I've battled countless beasts and demons. I am a captain of the Henslemen, after all. I got promoted and now I'm here, guarding our beloved queen." He stopped talking and stared out at the ocean. His dark hair whipped in the wind.

Ceychell leaned on the balcony next to him and smiled. "I imagine it's hard to deal with all the attention."

"It can be quite taxing, really," he said. "You know, you really are beautiful. Possibly the most beautiful person I've ever seen. I am amazed kingdoms aren't fought for you."

It was *almost* as if Neandra sobered for a moment. When he leaned in for a kiss, she backed away.

"I see, you are shy. My mistake."

Ceychell glanced down and saw the twin sabers on his hips. She remembered Miraden's letters about how good he was with them. "Oh, not really shy," she said and began unfastening his belt.

"Ah… I like where your mind is going," Neandra said.

"If only you could read my thoughts," she said. She slid his belt off carefully and laid it on the limestone floor of the balcony. He leaned his back against the balcony, put his arms along the rail, and closed his eyes. She turned and whispered to Simigrin, "Freeze his arms?"

Simigrin's eyes widened and she nodded.

"Ladies… I'm so glad I found you," he mused.

Ceychell leaned in and said, "Thank you, people's hero." He tried to kiss her again, but she leaned back. He tried again and she bent to the side.

Frost spread from Simigrin's hand to the balcony railing and thickened to ice over his hands and arms.

"What in—" he said before Simigrin put her hand over his mouth. Frost formed around her hand, under his chin, around his mouth.

His eyes widened, and he jerked back and forth, bucked and tried to bend away from the rail. Ceychell picked up his sabers and tossed them over the side. They plummeted down, clanged off the rocks, and into the ocean.

"You don't remember me?" Simigrin said. Neandra stared at her and tried to scream but the ice muffled his cries. "You not only left us for dead and tried to strand us at the Baron's keep, but you took our horses and likely our reward." Simigrin kicked him hard in the groin. Neandra howled and sank, but was suspended by his frozen arms. "That's from me," she kneed him again, "And that's from Miraden."

Neandra's eyes teared. He jerked his head and tried to speak.

Ceychell thought he might be begging. It sounded lovely.

"You don't know who I am, do you?" She stroked his frozen cheek. He shook his head. "I'm Ceychell. You were going to kiss me goodbye, remember?" Neandra's eyes darted back and forth. "You remember throwing my letter into a chasm?" She grabbed his collar with both hands and yanked him toward her. "You cost me Miraden and I should cut your damn throat!"

"Alright," Simigrin said, "We can't linger here too long. Get your revenge and let's go."

Neandra screamed and shook his head. Tears ran down his icy cheeks.

"No," Ceychell said. She raised her leg, put her foot on the rail next to Neandra's face, and drew Hellshy from its sheath. "I want more."

"What are you doing?" Simigrin said.

"You threw away my letter and ruined my life!" Ceychell screamed. "For that, you'll—"

"Ceychell!" Simigrin tried to grab her wrist but missed. Ceychell jammed Hellshy's jagged blade into Neandra's heart and twisted it. Neandra's scream was muffled by the ice. He buckled on the wall while Ceychell twisted the blade. She wanted him to feel how much she hurt, how much pain he'd caused her. Then she ripped the blade out of his chest, laid it on the rail, bent down and grabbed his feet, and flipped him over the wall. He screamed and slammed against the other side of the railing, his dislocated shoulders still frozen in place. Blood gushed from his chest onto the balcony and down the cliff.

"Ceychell!" Simigrin hissed. "No one hates him more than I do, but you're murdering him. Are you really a murderer?"

"I love Miraden, more than anything in the world," Ceychell yelled. "And this is what he gets for ruining that!"

"Killing Neandra isn't going to change Miraden's mind. If anything, he might resent you for it—it might even terrify him!"

The ice was starting to crack around Neandra's arms. He groaned and his eyes rolled back in his skull momentarily.

"He is my best friend!" Ceychell yelled. "And now he may die! We should have never come to help you. You mages brought the ashenkin here! And now he's fallen for you, a bloody mage." Ceychell picked up the dagger from the railing and stared at Simigrin.

"We didn't bring the ashenkin. I have been trying to stop them! You're a mage, like it or not. You are one of us!"

"I know the truth! Umorogrin has poisoned your minds. I've seen how you manipulate Miraden. You don't even want to save him. You just want the crown for your *Lord*. I don't trust you!"

Simigrin shook her head and backed away.

Neandra's muffled screams were fading and his head was wobbling to the side. Ceychell whispered a few words and flicked her hand. Flames burst from her fingertips and licked the ice. He stared up at her from the corner of his eye.

As the ice started to break apart, Simigrin lunged forward and grabbed Neandra's wrists. Ceychell shoulder slammed her away, the ice broke apart, and he fell.

A moment later, they heard a dull splash.

"You are the real monster," Simigrin said.

Ceychell stared her down and considered throwing her over next. "We need to get to the kitchen. But this *isn't* over."

THIRTY

THE FADING RUSE

LOVO POURED SOME WATER ONTO a kitchen rag while Ceychell wiped off her arms. Simigrin shook and stared into space. Miraden had not seen her so disturbed since they were in Bleak Gale Pines. He wasn't sure who to help first.

"Are you hurt?" Miraden whispered.

"No, I'm fine," Ceychell said, not seeming fine at all. "Did you get the horn?"

"How about you, Simi?"

"I'm fine," she said, but she seemed even less "fine" than Ceychell.

Miraden suddenly realized he never had a moment to check inside the box. He pulled it from his sack. The other three stared at it. It was beautiful, smooth, black as tar, and heavy. The seal between the lid and the box was so perfect it was nearly invisible. He only found it because it must have jostled slightly open in his pack. He held the bottom and let Lovo remove the top. Inside was the horn, but it was not from a bull or any animal he'd ever seen. Though it must be hundreds or thousands of years old, it looked like it could have been made yesterday. It was white, cracked, and larger than a bull's horn. Three thin, black metal bands were wrapped around it without rivets or nails. When he held it up, it hummed.

Lovo put his hand on Miraden's shoulder and hugged him.

"Good job, Miraden," Ceychell said. When Lovo finished his bear hug, she hugged him and whispered in his ear, "Let's get you back to Fe Jet." He hugged her back and didn't want to let go.

"What about the crown?" Simigrin asked.

Miraden had nearly forgotten about it, and now doubted they should even bring it back to Umorogrin. He also debated telling Simigrin about her mother. "The queen said—"

A ruckus erupted outside the kitchen door. The four companions hushed and ducked behind the shelves as a pack of people entered the kitchen.

Weapons bounced against armor and heavy boots clapped the kitchen floor for a long moment until they were out the far door.

Chintaja poured a little more water onto Ceychell's arms while she tried to rub the rest of the blood off of them. "The queen's words will have to wait," Chintaja whispered, "We need to get out of here, now."

"He's right," Lovo said. "We could be trapped or, worse, have to take the road south."

Miraden pulled off his cloak, rolled it up and handed it to Lovo. "Let's go."

Lovo took Miraden by the arm, Chintaja took Ceychell and Simigrin's arms, and they hurried out of the kitchen and into the guild hall. It was mostly cleared out. The barkeeps were gone. Fewer than ten patrons and only seven Henslemen, a few of whom looked over at them, were left.

Someone said, "What are they still doing here?"

"Trying to make a little extra money," Chintaja said and kept walking. "They were so busy they didn't hear the word to clear out."

"Orders are out that nobody leaves."

Miraden finally looked over. Three Henslemen walked toward them. About twenty more stared at them.

"We're taking them down to the dock," Lovo said. "We'll be right back up."

"Orders are orders, brother," a Henslemen said. He was Miraden's height, dark-skinned and muscular. He walked toward them.

"I *am* following orders, brother," Lovo said. He stepped up to the Hensleman, and they stared each other down for a moment.

"Yeah? Whose orders?"

Miraden felt a surge of sickness and swallowed it down. He hoped Lovo knew what he was doing. Fighting their way out seemed unwise.

"I don't remember, one of the captains yelled to get *them* out of here immediately. Stuffy old guy, he was in the gallery," Lovo said.

The Henslemen clicked his tongue and nodded, then backed up. "Alright, get them out of here."

When they reached the cave, a ferryman in a black robe was waiting for them on the dock next to an empty rowboat. Chintaja dropped several coins in the man's hand, and he waved for them to get in. Miraden struggled and threw up into the water. Lovo patted his back.

"Better now than in the boat," Lovo said. He helped Miraden clamber into the rocking boat.

There were only two oars, and Lovo pulled them quickly away from the dock.

"Thought you were coming right back?" the Henslemen who'd tried to stop them yelled. He and two other Henslemen in boiled leather with a yellow sash on the arm were standing on the dock and loading their crossbows.

Simigrin and Ceychell's books popped out of their invisible sacks.

"Let me get this before you cause us more problems," Simigrin said, pushing Ceychell back down on the bench. Miraden's bow was still strapped to Lovo's back. He pulled it off and fired it. A bright golden arrow flew toward the three Henslemen but missed.

Then he heard a loud whistle and ducked down. A ball of ice had formed at the tip of Simigrin's staff. She cast it into a shield around the boat. The Henslemen's bolts struck but didn't penetrate the ice.

Ceychell stood up, rocking the boat slightly.

"What are you doing?" Chintaja asked.

She thrust her palm forward. Nothing happened. She whispered something Miraden couldn't hear; the book warped and shuddered and nothing happened again. He leaned over the boat so he could see past the ice shield. The Henslemen were reloading and shouting.

Ceychell yelled something in another language, and thrust her hand out again. An explosion sent fire vomiting out of the mouth of the cave, and the entire cliff face shuddered.

"Looks like you killed them too," Simigrin said.

Ceychell sat without looking at her rival. "I did what needed to be done."

"Just like murdering Neandra?"

Miraden stared at Ceychell for a moment and said the only thing he could think of: "What?"

"We saw Neandra in the guild hall," Simigrin said. "We were hazing him for a bit of revenge but Ceychell decided to 'do what she needed to—'"

"Shut it," Ceychell said.

"She tortured and murdered him, Miraden," Simigrin said.

Everyone looked at Ceychell, but no one said a word. Miraden hated Neandra, thought he may even deserve to be killed, but... Ceychell? Her face was painted in anger. Miraden felt like he was looking at someone he didn't even know. He was dizzy and nauseous. He put his face in his hands and tried to fall asleep.

When he woke up, he was being carried on Lovo's back. It was still nighttime. He was so queasy he didn't want to keep his eyes open, but he was too curious to close them. Lovo was carrying him onto their ship, he thought. Ceychell, Simigrin, and Chintaja were just behind him. He recognized the port at Sentry. "Are we leaving?" he asked.

Lovo set him down on the deck of the boat. He closed his eyes and tried not to vomit. Something wet wiped against the side of his face. He reached over into a mound of fur and was licked again. Tundra whined and leaned her massive head against him. Then she lay down beside him. Simigrin and Ceychell walked toward opposite ends of the boat.

Lovo handed him a wineskin of water. "We are heading south, buddy. We need to get you to Fe Jet before it's too late."

Miraden sipped the water. It was cool and delicious. He remembered what Ceychell had done and it troubled him. "Are they still chasing us?" he asked.

"They will be. We'll have to come back for the crown, and we'll need you alive."

Miraden gestured for Lovo to lean in close and whispered, "I got the crown, too. Don't tell them. I think Simigrin may steal it."

Lovo gave Miraden a sidelong look. "I don't think she wants to steal it. Get some rest."

Miraden leaned over against Tundra. He was about to close his eyes when Simigrin rushed over.

"Miraden. Miraden… "

THIRTY·ONE

A HARD BARGAIN

CEYCHELL STARED UP INTO THE blackness of night. The ship headed north, away from Sentry and past Queen's Edge. Figures flickered past the battlements, she could see their shadows and their torches. The wallwalks were busy, but no alarm was sounded. They sailed past without event.

Ceychell stared at the black horizon. It was a cloudless, moonless night. She worried that Miraden wouldn't make it. She relived murdering Neandra and she'd wished it wasn't true, but she enjoyed it. He deserved it. She felt a cold sickness inside her that made her want to vomit, but she pressed her eyes shut and repressed the urge.

A flash of heat washed over and a thirst hit her throat. Pressure built behind her eyes and skull, it was painful. A gust of hot wind shot sand into her face, so she turned away from it and waited for it to pass.

The ground was rippled, cracked, and flat. It stretched endlessly, like it may have been a sea at one time, but now it was just orange and blue sand.

She started walking, wondering when Carbrojl would show up. She couldn't shake the thought, she recalled tossing Neandra off the castle wall and being branded a murderer. *A murderer.* She'd never thought of herself as a bad person, but when Simigrin called her "murderer," it stuck.

Miraden was getting sicker. She hoped they could get to Fe Jet in time to save him. She realized how infatuated she had become, and how easily she stole his sense of adulation. She still felt wounded by his rejection of her, but the thought of losing him threatened her with emptiness, an emptiness he often expressed how he felt to her through his letters. She considered lying down on the baked sand and waiting for it all to pass, but she couldn't, Miraden still needed her help.

At last Carbrojl arrived, standing in the ripples of the heat coming off the sand. She knew he'd be waiting for her.

"You've come to me once again, my child," he said.

"You've brought me here again. Why?" she asked.

"I bring you because you desire it. I see your dreams and know your thoughts. I know what you desire."

"Even if that were true, you couldn't give me what I want. You and the mages have ruined our world."

"Indeed. But you can stop all of that. You have the power."

Ceychell stared at him. "How?"

"The crown, my dear," he said. "It will grant you all my power. The power to free the children. The power to channel all of my spells in that book. The power to save your village. Perhaps even the power to get back Miraden."

"I don't want Miraden's love if I need a spell to get it," she said. "I left my home to find myself, to fight for a good cause, to fight for love, just as he did for me. But unlike him, I failed. I failed *him.*"

"You've not failed, not yet. Your friends work against you. Simigrin will take the crown and give it to Umorogrin, and he will sever my bond with your world. Our bond. You will lose all your power and die. And fail *him*."

"Why would I die?"

"You have a soul of fire. Don't you know by now what that means?"

"Yes, it means I have a tie to your world."

Carbrojl lifted his hand, her hand lifted and went into his. She tried to resist but couldn't. He ghoulishly smiled. "No, Ceychell. It means you have a tie to *me*. It means you were born to wield great power, and unlike my clerics, who pretend to serve me, you draw directly from my power." He squeezed her hand into a tight fist. "You may be the last who can do so."

"I don't want to wield great power. I want to go home, and I want Miraden to come with me."

"Then you must stop the ice mage, or she will take him from you. You need me, now more than ever. Do not cast my aid away or you will lose everything. Your destiny is your choice. You just have to choose." He touched her arm, and a blissful electricity shot through her body.

Ceychell blinked and was again staring at the black horizon. The waves rocked the ship and wind blew her hair about. She removed a wineskin from her bag and downed all the water in it. She coughed, wiped the surfacing tears away and looked back to Miraden.

Lovo was on her left; Miraden and Tundra, looking droopy eyed, on her right. Miraden was pale green and wheezing. She pulled him toward her, put her hand on his chest, and ran her fingers through his hair. He looked in pain, shivering and sweating.

"I know you love him." Simigrin had crept up behind her. Her eyes were puffy and surrounded by dark rings, her hair was a mess, and her dress was wrinkled.

"You're right," Ceychell said, even though she didn't want to talk to Simigrin. "I am the only one who truly loves him. I'd do anything for him, even if it meant unleashing Fe Jet on the world."

"Do you think he'd do that for you?" Simigrin asked.

Ceychell was stunned by the question. Was she blinded by her own obsession? *Would* Miraden save her?

"Would he let thousands, maybe millions of lives be lost for your love?" Simigrin added.

Ceychell shut her eyes; clenched her teeth and felt the same rage swell in her chest as it did before she killed Neandra. "Before *you*, he would have." Ceychell said, shaking her head. "You know, I really liked you. You were a hard but fair teacher, but I really thought we had become good friends. Now that I know Umorogrin's secrets, I think you poisoned Miraden with your lies."

"You're wrong," Simigrin said without hesitation. "I want what's best for him, just like you do."

"You were going to let him die."

"I told him how to find the horn. Not you," she said and walked away.

Was it another lie, or did she really help Miraden? Maybe Simigrin was being lied to, too.

A day and a half later they reached the port town of Andora at the northeast edge of the Syindella Channel. It was small, with two docks and a fort, some trading posts, fishermen, and merchants. Beyond the town was a range of short, craggy mountains. Between the two tallest peaks, flatlands could be seen all the way to the horizon.

Miraden was up and chatting, even laughing for a moment, with

Lovo and Chintaja. Tundra was Miraden's height sitting beside him on her rump. She was licking his face and holding him with her huge paws.

They were only stopping for supplies but Ceychell feared that Miraden's time was running out. They still had a long trek through the tunnel back to Fe Jet.

"Everyone ashore," a sailor hollered.

They walked up the dock to the trading posts and purchased water and linen robes with hoods for the heat. The linen vendor was a thin, old dark-skinned woman with a linen head wrap and blue hair. She welcomed them with a smile. Even recommended they climb a short cliff for the view and the best food in Andora. They all agreed they needed a real meal, so they went.

The eating spot was near the edge of the cliff. They could look down at the channel for dozens of miles. She wasn't sure how high, but she felt like she was sitting back on the Kaehrnstone looking down on Baregorin forest stretching out as far as the eye could see. Except, instead of trees, there was a wide channel. Far to the south were heatwaves and a hint of desert beyond the southern shear wall.

They sat in a large tent at the edge of the cliff with a view of the channel all the way to the western horizon. There were only two other tables, and one person sat at each. They really hadn't talked much on the voyage down from Sentry. Ceychell figured they were all just exhausted, and eager to get Miraden to Fe Jet. Going back to Sentry was the last thing on her mind—she pulled her hair up and raised her chin to let the cool wind blow on her sweaty neck.

The house specialty was grilled lizard and freshly boiled spiced and mint tea, so they ordered enough for the table. Miraden hardly ate his lizard and gave most of it to Tundra lying next to him. After they ate, they sat quietly and stared at their tea until Simigrin spoke.

"It's going to be even harder to get the crown now." She put her elbows on the table and slumped her head into her hands.

Ceychell noticed Miraden glower when Simigrin spoke. Who could blame him, she doubted he would go back.

"It is amazing we left with our lives," Chintaja said. Lovo nodded.

Ceychell said, "If we stay here too long, one of us might not be able to say that." A tense moment passed, but no one challenged her.

"I got the crown," Miraden blurted.

A surge of joy filled her. Ceychell hugged him. "You did? You're always full of surprises!" She couldn't wait to get home.

Simigrin leaned back in her chair and pushed both fists in the air. After a happy scream she yelled, "Well done, Miraden!"

Miraden paused in thought for a moment, and then said, "Yes, now your master will have it. But I thought of tossing it in the ocean."

Simigrin's head jerked forward. "What? Why?"

"The queen said Umorogrin deceived her," Miraden whispered. "He caused the ashenkin problem, and now he's trying to cover it up. Just like Ceychell said."

Simigrin looked like she'd seen a revenant sitting next to her. Her eyes twitched as she slowly turned to look at Ceychell who coolly stared. It was about time.

"She said the Henslemen keep her prisoner in her castle. They aren't protecting her. And they're spreading Mandera Spores to make everyone sick, and then blaming the ashenkin. It's all a big lie."

"Mandera Spores, ugh!" Ceychell said. "That's what that rusty stuff was on the houses in Sentry!" How could she have not thought of that? It was so obvious now. It can be easily treated, but not if people were led to believe it was the Devil's Bargain. "Of course. The Henslemen are Carbrojl's clerics! It all makes sense!" Carbrojl was right all along.

"Miraden... how—" Simigrin said.

"There's more," he cut her off. "Umorogrin may have felt guilty to contact Carbrojl to save Kalionite…" he paused and looked down at the table. Ceychell knew that conflicted gaze. Whatever it was, she knew it was big.

"And?" Simigrin said. Miraden jerked as she grabbed his arm. Her eyes were wide open.

"Because they'd already taken her second daughter, and she was left with no heir. Her second daughter, Simi."

Everyone looked at Simigrin in shock. None could be more shocked than her. "This can't be," she mumbled and teared. She covered her mouth.

"There was a painting of a man in a blue robe taking her baby, I saw it," Miraden said.

"So you are the heir to Queen's Edge?" Chintaja said.

"None of that really matters though, does it, right?" Miraden said. "As long as I give you the crown?"

Ceychell stared at her. "That *is* why you're here, isn't it?"

"Why are you blaming me?" Simigrin shouted and slapped the table. "I'm in this to stop the ashenkin. This is all a lot—" she shook and angrily wiped tears from face, "a lot to take in. I'm not some evil spy!"

"Hold on here," Lovo said, pinching a scrap of lizard off Miraden's plate. "Lay off Simi. We are *all* here to get the crown, right? Just because Lord Umorogrin didn't give us the truth doesn't mean we are enemies. He said the crown is the key to stopping the ashenkin, and it's our best lead. So let's put all this behind us, and confront him after he stops them." Everyone took a moment but slowly nodded in agreement. "But first, we need to get back to Fe Jet."

"Right," Chintaja said. He stood up from his seat and put on his helmet, pulled a thick dagger from his belt, and pressed it against Simigrin's throat. Lovo pushed himself back from the table, and Chintaja drew his longsword with his free hand and pointed the tip at Lovo's eye.

"What is this?," Lovo said, trembling with rage. "How could you?"

"Sorry, Lovo, but I have orders and an estate to collect, and I'm certainly not going to cross the channel and bring the horn to Fe Jet. Come with me. We can leave these fools here and live as nobles in Crestain. A vineyard, feasts, and servants. Think of it, Lovo."

Tears rained down Lovo's cheeks as he stared at his close companion. He balled his twitching fingers into fists.

Chintaja pleaded, "You said you always lived in poverty, always dreamed of the good life. *We* can have it. You and me. These people aren't your friends, they use you."

Lovo looked back at Ceychell, then Simigrin, then at Miraden. Miraden sat still and stared at him without a word.

Chintaja stared straight at Ceychell and tapped Simigrin's throat with the dagger. "Hands on the table, hothead." Ceychell slowly slid her hands onto the table. "Alright now, Miraden. Give me the crown. And while you're at it, the horn too."

"Okay. You win," Miraden said. He reached toward his sack, looking like he was about to vomit.

Ceychell hoped Miraden would not give up so easily. She certainly wouldn't. But the knife was firmly pressed against Simigrin's neck. Simi hissed as the sharp edge of the blade pushed on her skin.

"Please, let us keep the horn." Simigrin pleaded. "Miraden will die without it."

"There is no way I'm letting you take the horn south. Besides, he won't make it back to Fe Jet anyway," Chintaja sneered. "Look at him. He's practically dead."

Miraden's hands tremored but he managed to set the crown on the table. Ceychell stared at it, thinking how she could snatch it and get them out there. It was such a simple thing, gold with a single emerald. She wondered how much power it possessed. She could use it to escape to a better place with Miraden. She would use it for good or not at all. She wanted it so badly it made her sweat more.

"Good, now slide it over," Chintaja said. Miraden pushed the crown across the table.

"Now, Simi, put the crown in my sack." He slid the knife harder against her throat, and she straightened and picked up the crown. "Nice and smooth, Frosty."

Tundra awoke, clambered to her feet and growled loud and deep.

Chintaja didn't even look at the bear. "Keep your pet calm, Miraden, or you'll have to reattach Simi's head."

"Easy, Tundra," he said. "Easy." Tundra let out a low growl. She was so large and so close that Ceychell figured she could tackle Chintaja and he couldn't stop her. She didn't want her to listen to Miraden. "Hold, Tundra. Stay with me," Miraden said.

Ceychell concentrated and took a long slow breath, and without moving her hands from the table, slipped Hellshy from its sheath on her thigh, down to the ground, around Simigrin's feet, and behind Chintaja's greaves.

Miraden sat the black box on the table. "Please take your knife off her throat.".

"Slide it to me and I might let her live," Chintaja said. "Last chance, Lovo," he grumbled, poking the big man's chest with his sword tip. "Please, come with me. You don't want those monsters unleashed in the south. And we will have enough coin to live a good life."

Ceychell brought Hellshy up behind Chintaja's back toward his neck... and nicked his hair. Chintaja stepped back and slapped Hellshy away with his knife. Lovo kicked the empty chair into Chintaja, crashing into the knight's leg. Then Lovo sprang to his feet and drew his mace.

Tundra bounded toward Chintaja.

Miraden stood up, nearly fell, steadied himself on the table, and reached for his bow.

Ceychell and Simigrin stood. The other people in the restaurant scrambled, screaming.

Lovo swung his mace at Chintaja's head; Chintaja parried it with his sword against the haft. As they stood there, locked in a stalemate, Simigrin shot a blast of ice at Chintaja's face. Chintaja shielded himself with his knife arm, and the ice wrapped around it an inch thick. Tundra lunged and swung her massive paw just over Chintaja's head. Lovo pulled back his mace and swung again; Chintaja ducked and punched his frozen arm into Lovo's gut.

Lovo doubled over, and Chintaja whipped his blade down at the back of Lovo's neck, but a blast of light shot through his shoulder and knocked him back from Lovo. The big trainer screamed as blood gushed from his arm. Then Tundra slapped him over the cliff.

"No!" Simigrin screamed. She and Ceychell ran to the cliff edge. Chintaja was halfway to the rocks below the cliff. The two women thrust out their hands. The crown slid up from Chintaja's pack, but he grabbed onto it, and dangled in the air as the two women tried to wrest it from him. Their arms shook and strained. The crown rose, but Chintaja rose with it.

"Fry him," Simigrin said.

"Let me up!" Chintaja screamed, "Please! I'm sorry!"

Lovo joined the women at the edge of the cliff and looked down at Chintaja. His eyes were still glassy with tears.

"Look away, Lovo," Ceychell said

"No. I won't," the big man said.

"It's for the best, Lovo" Simigrin said.

Chintaja was nearly up to the top of the cliff. He had three fingers barely on the crown; his icy frozen arm hung below him.

Lovo knelt and reached down, "Grab my hand!"

"You have to grab me," Chintaja hollered. "I'm slipping!"

Ceychell poured her energy into pulling in the crown, clenching her teeth and trying to keep her arms from trembling.

Lovo grabbed Chintaja's wrist. The crown flew up over Ceychell and Simigrin and sailed back toward the tent.

Blood poured from Chintaja's shoulder, down to his feet, then to the crashing waves far below. "Pull me up, Lovo. Heal me, I beg you!" Chintaja said.

"Goodbye," Lovo said and let go. Chintaja screamed as he plummeted to the channel far below him.

Ceychell scrambled toward the tent, but Miraden was already there. He picked up the crown, put it in his bag, and walked past Ceychell and Simigrin to Lovo, who was on all fours crying. "I'm sorry, big guy. I'm sorry." Miraden held Lovo and let him cry it out.

They didn't stay in Andora long. They had to get across the channel but the sailors from Sentry refused to give them a ride now that Chintaja was gone. It didn't take much convincing after they paid a few hydra to a fisherman to bring them across.

As they approached the small fishing village of goat people on the other side of the channel, Ceychell saw they were arming harpoons on their fishing ships.

"We are on a mission for the Lorden!" Lovo yelled.

"Don't shoot!" Ceychell and Simigrin both yelled and waved her hands. It seemed to have worked because no harpoons were fired.

They unloaded at the dock, and the fisherman waved goodbye and sailed north.

The goat people crowded around them; they seemed to be angry. Ceychell saw the goat woman she'd originally talked to and said,

"We need to get to the Lorden as fast as possible. She's expecting us"

The goat people looked at each other in confusion then parted for them to pass.

"Come," the goat woman said and waved to them to follow.

They followed her to the tunnel entrance. It was just before nightfall and Ceychell was getting tired. They were all tired.

"How are you feeling, Miraden?" Ceychell asked. He slouched and shuffled more than walked. When she put her hand on his shoulder, he collapsed to the ground.

"Miraden!" she shouted and knelt to help him. Lovo and Simigrin crouched over him as well. He was wheezing every breath and staring vacantly at the tunnel wall.

Simigrin put her hand on his head. "He is burning up. We have no time to rest. We have to get him to the Lorden."

"It took at least three days to walk from her palace," Lovo said. "Even if we moved fast…"

Simigrin lifted Miraden off the ground. "We need to try, come on."

Ceychell helped lift him but she knew they could not move fast enough with Miraden barely able to walk. Lovo took Miraden's gear off and lifted him onto Tundra. The bear made a little chirp and seemed to nod her head.

"C'mon, Tundra. Follow me," Lovo said. He pulled a chunk of smoked lizard out of his pocket and let her smell it.

Simigrin shook her head. "No, we still won't make it. I am going to take a risk and put you into a sleep, Miraden. It may slow the poison enough to buy us time."

"Don't do that!" Ceychell said. "The Lorden said he will fall into a final sleep. You could kill him."

"We are several days away—he will die before we get there. Do you want to make that call?"

Ceychell looked at Miraden. He was nearly green and barely

breathing into Tundra's neck fur. "No, do it."

It was a tense and exhaustively long walk through the tunnel. Ceychell was beyond tired; the others were sweaty, miserable, and silent. Miraden peacefully slept on Tundra. Ceychell held one of his hands; Simigrin held the other. His hand was still warm, which gave Ceychell hope.

Finally, when Ceychell thought she couldn't possibly take another step, a light appeared at the end of the tunnel. The four companions were too tired to celebrate. They raced toward it, and eventually a doorway, lit by a single torch and guarded by two scorpion guards, appeared at the end of the tunnel.

"Get the Lorden!" Simigrin yelled. "We need her help!"

"We have the horn!" Lovo shouted.

One guard opened the door, and the other disappeared inside.

Simigrin reversed the spell, and Ceychell poured the last of her water onto Miraden's head. His eyes were closed and his head lolled back and forth with the lumbering sway of Tundra's pace.

The guard took them through the doors, down another tunnel, and into the great throne chamber. The Lorden came down the steps toward them with an entourage of guards.

"Lorden Flisstriq," Ceychell yelled! "We need the antidote immediately. We have the horn!"

The Lorden slithered up to them, her guards right behind her. "You have the horn?"

"We do," Ceychell said. She pulled the box out of Miraden's pack and slapped it into Lorden Flisstriq's hand. Her eyes widened as she opened the box. The torchlight flickered off the Lorden's serpent eyes as she gazed at it.

"Extraordinary," she said, staring at the relic. "You actually got it."

"We had a bargain," Simigrin yelled. "Miraden is dying. Please give him the antidote."

"We did have a bargain," the Lorden said. "Hold him up to me." They picked Miraden up from Tundra's back. The Lorden leaned forward and bit him on the neck.

"Is that the antidote?" Lovo asked.

"Is this a joke?" Ceychell asked.

The Lorden pushed Miraden's eye open and bent over to look into it. "He will fully recover in a few days. The antidote is the same venom, given when the victim has fallen into a coma. He will probably be immune to most poisons after this. He should thank me."

Ceychell screamed. Her voice unnaturally shook the entire room. Dust fell from the ceiling, torches went out, everyone held their ears. She turned and roared, "Thank you, *great* Lorden, for nearly killing my friend!" She wondered if she could work up a blaze of flames fast enough to burn the Lorden right there, but she knew they wouldn't get out of Fe Jet alive.

The Lorden held up her hands when the guards advanced. She shook her head. "I'm curious," the Lorden said. "Did you get your crown?"

"We didn't have time, just the horn," Lovo said.

"Hrmph. It matters not," the Lorden said.

The scorpion guards circled around them.

"Are we your prisoners again?" Simigrin asked.

"You've done a great thing for my people, yet you humans are our enemy. What would you have me do?"

"Let us go?" Lovo mused.

"We still have to get the crown," Simigrin said.

"If I let you go," the Lorden said, "you will warn your people that I am no longer their captive."

"No one knows you exist. You're no one's captive," Simigrin said. "I simply cannot let you return north. You can either fight one another to the death to entertain my people, the winner can serve me for the rest of their days. Or, you can decide your own fate."

THIRTY·TWO

DISSENTION IN THE RANKS

CEYCHELL AND HER COMPANIONS WERE put into a square cell, watched by scorpion guards. They were given two clay pots: one filled with yellow and blue fruit, the other with water.

They had one day to decide how they would die, but they had not discussed it. Instead, Ceychell was trying to think of a way out of their mess.

Miraden had awakened slowly and was eating with the rest of them. He seemed groggy, but the color had returned to his face.

"Your bear," a guard said. They brought in Tundra on a chain leash. She was muzzled and looked drugged. When she saw Miraden, she lumbered up to him, and Miraden hugged her. After the guards closed the cell door, he took her muzzle and chain off and petted her.

"I'm so sorry that we don't have much longer together, Tundra," he whispered. The bear groaned and slumped against him. Ceychell teared up watching Miraden and Tundra console each other. They seemed to understand one another.

Lovo leaned toward Ceychell and whispered, "Maybe we should make a run for it. If we get through the tunnel, we can try to get a boat out again."

Those guards look like they can run much faster than us," Miraden said. "We'd have to fight our way out."

Ceychell had thought Simigrin was asleep, but she opened her eyes and said, "I could create a barrier or maybe even freeze them. If I do it in the tunnel, it might be hours before someone finds them."

"What if they smash through it?" Lovo said. "Or somehow sends notice to have the tunnel sealed?"

"Even if we made it through, we'd still face the desert," Miraden said.

"We are too exhausted to fight our way out," Simigrin said. "Even with Tundra." She could barely keep her eyes open.

Ceychell said. "What if we request to jump off the cliff? We would be out of the tunnel and could try to flag or steal a boat."

"The Lorden may not let us take the tunnel. And none of us would survive that jump, Ceycha," Miraden said.

Despite their dire situation, Ceychell was happy to hear him call her that again. "We won't jump," she said. "I believe I can create a portal to get us across the channel. But I think I'll need the crown."

Simigrin shook her head. "No, absolutely not."

"Why not?" Ceychell asked.

"That crown is evil. You even said that it was enchanted by Carbrojl. No one should use it. We already have enough problems now that they have the horn."

"Should no one use it?" Miraden asked, "Or are you saying that Ceychell should not use it?"

Simigrin paused for a moment and then pouted. "No one."

"That sounds risky, Ceychell," Lovo said. "What if the portal doesn't take us to the right place, or it fizzles? That's a long drop."

"Is it riskier than fighting our way out of a city in the middle of a desert?" she asked.

Lovo shrugged. "Guess not."

Miraden went to put his hand on the pommel of the axe Ormus had given him but they were stripped of their weapons. "How sure are you about this spell?"

"It's similar to one I already know. The crown will give me any power that I don't already have." She hoped. It was a long shot, but it was their only shot.

Simigrin rolled her eyes. "This isn't going to work. I'm not willing to risk my life on your magic."

"With the crown, I *know* I can do it. It has great power."

"No way," Simigrin said. "Please, Miraden. Don't agree to this. I say we ask to be stranded in the desert or something. We don't want to be stuck on the edge of a cliff with nowhere to go but down."

Lovo patted Miraden on the back. "I'll follow your lead, buddy."

Miraden shook his head. "Why is this my decision?"

Ceychell wanted to laugh. Miraden had changed, but not completely. "I'll take your lead, too, Miraden."

Simigrin hesitated, shook her head, and said, "I will follow you, Miraden."

THIRTY·THREE

THE GOLD MARCH

THEY WALKED THROUGH THE DESERT, a long sea of gold sand that blurred into the horizon, no trees, no rocks, not even bones. It was hot, oppressively hot, and windless. Miraden smacked his lips and thought about the wineskin of water he had at his side. Ceychell and Simigrin were at his sides, Lovo and Tundra behind him. They each got to fill their water before leaving Fe Jet, but he had to ration his for himself and Tundra.

Despite feeling better than he had in more than a week, he was desperate and terrified of jumping from the cliff, even if he fell into a portal. Ceychell's plan might work, but they didn't have a better one anyhow. He looked down at his hip where Ormus's axe should be resting, but they didn't return it with his pack. He had his bow, but no quiver of arrows—at least they didn't know about the magic string. He'd need it, if Ceychell's plan didn't work.

Fifty scorpion guards and a silver coach with barred windows followed them. Four great armored lizardmen carried the coach. They made it look effortless. The Lorden leaned out a window of the coach and watched them march. He couldn't quite tell, but it looked like she enjoyed it.

They walked for hours toward the cliff. Miraden was tired, dehydrated, and burning up. Ceychell wore her filthy red robe; her hair was a mess, sweat soaked and stuck to her face. He smiled at her; she didn't see it. She'd been such a loyal friend, even after he'd crushed her—she stayed true and wonderful to him. Was it because she felt indebted to him for saving Kyradel? Was it because she was still trying to regain his love? Or was it for a reason that wasn't obvious to him? He wished he could talk to her, but the guards had threatened to cut off fingers should they talk again.

Simigrin seemed to be nearly falling with every step. She used her staff to help her walk and kept her head down. Her blue robe was dirty and torn, her hood barely attached by threads. Her silver vambrace shone through a tear in her sleeve, and Miraden thought back to the day he'd given them to her. It seemed so long ago since he'd given them to her in Crestain. He loved her, and wanted to believe her, but the crown had become a barrier between them.

He gave Tundra some of his water and scratched her ears. He felt such a bond with her. She was as loyal as any friend could be. He was glad she was with him, but he was sorry that he'd brought her to such a dismal end.

When he turned to look at Lovo, Lovo grinned and nodded. Miraden didn't have to say anything—he knew Lovo had his back to the very end. Lovo deserved better than what Miraden had led him to.

They weren't allowed to rest until they stopped in the evening. They were not allowed to build a fire but the guards gave them more water. The four agreed in whispers to sleep as well as they could. They would need their energy.

Nevertheless, morning came too soon. Miraden was woken by a kick to his boot from one of the scorpion guards, who proceeded to wake the others the same way.

They walked for another day and a half, and by high noon on the third day, Miraden could see a long stretch of palms from one end of the horizon to the other. He suspected that was their destination but every step was so hard and slow. A shadow grew over him; he turned and shielded his eyes from the sun. A scorpion guard stood behind him with two spears.

"Pick up the pace, or I will smash you into the sand and let the insects peck you dry, by the Lorden's mercy," the guard said.

Miraden and the others didn't need any more convincing. Miraden sped up and offered the rest of his water to Tundra. She was dragging the most.

A few hours later they reached a stretch of lush palms, so tall they looked almost unreal, swaying in the breeze. Thousands of red, blue, and black birds perched on fronds so high up they were nearly out of sight and sang in beautiful harmony unlike anything he'd ever heard. Beyond the palms, the tall cliffs of Syindella Channel towered over the channel.

The grass under his boots was a welcome change after three days of dragging his feet through the sand. As he turned to check on his companions, he noticed Ceychell's red book was floating just above her bag. She nodded at him and tilted her head toward Lovo. He was holding the crown in front of his belly where the guards behind them could not see it. Miraden slowed down just a bit and let Lovo slowly catch up to him. Miraden reached back and felt the crown placed in his hand.

Ceychell stumbled on a tuft of grass and bumped into Miraden. She whispered, "I love you." When he slipped the crown to her, the emerald green and white of her eyes went black as coal and her hand trembled.

"Are you okay?" he whispered to her.

Simigrin whispered from behind them, "This is a bad idea,"

drowning out Ceychell's answer.

Miraden was first to the edge. The opposing cliff wall was a few miles away on the other side of the channel. He peeked over the edge at the sheer drop, some jutting rocks and the water far below. His heart sank.

Then one of the guards behind them yelled, "Stop!"

Ceychell's book floated in front of her stomach, rippling with heat. Her black eyes were ringed in red skin, as though her eyes were burning. She gritted her teeth into a grin and stared down at the crown. When she looked at him, Miraden stared into Ceychell's cinders and felt his heart sink. Giving her the crown was a mistake.

THIRTY·FOUR

THE LAST DROP

CEYCHELL'S HAIR WHIPPED IN THE wind. The sky was red, the grass was black. Her heart pounded in her chest. A burning wave pulsed up her arm from the crown. Miraden stood in front of her, terrified. Lovo and Tundra were by him.

She stepped up to the cliff edge, Simigrin beside her. As she stared down, the colors came back into the world. She saw the blue of the water, the browns and oranges of the cliff. It felt like her heart just shot into her throat; she couldn't breathe.

Simigrin was in tears. She shook violently then turned away from the cliff. She was so scared of heights, Ceychell hoped she could snap out of it, or the entire plan could fail.

Fifty guards stood in three rows holding their spears before the Lorden who stood on a throne that rested on the shoulders of four guards. She was smug, leaned on her fist and watched with a grin. Ceychell glared at her.

"I really liked you, Ceychell," the Lorden said. "It is a shame to kill such an adventurer."

"Pull it together," Ceychell whispered to Simigrin. She wasn't going to dignify the Lorden with a response.

"I'll give you one minute to start jumping in before I start pushing you in," the Lorden said.

Ceychell turned and stared down at her death. She looked over at Miraden who was looking at her and scratching Tundra's neck. The bear sat down beside him and let loose a sad moan.

Lovo put his hand on Miraden's shoulder and whispered. "I'm with you, buddy."

Miraden looked down the cliff, then over at Ceychell again. The way he stared at her she felt his love and his terror, she wanted to go to him.

She looked back at Simigrin who was shaking. "Simigrin, Simi!" Ceychell hissed. Simigrin breathed rapidly and shut her eyes. She glanced back at the chasm and then turned, wiped her eyes and grabbed her book out of her bag.

"You need to give us cover," Ceychell whispered.

Simigrin looked at her and screamed "Wait don't!" She reached her hand out in Miraden's direction.

Ceychell turned sharply and saw two scorpion guards shove Miraden over. Tundra roared and swiped one so hard she ripped the guard's arm clean off. Lovo grabbed Miraden and held his arm but Miraden was dangling over the cliff.

"No!" Simigrin screamed and thrust her hands out toward the rows of charging guards. She shouted her spell as a barrier of ice crystalized out of thin air, rapidly grew and surrounded them at the cliff. Long sharp spikes jutted out from the wall in all directions, a few guards were impaled before the rows could stop.

"Get through that wall! Kill them!" the Lorden screamed.

Ceychell released a ball of fire at the guard on their side that had all its arms. The fire detonated at his neck and blew him off the cliff. The guard missing an arm was wrestling Tundra, the bear bit its throat while the guard was clutching it with its huge claws. They shifted and knocked into Lovo and Miraden as they all went over the side.

"Miraden!" Ceychell screamed. She held the crown, concentrated on the portal spell, reached her hand down toward the river in the direction that Miraden, Lovo, Tundra and the guard were plunging, and opened a black gate. She looked across the channel to the top of the other wall and focused, another black gate opened on top of the cliff wall. She could hardly see it and couldn't tell if the group made it through.

Her body ached and burned while holding two gates open. She screamed, it felt like her flesh was boiling. Simigrin took hold of her hand, and held her book with her other.

There was a crash; a dusting of ice fell on them. Ceychell glanced back and saw the guards smashing through the wall, it would be seconds before it was down.

She exchanged a look of fear with Simigrin. The ice mage she'd been through so much with was standing right beside her clutching her staff.

"We can take them," Simigrin said.

Ceychell smiled and said, "Tell my sister I love her. Go save the world," she slapped the crown into Simigrin's hand and bumped her off the cliff.

THIRTY·FIVE

THE FINAL LETTER

MIRADEN FELL OUT OF THE portal. His heart raced uncontrollably as he crashed to the ground with Lovo, Tundra, and the guard. His head ached from a shrilling in his ears; his ears painfully popped when sound was returning. He couldn't breathe, he kicked and twisted and pushed past arms, claws, and fur before he finally wriggled free.

He removed his bow from his shoulder and drew the string. The scorpion guard clutched Lovo's throat, looked up and Miraden shot it through the head. The guard collapsed.

Miraden ran over to Lovo, "You okay?"

"I think so? We made it?" Lovo said as he pushed the guard off of him.

That's right, Simigrin and Ceychell were still on the cliff. Miraden shook the cobwebs from his brain. He rushed up to the edge of the cliff and saw someone falling toward the gate.

Simigrin fell out of the gate landing on Tundra. She shook and screamed. As she rolled off of Tundra's back, she curled in a ball and continued to shake uncontrollably. Miraden wasn't sure how Simigrin could have jumped with her extreme fear of heights. He was nervous to go to her. Then he saw in her hand the crown tightly clutched.

"No, no no no." Miraden muttered. He dumped out his bag, picked up his looking glass, and peered through it. The black gate he fell through on the other side of the channel was gone. The scorpion guards were lined up at the cliff edge staring back at him. Something exploded down on the water. Black plumes of darkness billowed from the channel then wisped up into smoke over the chasm. Then another, closer loud bang with a plume of smoke. The portal near Miraden blew away like dust.

Miraden looked around. Perhaps he had missed Ceychell coming through the gate when he was on the ground, but all he saw were Lovo and Tundra behind him and Simigrin crying. He looked over the edge of the cliff to see if she had fallen, but there was no sign of her. He fumbled the glass and nearly dropped it over the cliff. He desperately searched the cliff top where she stood and the water line where he fell.

"Nooooooo!" Miraden dropped to his knees at the very edge of the cliff. Lovo grabbed him from behind and pulled him away from the chasm. Miraden screamed through his tears and dug his fingers into the dirt. He couldn't go on without her. He screamed and screamed as he fell back into Lovo.

A horn, like no horn he's ever heard, blared a deep, dark note over the channel. It startled him for a moment; he knew it must be the Horn of Syindella.

"They're coming, Miraden," Lovo said. "We have to warn… everyone." He lifted Miraden off the ground. "I'm sorry about Ceychell," Lovo said, his voice was cracking, "but we have to go. There will be time to mourn later."

Miraden, red-faced, turned and caught up to Simigrin. She was seated on the grass, holding her legs to her chest and shaking. Her eyes were red and full of tears.

He looked at the crown and panicked, "Why!" he said. "Why would you take it from her?"

Simigrin screamed, "I didn't take it from her!"

"Why do you have it? You've been trying to keep it away from her this whole time!"

"That fall will haunt me forever! I would have never taken it from her, she gave it to me and pushed me off the cliff!"

"Why would she do that? She needed the crown for the spell."

She threw the crown at Miraden. "She gave it to me!" She stood up but was on shaky legs. "I wanted to keep it from her because Lord Umorogrin told me she couldn't touch it until she's ready or she would become a threat. Even after everything you and Ceychell said about him, I still trust my master. Please Miraden, you need to trust *me*!" He stared down at the crown at his feet; the prize for Ceychell's life. He hated it.

Miraden pointed at the scorpion guards across the channel. "The biggest threat in the world is now coming for us, and Ceychell could have helped. Now she is gone."

Miraden turned his back on her. It wasn't real to him; he couldn't imagine living without Ceychell. She was his family; she was everything to him. How could he tell Kyradel? What would Ormus do to him when he found out? How could Simigrin do this?

"Let's head west," Lovo said. "Perhaps we can catch a caravan heading toward Kander." Lovo wiped tears from his eyes and put his arm around Miraden. "C'mon buddy, Ceychell would want us to keep going." His voice broke at the end.

They walked away from the cliff, found a dirt road, and headed west along the flatlands, nothing but low shrubs and weeds as far as the eye could see. At least the heat wasn't overwhelming. After a few hours, a small trade caravan caught up with them.

Lovo approached the lead driver, a young man with a hook nose.

He wore furs and had a long scar that split his ear. "Hello, friend. You wouldn't happen to be headed to Kander Bondare?"

"We are," the merchant said. "Is, is that bear tame?"

"She is," Lovo said. Miraden couldn't speak. He just stared at the wagon, he didn't care.

The man beside the driver, a fatter man with fine green silks, leaned back to look at them and said, "Got anything to trade?"

"I'm a mage at the college," Simigrin said. "I can offer you five hydras when we arrive." The driver instructed them to hop into the rear cart half-full of barrels. As they rode, Miraden looked north and saw the Scorgis in the distance. It was charred and smoking. Lovo seemed to notice it, too, but they said nothing.

Simigrin put her hand on his, but he just stared out of the cart. He was dead inside.

Miraden lay against Tundra in the rumbling wagon. Simigrin and Lovo sat across from him. He was sick with anger, ruminating on what Ormus would say to him when he got back to Kaehrn. The man might even kill him. He had promised to bring Ceychell back safely. He held back tears as he envisioned telling Kyradel and Curasca the news. It killed him slowly, over and over again. Not only did he fail to bring back Ceychell, but he had unleashed the Lorden's horde. He failed himself. He failed everyone.

END OF BOOK TWO

SIMIGRIN'S STRIFE

CHAPTER ONE: THE UNFORTUNATE COVER-UP

THEY ARRIVED IN BONDARE NEAR the Corral. Miraden and Simigrin had hardly spoken in the past three days. Simigrin paid the driver while Lovo and Miraden stood beside Tundra. The shopping crowd gave them wide berthing, many stared fearfully at Tundra.

Miraden stood, staring through a group of merchants standing across from him. He saw Ceychell running from him, laughing as he chased her through the woods back home. It was late fall, the leaves were changing and frost crunched beneath his steps. She ran just fast enough for him to not catch her, be he knew she wanted to be caught.

"Hey, buddy. Is this your bag?" the hook-nosed merchant asked. Miraden no longer saw Ceychell, there was a dirty tent filled with a fresh catch of fish and three chickens across from him. He turned back to the merchant and put up his hand. The hook-nosed man nodded and threw him his bag.

The three companions and Tundra trudge up the mountain into the mist and thin air.

When they reached the great enchanted steel doors to the university, the doors opened for them, and they were ushered in by a host of anxious, excited mages. They welcomed Simigrin and showered her with praise. Miraden and Lovo walked just behind her in silence with Tundra plodding behind them. Miraden didn't want to see Umorogrin. He didn't want to tell them about the horror from the south they unleashed. He wanted to hide and vanish from the world once and for all. He was done with adventures.

They followed the mages into the great hall of the university.

Miraden reached into his bag for the crown and couldn't find it. He dug around, looked up and saw Lord Umorogrin shuffling quickly toward them.

Miraden thrashed around his bag.

"What is it?" Simigrin asked. "You didn't—"

"The crown isn't here!" he said.

"Master Simigrin! You have returned with Miraden and Lovo." He paused for a moment and stared at them. "What has happened?"

Miraden stayed quiet and let Simigrin explain. She told them about the horrible storm, being stranded at the Fjishers, going through the desert to Fe Jet, and stealing the horn and crown.

"The Horn of Syindella?" Lord Umorogrin gasped. His jaw trembled. It's like he'd seen a ghost. "If you have returned it to them, we are all in grave danger. And what's worse, you have allowed Ceychell to touch the crown before you brought her back here. Where is she now and where is the crown? I must see it."

Simigrin looked down and said, "Ceychell died saving us. Her portal burned out as she tried to cross the channel. I lost the crown."

Miraden stared in shock, he couldn't believe she took the blame. He wanted to run out the college to see if they could catch the merchant thieves.

Lord Umorogrin shook his head. "We needed her, desperately, to stop the ashenkin. Carbrojl has nearly robbed the world of all its children to build his army. Now, we can only hope she perished, for if she didn't, I fear she will have enough power to bring him into this world. Without my guidance, she would become the instrument of Carbrojl. And you've lost the very thing I sent you to retrieve."

"You can only hope?" Miraden screamed before he even realized he'd opened his mouth. "Ceychell meant nothing to you! Tell us, tell *me*, did you really cause the ashenkin to invade our world? Did you make a deal with Siennah and Carbrojl?"

The mages looked at Lord Umorogrin, incredulous, and some of them gasped while others whispered their fears. He straightened his back, and said, "Yes." Another wave of gasps from the mages.

"Did..." they all turned to Simigrin. "Did you take me from Queen Siennah?"

Lord Umorogrin sighed heavily and looked down. "All born with magic ability are brought here... regardless of their status."

"Was trying to save Kalionite you atoning for taking me?" she asked. Tears ran down her dark cheeks as her lips trembled. She looked on the brink of balling.

Lord Umorogrin sighed and said, "I—"

"Hi Miraden!" it was Kyradel's voice. Miraden would recognize it anywhere. She stood in the entryway in light leathers. Elsaria stood beside her holding a heavy pack. She wore bear furs and her hair was in a single long white braid over her shoulder.

Miraden was so shocked, he just stood there gaping at her.

She ran through the hall to him and pulled him into a bear hug. He held her and started to shake. He shook so badly she let go and looked at Simigrin, Lovo, and then past them. Then her jaw trembled and she yelled, "Where's my sister?"

GET A FREE WORLD MAP OF THE HER SOUL OF FIRE SERIES

I love writing. I really love worldbuilding, but what I love most is when people enjoy my stories. I want to stay in touch with you, not to send you spam, but to make sure that if you like my stories, that you get notified whenever I release a new book or have something special to send to my mailing list community.

I would like to share the world map with you. Also, as you can imagine, I'm working on the next book in the series and have a good deal of it written. As a member of my mailing list, I'd love to share part of it to give YOU insight on what's to come!

So, if you sign up for my mailing list at **jvfahl.com/#newsletter**, I'll send you this free stuff:

1. A map of the world in the *Her Soul of Fire* series
2. A future sneak-preview of Book 3.
3. Possibly more free stuff!

My promise: I **will not** spam you and you'll only hear from me when I have something to share that I think you'll be interested in. I do this because I love it, and I hope you will too, not for the spam and sales.

Thanks so much.

DID YOU ENJOY THIS BOOK? YOU CAN MAKE A DIFFERENCE

Your review is the **most powerful thing** I can earn to get more people to read my stories. I don't have one of the big 3 pushing my fantasy novels or NYT best sellers badge to my name, and that doesn't really matter to me. What I do have, is the potential for a real reader who enjoyed my story to leave a review for others and encourage them to read my stories. That's what matters to me.

Honest book reviews bring me other loyal readers. Your review is very important to me, **I cannot state that enough.**

If you enjoyed this book, I would be quite grateful if you could spend a few minutes leaving a review. It can be as short as you like on your favorite book site, whether it's amazon.com, goodreads.com, bookbub.com or one of your choice, it matters so much to ME.

Thank you so much, I truly appreciate you. And thank you for reading.

ABOUT THE AUTHOR

J.V. FAHL is the author of *MIRADEN'S FOLLY* (HER SOUL OF FIRE Series) and is working on another grimdark fantasy series as well. You can find him at **jvfahl.com**. He's on Twitter at **twitter.com/JVFahl**, on Facebook at **www.facebook.com/jvfahl** and if you really want to reach out to him directly, he'd love to hear from you: **jvfahl@thedarkwriter.io**.

J.V. Fahl has lived in all four corners of the United States, been to 20 countries, served in the US Navy, and now lives in the Smoky Mountains. He is always interested in hearing from his readers.